Mambo
in
Chinatown

Jean Kwok

RIVERHEAD BOOKS
A member of Penguin Group (USA)
New York
2014

RIVERHEAD BOOKS
Published by the Penguin Group
Penguin Group (USA) LLC
375 Hudson Street
New York, New York 10014

USA • Canada • UK • Ireland • Australia
New Zealand • India • South Africa • China

penguin.com
A Penguin Random House Company

Library of Congress Cataloging-in-Publication Data

Kwok, Jean.
Mambo in Chinatown / Jean Kwok.
p.   cm.
ISBN 978-1-59463-200-6
1. Chinese American women—Fiction.   2. Chinese Americans—Fiction.   3. Ballroom dancers—Fiction.
4. Family secrets—Fiction.   5. Family life—Fiction.   I. Title.
PS3611.W65M37   2014   2013043639
813'.6—dc23

Printed in the United States of America
1   3   5   7   9   10   8   6   4   2

Book design by Michelle McMillian

For Erwin, Stefan and Milan,
and to the memory of my mother,
Shuet King Kwok

Mambo
in
Chinatown

One

My name is Charlie Wong and I'm the daughter of a dancer and a noodle-maker. My mother was once a star ballerina at the famed Beijing Dance Academy before she ran off to marry my father, the handsomest noodle-maker in Beijing—or at least that's what she always called him before she died. Hand in hand, they escaped to America to start their family. Unfortunately, my mother's genes seemed to miss me altogether. I took after Pa, minus the good-looking part. And minus the manual dexterity as well: he never managed to pass his considerable noodle-making skills on to me, much as he tried. So at twenty-two years old I was instead working as a dishwasher at a restaurant in New York's Chinatown. Pa was their noodle master. Customers lined up at the back door to purchase packages of his uncooked noodles to take home.

Peering now through the window that connected the tiny dishwashing room to the kitchen, I could see Mrs. Lee standing by the back door. She'd put on extra lipstick for Pa, and she fixed her eyes on his tanned hands wrapped around the bamboo pole.

"Can you make them extra long for me?" she asked in Mandarin. She stood a bit stiffly, careful not to brush against the grease-covered doorframe.

Pa nodded as he hoisted the bamboo pole and lowered it once again onto the dough on the table. The end of the pole fit into a hole punched in the wall, just above the table surface. As he rolled the pole, the dough became thinner on every pass. It was hard work. I knew his hands were ridged with calluses. Then he sliced the dough into perfectly regular strands with his cleaver, and began pulling them by hand. He twirled them into a rope, then stretched them again and again. It was like magic.

He looked up to flash Mrs. Lee a smile. "Must be your birthday."

She actually giggled, a woman of her age. "You are an intelligent man."

I would have snorted, only the waiters pushed another plastic bus tub filled with stacks of bowls through the other window at that moment, the one connecting the dish room to the restaurant. Everybody knew it was good luck to have long noodles on your birthday since they symbolized long life, just as many of us in Chinatown remembered Mrs. Lee's husband had passed on a number of years ago. I dumped the food off the dishes, then piled everything in another tub. I was used to women complimenting Pa—but if you're trying to catch him for your own, good luck, lady. Pa hadn't dated since Ma died and probably never would; he was still in love with her. I hefted the heavy tub with ease, then hauled it over to the washing sink. I'd been working this job for years, ever since leaving high school, and I had the biceps to prove it. I ducked my head to look through the window again and see what Mrs. Lee was up to. I caught a whiff of ginger and garlic that one of the cooks had just dropped into a wok.

Pa had given the ends of the dough to his assistant and they'd stretched the noodles across the room while the other cook dodged them. Mrs. Lee beamed as Pa rolled up the finished noodles for her.

"You should join us. I promise the noodles will be tender," she said.

Pa gave her an old-fashioned bow from the waist as he handed her package to her. "You are very kind but I am so busy taking care of my two daughters. You know how it is."

"Of course," she said. Her bright lips drooped at the corners. "Next time, then."

"Yes, I wish you long life and happiness," said Pa, turning back to his assistant. "Get me a sack of flour from the basement, will you?"

I should have been the one helping him. Pa had brought me to the restaurant to watch and train ever since I was a child. Hard as I tried, I still dropped everything. "You have to coax the dough," Pa said, but I pummeled it instead. A noodle master has magic in his fingers. Mine were as clumsy as if I were always wearing gloves. Pa was tall and lean. His defined nose and cheekbones made for a strong face on a man, but those features were too sharp for a woman, according to my Aunt Monica and Uncle Henry. I was tanned like the rest of Pa's family, and for a Chinese girl, I was homely. I had learned early on not to attract any attention. Most of the time, I succeeded.

I wiped the sweat from my forehead. It was the afternoon lull but my legs were already starting to ache from the hours I'd spent on my feet since the early morning. I poured in some detergent, then turned on only the hot faucet and let it fill the sink. At the beginning, I couldn't bear to put my hands in the scalding water, even when I'd diluted it with some cold. I'd tried to use gloves until I realized the steaming water poured in over the tops of the gloves anyway when I submerged my arms. But if I was good for nothing but washing dishes, I'd resolved to be the best dishwasher I could.

I'd increased the heat day by day until my body adjusted. I didn't mind the way my hands and arms became reddened and chapped. It was the cost of my labor.

The rising steam combined with the August heat was stifling. I dropped a stack of bowls into the water, then plunged in my hands and forearms to soap them. My skin had become so rough now I barely winced anymore. The hotter the water, the faster I could work. Although the restaurant had a dishwashing machine, it was so ancient I had to make the dishes as clean as possible before loading it anyway, rather than waste time cleaning out the debris from the machine traps. Otherwise, I would have to check the dishes when they came out of the machine to know they were clean. Especially during the mealtime rush, every second was precious or we'd run out of clean dishes and silverware.

I pulled out another stack of dirty bowls from the bus tub and found a large roach hanging from one of them. I froze. I didn't want to drop everything into the soapy water and have to fish out the now-boiled roach. The bug took advantage of my confusion, racing up my hand and onto my arm.

I screeched. The dishes I'd been holding clattered onto the floor while I batted at the roach, trying to get it off my shirt before it reached my face. Suddenly, a white cooking cloth whipped the roach off of me. It landed upside down on the floor, thick legs waving, and a man's foot smashed it.

"You are the clumsiest dishwasher we've ever had!" said Mr. Hu, the owner of the restaurant. His round cheeks seemed covered with a perpetual layer of grease. "Clean it up right away!"

"I'm sorry," I said. "I was—"

"I don't want to hear it!"

Pa was standing in the doorway. "Mr. Hu, she works very hard."

Mr. Hu softened when he saw my father. Without Pa, his restaurant would lose most of its business. "I know. And she is strong too. Just get rid of this mess, okay? Dishes are expensive."

I started sweeping up the broken crockery right away. When Mr. Hu was gone, I said, "Thanks, Pa." Although I could understand Chinese, I couldn't speak it very well. Pa and I usually communicated in English. Sometimes he spoke Chinese and I answered him in English.

"Anyone can drop a soapy dish. That man needs a vacation." He gave me an affectionate pat on the shoulder, then went back to the noodle station.

If it weren't for Pa, I didn't know if the restaurant would have kept me on since there was no shortage of cheap labor. However, I did work hard and I knew the restaurant had gone through a number of dishwashers before I was hired. It was dirty work, even for Chinatown.

An hour later, I was sleeping across a row of chairs by the wall at the back of the restaurant. All of the staff took naps there during our breaks because our shifts could extend from early morning until late in the night, depending on business. If more customers showed up, the restaurant stayed open. Everyone ignored us as long as we kept our backs to the other tables, and if we didn't snore too loudly.

Someone tapped me on the side of my head. I jerked awake and peeled my cheek off the vinyl of the chair, annoyed and disoriented. "What?" I saw the yellowing wallpaper, then turned to focus on my little sister Lisa's heart-shaped face. "Don't touch my hair."

"Sorry," she said but I could tell she'd done it on purpose. "You wouldn't wake up otherwise."

I pushed myself up on one elbow and frowned at her. "Did you try?"

"No. I know from experience." When I rolled my eyes, she leaned in and whispered, "I found an ad for a new job for you."

I didn't find out what Lisa's job possibility was until after my shift. I'd shooed her out of the restaurant after her announcement, before she got me into trouble with Mr. Hu again for dawdling on my break. I knew she'd be waiting for me at home. Even though it was late by the time Pa and I arrived at our apartment, Lisa always tried to stay up. If she fell asleep, she'd wake up again when she heard us come in because she wanted to make sure we got home safely.

"What could happen in Chinatown?" I asked her once.

"Petty theft, knife fights, muggings, gang wars," she answered.

She had a point. She was only eleven but Lisa had always been precocious. Sometimes I watched her sleeping and wished I could keep her safe from the life I led. At the very least, I would have liked to keep her ignorant of how tired I was much of the time, but it was impossible to fool her. No matter how often I told her I was satisfied being a dishwasher, Lisa kept trying to find new opportunities for me.

To be honest, I didn't mind. I wished not for a new job or place but for a different life altogether, to change not the where but the how of things. Some people dreamed of going someplace else; I dreamed of being someone else. Someone who hadn't always been in the bottom half of her class at school. Someone poised, elegant and beautiful—like Ma had been, like Lisa would be when she grew up. It was Lisa who took after Ma, from the slight flush beneath her skin to that gliding grace when she ran. Sometimes I would look at Lisa and Pa and silently ask the gods, "Could I please not be born into such a good-looking family in my next life?" It wasn't easy being a cow among gazelles.

Every night, after saying good night to Pa as he retired to his tiny closet of a room, Lisa and I folded up the plastic table in the living room and put it in the corner. My mattress, with the sheets hanging off it, always leaned by the wall. We squeezed that in between the sofa and the pile of three little televisions stacked against the other wall. Only the top one worked, but Pa could never bear to throw away any of the others. "They will be maybe handy someday," he said. Then we pulled off the worn patchwork cloth covering the sofa, exposing the scorch mark I'd made when I left the iron on it once. We covered the sofa with a sheet, then piled on Lisa's pillow and blanket, which I had painstakingly sewn together from scraps. She was growing almost too tall to fit on the short sofa and I wasn't sure what we would do then.

Although I nagged Lisa to go to sleep before Pa and I got home, I secretly looked forward to those moments of peace at night: Lisa lying on the sofa and me on my mattress on the floor below her, when we chatted and read before going to sleep.

"How were Uncle Henry and Aunt Monica today?" I asked.

She made a face, then said, "Fine."

"You shouldn't be ungrateful," I said, "we're—"

She completed my sentence, "—lucky that they use me for free slave labor in Uncle Henry's office under the guise of taking care of me. I know." Uncle Henry was a well-known doctor of traditional Chinese medicine in Chinatown. Lisa helped out at his office with tasks like filing and cleaning after school until closing time, then she came home. Now that it was summer vacation, she was there full time.

I grinned before I could stop myself. "How did you become so obnoxious?"

"The same way you got so moralistic."

We stuck our tongues out at each other, even though I knew I was much too mature for such a thing.

"And I thought you wanted to be a doctor," I said.

"I know." She sighed. "It's good experience for me, even if he's not a western doctor."

"Come on, start reading," I said, passing her the paperback book.

Every night, Lisa had been reading *Pilgrim's Progress* aloud to me before we went to sleep. I'd actually started by trying to read to her but I had so much difficulty with it that she took over. In school the words "lack of motivation" had appeared repeatedly on my report cards, but my teachers never knew about the hours I struggled over my textbooks in the evenings. It was my tenth-grade English teacher who'd given us the list of Top 100 Classic Books and I was still determined to get through that list. I barely passed that teacher's class and she didn't notice me much, except to ask me a few times to try harder, but I worshipped her from afar, with her sharp wit and wild hair and gesturing hands. I never dared tell her how I fought at home to read her books, how after many hours I would only be halfway through the assignment. I could see the difference between Lisa and me from the moment she started to read, fluently and easily. Even though I was an "ABC," American-born Chinese, reading was like a foreign language to me.

My teachers had always wanted to talk to Pa, but he never dared show up to meet them. He thought his English was too bad and I think he was intimidated by them. He felt his lack of education as a noodle-maker. His brother, our Uncle Henry, was the oldest son and had been rigorously trained in traditional Chinese medicine, although he didn't have a medical degree. There'd been no money left for Pa. I'd once seen the father of another student at school, arguing with a teacher for his child. For a moment I'd allowed myself to think it was Pa and my heart had leapt. Once, Aunt Monica had come to the school in Pa's stead. She spent her time telling my teachers that I needed to help out more at home, that it was shameful my father did most of the cooking. When I told Pa, he'd politely refused her help from then on. This was why I made sure I myself went to all of Lisa's teacher meetings now.

As Lisa flipped open *Pilgrim's Progress* and started to read, I did my best to pay attention. My legs and arms felt heavy, my back ached from bending over the sinks. I was so glad to be off my feet. Before I knew it, Lisa was tapping me on the head again.

"Why are you doing that?" I protested, trying to pretend I'd been awake the whole time.

"I thought we were reading this to improve our minds," Lisa said. "How can we do that when you're asleep?"

"I'm not sleeping." I paused. "Anymore. And we're improving your mind at least."

"Before you conk out again, can I tell you about your new job possibility?"

I groaned. "Will you stop being such an optimistic little beaver? You know I almost never get hired. And when I do, I just get fired again."

"That's only because you haven't found the right job yet. Take a look at this." Lisa passed me a scrap she'd torn out of an English newspaper, probably from her school library. Pa only bought Chinese newspapers, which neither Lisa nor I could read.

I glanced at the clipping, then sat up. I read the ad out loud, "Wanted: Receptionist for Ballroom Dance Studio."

Lisa said softly, "A dance studio."

"They'll never take me," I said. "I'm a terrible receptionist, remember?" I had tried to work outside of Chinatown a few times but all the phones I was supposed to answer had so many buttons. The computer was a mystery to me since we didn't have one at home and I'd only had a few hours of practice at school. But the worst was when I had to write down appointments. That was when things most often went wrong.

The last time, I'd only been a receptionist at the accounting firm for a few days. The company was small and cheap, and when they needed an important package delivered to Midtown, they'd sent me instead of hiring a courier. Big mistake. As always, I got lost looking for the right bus. When I finally found it, I realized I'd left my wallet back at the office. Determined not to fail, I walked all the way to my destination. But when I finally arrived, I looked down at the thick manila envelope I was supposed to deliver and it was a stained and crumpled mess. I'd been kneading it as I worried my way there. And I was fired again.

"You may have changed by now. It's been a while." Lisa bobbed her head up and down, to show how sure she was of this possibility.

"I doubt it." But despite myself, I glanced up at Ma's photos. A dance studio was a magical place; it represented Ma's passion and talents. She'd died when Lisa was only three, but we both grew up poring over her photos. Ma, incredibly young at seventeen, in a dress of embroidered silk, poised on one leg with her body turned to the camera, a white fan flicked open above her head. An old Chinese newspaper clipping of a line of star dancers from the Beijing Dance Academy at a diplomatic event. Ma in the foreground, dressed in a dramatic costume from the Beijing Opera, curtseying to the white man in a suit.

Lisa didn't remember Ma at all, but I did. Ma had never danced again in public after coming to the U.S. with Pa. She couldn't speak English, didn't know anyone in the dance world, hadn't understood how the system here worked, and soon, her life had been swallowed by hard labor. But she'd trained me. There was only a few feet of space available to us, but Ma was determined. During the week, she worked long hours as a waitress at the noodle restaurant with Pa. As soon as she had a day off, she would push all of the apartment's furniture aside and teach me while Pa stood in the doorway.

I suppose it wasn't so much dancing as exercises she taught me. Stretches, handstands, push-ups, pirouettes, anything we could do in the limited space. I'm sure I wasn't very good but I felt strong and limber with Ma's hands correcting me, gentle but firm, pushing my hips, my arms, my neck into place. It was one of the few times I didn't feel like a failure at everything. Ma became someone else when we trained, someone fierce and merciless.

"We must do this now, while you're still young," she said. "This flexibility, this strength, will always belong to you."

I remember wondering why Pa always stayed to watch us even though his face was so sad.

Underneath Ma's photos stood a large jar labeled "Broadway Money" in Lisa's rounded handwriting. We'd pasted ads for different shows all around the sides. It was partially filled with bills and loose change. Lisa and I had been saving for years to go to a Broadway show with Pa. Seeing the dancers would bring Ma back to Pa, if only for an hour or two, we thought. Since we weren't sure when we'd have enough for tickets for all three of us, we hadn't decided on the show yet. I'd counted the money recently and we had just enough for a ticket for one person.

I looked again at the employment ad. Imagine working in a dance studio. I'd be able to watch the dancers every day.

Lisa's voice broke into my thoughts. "They're interviewing on Monday. What do you have to lose?"

I woke to the slight sounds of Pa moving around in our kitchenette. It was Sunday and Pa and I had the day off. There was no door, only an archway between the living room, where we slept, and the tiny kitchen, which contained the altars to Ma and our ancestors. Pa always made breakfast for Ma's spirit, even though it'd been eight years since she'd passed away. In fact, we never ate anything at home before putting it in front of Ma's altar and offering it to her first. On the altar was a close-up framed photo of her young face. Pa was lighting incense now and murmuring, "Here's your tea, dear one."

By the time Lisa and I had put away my mattress and all of the bedding, Pa had finished making egg drop soup and put our bowls on a small table in front of Ma's altar. Lisa and I went into the kitchen to bow to Ma and light incense for the gods. After Ma's spirit had eaten, we took the bowls into the living room and sat down at the plastic table to have our own breakfast.

As the oldest female in the house, I should have been doing most of the housework, but from the time I was a small girl I'd shown myself to be incapable of learning any domestic task Ma had tried to teach me. I burned myself whenever I tried to cook, and even after I'd swept the floor as well as I could, Ma had to do it again. Luckily, Pa was a great cook and we sometimes brought home leftovers from the restaurant. He didn't seem to mind the way I was, although Uncle Henry and Aunt Monica often reprimanded him for spoiling me.

As the three of us sat around the fold-up table, I stirred my soup to cool it, first clockwise, then counter.

Pa shook his head. "Some say for good luck, you need to stir clockwise. Some say counterclockwise. But doing both at random is definitely wrong."

"Sorry," I said. "I just had something on my mind. Pa, do you think someone could fill in for me tomorrow afternoon?"

He looked up, concerned. "Why? Are you sick?"

"Job interview." I knew we needed every cent the two of us could bring in together. A wave of guilt washed over me at the thought of losing good money for this interview, when I wouldn't be hired anyway. I started shaking my head. "I don't need to—"

"No, no," Pa said. "That's good, very good. You deserve a better life. What is the company?"

Lisa and I exchanged glances. "Computers," she said.

"They're very well known," I added. We both knew that Pa would worry if he knew it was a dance studio. Were they doing indecent forms of dance? Would men there want to corrupt his daughter? And so on.

"Ah, good," Pa said. "I will go to restaurant and tell Mr. Hu today."

An hour later, Pa left to do the shopping and chat with his friends in Gossip Park, our nickname for the large park in Chinatown. Lisa and I used the time to try to find something I could wear to the interview. We searched through all of the closets, and I thought it was a good thing Pa never threw anything away. In the end, buried in a garbage bag filled with clothing that had been given to us, we found a red dress. It was so long on me that I had to belt it around my hips to make it reach midcalf instead of my ankles.

My hair was not in the best shape. I'd recently allowed Mrs. Tam, who owned the beauty salon on our street, to have her way with it.

"I give you a big discount because we are neighbors," she said. "I know how to make girls beautiful. Trust me."

So despite the expense, I'd let Mrs. Tam do my hair instead of having Lisa chop it off the way she usually did. Mrs. Tam layered my hair in hopes of "bringing out its natural curl." With my thick, coarse hair, I wound up with a big ball of frizz on my head, chunks sticking up all over the place. At that point, Mrs. Tam wanted to perm my hair to make it look better, but thankfully, I didn't have the money for that.

"I found it!" Lisa pulled a long piece of red cloth out of an old suitcase. She came over to me and wound it all the way around my head, hiding most of the haircut.

Together, we looked at me in the mirror.

"Does the scarf match the dress?" I asked.

Lisa squinted. "Almost."

"I guess it's close enough." The big, sacklike red dress covered my entire body and it seemed as if I was wearing a red turban on my head, with the ends of the scarf trailing down behind me like a tail. "Do you think it's too much red?"

"No," said Lisa loyally, "you look like a gypsy, Charlie."

I gave her a quick hug. Then we stared down at my shoes. I was wearing my sturdy dishwasher shoes.

"They'll be fine," I said.

"I think you have to wear high heels," she said. "Isn't that what they dance in? It might make a better impression. And you have such pretty feet."

"Smarty-pants," I muttered as I got down on my hands and knees to search in the back of the closet again. Lisa knew my weaknesses. My feet, narrow and arched, were the one thing I'd inherited from Ma. Lisa used to call them "Cinderella feet" before I started wearing the sturdy shoes I needed at the restaurant.

I finally dug out the only pair of pumps I owned. The heels were scuffed and the black vinyl surface was peeling off at the toes to reveal light gray patches underneath.

"Wait." Lisa rummaged through the kitchen drawer until she pulled out a black permanent marker.

I used a pair of scissors to cut off the bits that were sticking out. Then I started drawing on the shoes with the black marker, coloring in all of the gray and scuffed parts. When I was done, the shoes still appeared awful if you looked closely. The colored-in areas had a completely different texture from the rest of the material, but from a distance I thought they looked all right.

"They're great now," Lisa said.

"You're just worried I'm going to chicken out," I said.

"Are you?"

I glanced at the photo of Ma, posed in her one-legged stance, then I looked at the redness that was me in the mirror. "I guess I'm as ready as I'll ever be."

Two

I could already tell in the elevator that I was out of my league. The building was on the Upper East Side, a world away from downtown Chinatown. I squeezed myself into the corner, trying to avoid my blurred reflection on the metal walls. The man standing across from me had streaks of gray in his hair and the shiniest black shoes I'd ever seen. His pants had been perfectly pressed. I was dripping with sweat, but he seemed collected and fresh in his crisp shirt. I took a deep breath as the doors slid open. We stepped out of the elevator together and he allowed me to precede him down the carpeted hallway to the gilded double doors. Another blast of air-conditioning hit me as he held a door open for me. Some sort of fast classical music was playing.

"Oh, my dear Nina," he said to the young woman sitting behind the reception desk. He had a hint of a Southern drawl. "Are they still torturing you like this?"

She looked up, one hand clutching her long brown hair, and

blew out a sigh. "Hi, Keith, I can't take this anymore. I just discon-nected someone by accident again. Go on in, Simone's already in the ballroom."

The man named Keith laughed, then glanced at me. "Maybe she'll rescue you."

Nina looked at me as Keith stepped through another set of doors. Her features flowed into each other so smoothly that she seemed to have been carved from marble. "Are you here for the position?"

"Yes. I'm Charlie Wong." How did they both know I wasn't a dance student? I shifted my weight from foot to foot, trying not to look as nervous as I felt.

"I thought you'd be a guy." She looked down to check her list. I couldn't help staring at her a little when she couldn't see. She was probably one of the most beautiful women I'd ever seen and she was doing the job I wanted. Nina found my name, then gave me a quick genuine grin. "Glad you're a girl, though. Just go through those doors into the ballroom, hang a left and the manager's office is tucked in the corner," she said, pointing. "And watch out, they're doing quickstep."

I had no idea what she was talking about but as soon as I stepped through the next set of glass doors, I shrank back as a dancing cou-ple ran toward me at full speed. They pivoted gracefully out of the way, staying in place while they did a series of little synchronized kicks in time to the music, and then raced off again.

I realized I was standing on the edge of the main ballroom. It was the sort of room that felt as if chandeliers were hanging from the high ceilings, although there weren't any. Perhaps it was the wood paneling, or the tasteful lighting. A few small tables were placed against the right wall and several couples sped across the room coun-terclockwise. Some were posing in front of the floor-to-ceiling mirrors, which covered every wall except for the one by the tables. In the distance, I could glimpse my reflection. I resembled a ball of red yarn.

I couldn't seem to start breathing again. To the left of me, set in the corner of the ballroom, was a closed door. I started to walk toward it, feeling the dancers notice me with just a tiny angling of their heads, a swivel of their hips to position their bodies so they could keep me in sight. I clenched my jaw and knocked on the door.

It cracked open and a tall African-American woman with pronounced cheekbones peered out. "And you are . . . ?"

"Charlie Wong."

She pulled the door the rest of the way open. She had short tight curls that accentuated her oval face and a body rounded with pregnancy. As she stepped aside to let me pass, I saw her eyes flicker to the cloth wrapped around my head.

The office was small but luxurious. Framed photographs and posters of dance couples in different poses covered the walls. I stood in front of the massive desk until the woman seated herself behind it.

"I'm Adrienne," she said. "Sit down."

I took a seat, then we studied each other for a moment. In her tight sleeveless white top, her stomach bulged but her arms and shoulders were muscled and sinewy. She didn't blink as she gazed at me. Her eyes were tilted, a light hazel, striking against the dark creaminess of her skin. She was clearly someone who did not suffer fools gladly. I fumbled in my bag for my résumé. It was a bit crinkled when I pulled it out and I braced myself for what she would say when she read about my old jobs that had ended too quickly. To my relief, she hardly glanced at it before tossing it onto the pile on her desk.

She steepled her fingers together. "Why don't you tell me a bit about yourself?"

Images of Lisa, Pa, the noodle restaurant, my high school, rushed into my head and strangled my voice. What could I say that would be relevant to this beautiful place, these gorgeous people? "I'm not sure where to begin."

"Why don't you start by telling me why we should hire you?" The door behind me opened and a man stepped in. "Ah, there's Dominic."

Dominic had pale skin in contrast to his dark hair and eyes. He was wearing a light suit that appeared simple but must have been expensive from the way it fit him, as if it'd been poured over his body. He arched one spidery eyebrow at me in what seemed to be both a question and a challenge. He then leaned silently on the wall behind Adrienne next to an enormous poster: a stunning dark dancer poised in the arms of her partner as if she were about to take flight. I realized the poster was of the two of them.

She saw the understanding in my eyes. For the first time she smiled. "I haven't always been five months pregnant, you know. That was taken after the first time we won the American Ten Dance title."

Although I had no idea what that was, I nodded. I hadn't even known there were ten dances. I swallowed, then tried to answer her question. "I don't really know why you should hire me over all of the other people who are probably dying to work here."

Adrienne gave a snort caught between surprise and laughter. "Well, you're honest, I'll give you that." She leaned back in her chair and stared at me, then said, "So what's Charlie short for? Charlotte? Charmaine?"

I cleared my throat. "Umm, nothing. It's just Charlie."

Neither of them said anything for a moment, then Adrienne continued, "What's your deal, Charlie-short-for-nothing?"

When I gazed at her blankly, she linked her fingers across the top of her belly and said, "What do you really do? Tap dancer, writer, musician, fire-eater?"

"Dishwasher."

Her full lips quirked. There was a pause, then from behind Adrienne, Dominic said, "Interesting." He had a slight foreign accent. I couldn't tell if he was being sarcastic or not.

Adrienne asked, "And after your day job?"

"It's actually a day and night job," I said.

Now they both choked back a laugh.

While I was trying to figure out if I should say something else or not, Dominic asked, "Do you have any administrative experience?"

"I've worked in three different offices as a receptionist," I said with perfect honesty. I hoped they wouldn't check my résumé, which would reveal I'd only lasted a few weeks at each job before being fired.

"Have you ever had any dance training?" Adrienne asked.

I wished I could claim something that would impress her, anything, but I had to be truthful. "No."

"Really? No ballet lessons as a child, no secret dreams to become a dancer?"

Surprised and appalled, I said, "I'm the clumsiest person you ever saw. I could never dance."

"Everyone can dance," she said automatically, as if she were quoting something she'd learned by heart. "That's the Avery Studios principle. But we are indeed not hiring any dancers. Is that clear?"

"My mother was a dancer," I said. "But I didn't inherit any of her talent. I'm more like my father."

"What does he do?"

"He's a noodle-maker in Chinatown."

Now Adrienne smiled. "Charlie, why in the world do you want this job?"

I didn't allow myself to think. I didn't know how to get this job, which I didn't deserve in any way, so I told them the truth. "Because this place is so beautiful. If I worked here, I'd be able to be around the dancers. Because it reminds me of my mother, who died when I was fourteen."

Adrienne's face had grown serious. When she finally spoke, she addressed Dominic instead of me, and her voice was almost a whisper. "What innocence. Were we ever this young?"

I forced myself to continue. "I'm already twenty-two. But I promise that if you give me a chance, I'll do everything I can to deserve to stay here. I'm probably not the best receptionist you've interviewed. But I think I want this job more than anyone else."

They were silent, then she said, "Could you step outside for a moment?"

Since they hadn't told me where to go, I went out into the ballroom and stood beside the door of the office. Keith and a tall blond woman were pivoting around the room in perfect little circles together, as if they'd stepped out of a black-and-white movie. In my haste to leave the office, I hadn't closed the door properly and it swung open an inch. I leaned against the wall, realizing I could hear Dominic's voice.

"I like the last one better," he said.

"The brunette? She's too dramatic. Trust me, she's an actress or something in her spare time. I'm tired of hiring a new receptionist every six months. Everyone only wants to work here because it's a dance studio. We attract every wannabe in New York City, and goodness knows there are enough of them. We're like a rest stop."

"Fine, but does it have to be her? I mean, look at her."

I froze. I was sure they were both gazing through the window in the door, where they'd be able to see my reflection on the mirrors of the opposing ballroom wall. I pretended to be fascinated by the dancers passing by.

There was a pause, then Adrienne said, "She's okay." Another long silence. She continued, "She has no dreams of being discovered. And she's got experience."

Dominic finally spoke. "Is that a towel on her head? Come on, the receptionist is the gateway to our studio. She's got to look representative."

"Dominic, we've already got enough sex appeal here to sink the freaking *Titanic*. She just needs to look decent, and she needs to not leave to go join the circus after two weeks, like everyone else."

"I think you're going too far."

"I like her," Adrienne said. I couldn't help my sudden smile. "The dancers are constantly grumbling about needing to man the front desk. Clients are becoming unhappy and we're losing money. We get that cloth off her head and if she doesn't look insane, we hire her, okay?"

There was another silence, which I assumed was Dominic's surrender, and then Adrienne pulled the door open and said, "Can you come back in here, Charlie?"

I felt my pulse pounding in my throat as I stepped back in.

Dominic said, "Would you please take that—thing—off your head?"

I tried to keep my hands from trembling as I unwound the long red strip of cloth. In my mind's eye I saw my hair as it burst free: bushy, unevenly cut, tufts sticking out at random.

Did Dominic flinch?

"Now I see why you're wearing the scarf," Adrienne said. She came over and studied me. "The face is nice, though, now that I can see it without being distracted by all that material."

To my surprise, she took hold of my shoulders and gently moved me so that the light from the window in the door fell upon my face, an object for them to examine.

"Good bones," Dominic said. "No makeup."

I winced.

"She doesn't have bad taste," Adrienne said kindly, "just no taste. She's a blank slate. The dancers can help her."

Dominic sighed. He pulled Adrienne close and pressed a kiss to her temple.

I was hired.

It was late afternoon and I knew Lisa would be at Uncle Henry's office in the heart of Chinatown, street number 88, which many people thought was lucky. It was one of the reasons he was so successful. After taking the elevator to the third floor, I stopped in front of the sign that read "Traditional Chinese Medicine, Henry Wong" and collected myself. Uncle and Aunt would frown upon anything less than serious behavior. I opened the door to find Lisa sitting behind the reception desk. The room was crowded with Chinese people who were waiting to see my uncle. Lisa ran to me as soon as I entered.

"I got the job!" I said, trying to keep my voice low while jumping up and down with excitement. Lisa leapt into my arms and gave me a hug. The top of her head came up to my nose now.

"I knew you would, Charlie!"

"Where's Aunt and Uncle?" I asked, looking around.

"Uncle's with a patient and Aunt went out with the Vision."

"You're taking care of the office alone?"

"Now that they've got Dennis, she goes out more often."

Lisa had mentioned a new assistant. I lowered my voice so that none of the patients could hear us. "I hoped this job would mean you wouldn't have to come here anymore, but the hours are from one thirty to ten thirty in the evening, so I still won't be home after school. I'm sorry."

She looked downcast for a moment, then whispered back, "Don't be silly. Even if you were home, Pa would make me come here." It was true that our family owed Uncle a great deal. He had paid numerous medical bills for Ma. "Besides," Lisa added, "I need the experience anyway. It'll help for college."

It was just like her to find the bright side. I wasn't so sure I would have been comfortable working here. All around us were large glass jars containing wolfberry fruit, dried antlers and dehydrated lizards.

"What's that?" I pointed at a new jar, prominently displayed behind the desk. It was filled with what looked like pale, fleshy roots soaking in a light-colored liquid. We walked over to it, still keeping our voices down.

"Snake penises in wine," Lisa answered.

"Are you serious?"

"Extremely. The whole thing had to be specially ordered and the snake penises cost fifteen hundred dollars a pound. I could sneak you a glass if you want."

I gagged. "Very nice of you. I never knew snakes had such large . . ."

"Probably from very big snakes. We don't tell the patients this but they often cut it off when the animal is still alive."

"Is that legal?" I looked away from the jar.

"There are many things that are not legal but commonly accessible if you know the right people." Lisa imitated a commercial. "Snake penis wine is sure to warm your kidneys and enrich your qi, not to mention what it'll do for your sexual prowess."

I tried to stifle my laughter. "You shouldn't be talking about such things."

"What? I have to listen to it all the time. Half the stuff here is for helping those old guys in bed. Look here." Lisa pointed to a jar of dried seahorses. "Also a popular choice to improve your virility. Only four hundred dollars a pound. Ironic that it's actually the male seahorse that gets pregnant, isn't it? Doesn't seem too manly to me. But who am I? I just keep my mouth shut around here. If I were to speak, I'd tell them to just go get some Viagra."

I snorted and covered my smile. "Well, I still believe in this stuff when it's used right. If Uncle sells it, I'm sure it helps. Don't you remember, that milk-vetch root soup cleared up my skin?"

Lisa didn't answer. I started walking around the jars, reading their labels now. It'd been a long time since I'd been here, since my hours at the restaurant usually didn't allow me to visit. I passed a jar filled with dried, dark red centipedes, and one that appeared to hold a large baked cobra. "But I don't know why they have so many poisonous animals in here."

"Because 'poison fights poison.' That's what they believe." Lisa shrugged. "I personally think it'll just give you a stomachache and some really weird dreams."

"Lisa." It was Uncle Henry, standing in the doorway. There was a young man next to him.

Her smile vanished immediately. "Yes, Uncle."

"Uncle Henry," I said, greeting him with the honor due an elder.

"Charlie, so glad you stopped by. Have you met Dennis? He has an undergraduate degree in pharmacology and has been opening my old eyes to modern science." Uncle smiled at me and his face changed from stern to handsome. As always, he wore a dark green Mao suit, buttoned up to the neck.

Dennis shook my hands. He had a shock of black hair, full lips and bushy eyebrows. "I'm really learning a great deal here. It's fascinating."

I decided not to mention my new job. If it didn't work out, I didn't want Uncle's pity and it wasn't much anyway, not compared with what someone like Dennis could do. I'd always wished I could be better than I was for Uncle. In high school, the only respect I ever got from the other kids was for being Uncle's niece.

Uncle Henry had a softer version of Pa's features. I'd heard matrons whispering, "What a fine figure of a man Doctor Wong is," even though most of his hair was gray by now. He was a traditionalist and refused to consume any sort of non-Chinese food. If he hadn't had rice, then he hadn't eaten. He and Aunt Monica had never been on a vacation away from their house. He didn't see the point of wasting money, he said, although he would like to return to his home, China, some day. I remembered that when I was a child, he'd often paid special attention to me. He was the one who would sit at our plastic table in our tiny apartment and try to explain fractions to me. When Aunt Monica got impatient with me for not catching on faster, he would soothe her by saying, "Charlie is trying." But that had changed as I'd grown older.

"We need an extra pair of hands for a moment, Lisa," Uncle said. When Lisa followed them down the hallway, I trailed after her.

He opened the door of the examination room to allow Lisa to enter and I saw a woman lying on her stomach, acupuncture needles protruding from the smooth curve of her naked spine. The smell of mugwort drifted out to me. Uncle stepped in behind Lisa and Dennis, then turned to me with a smile. "Would you please watch the front office for me for a moment, Charlie?" With a little nod, he closed the door in my face.

It was clear he remembered as well as I did the day I'd been fired from his office. When I was around twelve, before Ma had died, they had tried to have me help in his office just as Lisa was doing now. "I would be happy to teach Charlie," Uncle Henry had told my parents.

I remembered Aunt Monica standing over me with her hands on her thick hips. "How could you have dropped the vat of rat fetuses all over the waiting area? Do you know how much that's worth? And we'll never get the oil stains out of the carpet."

After that, I'd been banned from working in the office. I felt guilty that Lisa had been stuck with the job simply because I'd been no good at it. But at least she wasn't a dishwasher. I would do anything to keep her out of the restaurant life.

I'd been sitting behind the desk in the office a few moments when Aunt Monica and the Vision walked in, trailed by Todd, the Vision's assistant.

I stood and greeted them. "Aunt Monica, Mrs. Purity, Todd," I said. Behind her back, everyone called Mrs. Purity by her true title, the Vision of the Left Eye, but none of us dared do it to her face. Like most children in Chinatown, I'd been taught to be afraid of her. She was considered the most powerful witch in the area, and people believed witches bound the souls of young children to themselves to serve them. Witches needed souls who would do their bidding to travel in between ours and the spirit world. They were even suspected of murdering children to gain their souls. As kids, we'd been forbidden to be alone with her.

The Vision was small, her back more crooked than I remembered, dressed in too-short cotton pants and a flowered shirt, looking just like the hundreds of old ladies in Chinatown. She carried a red plastic handbag. Her face was shaped like an iron with a small

pointed forehead and blunted at the chin, the brown skin unwrin-
kled and unflinching, and set deep in one socket was that wandering eye, roaming loose in the blankness of her face, staring where it
would.

Aunt Monica gave me a controlled nod. Her lips were screwed
tight, her eyes cold under reddened, hooded lids. Her hair was
white and had been for years because Uncle Henry didn't want her
to color it. He said the dyes caused cancer. It was well known that
they'd been desperate to have children, especially a son, but they
had not been successful. I remembered from my childhood that
their house had been filled with fertility Buddhas and ancient
drawings of plump, healthy boys. They believed that this would
help bring a male child into their life. Aunt Monica had followed a
diet of coconut and eggs, so the baby would have smooth white
skin, and had stopped watching animal shows on television for fear
that the baby would emerge looking like an ape. But no child came
at all.

I'd always suspected that Uncle's own desire for a boy was
the reason my Chinese name, Cha Lan, meaning "beautiful orchid," had been turned into Charlie in English. Everyone knew
it was easier to be accepted with an American name, so after choosing a Chinese name for a child, many parents would ask English-
speaking friends and family for suggestions for an American
equivalent. I'd been the one who had suggested Lisa when my little
sister had been named Lian Hua, "lotus flower."

After I'd figured out from Uncle's behavior that boys were more
desirable than girls, I'd asked Pa, "Did you want a boy too?"

Pa beamed and said, "When I could have two girls who remind
me of their ma? Of course not!"

Ma had hit him playfully, saying, "You are a charmer."

"I got you to come with me, didn't I?" said Pa. But then their laughter had died. Ma's face had grown tight, as if with grief for something she had lost.

Todd, the Vision's assistant, gave me a friendly smile. He was tall, with hair that was shaved high up behind his ears in a partial mohawk. Despite his hairstyle, there was a sweet light in his eyes. I remembered him as a solitary kid from high school, where he'd been a few grades ahead of me. He'd been working for the witch for a while now. He was wearing neon green sneakers, and kept tossing the top of his mohawk out of his eyes as he cracked his gum. He was the least mystical person I could imagine. I didn't know why the witch put up with him, except that possibly he was useful for carrying heavy things. "What's up?" he said.

"I'm all right. You?"

"Yeah, I get by," he said.

The Vision had her functional eye aimed directly at me. "This is the older daughter."

"Yes," said Aunt Monica in the half whisper she always seemed to use with the witch.

The Vision reached out and took my hand in hers. Her skin felt cool and slightly damp. The waiting room was full and I realized the Vision was going to impress us with her psychic abilities. I tried to pull my hand away but she held on and closed her eyes. She spoke loud enough for everyone to hear, "No boyfriend, husband or mate."

My chest tightened with fear. It had been a while since I'd dated anyone. How did she know? And what was she going to say about me?

"You are without equal," Aunt Monica said to the witch.

The Vision continued. "You must take your own blood, your menstrual blood. You take the papers you catch the blood with and wait until the night the moon disappears altogether. That night, you lay the papers on the roof tiles of the man's house. Anchor them with a stone. Let them dry for seven days and seven nights under the sun and the growing moon. Then crumble them into ash and put them in his coffee."

I choked and yanked my hand out of hers. Everyone around us looked impressed. The witch paused. Her eyes were open again. I managed to nod.

"When he drinks it, he will know no one but you."

My cheeks were on fire. Obviously the witch had looked into my future and seen that the only way for me to ever get a boyfriend was for me to bespell him with a used tampon, and now half of Chinatown knew that as well. Todd chewed vigorously on the gum in his mouth, trying not to laugh.

Aunt Monica stared at the Vision. She clasped both of her hands around the Vision's and said, "Thank you for this wisdom."

"I could do no less for your niece," the witch answered. "If she should need a beauty potion—"

"I have a new job," I blurted, desperate to change the subject. I also knew how powerful the Vision was. While I'd already given up on my love life, I still had some hope for the studio now.

"I know," said the Vision. "It will amount to nothing."

Her words fell upon me like stones. She blinked and turned her normal eye to me. Her face cracked into a smile. "Do not take it so hard, girl. A husband is a fine thing to have. Use the spell."

Lisa, Dennis and Uncle Henry came out of the examination room at that point, followed by their patient. She seemed to be in her late thirties and was dressed plainly, with a dirty air filter mask sticking out of her bag. I guessed she was a garment factory worker, possibly a seamstress. She bowed low to Uncle Henry. "I couldn't move my arm without pain before I came to you. Now I'll be able to work again. However much I owe you, it cannot repay my debt."

Uncle Henry spoke in a voice so soft that I could only hear him because I was standing right next to them. "I know your husband just lost his job. There is no charge."

She pressed her lips together and I was afraid she'd burst into tears. Wordlessly, she pressed his arm, then left. A few of the patients were already crowding around the Vision as I waved goodbye to Lisa and exited the office. My uncle's patients and her clients often overlapped. While I was walking back to our apartment, I was filled with pride for my uncle. Turning over in my head the Vision's bleak words about my future, I wished I had inherited some of his gifts.

Three

Ithd been a quiet evening at the noodle shop and I peeked out to see that there were customers sitting at only two tables. I had to finish out the week at the restaurant before I started at the dance studio on Monday. Mr. Hu had grumbled about finding a replacement for me, but we all knew he'd find someone without much trouble. Now I hoped the manager would close the restaurant when the last customers left. Pa had already started cleaning the kitchen. My shoulders and calves ached, as they always did by this time of night. The door swung open and my friend Zan entered.

She saw me right away and came over with her loose and graceful stride. "Can you take a break?"

Mr. Hu had already gone home. I knew the manager wouldn't report me if we snuck into a booth near the back. "Come on."

As we slid in, Zan pulled off the headband she used to keep her hair back. Her hair was plastered to the top of her head and several strands stuck to her forehead. But where it'd been free of the band, her hair was thick, black and glossy. I always wondered how it was that I seemed to be the only person who noticed how beautiful Zan was, even though she never wore a speck of makeup. I guessed most people didn't look too carefully at the girl who ran the egg cakes cart.

I groaned when Zan set her tattered copy of the *New York State Driver's Manual* on the table. "You don't own a car. I don't own a car. We don't know anyone who owns a car." I thought of Uncle and his precious Mercedes. "No one who would ever let you practice in it anyway."

She shoved the book in my direction. "Doesn't matter. Come on, test me."

"Why don't you become an accountant or something?"

Zan raised her eyebrow at me. In high school, Zan and I had been poor students. I had so much trouble with letters and Zan couldn't do math. We'd tried to help each other but that'd been like the blind leading the blind. "I'm going to get my commercial driver's license and I'll be waving at you from one big truck someday."

I'd heard it before. I didn't want Zan to waste her time. I knew she wanted out and somehow she'd grasped onto this idea of becoming a truck driver. She was in that egg cakes cart, rain, snow or shine. Her mom ran the one on Mott Street, and when Zan left high school, her mother had bought a second cart with their life savings so that Zan could operate it on Canal Street. "I just don't see how you'll ever—"

Dampness shone in her eyes. "I will."

I placed my hand over hers. "You're right. One step at a time." I flipped the book open and read aloud, "Under normal conditions, a safe following distance . . ."

We both looked up when the door opened again. A group of Asian college kids streamed in, and to make things worse, I picked out Grace Yuan and Winston, my ex-boyfriend. Grace saw me and lifted her hand in an awkward half-wave, then dropped it again. She looked away. Grace and I had been best friends long ago, when we were little girls. Ma's mother, my grandmother, had been a Yuan too, a distant relative of theirs, so our families had always been friendly. I loved Grace's grandmother and called her Godmother. Grace was a year younger than I was. The funny thing was that it was after I got left back in fifth grade and we were finally in the same class that she started ignoring me.

Zan quickly set her book upright to partially hide our faces. I said, "It won't work, but thanks. This means I'll have to go back to my dishes anyway."

She pressed her lips together. "They're going to hang out with their cheap orders for hours and you'll have to wait until they're done showing off to each other before you can go home. Just because they've been out partying and have nothing else to do."

"It's a part of the job. Hey!" I suddenly realized I hadn't told Zan my big news about the studio. I quickly sketched it out for her and she scrambled over to my side of the booth and hugged me.

"I'm so happy for you!" Her face glowed. "You're going to be fantastic."

"I'm scared."

"You can do much more than you think, Charlie. I know you."

I gave her a quick squeeze, then caught the manager giving me the evil eye. "I have to go." The group of cool kids was staring at us as well. Grace was sitting so close to Winston that her long curls brushed against his fraternity T-shirt. I knew their romantic relationship had ended years ago but it still stung to see them together. His mouth opened, as if he were going to call something out to me, then he shut it again.

Zan said, "Come by the cart when you can. I'll miss stopping by to see you here." She went past the group with her head high, and none of them said anything to her, not even Grace or Winston. It was as if Zan didn't exist. I hated them for that.

I stomped inside and started scrubbing some pots I'd left to soak. A few minutes later, I heard someone come in to use the bathroom. It was so grimy, most customers avoided it if they could. Probably one of those kids needed to throw up after drinking too much.

"So how are you doing, Charlie?"

I whirled around. Winston was leaning against the door jamb, tall and lanky. I said, "That's dirty. I wouldn't do that if I were you."

He straightened up, brushed off his shoulder.

I took a breath. "I'm fine. Did you come to use the bathroom? It's right there."

"Yeah, yeah. See you, then." He ducked into the tiny bathroom.

I turned back to the sink and made myself ignore him when he left. Winston and I had been friends since seventh grade. The Winston I'd cared about had been a short, scrawny kid with bad skin who used to laugh so hard at some dumb joke, he'd bend over double. In the months after Ma died, Winston and I spent more and more time together. One afternoon when we were fifteen, his ma was working at the bank and we were at his apartment alone. He kissed me. We hid our new relationship from our families, of course, because even though Pa had never spoken to me about dating, I knew it was forbidden. But being with Winston seemed so natural. It never occurred to me that anything could change, until a year later. That was when Winston shot up by a foot, his skin cleared, and Grace and her friends gathered him into their crowd. He seemed to date every cool girl in the school after that, but it'd hurt twice as much when he and Grace were together.

Rationally, I understood. He'd been a teenage boy and suddenly, the prettiest girls in the school were fawning over him. Grace was petite and vivacious, all laughter and bubbles. But I'd been left dumb and gasping like a fish at market, and the memory of that feeling still seared. Somehow I never saw these things coming. Hiding my love life from Pa, I'd dated a few different guys since, and even went steady with someone for a while, but no one could compare to the way I'd felt about Winston.

Pa poked his head into my area. "Was that your old friend Winston?"

I kept my head bent over the sink full of dishes. "Yep."

"Why you not invite him over sometime?"

"Sure, Pa. Sometime."

Zan, perched on our couch, was watching Lisa and me circle our small apartment with our cheap butterfly nets, trying to catch flies. Zan unexpectedly had this Saturday afternoon free because one of the wheels on her cart had broken off at lunchtime and it was being fixed. I'd convinced her to come with me to the tai chi class I attended but Pa wanted us to rid the apartment of flies first. He had occasional Saturdays off, and when he was home, he liked to improve things. The problem was that our place was so cluttered with papers and piled-up boxes that the flies had millions of hiding places. We'd turned off the fans to lure the flies into the open, which meant the apartment was sweltering.

Lisa was tiptoeing up to a fly that had landed on a stack of clothing. She swung her net and the fly took off.

"Why don't you just whack them with a newspaper, like everyone else does?" Zan asked, fanning herself with a piece of paper.

"No," Pa said, cradling his pillow in his hands. He was balanced on one of our folding chairs. He stayed focused on the mosquito on the ceiling. "Life is precious."

Zan snorted. Her father was a butcher at the live poultry place on Canal Street.

I said, "Be careful, Pa."

With a quick movement, he flipped his pillow hard toward the ceiling. It bounced off and he caught it again. Peering at it, he said, "Got it. Filled with blood too. Need to wash the pillowcase now."

Zan said, "But you just killed that insect!"

Pa sighed as he climbed off of the chair. "I know. In a court run by mosquitos, they would probably find me guilty. They are only taking a little blood after all. No reason to kill another living creature. But they're biting my daughters. I cannot stand it."

"And they're too little to be caught by the butterfly nets. We used to try," Lisa said.

"At least it's a soft death," Pa said.

Zan said, "I don't think it feels so great to the mosquito."

"It's a pillow," Pa said. "I think it is not a bad way to go."

I caught a glimpse of Pa's face and quickly changed the subject before he started feeling so sorry for the mosquitos that he stopped allowing us to kill them. "Oh, there's that fly."

"Where?" Lisa zeroed in on her target again.

"It is not easy to be a Buddhist," Pa said.

Zan wrinkled her brow. "But you guys eat meat. How does that fit in, Mr. Wong?"

"You're right. It doesn't." He smiled and shrugged. "But my girls are growing and they need the nutrients. And because I am weak and like the taste. As I said, life is complicated for a Buddhist, especially when you are Chinese too."

"You don't need to eat meat for the nutrients," Lisa said. Then she swung her net and called, "I caught mine!" She waved her butterfly net around in circles, so the fly couldn't get out. Pa quickly pried one of the screens off a window, Lisa ran over and stuck her net out. We watched the fly zoom away.

Pa replaced the screen.

Zan looked at me. "How do they all get in here when you've got screens on the windows?"

"Some of the screens have rips in them," I said.

"Remember last summer when the apartment got invaded by ants?" Lisa said.

"Ugh! Don't remind me," I said.

Lisa turned to Zan. "This colony of ants showed up in the kitchen but Pa didn't want to kill them so we would just shoo them away. We could literally see them getting bigger and stronger by the day. We tried cinnamon, garlic, vinegar . . . Nothing helped."

I interrupted. "Of course it did. The mint worked, and after that, they all left." I gave Lisa a look to shut her up. She widened her eyes, remembering I'd secretly bought a bottle of insecticide and sprayed the entire apartment while Pa was at work.

I could tell Zan had figured it out by the mischievous look in her eyes. "How strange," she said innocently, "I never knew mint repelled ants."

I glared at her. "Lisa found it on the Internet." In recent years, Lisa's school had begun lending all of the kids laptops for use in their classes, something I'd never had, so Lisa was our technology expert.

Pa nodded. "Very wise, that Internet." To Pa, the Internet was a sort of prophet.

"Why don't you do something useful, like help us catch the last fly?" I said to Zan. She grinned and took my butterfly net. Within a few minutes, she'd caught the fly I'd been stalking.

As we watched it zip away, Zan said, "Have you ever thought that you're just releasing flies into the world, where they can have babies and bother more people?"

Lisa giggled. "I hope they have fun."

I grabbed Zan's arm. "Come on, let's get Godmother Yuan and go to tai chi class."

Zan and I walked a few blocks over to Godmother Yuan's building. We linked arms to fight our way through the crowds, squeezing past stands of live crabs and dismembered eels, the carp lying limp in the blazing sunlight. Especially during the weekends, there seemed to be almost as many tourists as Chinese in Chinatown. We dodged one white couple who were pointing at the roasted geese hanging in the window of a restaurant, then turned the corner onto the twisty little street where Godmother lived.

It was a bit quieter there and the sharp scent of incense filled the air. Godmother lived on the second floor, above a religious store that sold joss paper, urns and idols, where incense was always burning. Even though she wasn't really my godmother, I called her that as a sign of affection and respect. Godmother Yuan was a tai chi master. She'd been our friend for as long as I could remember. When Ma died, Godmother, her face covered in tear tracks, held my hand at the funeral as she cradled Lisa on her lap.

Zan dabbed at her sweaty forehead with a tissue as we climbed the stairs. "Should I call her *sifu*?" *Sifu* meant "master" and it was what most of Godmother Yuan's students called her.

I shook my head. "You're not a regular member of the class. Just 'Mrs. Yuan' will be fine."

Zan smiled. "Do I have to call you *sifu*?"

"Ha! I'm just the helper."

I stopped in front of Godmother's door and knocked.

Her voice came from within the apartment. "Charlie, you know my door's unlocked."

Zan's eyebrows shot up. "Is she serious?"

I said softly, "Nothing anyone can say will convince her to do otherwise. She says her door's always open to her students and friends. It's never been locked, not even when her husband was alive."

I turned the doorknob and the door swung wide. Out of politeness, we didn't enter. Godmother was walking toward us with her bag over her arm. She was short and round, with a white permed head of curls, like a dandelion, but I knew how strong she was because I'd sparred with her in push-hands training. She wore simple, loose clothing that allowed freedom of movement. I'd never seen her in a dress. It was a well-known Chinatown rumor that a few gang members had tried to take her purse once and she'd sent them running with a few blows.

"Do you remember my friend Zan, Godmother?" I said. Godmother spoke Toisanese and I only spoke Mandarin, so we always communicated in English. Her family had been in the U.S. so long that her English was better than Pa's.

Zan bowed her head and said, "Mrs. Yuan."

Godmother said, "Of course I do. Are you joining us today?"

I said, "Would that be all right? It's only this one time. Zan can't make it to your other classes at the Tai Chi Association or Senior Citizens Center."

"Any friend of yours is welcome. I wish you could help me with those other classes too, Charlie," Godmother said as we headed down the stairs. She turned to Zan. "She is my best student."

"Oh, that's not true," I said. "I've just been doing it for so long."

"Are you coming to tai chi in the park this Sunday?" Godmother always asked me this.

"I would like to but it's too early for me."

"When are you going to stop that dishwasher job? It keeps you up until all hours. 'If you do not change direction, you may end up where you are heading.'"

"Is that from a Hallmark card?"

"Who? No, it's Lao Tzu."

I glanced at Zan, signaling her to be quiet. "Actually, I'm starting a new job on Monday. As a receptionist. In computers." I couldn't risk Godmother telling Pa the truth.

Godmother stopped walking so abruptly, I almost tripped. "Really." She fumbled in her purse until she found a new red envelope. "I always keep a couple in here, in case I run into one of my grandchildren." She took out two wrinkled five-dollar bills from her wallet, folded them carefully and put them in the envelope.

"Oh no, Godmother, it's not necessary." I knew how little she had. She was well respected but she taught most of her classes, including the one we were going to, for free. Most positions at the Yuan Benevolent Association were volunteer.

She pressed the red envelope in my hand. "For good fortune."

"Are you sure?"

"You must take it or it will be bad luck."

"Thank you." I bent over and kissed her cheek. I thought about what the witch had said. "The Vision told me my new job will amount to nothing."

"Hush! Don't repeat the words of that old potato."

Zan and I laughed. It was well known that Godmother and the Vision had an ongoing feud, due to some insult in their youth everyone else had forgotten.

"Another Lao Tzu quote for you: 'When I let go of what I am, I become what I might be.'"

"I hope you're right."

We climbed up the stairs to the Yuan Benevolent Association. The Benevolent Associations had been formed originally to help families abroad. This one occupied the third floor of a building, and was a place where all members with the Yuan surname could gather and gossip. There was often free tea and food, plus social events like mahjong evenings and these tai chi classes. I wasn't allowed to be a full member but they tolerated me because my maternal grandmother had been a Yuan before her marriage. After they wed, girls were no longer considered an official part of the family.

Godmother Yuan tapped me on the shoulder. "I'll never understand why you don't join the Wong Benevolent Association. They're so powerful, many times the size of ours. They just helped that Wong girl from Hong Kong pay her way through college."

I'd said it before. "I'm the wrong kind of Wong, remember? I'm a northern Wong. The Wong Benevolent Association belongs to the southern Wongs. Their name is even written with a different character. Anyway, I don't think I'm cut out for college."

"Nonsense. 'A genius always presents himself as a fool.'"

"Umm, thanks, Godmother. I think."

Zan was grinning.

Godmother opened the door and we entered a large room with windows that faced the street on one end. We could hear the constant rumble of traffic as the ceiling fans whirred. A few older ladies were already moving the tables and chairs out of the way. Some chairs were set up at the side of the room for qigong work. At the other end was the platform with a statue of the Yuan ancestor on what we called the "god table." Godmother went to light incense and pay her respects to her ancestor. The smell of roast meat and rice drifted into the room from the restaurants on the street. More people trailed in.

Every time I came to tai chi class I thought of Ma, who had started me on it so young. She believed it was important for balance and health. As with acupuncture and other forms of healing, one of tai chi's goals was to mend and stimulate the circulation of qi throughout the body. The spiraling, circular movements brought the person back into mental and physical balance. As it was both a martial art and a form of meditation, it unified body and soul. I always enjoyed the tai chi classes because I felt centered afterward, and it was one of the few times when I felt at home in my body. I'd tried bringing Lisa too, but she didn't like it.

Godmother nodded at me to begin the class. I led Zan to a spot near the front where she could see the lesson, yet wouldn't feel too exposed. I felt comfortable in my large T-shirt and loose pants. I announced that class was about to begin, and when everyone had lined up, Godmother walked to the Yuan ancestor's statue. The students all turned to face the statue as well. She bowed and we followed.

Then the students turned back to me as I started the class. I always did the warming up and cooling down for Godmother. That gave her the chance to walk around the room, "smiling from the heart" at the students, as she put it.

"Stand upright and relax from head to toe. Find your center." I bent my knees and allowed my arms to float upward, then down again. We stretched our spines, then hips, knees and feet, turning the legs inward and outward. I enjoyed teaching, even in this mild way.

After the warming up, I led the students into a few dynamic exercises like Lifting the Sky, where we stretched our linked hands toward the ceiling, to get their energy flowing. I was surprised to see Zan having trouble with many of the exercises, especially since she was usually so coordinated. Of course she was new at this. Then Godmother came to the front of the class and took over. She reviewed the tai chi movements we'd done last week, then moved on to a few new ones. I stood next to Zan and followed along, losing myself in the flowing movements.

After that, the class split into two groups. The most advanced students went with Godmother to do qigong, while I helped the rest in push-hands training and tai chi sword and fan.

Godmother caught my eye and sent me a questioning look, and as always, I shook my head. Godmother always said, "External strength is supported by internal power," meaning that learning tai chi with qigong was ideal, but I didn't dare explore qigong any further. Qigong was becoming aware of our internal life energy, allowing it to flow throughout our bodies for healing. An essential part was feeling all your emotions and letting them go. When I thought of Ma's death and my disappointing life, I knew I wasn't ready for that.

Zan was breathing hard. "It looks very easy when you do it. I feel so clumsy."

"It just takes time to learn because you need to control all these muscles in order to make it smooth." I saw two men in their fifties starting to become aggressive with their push-hands exercise. "Come on, I have to break that up."

I went over to the students and separated them. I stepped in for one of them and connected to the other man's wrists with mine. "Push-hands is not about shoving each other." I began to move our linked arms in a circular direction. "We are questioning and answering each other. Meet the incoming force with softness, move with it, then redirect it." I stepped back and allowed them to try it again. Both men bowed to me before resuming the exercise.

Zan was staring at Godmother's group. "What in the world are they doing?"

At the beginning, they'd sat in a circle, discussing meridians and healing, but now they were standing with their eyes closed, their limbs twitching and swaying. Godmother had her hand spread, fingers vibrating, over one woman's head and was directing the woman's movements like a puppeteer, though not actually touching her at all.

"Flowing Breeze, Swaying Willows," I said. "It's pure energy flow."

One man started to convulse, then began to wail, a high animal sound. Another woman shook her head violently from side to side. None of the other students seemed to notice.

"That's the freakiest thing I've ever seen," Zan said.

"I know. That's why I'm not really such a good tai chi student. I don't want to develop my qigong."

"I'm with you. Why are they doing that?"

"They're cleansing the negative energy from their bodies. They're not controlling it, it's flowing through them. When there's a blockage, it needs to be cleared from the body. It restores the natural balance."

I thought of the few times Godmother had tried with me. I'd felt such a rush of grief and disappointment in myself, I'd had to stop. If I let my fear take over, there'd be no way I'd make it back to that dance studio on Monday.

Four

O n Sunday, Pa, Lisa and I went to temple to pray that my new job would be successful. The monks often put beautiful accessories on the golden idol of Kuan Yin, goddess of compassion, and today she had been clothed with a blue lace shawl. Kneeling in front of her, I'd whispered, "Please let me do it right this time."

Since I didn't have to be at the studio until the early afternoon, I had the mornings free.

"Maybe we could start reading *Pilgrim's Progress* in the mornings now," I said to Lisa.

"Umm, why don't we wait and see how it goes with your new job? You'll be so busy for a while. Maybe we should take a break with the reading."

Sometimes I wasn't sure that Lisa wanted to improve her mind. She saw my look and said, "Just a temporary one, Charlie."

Lisa hugged me tightly before she left for Uncle's office. "You'll be great. You're so much better than you think you are."

Then Pa had stuck a bobby pin with a small red rose on it in my hair. "Red always brings good luck," he said. "And you shouldn't leave your hair just free like that. It's too wild." It was also because in times of mourning, Chinese unbind their hair as a sign of grief, to leave it loose and untamed. Pa was afraid that wearing my hair like that would bring on a period of despair. I wasn't superstitious, but I kept the bobby pin in my hair. It felt like wearing a bit of Pa's love.

Once Lisa and Pa had left, my fingers began to feel numb with fear again. Images of that glamorous studio flitted across my mind. This time, I would pay attention as best I could. No more stupid mistakes. This was my chance: no more immersing my hands in boiling water, no more shifting from leg to leg for hours to relieve the deep ache in my back, no more grease underneath my nails, no more lifting tubs filled with so many ceramic plates it felt like hoisting sandbags.

I dressed carefully, applying two heaping palmfuls of gel to flatten down my hair. I decided to wear pants: they couldn't possibly go over as poorly as the dress had. The pants were somewhat baggy but plain and black, and I paired them with a big, pink cotton shirt patterned with large roses to match the flower in my hair. I wore my one pair of heels, relieved to find that the bare patches I'd colored in were mostly hidden by the pants.

Adrienne had asked me to come to the dance studio at one p.m., a half hour before it opened, to have the chance to get settled before everything began. I was hoping to have some quiet time. When I arrived, the reception area was dark and empty as I'd expected, but lights shone from the ballroom. I tentatively poked my head inside the double glass doors.

"Hello?" When no one answered, I pushed through to the next set of doors and peered into the main ballroom.

It was a blur of lights and people. A couple on the floor was dancing as Adrienne circled around them, analyzing and stopping them at different points. Two young women sat by the tables, watching.

I recognized the receptionist from last week, Nina, dancing with a broad Latin man. She wore a burgundy spaghetti-strap leotard with gray sweatpants rolled down to her hips, and high heels. Her shoulders and arms were tight with muscle, and as I watched, she did a series of high-speed turns around her partner. She stopped in between one heartbeat and the next. So, not a receptionist after all. She must have been a professional dancer filling in at the desk until they could hire someone.

Adrienne now stepped in to talk to them both. A beautiful loose, wide-sleeved shirt draped gracefully over her rounded middle. Then she caught sight of me through the doors and gestured for me to come in. "I'll be with you in a few minutes," she called.

"I'm early anyway," I answered, entering the room.

"Hallelujah, you came!" Nina said, her hands clasped together in mock prayer. "Please don't leave or they'll make us take shifts playing receptionist again. We're just running over because we're struggling with the turns. I'm Nina and this is Mateo."

Mateo, medium height with dark skin, was dressed in a black T-shirt and sweatpants. He extended his hand to me. When our palms touched, he looked down at them quickly as if he'd been startled, but said nothing, only gave me a quick smile. He turned to Nina and put his hand on his hip. "You're off balance, sweetheart. Don't blame me."

Adrienne shook her head. "Not true." She used her finger to draw a line from Mateo's belly button up through his head. "Your arm that is leading her is off the alignment of her center. That's why she's having trouble. Do it again and I'll show you how it should be done."

I was relieved the center was important here too, something Godmother always told me in tai chi. It made me feel a bit more comfortable in this unfamiliar world. They repeated the move with Mateo doing the lady's part, Adrienne teaching. Then Adrienne took Nina into dance position so that Adrienne was doing the man's part. "Nina, you're spotting straight during the triple but I think you should spot him instead. It'll give this segment a more intimate look."

Nina nodded and did the step with Adrienne. She spun and spun, then said, "What a difference!"

Finally Adrienne allowed Nina and Mateo to try the move again together. They executed it perfectly.

"It was my fault, my dear," Mateo said to Nina. "Forgive me?" And he bent and gave her a kiss on the cheek.

I looked down. Some women were so lucky. I had never seen anything like this place. I felt a flash of sadness for Ma, who would have amazed them all, I thought, if she'd only had the opportunity.

Adrienne came over to me. "Charlie, I'm all yours now."

We walked toward the two young women who were sitting at one of the tables set against the wall of the ballroom. I recognized the tall blonde from last week. Now that I was closer, I could tell that although she made a stunning impression from a distance, she seemed to be wearing heavy foundation. She sat straight, her collarbones protruding under her open black cocktail dress, and lean legs crossed.

Her companion was petite and dark, with short black hair. Unlike my hair now, her cut accentuated her large dark eyes and crimson lips, pulled in a half smirk. They both looked me up and down but didn't say a word.

Adrienne said, "Charlie, this is Simone and Estella, two of our dancers. Charlie is our new receptionist." Adrienne gazed at us, clearly expecting us to shake. Simone, the blonde, extended a languid hand to me and I took it.

I felt the softness of her palm, then she jerked it away. "Do you have a skin disease or something?"

"Simone!" Adrienne sounded furious.

Everyone stared at my right hand. It was red and callused, the skin broken and bleeding in a few places where the chapped skin had cracked. I was so used to everyone else at the restaurant having a body shaped by manual labor that it hadn't occurred to me that my hands were unusual.

Adrienne put her hand on my shoulder and said, "That's just a holdover from her last job. Come on, Charlie, I'm sorry to have kept you waiting."

As I walked past the two women, I didn't miss the way they stared. Adrienne hissed, "Put some cream or whatever on that and get your skin back to normal as soon as possible, do you hear me?"

I nodded.

"I'm going out on a limb by hiring you. You have to look presentable and those hands are ridiculous. If necessary, slap some makeup on them."

"I'll fix them," I promised, mortified.

Adrienne took me to my desk and showed me the phone system. "We have an accountant who comes in every week to settle the accounts, and Dominic and I handle most of the administration and billing, so your job is really to welcome the students, handle all of the bookings for the dancers and group classes, and take telephone calls. We're on social media and have our own website but we still hire an old-fashioned telephone call center off-site that does the recruiting for our introductory classes. It's so competitive in New York that we find we need every extra bit of help we can get."

Adrienne brought out the appointment book and the sheets I needed to make for each dancer with their schedules. "We want every student to feel welcome from the moment they hear your voice on the phone. It's very important to us to have everything run smoothly, from the first contact throughout all of the bookings for the lessons."

The telephone caught my eye. It had many buttons. Adrienne saw my trepidation and said, "There's an instruction sheet on how the phone system works."

I swore to myself I'd study it every chance I had.

Adrienne took me on a tour of the studio. Behind the reception-ist's waiting room was another office, which Adrienne explained was used by the accountant, Dominic or her. The black leather couches in the reception area were for students or dancers on their breaks. Then there was the main ballroom, with her small office nestled inside it, and positioned at the end of the main ballroom was another door. We stepped through it into a smaller ballroom, with its own sound system and mirrored walls.

"We can use this room for wedding couples and group classes, also when students are rehearsing special numbers that require spe-cific music," Adrienne explained.

"How much are the private lessons here?" I wondered if I'd ever be able to take a few myself.

"A hundred and twenty dollars," Adrienne said.

"For a package?"

"No. Per lesson."

I almost choked. What kind of world was this? Godmother's paid tai chi classes cost that much for several months of training.

Adrienne gave me a small smile. "Our dancers are some of the best in the world. We train our professionals with internationally renowned dancers like Julian Edwards, who will be coming in later. He's not a part of our staff. He travels all over the world, giving coaching sessions to top professional dancers. We're lucky he visits us regularly." She had reached a door inside the small ballroom and she opened it. "The teachers' room."

I looked in to find a room filled with lockers on the wall, reminding me of my old high school. People had stuck posters and photos onto the fronts of their lockers. It smelled nice, like an expensive department store. There were small machines for coffee and tea, a microwave, a minifridge, a full-length mirror propped against the wall, and at the end, another door that was propped open. I could feel a slight breeze from outside.

"That door goes onto the roof of the adjacent building," she said. "No smoking inside, so the smokers go out when they need to. You don't smoke, do you?"

I shook my head.

A number of folding chairs were set up in the free space of the room.

Mateo stuck his head in through the door. "Should I start grabbing some of the chairs for the meeting?"

I looked around at the staff sitting in a circle in the small ballroom. Muted spotlights hanging from the ceiling gave the room an intimate glow. Nina and Mateo were already there, still bickering about something from their rehearsal. The blond Simone was next to Mateo, then came the petite brunette, Estella. A couple I didn't know sat by Estella. Adrienne had saved a seat for me in between her and Dominic, who had just arrived.

Dominic stood up. "I think most of you have met Charlie, our new receptionist."

Adrienne said, "Except for Viktor and Katerina, who are both from Russia." She indicated the other couple. The tall man gave me a nod and the woman, who had a riot of chestnut curls, smiled at me in a friendly way. Everyone was watching me. I sat on my hands without thinking, trying to hide them.

Dominic said, "We hope she will be staying with us for a long time. Be nice to her or she will leave and we will make you answer the phones again." He went over some sales numbers from our studio and others in the Avery chain. Apparently this studio was doing very well, except they were not keeping enough students from the introductory group lessons.

"What is going wrong?" Dominic asked. "Estella, since you most often teach the intro groups, can you tell me? We need to make sure they have a good time and want to return for private lessons."

The flush on Estella's cheeks made her look even prettier. She spoke with a faint French accent. "I do not know. I teach them. I do not tell them they are the clumsy elephants they are. I keep my mouth shut. I cannot help it if people do not want to continue."

Adrienne broke in. "But you see, that attitude has to change. You're calling them derogatory names."

"Not to their face."

"But in your mind, and they feel that. These are complete beginners. I need you to treat them with warmth and kindness."

Estella pouted. "Let someone else teach them, then."

Dominic said, "There is no one else. Nina is booked all of the time, Simone and Katerina usually have their competition students, the men are already overloaded with students in the evening hours. Please, Estella, try to be a bit nicer to the students." His look was gentle.

Estella's lips curved in a reluctant smile. "Yes, I will try."

Then Adrienne said, "Remember that there is a party this week for the students on Thursday evening and the theme is Hawaiian, so please don't come dressed like a belly dancer or an Egyptian. One last point. While we are very happy about the affection between our students and our staff, there is a line between dancing and hanky-panky. Please remember that. Thanks, everyone. Get dressed now, as our first students will be coming in soon. Charlie, if you could please wait for us for a few minutes in the ballroom while Dominic and I finish updating the accounts from last week. Then we'll get you started."

Estella and Simone had taken up their former places at the table in the main ballroom since they were already dressed for the day. I took a seat at the table next to theirs but none of us said anything to each other.

A man with blond wavy hair was waiting by the mirror. I imagined he was Julian Edwards. He had a prominent nose, and a pronounced cupid's bow above a full underlip. There was something in his walk—his weight low and centered—that reminded me of God-mother, though he was much younger. The Russian couple, Katerina and Viktor, entered the ballroom and greeted him. They took dance position and began to move across the floor.

Julian watched for a few minutes, then stopped the couple in midstep, very close to where we were sitting. Although they'd been gliding across the room a moment ago, they froze the moment he touched them, completely balanced. Katerina's leg was extended behind her red Lycra dress with her toe pointed, her head arched back. Viktor, extremely thin, all long arms and legs, made me think of a giant stick insect.

"Viktor, if I may." Julian gently extracted Viktor from Katerina and took his place. Then he placed his hands on her shoulders and arched her back slightly more, turned her head a fraction to the left. "You have a lovely position, Katerina, but we need a bit more stretch here to balance the pivot turns." There was something British in his voice.

He stepped away and allowed Viktor to take position again. At his nod, they resumed as if nothing had interrupted them and flew across the ballroom. They looked like a fairy tale come true as they flowed across the floor, their long strides eating up the ballroom, Katerina's expression a blend of joy and passion.

Now that they were out of hearing distance, Simone and Estella spoke to each other in mock whispers. I watched them in the mirrored wall facing us.

"Julian has such . . . line," Simone sighed.

Estella giggled. "I'd do a dip with him anytime." They both laughed. "You have to admit," she continued, "Viktor and Katerina look good together."

"Of course, they've been dancing together since they were five or something in Russia. He's a powerful dancer but Katerina . . ."

"She is big, isn't she?" said Estella.

"She would never have been allowed to keep all that weight at Juilliard," Simone said. I studied Katerina. She was tall, broad-shouldered and voluptuous. She was more athletically built than the model-thin Simone, but to my eyes she was stunning.

"You're so bad," Estella said with a laugh.

I barely knew I had spoken aloud: "I think she's lovely."

Both women glared at me. "Were we talking to you?" Simone said.

I'd just arrived at the studio and they already disliked me.

A few weeks passed, and Uncle and Aunt were taking us out to dinner because it was Uncle's birthday. The glamour of the dance studio had already rubbed off on me a bit. I chose a dress with an open neckline that evening and put on lipstick. The dress was quite modest but revealed my neck and collarbones. I understood the moment Pa paused that I'd done wrong.

"Don't you like it?" I asked, already knowing the answer.

"You look like a dancing girl," he said.

"Ma was one," Lisa said.

"Your mother was a dancer," he said. "There's a difference."

"She wore beautiful clothes too." I glanced at the photo of Ma onstage.

He sighed. "Your mother was a very lovely woman." His face softened. "And she was already married to me. Come on, put on something befitting a modest girl. And maybe you should wash your face too."

I felt the familiar knot of anger rise in my throat and swallowed it down again. Did he have any idea what other young women my age were wearing? What they were doing? I was too old to be living at home with Pa. He was so protective, he wanted to keep me away from boys until I turned twenty-five, at which point he would expect me to somehow be married. There was no in-between phase.

But I didn't think I could leave my family. Lisa needed me, and I couldn't leave Pa with all the bills to pay alone. My sister had been only three when our mother died of a massive stroke. At fourteen, I was the one who'd comforted Lisa on the nights when there was no one to hold either one of us anymore. Pa had shrunken into himself. He could barely care for himself, let alone two young girls. He would just scratch the back of his head, rub his eyes like he had something in them, then retreat to his own room again.

When Ma was alive, I used to breathe in her scent. On the surface was the oil and sweat of the restaurant, but underneath that was her smell, cool and lemony. I still floated in that bubble of loving her with everything that I was. I had Pa but I loved him in a different way. After Ma's death, everything had changed. It was afterward that I truly hated school and my classes became so difficult. The other kids ignored me, the teachers found me to be a silent problem, sullen and unresponsive at the back of their rooms. I'd had Winston, Zan and another friend, Mo Li, but then Winston had left me as well. I couldn't do chitchat with a big crowd of girls like Grace could. I was tactless, too honest, hopeless at pretending, and I was also miserable. I just did my best to hide away in my baggy clothing, and Pa had no idea how to guide me to become a woman either, which was just fine with me. There'd been a few boys in high school who'd liked me anyway but none of them turned into anything serious, especially since I had to hide the relationship at home.

And now here we were. I obeyed Pa and put on a shapeless top that covered my neck, and a thick pair of pants. I gritted my teeth and took off the lipstick as well. Pa nodded in approval when I came out. Lisa made a face at me behind his back and we wrinkled our noses at each other.

Then, at the last minute, just as we were supposed to leave, Lisa said, "I'm not feeling so well. Maybe I should just stay home." She was hardly ever sick. And we so rarely got to eat at a restaurant, I knew she must really feel lousy to decide to miss it. I went over to her and smoothed out her hair. Her forehead felt sticky underneath my hand.

"Are you all right?"

"I'm not hungry," she whispered, "and I see Aunt and Uncle every day anyway."

I said, "Maybe she's tired since school's just started again."

Pa shook his head. "You have to come, Lisa, we cannot disgrace ourselves this way. This is an important day for Aunt and Uncle and they have reserved a table at the restaurant. We are their only family. We cannot let them down. I promise we won't stay too long."

But we both knew we would. Pa always forgot his promises once he was with Uncle Henry and they were chatting and laughing about old times.

I was surprised to find Dennis seated next to Uncle Henry at the restaurant. Uncle even had an arm slung around the back of Dennis's chair, laughing at something he'd said, while Aunt Monica beamed. It was unusual for an assistant to be invited to a family event, but I understood. Dennis was becoming the son Uncle and Aunt had never had.

I sat between Dennis and Lisa, and when we were choosing what to order, I said, "How about Peking duck?" I knew that was Lisa's favorite dish.

The older people gave me disapproving looks. "Charlie," Pa said. "We never have duck for a birthday celebration."

Of course. Duck eggs were used in funeral rites and thus duck was bad luck at other times. For a birthday, the "three lives" were acceptable: chicken, pork and fish. Noodles were always necessary too, to represent longevity of life. They ordered pork in black bean sauce, noodles, a soy sauce chicken complete with head and claws to symbolize wholeness, a tofu dish and a whole steamed carp. Although Pa loved fish with bitter melon, nothing bitter was permitted on a birthday, lest the taste bring bad luck in the year to come. Pa, Aunt and Uncle started to drone on about their times in China and the people they'd known then. I felt overwhelmed with shyness next to Dennis. Even though Lisa and he worked together, they didn't speak either.

Finally he said to me, "So are you still in school?"

"No." There was an awkward pause. I didn't want to discuss my dishwashing job or the studio. I made an effort. "You did your degree in pharmacology?"

He brightened. "Yes. I'll probably go back to school for my master's in a few years but I wanted to explore my options before I did. So much of eastern medicine is uncharted territory."

At that moment, the inevitable noodle dish arrived. Uncle took a bite and said to Pa, "Ah, these are good but nothing compared to yours."

Pa roared his great laugh. "You put the tall hat of flattery on my head. I am an illiterate man, you are the one of learning. Older brother, you are doing so well. Are you ever going to expand your office?"

"This is my home. No, I don't want to leave Chinatown. These are my people. I live for them." I could tell he meant it.

Dennis smiled. "Your dedication is admirable, Mr. Wong."

Uncle Henry patted Dennis on the arm and spoke to Pa. "This young man can practically run my office without me already. He has already taken over some of the more standard cases, which frees me to visit patients at their homes."

"Here, eat more," Aunt Monica said, heaping my plate with a pile of mushrooms, which I didn't like. But since mushrooms brought good luck, I would be in trouble if I didn't eat them on Uncle Henry's birthday. I started chewing my way through the pile. She eyed me. "You don't look very well."

I was embarrassed she'd said that in front of Dennis, who was politely pretending not to listen. "What do you mean?" This was so unfair. Pa had made me take off my makeup and now I was going to get crap because I didn't look pink enough.

"You are skinny and anemic," she said.

"Maybe I have something for you," Uncle Henry said.

"Oh no. No," I said. I knew what this would mean: a gift from his office. I'd already consumed enough strange animals boiled in bitter herbs. "I've just started a new job. That's the only reason I am more tired than usual. It will get easier soon."

Pa said with pride, "She is working in an office."

"Really?" Uncle made an impressed face. "Going up in the world, eh? What are you doing?"

I took a deep breath. "Data entry. Some telephone work. In Midtown."

"Oh, good, good." Uncle dug out the eyeball of the fish and put it in Pa's bowl. "What a delicacy, eh? Take more, brother. But especially if you are starting something new, you need more energy. In fact, both of your girls look a bit pale."

Lisa was resting her chin on her hands, as if she was exhausted.

Uncle said, "I have a fresh shipment of Tibetan caterpillars."

"No!" I said.

Aunt Monica glowered at me. "Silly girl, those caterpillars sell by weight for twice the price of gold. They can cure infection, inflammation, fatigue, phlegm. Even cancer!"

"Really?" Pa's eyes widened.

I nudged Lisa underneath the table for help, knowing that we would be force-fed the valuable caterpillars if we didn't stop this now. I didn't care whether they worked or not, I still didn't want to eat any worms.

Lisa raised her head and said, "I feel just fine."

"Harvested by nomads," Uncle Henry said. "The caterpillars only live in the grasslands above ten thousand feet and are infected by a parasite, a type of fungus. The fungus kills the caterpillar, then feeds on its body. That is why they are so powerful." Uncle waved his chopsticks at Pa for emphasis. "I will give you a few. Boil them with ginseng until the soup condenses to the size of one rice bowl. It'll be nice and concentrated."

Lisa and I exchanged a look. We were sunk.

"Amazing," Dennis said.

"Why don't you take them?" I said.

Pa gave me a quelling look. "We cannot possibly accept them for free, brother. No, you must eat too. We will pay full price."

"Ridiculous, you are my own family. A token amount is enough, one dollar per caterpillar."

"That is insane. We must give you at least ninety percent, how else will you survive? You will go out of business like this."

This reverse haggling went on for a while, with Pa fighting to chip in more and Uncle arguing for him to pay less, until they arrived at what they both secretly felt was the right price for a family member, about sixty percent of the retail price. Lisa and I were used to this. At the end of the meal, there would be a similar fight over the check, with everyone struggling to pay until the person who was actually supposed to get the check won. In this case, it would be Uncle who paid since he had invited us. It all seemed senseless to me but it had to do with honor. Even though Uncle's medicines were so expensive, half of Chinatown credited him with saving their lives.

"How do you really feel?" I asked Lisa in a low voice.

"My head hurts. We're not going to leave early."

"I know. He always forgets. But let him have a good time. I guess he doesn't have much else."

Lisa sighed and we both looked at Pa as I put my hand over hers and she gripped it. She spoke in a low voice. "I'm glad I have you, Charlie. Sometimes I'm scared."

This didn't sound like Lisa. I tried to get her to perk up. "You should be afraid of that caterpillar soup."

She smiled for the first time that evening. "Believe me, I am."

Five

I fidgeted in Mr. Song's shoebox of an office at the middle school, waiting for him to appear and wondering why he'd asked me there. He was Lisa's guidance counselor. Lisa was never in trouble. When she was younger, she used to have anxiety attacks when she didn't get a perfect score on a test or when she couldn't understand how to do something, but that hadn't happened for a while now. His desk was cluttered with stacks of folders. A few books on the shelf partially covered a ribbon with printing on it. I nudged them away to read "Cornell." Mr. Song had a photo of a beautiful Asian woman in a bridal gown on his desk, probably his wife. I patted my own puffy hair, trying to tame it.

He stepped into the room, dark and handsome, and I understood why he needed that picture. It must have been to keep the swooning teenage girls away. "I'm sorry to have kept you waiting."

I blurted out, "Is Lisa in trouble?"

"Oh no! I hope I didn't worry you." He sat in his chair and rocked back. "Due to Lisa's test scores coming into our sixth grade, we'd already flagged her as a student to watch. I know she's just settling into our school now but something her English teacher showed me really gave me pause and made me think we ought to sit down and discuss her future."

He pulled out one of his folders and flipped through the loose handwritten pages. "The teacher asked the class to describe snow to someone who lives in the desert, someone who has never seen or felt snow before. Let me read you a few typical responses. 'Snow is white, cold and fluffy. It forms a blanket over everything. You can find it in your freezer.' Or 'Children jump and play in snow, bundled up in their winter clothing.'"

I was tense. "What did Lisa write?"

He took out a page he'd marked with a yellow Post-it note. "Light snow is like a dance of fairies: wild, chaotic and free. Heavy snow is sorrow, blanketing your eyes until you are blinded by it. Melting snow is a long glide of tears for the loss of someone you never had the chance to know."

I blinked the emotion from my eyes, keeping them averted so Mr. Song couldn't see. And I'd thought Lisa didn't care about not having a mother. "I'll get her to rewrite it. The teacher probably wanted—"

"No." He leaned forward. "Lisa is extraordinary."

I exhaled. "Yes, she is."

"We have our own honors program and she's already enrolled in it. However, I can't help but feel that a child like this could truly blossom in the right environment. We are only a middle school. She'll need to leave in a few years anyway. Have you ever heard of Hunter?"

"Hunter College?" Lisa couldn't be that advanced.

"No, Hunter College High School. It's a laboratory school for intellectually gifted students."

I swallowed. "We couldn't afford—"

"It's free. The school's from seventh to twelfth grade. The test for admission is this coming January and is extremely competitive. The kids need to already be in the top percentages in both math and reading before they're allowed to take the test. Lisa qualifies. Out of about thirty-five hundred kids who take the test, less than two hundred are admitted. The admission rate is only about six percent."

Lisa was such a perfectionist. If she tried and didn't make it, she would be crushed. "Is it worth it? She's just settling in here."

"I know. It's just that Hunter is such a special place, offering her all of the support and facilities to develop her gifts. She'd be among bright, creative kids. I have a feeling she'd thrive at Hunter."

I studied his glowing face. "Did you go there, Mr. Song?"

He coughed into his hand. "I see Lisa is not the only intelligent one in your family."

"Oh no. I was a hopeless student when I was here."

He looked sad. "Then I believe we failed you."

I'd never thought of it that way. "How long have you been here, Mr. Song?"

"Just a few years."

I was still puzzled about what a man like this was doing in our Chinatown school. "Are you Chinese?"

"Korean. You're trying to figure me out, right?"

Taken aback, I nodded.

"I want to make a difference to the kids here. Contrary to popular opinion, I'm not the only one." He stood and extended his hand. "Please talk to your parents about allowing Lisa to take the Hunter test. A few of her peers have qualified as well. Just give her the chance."

I managed to get to Pa's noodle restaurant before the noontime rush. When I gestured to Pa from the back alleyway, he nodded at his assistant to take over and stepped outside to talk to me.

"What did the teacher want?" he asked.

"He thinks Lisa is gifted. He wants her to take a test for a special school."

"Where is this school?"

I knew what Pa meant. "I think it's not in Chinatown." He wanted to keep us close and protected.

He shook his head. "Is this necessary?"

"She doesn't have to take the test but Mr. Song felt it would be a great opportunity for her if she got in."

"How would she get to this school? Take the subway alone? Now she can just walk. This city's not safe for such a young girl."

Sometimes it felt as if Pa was still living in China, while Lisa and I were in America. "It's for her future. Things are very competitive in this country. She could maybe get into a top college, and the right preparation could change her life. And Mr. Song said that she might not be accepted at all."

Pa bristled, as I knew he would. "Lisa is very smart!"

"There are a lot of bright kids. Other students from her middle school will try for a spot too. There's a good chance she won't be admitted. But Pa, we need to give her the opportunity. Otherwise, she might end up as a dishwasher like me."

"Okay, okay," he said, waving his hands. "Let her try. Then we will decide what to do."

I tried my hardest at my new job. I made a copy of the phone instruction sheet and took it home to study. For the first time, I understood how all of the buttons worked and made sure I could connect people and put them on hold. It worked most of the time until I was under stress, with students in front of me and someone on the phone line, and then things would go wrong.

My main problem was the written work. Somehow, I would mix up times in the schedules. I checked and double-checked whenever I could, which meant I caught most of my own mistakes, but when I had a student on the phone who was in a hurry and dictating the changes to their appointments at lightning speed, I didn't always manage to correctly record what they'd said. Even when I repeated it back to them right, I sometimes wrote it down wrong. I started to come to the studio early on a regular basis so I had more time to make up the sheets for each of the dancers with their schedules for the day. I filled them in twice: first in pencil, then after double-checking with the main appointment book, I finally put everything in pen.

Several times, Simone had stormed up to my desk. "Where is this student I'm supposed to have now?"

"I'm so sorry, let me check."

"You are supposed to get it right the first time! Why else are they paying you?"

She normally didn't waste too much time on me, thankfully, and stomped back into the main ballroom, where she could practice again. Although I made mistakes with the others' schedules as well, everyone else remained quite kind to me, even Estella.

Adrienne managed the business part of the studio while Dominic was its artistic soul. He taught most of the dance sessions for the professionals, except when they'd have a guest coach come in from outside the studio. Adrienne gave coaching sessions as well, but Dominic was the world-famous choreographer. He went through the studio making small adjustments to student and professional alike.

"We are so lucky to be at Adrienne and Dominic's studio," Katerina told me once. "They were the reason we came from Russia. Every day, we can be trained by them."

Whenever I entered the studio, I breathed in the smell of it: airconditioning, cologne and perfume. No food smells, no garlic oil, no dirty dishes waiting for me. I loved that my clothing no longer smelled like food. I smeared my hands with moisturizer every night and the skin began to knit together, the ridges in my nails filling out.

When a student came in, he or she would report to me, then sit at one of the tables in the ballroom until the teacher was available. When I saw a teacher correcting a student's body, moving a hip or shoulder back into place, I thought of Ma, and how safe I'd felt when she'd done that for me. I knew I would never be able to afford the lessons, and yet I spent as much time as I could watching at the glass doors to the ballroom, struggling to decipher the mysteries of dance.

Mostly what I learned instead was the rhythm of the studio. Dance session was held daily in the early afternoon for any professional who wasn't booked, and the sessions were taught by Adrienne, Dominic or an outside coach. I learned many dancers retired in their thirties or early forties. The ones who had won national or international titles became coaches and judges. The bulk of the student lessons were taught in the evenings, after people got off work.

Social dancers came in for a small set of lessons or to reach a goal, like learning how to salsa in time for a party. Wedding couples usually wanted to avoid the "clutch and sway" syndrome for their first dance. Serious students, on the other hand, returned regularly. Some of these were social dancers, people who loved being at the studio every week to dance together. Most were competition students. Mateo's Japanese student, Okina, booked double lessons several times a week with him. I heard that she had been winning competitions for years. Keith was Simone's competition student and he was by far the best male student in our studio. Katerina and Viktor trained regularly with their serious students as well.

I also finally figured out that Mateo and Nina weren't a couple off of the dance floor.

"You see him?" Mateo asked me when a good-looking guy wearing a T-shirt underneath a leather jacket strode into the ballroom. Estella greeted him and they stood chatting near the glass doors.

"Is he one of Estella's competition students?" I answered.

"Oh yes, and she's possessive too. Rushes to put on more makeup before he comes. He's a big television producer, does half of the daytime soap operas. But he just doesn't know that he's gay yet. I can tell. If he ever got a chance to try me, he'd leave her skinny butt in a second," Mateo said. He stood up and walked deliberately toward the pair, swinging his hips. As he passed, I saw him turn his head and catch the guy's eye, giving the man a long wink that made him flush as red as his T-shirt. Estella's lips thinned. Mateo glanced back at me through the glass and pretended to fan himself.

My favorite time of day was before the studio opened, when the professionals were rehearsing. I thought to myself that this was when their true selves were revealed. When they were lounging around in the waiting area during the day, they were diminished, as colorless as the rest of us ordinary people. But then they stood up as dancers and started to move, and it was as if a light shone from within them. I held my breath at their swiftness, strength, grace and power. They were dressed in their rehearsal clothing then—sweats or plain T-shirts—but were all the more breathtaking for it.

I realized that the professionals were not physically flawless. Nina really did have a perfectly proportioned face but Simone had bad skin underneath her makeup and her features were oversize. Estella's nose was very sharp. Viktor had a long awkward face with uneven teeth. Mateo's head was completely square and Katerina's features were as full-blown as the rest of her.

Yet when any of them walked into a room, heads turned. Their attractiveness had more to do with how they moved, how they held themselves, than how they looked. Sometimes I would see Viktor on break, slumped in a chair like a puppet without a master, but then later he would flow across the dance floor with the controlled power of a storm. I began to see beauty as something that could be unleashed from within a person rather than a set of physical features like a perfect nose or big eyes. This was true of the students as well. It didn't seem to matter whether they were tall or short, fat or thin, they all transformed within a few lessons. Something to do with the magic of coordinated movement, the choreography of two people together, the achievement of control over their bodies.

Ma had said to me, "In the west, they believe in separation of body and soul. They think that the soul separated from the body will find enlightenment, but for the Chinese, we strive for unity. If you look at a child, you can see they are still struggling in their bodies, trying to master them. It is when you become one with your body and soul, that is when you will be whole. That is beauty." I'd never fully understood the truth of that the way I did now.

Later, for lessons, the male dancers would change into shirts and ties that they kept in the teachers' room and the women would put on skirts or tailored pants, but during their own rehearsals, they were free to be as they were. They weren't trying to be polite or charming. Viktor and Katerina cursed each other in Russian across the floor when parts of their routine didn't work.

I said once to Nina, "You and Mateo look different when you're on the floor together. It's like you are *more*."

She nodded. "When we dance together, we are at the edges of who we are. We have to push our own limits to find out who we can become, together." Then she'd shaken her head and said, "Now I desperately need some more coffee."

Sometimes Simone practiced with her professional partner, Pierre, who was from Haiti. They were a breathtaking couple, with her white-blond hair against the ebony of his skin. Most of the time they rehearsed at his studio down in the Village. Simone, Pierre, Nina and Mateo were mainly Latin dancers, while Katerina and Viktor specialized in the smooth dances like waltz or foxtrot.

Every day, I watched the dancers, hungry for something I hadn't known I wanted, holding my breath for the day I would make a mistake so great I would be asked to leave.

As Estella and Simone lounged on the chairs in the reception area, I kept myself busy checking the appointment book. They were whispering to each other. I usually enjoyed it when the dancers hung out in my area but this looked serious. I'd seen Estella called into Adrienne's office earlier and Dominic had followed them. I wondered what was going on.

The doors to the ballroom opened and Nina stepped in. "I'm going out now. You want me to grab you some pizza, Charlie?" I was surprised by the type of food most of the dancers brought back to the studio: Chinese takeout, burgers and pasta. Nina had told me that the amount of exercise they got burned off the excess calories. Simone and Estella were the only ones who always purchased salads from the deli on the corner.

"I brought something from home." I'd hidden a box of rice and leftovers in the fridge.

"Smart," Nina said. "I should do that more. It's hard planning ahead like that with the little guy at home."

I stared at her. "You have a child?" Nina appeared so young.

She smiled. "Here, look." She came around behind the desk, pulled out her cell phone and started showing me photos. "That's Sammy." There were pictures of Nina making funny faces with an adorable toddler who had her thick-lashed eyes. None of them included anyone who looked like he might be the father. I still couldn't believe she was a mother. She didn't look like any other mom I'd ever seen.

"He's wonderful," Nina said. Her eyes lingered on my stocking feet. I often removed my heels behind the desk when no one else could see. I'd been flexing and pointing my feet automatically because the shoes hurt so much, but now I stilled them. Would she notice how old and worn my one pair of pumps was?

Nina flipped her hair out of her jacket. "Sure you don't want anything?"

"Yeah."

"You should come out with us sometime. Leave that desk behind."

Warmth rushed through me. I nodded, then looked away as the phone rang.

That afternoon, I stepped into the teachers' room to find Estella huddled by the fire escape at the back, crying. Simone had her arms wrapped around her.

"What do you want?" Simone's lip curled.

"Estella has a phone call," I said. "It's from her competition student. He said he couldn't get through on her cell."

Estella ran a tissue underneath her smeared mascara, powdered her face quickly and then stepped out.

Later that week, I was handing Nina a mug of coffee when my fingers slipped and I spilled it. It didn't burn me but splashed across my orange shirt.

"I'm so sorry, Charlie," Nina said, dabbing at me with a paper towel.

"It's not your fault. I did this to myself." We tried wetting the stains. They didn't budge. I rubbed at them with all my strength. What would happen when the others saw me? "I can't go through the whole day like this."

"Come with me," Nina said, and led me to the teachers' room. She pulled a light cotton cardigan out of her locker. "I use this to warm up before rehearsal."

When I slipped off my wet shirt, I caught a shift in Nina's face, a widening of her eyes. I quickly changed into her cardigan and buttoned it up all the way, conscious of my worn T-shirt underneath. It even had tiny holes in it. I hadn't intended for it to be seen by anyone. Even though she was a bit shorter than me, her cardigan fit me fairly well.

Nina didn't say anything about my clothing and just gave me her usual smile. "I like that on you."

The biting October rain cascaded over the small yellow and green canopy of Zan's cart. It hit the back of the plastic poncho Zan was wearing and poured off of her in a constant stream. When I could, I tried to stop by her cart before I left for the studio. Despite the weather, several customers stood in line, huddled underneath their black umbrellas. I watched her as I waited for my turn.

She wore fingerless gloves, which she used even during the bitter New York blizzards. If her entire hands were covered, she couldn't get her work done quickly enough. She brushed oil on the rounded indentations of the hot egg cake molds, then ladled in the pale golden batter she kept in a large plastic tub. Deftly, she flipped the molds as the batter started to set. When the cakes were crispy, she eased them out with a fork onto a scratched steel pan. Then she jabbed at the egg cakes with tongs to separate them and counted them with lightning speed one by one into waxed paper bags. One dollar for twenty egg cakes. Then it was on to the next customer and she would do it all again.

When I finally stood in front of her, I said, "Hey, you want me to take over for you so you can take a break?"

She smiled. "Thanks, Charlie, but I'm all right." Zan and I had this interchange every time. She always refused whatever I offered. I didn't know how she managed to use the bathroom or eat lunch.

"Do you want my umbrella?"

"I don't have a hand free to hold it but it's nice of you."

I glanced behind me. There were only three other customers in line. I stepped around her and held my umbrella over her. "I'll wait until you're done with the others."

"You're a pal." Zan turned her attention to the next man in line. I looked around. The fried tofu cart was a few yards away from us. The man who ran it dumped more tofu into the hot oil as I watched. The smell of grease mingled with the damp musk of Zan's wet clothing. Her cart was sandwiched between the fried-tofu guy and the steamed-food lady. That cart offered rice noodle rolls, pig skin, fish balls, beef tripe and lo mein. It worked out, since people would get their lunch from the steamed-food cart, then come to Zan for egg cakes for dessert.

As Zan was serving a well-dressed woman, a man in a rain poncho stuck his head in and hissed to Zan's customer, "Chanel, Gucci! Just like the real thing!"

"Get out of here!" Zan snapped.

Finally, there were no more customers.

Zan said, "How's the new job?"

"I'm barely managing not to get fired."

She chuckled. "So what else is new?" She looked up, and for a moment, she met my eyes. "The important thing is, are you happy?"

I blinked as a horn blared and a passing car splashed us both. "I am. I love it there. It's a whole world in itself. I can't believe I'm free of the noodle shop. I feel like I'm going to mess up, get fired and wind up doing dishes again."

"Well, I was pretty impressed with you in that tai chi class. I never knew you could move like that."

"That's just a bunch of exercises. Anyone could learn. How's it going with your learner's permit?"

"I need to be really ready."

"What are you waiting for? You know that written test inside out."

"Come on, I was never that good at tests and it's so expensive. I'm allowed to retake it for free but if I flunk the first time, it'll just seem like a bad sign. And you always said the driving thing was a dumb idea."

"I guess I'm figuring out that if I can stumble along in a dance studio, you can pass that test."

Zan grinned. "Maybe."

"Lisa has the chance to take the Hunter test. You know, one of those special schools for gifted kids."

"Wow." Zan stirred her batter, not meeting my eyes. "You ever mind?"

I knew what she meant. "Not really. Sometimes. We can't all be special."

Rain poured off of her rickety metal cart as an elderly woman approached. Zan gave my arm a quick squeeze, then turned to help her next customer.

It was Monday again. All of the staff sat on the folding chairs in a circle in the smaller ballroom. Estella wasn't there. There wasn't even an empty chair for her.

Adrienne started to pace. "I think we already know what has happened and I want to make clear what our company policy is. There is to be absolutely no fraternizing with the students. It's in all of your contracts. Are we clear on what that means?"

I tried to remember what my contract had said. I'd barely read it before signing since all of the tiny print had seemed to swim before my eyes.

Mateo put his hands together in a wicked gesture. "No doing the nasty."

"Thank you for that visual clarification, Mateo." Adrienne continued speaking, "I've been in this business for many years. I know how it goes. We love our students. Our students love us. We dance with them, we teach them, we care for them."

Dominic stood up and took over as if they'd rehearsed it. "Some students will fall in love with you, especially the ones who are single and alone. This is normal. Maybe you will even fall in love with some of your students. However. We. Do. Not. Screw. The. Students."

He paused to let us take this in. "It creates an unsafe atmosphere here in the studio if the teachers start dating the students. Our students deserve better than that. They come to be taught in a professional way. Yes, ballroom dancing has to do with fun, romance and sensuality. That is a part of its power. We are here to teach them to harness that energy. However, there is a line we must not cross. The staff at Avery Studios may not become romantically involved with the students. Absolutely all staff, no exceptions." He turned to look at me.

"Me?" I said, confused. "Who would I sleep with? No one wants to do me." I could feel my face turn hot.

Nina burst out laughing while a couple of people chuckled.

Late that afternoon, when Mateo and Nina were sitting in the reception area, waiting for their students to come, I asked them, "Was it Estella's competition student?"

Nina answered, "They've been carrying on together outside of the studio for so long. It was totally obvious. I think Adrienne and Dominic were trying to give them the benefit of the doubt but she only got in deeper. She's in love with him. She thinks they're going to get married."

"Don't you think so?"

"I don't believe in men's promises anymore," Nina said, tossing her head. Mateo kicked her. "Except for yours, darling." Her tone was light but I could see the strain on her face. "I think she's making a huge mistake. I even told her, but she wouldn't listen. She's lost her job, her career, all for this guy."

Mateo put his arm around her and gave her a quick hug. "Just let out the pain, baby. And he's secretly gay too."

Nina laughed. "Shut up."

Mateo said, "It's dumb all around. She should just have made him quit taking lessons here first. Everyone knows it's impossible to police your relationships after the student's gone. No one cares then."

"Are they going to replace her?" I asked.

"Of course," said Mateo. "We're understaffed for the number of students we have anyway. What we really need is another man."

"No, we don't!" Nina said. "Enough men. You're just looking for some fresh meat."

Mateo shrugged. "Can't blame a guy for trying. But I heard Ms. Simone and Adrienne fighting after the meeting."

"Why?" Nina asked.

"About Pierre, of course."

I had to think for a moment. "You mean Simone's partner?"

"Sure. She'd do anything to get him in the same studio. Making a commitment . . ."

Nina pitched in. "And it'd be a lot easier for them to find time to rehearse. Plus, I'm sure he'd love to come here."

"Why?"

"We're the most successful studio in New York City." Nina shrugged like it wasn't a big deal. "It's because Adrienne and Dominic are so smart. They're good to us too. They pay a fortune to bring in people like Julian Edwards for the entire staff. So what did Adrienne say about hiring Pierre?"

Mateo struck a pose and began to imitate Adrienne. "This is ballroom, my dear. I do not need the drama, not until I'm sure you'll stay together. Dance couples, one moment they're all over each other, the next they're slamming doors and refusing to appear

in the same show together. So if I were you, I'd get myself to rehearsal instead of complaining to me."

I tried to keep a straight face but then I heard Nina snorting with
laughter and I couldn't stop myself from giggling.

"You're preaching to the choir," Nina said.

"So who are they going to hire?" I asked.

Nina shrugged. "Beats me."

Six

Lisa and I stared into the vat filled with live frogs. Some were black, while others were olive with black markings. As we watched, the fishmonger scooped out the largest one, a mottled purple-black frog, and popped it into a plastic bag. He tied the handles together. The bag writhed as the frog kicked. The customer dropped the bag into her large shopping tote and left, looking satisfied.

Lisa said, "Can we buy some vegetables now?"

I signaled the fishmonger for a few pieces of sea bass, which were fortunately already dead. Then Lisa and I took our time looking at the different produce stands. Lisa's red wool jacket brought out the gloss in her hair. It'd taken me weeks to save up for the sneakers she wore, the ones she'd wanted so much because the other girls had them. I didn't care about clothing for myself but I loved making Lisa happy. She stuck her finger in a pile of hairy rambutan. I shook my head, silently telling her not to touch. Then she paused over some bitter melon.

"Do you want one?" I asked. "I thought you didn't like them."

"I don't. But Pa does, especially with salted black beans and fish. I'm trying to expand my tastes now that I'm becoming more mature."

I laughed. "Good move." I studied the rough, pockmarked skins of the bitter melon. "These are really light green. That means they're going to be old and bitter."

Lisa made a face. "Pa can soak them in salt water. Maybe I'll just have a taste and you guys can have the rest."

"Oh, thanks a lot!" But Pa did love them and we hardly ever ate them at home. I bought one and then we went to the soy man to pick up some sweetened soy milk and fresh tofu. Our grocery money was dwindling by then but Lisa looked with so much longing at the containers of *doufu hua,* sweetened tofu pudding, that I bought her one.

On our way home, we passed Gossip Park. It was a beautiful autumn day so we sat on a bench just inside the park and I opened Lisa's pudding for her, then dribbled the syrup on top.

She paused with her spoon over the plastic bowl. "Don't you want any?"

"No, you go ahead."

She happily gobbled everything up. When she was done, she wiped her mouth with a paper napkin and sighed. A tall girl with her hair in two long braids passed by on the street behind us, arm in arm with her mother.

I said, "Hey, isn't that your friend Hannah?"

Lisa scrambled around to look, then sat down again. "Yeah." They'd already gone down the block. "She's taking the Hunter test too."

"Anyone else?"

"A white kid named Fabrizio. I don't know him that well. Hannah's studying with her parents for it every night."

A pang passed through me. I tried to sound casual. "What are they doing?"

Lisa rolled her eyes. "You know. That family lives to do homework together. It's the way they have fun. They're like, 'Oh, I know the answer to question number three!'" Lisa pretended to shoot her hand in the air. "When we were in elementary school, I overheard her mother complaining to the teacher because Hannah had homework over Mother's Day weekend. She said, 'When Hannah has homework, I have homework.'"

"Well, at least they care about her. What do her parents do?"

"Her dad is a dentist and her mom works in the bank. Hannah's always showing off that both of her parents speak perfect English."

"Well, I'm going to help you prepare for the Hunter test too."

Now Lisa looked worried. "That's okay, Charlie. I'll manage."

"No. I'm going to figure out what we have to do and then we're going to do it."

That night, I woke suddenly on my mattress on the floor. Lisa was sitting up on the couch next to me. My heart pounded in my chest. Something was wrong.

"Lisa, are you all right?"

She didn't answer. She started feeling around in her sheets with her hand. Finally she spoke in a small voice, looking astonished, "I peed in my bed."

Relief poured over me. "Oh, that's nothing. I'll help you." I turned on the light, then we took the sheets off together and rolled them up. "I'll wash them at the laundromat this morning after Pa goes to work and he doesn't have to know."

"I don't know what's wrong with me," Lisa said. "Next thing you know, you'll have to give me a bottle at night like a baby. I'm sorry."

"Don't worry. I bet you're just nervous about the test and everything else that's going on." I ruffled her long hair. "Good night, sweetie." I gave Lisa my blanket and she rolled over and went back to sleep.

I stayed awake for a while. Lisa was so smart, I often forgot she was only eleven. She hadn't wet her bed in years. But her body was changing now and it made sense she would hit some rough spots along the way. Maybe my new job and this exam were causing her more anxiety than I'd realized. I knelt by the sofa Lisa slept on, felt her soft rounded forehead, and brushed it three times with my left hand to ward off evil.

Later on that week, the studio started holding auditions for a new dance teacher. The phone rang off the hook with requests for information. On the day of the first audition, the entire ballroom was packed with men and women of all different sizes and descriptions. Some women had their hair up in buns like classical ballerinas, some were dressed in outrageous outfits with bare midriffs and feathers.

"Oooh, I like the one with the low-cut green leotard and pink shorts," whispered Viktor, wagging his eyebrows at Katerina. "Maybe we have to get you same outfit. I think it is very American."

She burst out laughing and wrapped her arms around his waist. "You are an idiot."

Nina and Mateo put on microphones and went to the front of the room to demonstrate. Adrienne and Dominic stood to the side, watching. Even before the group was supposed to do the combination, some people were marking it with their bodies, flinging their arms and legs around wildly regardless of who might get hit. They learned a few short combinations, then the entire room did the routine together, then Nina and Mateo had them do it in groups of ten. I couldn't tell the difference between any of them, only when someone went the wrong way. People paired up with each other, becoming flustered as they didn't know how to lead or follow.

It was a sort of controlled chaos. I noticed Dominic, Adrienne, Mateo and Nina circulating through the crowd, whispering to certain people. Somehow they picked out a group of thirty-five people who were invited back to take the two-week training course, which was actually an elimination class. Every day they decided who would be allowed to return the next day.

I heard the dancers discussing the candidates after every session in the reception area. Adrienne said that mainly what the studio needed was someone to teach beginning students and groups, so personality was vital. They wanted someone who could dance well but was also approachable, whom students could identify with.

"I like the redhead," Mateo said.

"He's handsome but arrogant. I'm afraid he's going to turn into another Estella," said Adrienne.

"What about the other one, that one with the endless legs?" Nina asked.

"Too tall, and bowlegged too. She's going to tower over half of the male students," Dominic answered.

"I have my hopes set on the blonde. She's a quick learner, good technique and a great personality," Adrienne said, but that woman didn't show up the next day. She'd gotten cast for a Broadway show.

On nights after Lisa was asleep, when I wasn't too exhausted by my day, I stayed up to work on a present for her. I wanted to give her something after she took the Hunter test to let her know how proud I was that she was trying, and also so that if she didn't get in, she would have some consolation. Although the January test was months away, I knew how slow I was. I bought a ball of shiny purple yarn with glitter woven through it. I'd seen other girls in her class wearing long sparkling scarves. Years ago, Zan had shown me and our friend Mo Li how to knit, but while Zan's stitches had been perfectly uniform, mine were lumpy. I had caught a slight cold and my throat was bothering me, but even as I frowned over my attempted scarf now, I tried to keep my spine straight and neck long, like the dancers at the studio.

I glanced at the photo of Ma and our jar of Broadway show money. Now that I was earning more as a receptionist, I gave Lisa a dollar to put in there every week. I still gave most of my paycheck to Pa. He was trying to save money for our future too. I'd tried to convince him that he didn't need to provide us with dowries anymore but he'd said, "Dowry, college, same thing."

Lisa continued to sleep badly, waking up exhausted and pale. She had nightmares and was now wetting her bed once or twice per week. At first, I'd put extra cloths underneath her sheets to keep the urine from soaking into the sofa, but soon I bought her some waterproof bedding from the bit of my salary I kept for myself.

Now she started thrashing on the couch. I dropped my knitting and hurried over to her. I held her and pressed my lips against her temple. "Lisa, you're dreaming. It's okay, it's not real."

She blinked, stared at me, then sat up. She hugged me tight. "Charlie, I wish I could always be with you."

Startled, I was silent a moment, then I hugged her back. "I'm here. Are you feeling all right? Is there something wrong at school?"

Lisa just held me. Then she said, "No."

I pulled away to stare at her slender face in the dim light, so much like Ma's with its widow's peak and pointy chin. "Really? You know you can tell me."

Her eyes began to redden but she didn't speak.

"There is something. What is it?"

She sniffed and looked away. "Nothing you can help me with."

"It's the stress of the Hunter test, isn't it? You don't need to take it."

"No, I'm fine about that."

"You don't have to go to that stupid school. Or is it because you don't feel prepared?" I'd meant to get some books to help her study but didn't really know where to start. Every time I saw a textbook, I felt a cold lump in the pit of my stomach, remembering all of the times I'd struggled myself. I had to pull myself together for Lisa. I was a bad sister.

"Really." Lisa laid a hand against my cheek. "I'm okay and the test's not the problem. I promise."

I placed my hand over hers. "Good. Then we'd better get you back to bed."

"How often is this happening?" Pa stood in the doorway of the living room. He looked older than usual, his disheveled hair stood on end.

I looked at Lisa. Her eyes begged me not to tell him. "First time," I said.

The next morning, Pa brewed the caterpillar soup for us. He had kept the caterpillars in an airtight box loaned from Uncle Henry all this time because Lisa and I had refused to eat them, but now he was adamant. We all sat around the small table with bowls of the viscous liquid in front of us. It was gray mixed with brown and smelled like dank earth. Thank goodness Pa had strained the caterpillars and herbs out of the soup. He must have known that if we'd been confronted with the bodies, we would have refused no matter what he said. But I had seen the little worms as he'd dropped them into the ceramic pot.

I stared at my bowl. "Are you really sure this works?"

"It's unscientific and unhygienic," said Lisa.

"Lisa." I didn't want to drink it either, but I didn't want her to be disrespectful to Pa. It was too late to avoid the soup now.

She continued as if I hadn't said anything. "This could result in our getting parasites. In the best-case scenario, we'd throw up from disgustingness."

I breathed in. "Come on, Uncle Henry just cured that new delivery boy from the noodle shop of asthma, remember? He knows what he's doing."

"He used acupuncture. That guy didn't have to drink worm soup."

Pa's angular face was firm. "This worm soup cost us almost a hundred and fifty dollars."

Lisa swallowed and glanced at our Broadway show jar. A hundred and fifty dollars was a huge part of our household budget. I knew what she was thinking. We could almost have saved for another ticket with this amount. But I thought of Lisa and her nightmares. Maybe it would work. I'd drink the soup because that meant she would too.

"Drink up," Pa said. "This is good for all of us. I will too. It is only because of Uncle Henry's kindness that we have access to such powerful medicine."

Lisa and I had years of experience drinking this sort of thing. We waited for the soup to cool, then held our breaths and gulped it down as quickly as possible. It tasted vile: bitter and slimy, with an undertone of mud. Then we ran to the sink and washed our mouths out with water.

"That is a waste," Pa said.

"I want a glass of soda," Lisa panted.

"Not allowed," said Pa. "The bubbles will counter the power of the soup."

I was heaving like I was going to vomit. I wanted to, only Pa would be so disappointed.

"Here." Pa gave us each a piece of dried salted plum. It was a relief to have another taste in my mouth.

"They were boiled so long, all the germs in the caterpillars must have been sterilized, right?" Lisa said.

"Sure," I said. "Can we talk about something else now?"

Pa said, "I think I feel stronger already."

The next morning, I woke up and my cold seemed to have been cured overnight. Lisa, though, remained unchanged.

For the first time in my life, I now rode the subway every morning, rocketing north out of Chinatown. I descended into the station in one world, and I emerged, half an hour later, in an entirely different one. Riding the subway was fascinating to me, watching all of the people get on and off. As the train went uptown, the number of Chinese people in the car decreased. They were replaced by men and women in long black coats, reading their cell phones. When I spotted a subway car ad for lupus treatment, I bit my lip, wondering if Lisa had some disease like that. What if she was really sick? No, she was a young healthy girl. She was just stressed.

More people got on and off. I particularly studied the other young women who seemed to be, like me, on their way to work, yet in some ways looked so different. Many of them wore simple clothing that somehow still managed to be attractive by the way it fell over their bodies. They all seemed to have the same types of flat shoes or black boots and oversized bags. It felt as if the rest of the world knew something I didn't, like they were dancing the tango together while I was doing freestyle, flailing away by myself.

At the studio, I'd grown more comfortable since Estella left. Simone still intimidated me but she kept more to herself. The class of potential new dance teachers had recently petered out: Adrienne and Dominic had narrowed it down to three people, but then all of them had dropped out for one reason or another. One had gotten a job at another dance studio, another decided to move out of New York, and they couldn't reach the last one at all. Now they had decided the upcoming period was too busy with ballroom shows and preholiday preparations to start another audition process, so they would wait until after the New Year to hire someone.

Adrienne was in the office every day at seven months pregnant. And I was still making mistakes. When I was under stress, I would sometimes forget how all of the buttons on the phone worked.

I had so much trouble with writing things down that Adrienne had said one day casually, "I think you may be dyslexic. Have you ever considered that?" I remembered a teacher in high school had mentioned that possibility to me as well, had wanted to talk to Pa about testing he'd need to approve. But Pa had been too nervous to come to school and I didn't want Uncle Henry or Aunt Monica to think I was somehow damaged goods, so I'd told Pa that the problem had been solved. I couldn't even really explain what dyslexia was to him either, since I wasn't sure myself. But in any case, it was not a positive sign if your boss thought you might have a learning disability.

I overheard Dominic talking to Adrienne about me in the office next to the reception area. "She cut off Giovanni on the phone." Giovanni was the Avery head of our entire region.

"No. Was he angry?" Adrienne sounded horrified.

"He seemed to think it was funny. Said she had a sexy voice but maybe we should hire someone who could actually do the work."

"Sexy?"

"I know, but on the phone you can't see how she's hiding in her baggy clothing."

I was mortified. I'd hoped the glamour of the studio had rubbed off on me and that I was becoming a bit stylish since starting work there. Aunt Monica had told me I was too boyish and muscular, so I tended toward clothes that helped compensate. Pa taught me to cover my legs at least below the knee, midcalf if possible, and now that it was cold out, I was wearing a few layers underneath my clothing to add to my thin coat. I spent as little as possible on my own clothing, knowing how important it was for Lisa to look nice at school and fit in with the other girls. I didn't want her to be as unpopular as I'd been. Most of my dresses and more formal clothes were hand-me-downs from Aunt Monica or leftovers the local ladies had saved for us from the garment factory.

Growing up, my only female role models had been Aunt Monica and Godmother Yuan, and even though I'd known Aunt Monica's taste for shiny fabric and large flowers was not the epitome of elegance, it was probably unavoidable that it would influence me a bit. Zan and Mo Li weren't much help either; then, they'd been just as clueless as I was. But it was obvious even to me that neither the dancers nor the students at the studio dressed the way I did. The students' clothing was plain but sleek, while the dancers, of course, wore flashier, more clingy clothing. It was so confusing. I'd never really cared about how I looked before. Once again, I longed for a mother I could talk this over with.

I remembered a time Ma and I had been at Aunt and Uncle's house in Queens. I was about ten years old. It was before Lisa's birth. We were waiting for them to come home and Ma had taken me into their bedroom, then opened Aunt Monica's jewelry box.

"Should we?" I asked.

She'd giggled like a child caught in the act. "No. This is very naughty of us."

Then she'd put a gold bracelet on her slender wrist and a jade necklace around my neck. She held up her arm, allowing the sleeve of the shirt she wore for waitressing to fall away, revealing the curve and muscle of her skin, her fingers unfurling like the petals of a flower as she watched herself in the mirror. Then with one arm high and one bent in front of her like a branch in the wind, she'd whirled into a series of turns, one after another after another, until suddenly she stopped with her arm still high, facing herself in the mirror. Even then, I understood it wasn't the bracelet she longed for but the space that went with such a piece of jewelry, the room and time to dance again.

"I am like a little girl here, Charlie," she said. "Playing at dressing up. Just the weight of this thing makes me remember."

I'd hardly dared make a sound for fear of disturbing her strange mood. I was afraid to frighten her into silence again but I wanted to know. "What, Ma? What do you remember?"

She gave a little laugh and said, "Lights. The smell of powder. An empty stage and my arms and hair weighed down with jewelry and clips. Everything made to catch the light."

"Like you," I said.

She'd caught me up in her arms then and held me. "You, you are my light-catcher." And then she'd tickled me until I couldn't breathe and when we were done, we both put back the pieces of jewelry we'd borrowed.

Even now, I wished I'd been old enough to buy her jewelry, to dress her up one more time before she died.

Then I made another big mistake. I'd booked Simone for the beginners' group class on Tuesday evening but didn't realize she had an extra lesson with her private student Keith then. They were getting ready for an upcoming showcase at the Copacabana and she couldn't move him. And now no one else was free to teach the group, either. This emerged at the Monday meeting, and to make things worse, dance coach Julian Edwards was present because he had to finalize details for the show with the dancers.

"Who is responsible for this?" Dominic roared.

I could feel everyone trying not to look at me.

"I'm really sorry," I said.

"This is the final straw, Charlie," he said. "We gave you a chance but there have been so many issues."

Adrienne laid a hand on his arm. "We're already looking for a new dancer, Dominic. Unsuccessfully, I might add. Let's not have to find a new receptionist at the same time, okay?"

Dominic took a deep breath. "This is a big problem. We are understaffed. The class tomorrow evening, it is already booked full and there's no one to teach it. All those prospective students. Can't anyone move their private students?"

Everyone looked away. My heart was pounding from my near-firing. I would be back at my old dishwashing job soon. I would have to leave the studio, Nina, the whole ballroom world.

Mateo spoke up. "It's one of our busiest nights. Everyone's got their regulars coming in then and the show is this weekend. We can't reschedule anyone right before the Copacabana event."

There was a pause, then I made myself speak. "Is there anything at all I could do to fix this? Maybe I could help teach it?"

"What?" Dominic cocked his head as if he was sure he'd misheard me.

My cheeks were on fire. "I don't know. Never mind. I really want to help if I can since it's my fault. It's just that I've assisted in tai chi classes . . . I thought . . ."

Nina said, "I think it's a good idea."

"She's not a dancer." Dominic shook his head.

"Maybe true," Nina said slowly, "but they're all beginners. No one could be worse than they are. All we do is show them a few basic steps. A walrus could teach the class and they wouldn't know the difference. I've done it. Believe me, I know what I'm talking about."

I felt dizzy and cold all at once. What had I done? I couldn't teach ballroom. Were they really considering it?

Adrienne murmured, "It's an idea."

Dominic said, "Adrienne, I love you more than life itself but when it comes to the dancing I must decide. Absolutely not."

Adrienne continued as if he hadn't spoken. "How could we cover Charlie's job?"

Nina said, "We can put the phone on the answering machine then. Most of the check-ins at that time are for the group class anyway. We all welcome our own students for that lesson, and Charlie checks off the students in the group as they come in. Problem solved."

"I didn't mean to teach it alone," I said. "Just that maybe I could help."

Adrienne said, "Well, there's no one to do it with you, Charlie. Dominic and I are both booked to give coaching sessions then. You'd be on your own."

Dominic said, "I am artistic director here and I am putting my foot down."

"Are you trying to upset a very pregnant woman?" Adrienne patted her large stomach. "Sweetheart, this is just a temporary solution. It could work for this one time."

Dominic looked like he was having trouble swallowing. "Darling, I can't allow this. We have standards to maintain."

To my surprise, Nina got up and walked over to me. She knelt at my feet and slipped off my pumps. "Dominic, take a look at this."

She stared at my Magic-Markered pumps in her hands with disgust. "What have you done to your shoes?" Then she tossed them aside and stretched out my foot, pulling up the material of my pants so you could see my leg. "Point."

"What?"

"Point your foot."

I did, my toes lengthening, the arch high and pronounced as it always was, just like Ma's had been.

She held my foot and turned my leg out. "Don't sickle your feet inward, turn them outward." Then she looked at Dominic as if this said it all.

Everyone was staring at my foot. "How did you know?" Dominic asked her.

"She takes off her shoes underneath the desk at the end of the day," Nina said.

Dominic walked over to me and said, "Stand up."

When I did, feeling awkward in my shoeless feet, he held one of my arms out to the side. "Could we possibly get some of this cloth-ing off?"

I was wearing a thick button-up sweater over a thin man's un-dershirt that I'd stolen from Pa.

"May I?" he asked.

I glanced at Nina for a moment. She nodded slightly, so I started to unbutton my sweater, conscious that I was wearing only a worn tank top underneath.

After I'd slipped my arms out of the sleeves, Dominic looked at me impassively, like a doctor. "Stand up straight. Hold out your arms."

I held in my breath and stood as Ma had taught me all those years ago. Shoulders down, arms held from the back, neck long.

"Make a fist," Nina said.

When I did, I could feel the muscles in my arms and shoulders tense. The entire circle of dancers was still.

"She can beat you up, Dominic, better watch what you say," said Mateo.

"Where did you get a body like this?" Dominic asked.

"Dishwashing. I'm more bony than anything else."

Nina said, smiling, "I couldn't believe it either when I first saw her. She spilled coffee on her shirt and I loaned her my sweater. And those feet."

I looked down at my toes. "What about my feet?"

Katerina spoke up. "I would kill for feet like yours. Any dancer would."

I didn't understand. They were the same feet that had stood at a sink for years.

Dominic said, "Why in the world do you dress the way you do?"

My expression must have shown my hurt.

He ran his hand over his face like he was in pain. "Even if we do entertain this ridiculous idea for a moment, who could possibly teach her the basics? Simone?"

Simone threw up her hands. "Come on, why me? I'd miss the dance session with Julian. She's not a dancer. Look at her!"

Nina took a breath, her eyes flashing, but before she could speak, a voice came from the corner.

"I'll do it," said Julian. He folded his arms and leaned back in his chair, inscrutable.

There was a collective gasp. Adrienne struggled to speak. I had never seen her at a loss for words before. "Julian, that is very kind of you but we need you for our own training today."

"I have time afterward and I'll do it for free." Now we all gaped. I'd seen Julian's checks and knew he charged five hundred dollars per lesson.

I spoke the thought on everyone's mind. "Why would you possibly do such a thing?"

He smiled. "When you get to be where I am, you've seen it all. I've held so many international titles, coached almost every top professional dancer. I enjoy a new challenge. It would be interesting to teach someone fresh. Someone with potential."

Everyone was now staring at me. Julian Edwards had labeled me as someone with potential. Simone looked like she had something unpleasant in her mouth, but Nina had the biggest grin on her face. I could feel my heart in my throat, a distant thin pulsing.

Dominic said to Julian, "You are trying to kill me, old friend."

Julian's eyes were filled with mischief. "And enjoying every moment too."

Adrienne said, her face blank, "That's settled then. Nina, you're going to talk clothes with her, then Julian can try to teach her a few steps."

"Clothing?" I said.

Adrienne said slowly and carefully as if I were stupid, "You won't be sitting behind a desk. Even for one class, you're part of the dream that is Avery Studios. You need to look the part. As much as you're able." She shifted her gaze to Nina. "Good luck."

Seven

After the meeting broke up, Nina took me into the teachers' room. "I need to join that dance session so I don't have a lot of time. But I can't wait to get you into something else. You'll need it to dance with Julian."

She brought her hands down and felt the ridges of my pelvic bones through the heavy pants I was wearing. "You're half the size of these things."

"I know you would have helped me even if Julian hadn't spoken up. I really appreciate it."

"You're welcome." Nina's smile was lovely. "Let's get you out of your clothes. No offense, but where do you get this stuff?"

I felt awkward. "Mostly hand-me-downs."

"You look like a matron." Nina was examining my reflection in the full-length mirror.

"That's who the clothes came from."

She started to laugh. "You need some better friends, honey." She walked to her locker, dug through her bag, then pulled out a soft blue garment. "Try this on. It's one of my rehearsal dresses. It's clean and Lycra, so it should fit you. Don't be shy. It has built-in panties so you need to step into it."

I tried not to look her in the eyes as I stripped down to my plain cotton bra and underwear. "Will anyone come in?"

She walked over to the door and stood with her back to it but her eyes were unwavering as she watched me. "Will you look at that?"

"What?"

"I still cannot believe how much crap you were wearing over that body. Stop a moment."

Nina walked over to me and stared at my bra, which was also a hand-me-down from Aunt Monica. I'd never noticed how it fit before. I knew my aunt was bigger in front than I was, but I thought I'd fixed that by shortening the bra straps.

Nina poked her finger into the bra cup where it bulged around my breasts. "This is all empty air. That thing is way too big for you. When you wear a bra, your breasts are actually supposed to make contact with the cups." She pulled out the frayed label from underneath the band, then stared at me and said, "Why on earth are you wearing a D cup? You're probably like a B or less."

"Someone gave the bra to me too, and I never paid much attention." I stepped into her dress and slipped my arms into the sleeves.

We both stared at my reflection. The dress was much lower than anything I owned and I tried to tug the V-neck higher, to no avail.

"Stop that," Nina said.

"I don't want to show any cleavage."

She peered at my chest. "You don't have any. It's just skin."

The dress flowed down my body, ending halfway down my thighs and flaring out at the hem. Instead of making my body look sticklike, it made me curvier, more feminine. The low neckline defined the line of my neck and arms. I'd hardly ever seen myself so exposed before. "I feel naked."

Nina came and adjusted the dress a bit for me, pulling it more smoothly over my hips. "Come on. The others have to see this."

When she dragged me into the main ballroom, barefoot, Mateo caught sight of me first and let out a long whistle. "Get a pair of heels on those legs."

Julian paused the dance session he was teaching to the professionals. Everyone stared.

I fiddled with my skirt as Adrienne came out of her office and leaned against the doorway. "Well, what do you know." She walked to me and looked me over. "What size shoe are you?"

"Seven and a half," I said.

"She can't teach without dance shoes," Adrienne said. "I think she'll kill herself in her usual pumps. Who's close in size?"

Simone avoided our eyes. Katerina said, "I'm an eight. I'm only teaching smooth today. She can borrow my Latin shoes for the lesson."

"Go get them," Mateo said. "I gotta see her in them." I looked in his direction to see Dominic and Julian looking at me. Julian had a faint smile on his face. Katerina went into the other ballroom, returning with a glittering pair of sandals in her hands.

I sat at one of the tables and Katerina put the shoes on my feet. The soles of the shoes were made of suede. One of the straps was so long, she wrapped it all the way underneath the bottom of the shoe before buckling it. She glanced up at me. "Don't look so scared. They're designed for speed and balance. That's why the heel is set underneath the center of your foot's heel instead of way back like some other shoes. You've got such high arches, they'll fit you fine."

Adrienne said, "Stay here and get used to those shoes, Charlie. Watch the dance session. Julian will teach you right afterward. I'll take over your job until then."

I stood up in the shoes, nervous, but when I walked a few steps, I realized I was much more stable than I'd ever been in regular heels. Instead of my ankles wobbling, my feet felt like they were solidly on the ground. From a distance the nude sandals appeared to be a part of my legs. I sneaked another glance at myself in the mirror. For the first time, I did not see a dishwasher.

Julian stood next to me so that we were both facing the mirror. Thank goodness we were in the smaller studio so we had a bit more privacy. I saw the other dancers pausing as they came close to our door, deliberately swinging their partners into dips so they could wink at me through the glass window.

"I'm going to teach you just a few steps. That's all you'll have time for. First we'll do men's, then ladies' parts."

"I have to learn men's parts too? I'll need to lead and follow?" This hadn't occurred to me, although I had indeed seen the dancers teaching both genders. Somehow I'd had the idea that maybe the male teachers stepped in for that.

"You'll be leading better than most men by the time we're done." Julian went to the stereo and turned it on. Sinatra started singing.

"This is a foxtrot," Julian told me. "Listen to it. One, two, three, four . . . Can you find the beat?"

"One, two, three . . ." I'd never been good with rhythm.

"No, feel the music. Don't worry about the numbers." He came over and took my hand in his. His was large and warm. Dancers always found it so easy to touch people. Pa avoided touching either of us if he could help it since it wasn't proper. I tried not to flush.

Julian closed his hands around my forearms and had me do the same to his. "This is called double hand hold." He closed his eyes and started swaying to the music with me. "Your music is not in your ears. It is in your partner. Listen to your partner."

He waited until we were swaying together, then he took off his cuff links, set them on the stereo and folded up the sleeves of his shirt. I looked down and saw tattoos of dragons swirling up both of his arms, underneath his formal shirt. He linked his arm through mine.

"First get the class just to start walking. Remember, they've never done any ballroom before."

"Neither have I."

"Right. You'll get along just fine then, won't you?" He gave me a smile, then started strolling forward and backward, side by side with me, both of us starting with our right legs.

"Dancing is just like walking. Don't let anyone tell you otherwise. If you can walk, you can dance. And if you can learn to walk properly, you can do any dance."

"I'm not that good at walking either," I muttered.

He heard me. "I bet you're good at sports."

I looked at him in surprise. I thought about my old gym classes at school. "I'm all right."

"You're extremely smooth. You're already rolling through your feet. But your steps are too wide."

I deflated.

He continued, "Lots of athletes have that. Like they're trying to get a ball to the other side of the ballroom. Usually, they're hairy gentlemen, though."

I choked a bit as he looked at me sideways.

"So you're special. As a dancer, you don't have to arrive at a destination, you only have to travel beautifully."

I pressed my lips together, dubious.

One side of his mouth tugged upward. He took me by the shoulders so that I faced the mirror. "You are lovely. Once you realize that, everyone else will be able to see it too."

I felt my blush sweep up all the way to the roots of my hair.

"I didn't know Chinese people could turn that color," Julian said conversationally. Then he took my arm and started walking with me around the small ballroom again.

"Now take two steps forward and a little side step. Slow slow, quick quick. Slow slow, quick quick . . ." He had his hand on my back. Then he turned to the mirror and said, "Now watch me and imitate everything I do. Sidestep, then close your feet. Good."

He started to show me the basic box. Thanks to learning movement in the tai chi classes, I could copy him pretty well, but after a few steps, I couldn't remember if I was the man or the woman.

"Julian, which leg am I on now?"

His smile was enigmatic. "The leg is irrelevant. Remember, it's not the steps. It's the feeling. That is dancing. Amateurs, they dance steps."

Julian let go of me and pretended to dance, jerking his arms and legs independently of his torso. "Left, right, left, right, like a robot."

Then he integrated his body and became a great flowing animal again. He rippled from his stomach out to his chest and then through his arms and legs. "A true dancer dances center to center." He drew a line in the air from his torso to mine. "We dance heart to heart. I am still amazed by the number of students who believe steps are dancing. The steps are nothing. A true dancer moves with her body, her center, her heart, and the legs are only there to catch her so she does not fall. If the movement of the center is correct, the feet will be where they need to be."

This I understood. Godmother had trained me for years to feel my center. I breathed in and found mine.

He put his hands on either side of my waist and swayed me so that I naturally took a step forward. It was my left leg I needed to stand on. That was clear now.

"There are two main types of ballroom dance: standard and Latin. In the U.S., those styles are called 'smooth' and 'rhythm' but people tend to use the terms interchangeably. Of course, there are technical differences between international and American style, which you don't need to worry about yet. For now, there are two sorts of walk you'll need to learn. A standard or smooth walk." He released me and glided forward and backward on his feet, taking long, smooth steps that led with his heels.

"And a Latin or rhythm walk." Now he pushed his weight onto his feet, rolling his hips, grinding his feet into the floor. "Do you see the damage on Katerina's shoes?"

I looked down and nodded. The inside surfaces of both shoes had holes in them, although the sandals in general looked fairly new.

"They are the result of Latin technique." He stood behind me, both of us facing the mirror. I didn't want to think what Pa would say if he could see us now. I could feel the heat of Julian's body behind me. He put his hands on my pelvic bones, at the corner of my hips. He had to bend down so his cheek was nearly next to mine, then shifted his legs together with mine. "One leg straight and one leg bent. Switch. Roll through your feet. Now, other leg. One straight, one bent." He gently pushed my hips back and forth, rolling them. "Weight transfer and release. Hold your top still. Very good."

He straightened and released me. My face, neck and ears must have been glowing. "That is what Latin feels like. Like the heat of the sun on your body, while you're drawing in the sand with your toes. Now, waltz."

He took a few steps away from me. He stood proud and held his hand out to me as if he were a prince. My head swam. I went over to him.

"No," he said. "Let's change places for a moment." He pretended to be me. "We begin a waltz like this." He threw his head back, shoulders down, stomach in, extended his arm and glided over to me, then gently laid his hand in mine. He fluttered his eyelashes at me.

I laughed.

"Okay, once more." We changed places so that he was once again doing the man's part. I employed all of my muscles to glide over to him like he'd done. "Much better. Now, for the first time, we shall waltz."

As we started to dance together, he looked at me with some surprise. "You move very well."

It felt wonderful in Julian's arms. I knew it was only because he was a world-class dancer, but it felt like being in love. When he held me, it was as if my body knew what to do without any thinking at all.

"You make me seem graceful," I said.

"Do you think of yourself as not?"

"I'm clumsy. I drop everything. I can't sew or cook."

"Never confuse small and large motor coordination," he said, spinning us through the room. "Many dancers are awkward with their hands. That has nothing to do with their bodies."

"Really?" I thought about this for a moment. "Are you clumsy too?"

He broke dance position with his head to look directly at me. "I assure you I am highly skilled with my hands. Would you care for a private demonstration?"

Right. I shook my head quickly and kept silent for the rest of our dance. By the end of that lesson, I'd learned how to do the basic box and how to make it into rumba, foxtrot and waltz by changing the way my body moved. We'd covered the basic steps in swing, plus an underarm turn. I'd also done a simple turn in rumba and waltz. I looked up to see Adrienne watching us through the window in the door just before she stepped through it.

"You're wonderful, Julian," she said. "How is she?"

I stood there while they continued to talk about me as if I weren't there.

"She's a quick learner. Light on her feet," he said. "Absolutely no ballroom technique at all, which is to be expected."

Adrienne looked me up and down. "That doesn't matter. Nina's right, the beginners won't be able to tell. We just need to get through this one class."

Adrienne walked over to me and allowed me to take her in dance position, so that I was doing the man's part. Her stomach bumped against mine. "Show me what you've learned."

I took a deep breath, then did the steps Julian had shown me. I started doing a slow rumba box with her, then into an underarm turn. Despite needing to keep some distance between us because of her protruding belly, I could give her the lightest of impulses and she would execute the step, beautifully. I'd never seen a heavily pregnant woman move like this. Now that I'd tried to do the steps myself, I realized how good she was. She made it easy.

Someone clapped from the main doorway. It was Dominic. "Well, well, well. Maybe this won't be a total disaster after all."

I stepped away from Adrienne. "It was all Julian's work," I said, turning to him. "Thank you."

Julian gave me a formal little nod, reverting back to his role as renowned judge and coach. "It was my pleasure." Then he strode over to Dominic, put his arm around him, and the two of them walked off, discussing the upcoming showcase.

At home the next morning, after Pa and Lisa had left, I pushed all of the furniture aside to make a small clearing in the middle of our living room. I ran over the steps I'd learned again and again. Man's part, lady's part. It was hard to do without a partner. I felt confused. One moment, I thought I knew it, and the next, I was sure I'd mess everything up again. I went over to Ma's altar and lit a stick of incense. "Please, Ma, lend me your strength today."

We had agreed I would borrow Nina's dress and Katerina's shoes for the lesson that day. Before the class, Nina had me practice teaching her. We did a run-through in the small ballroom. It was much easier to practice with her because it was clearer where my arms and feet needed to be in relation to another person. I only needed to show the students a few steps and most of the class would consist of them practicing what they'd learned.

"You'll be fine," Nina said.

I couldn't seem to stop trembling. "I've never done anything like this before."

"You used to teach some, right? Just think of this as tai chi to music."

I tried to smile. "And after this, I'm never coming out from behind my receptionist desk again."

When the students arrived for the beginners' group lesson, many of them seemed even more nervous than I was. I waited for them inside the small ballroom, wiping my sweaty hands against my borrowed blue dress. I thought of Nina's words: tai chi to music, that was all. I could do this. There were about twenty people, ages ranging from midtwenties to almost sixty. About half of them were couples, the rest were mostly women who had come alone. I noticed one man in the back. In his workman's pants and boots, he looked as out of place among the sophisticated clientele as I felt.

Adrienne was chatting in a friendly way with the red-haired woman standing next to the man. They seemed to know each other. After a few minutes, Adrienne came up to the front. She introduced me, then left to teach her coaching session, with a little wink to me at the door. She'd given me the tags with their names on them, which I'd made earlier in the day because Adrienne believed it made the students feel more comfortable if you used their names. I checked my list and tried to match names to the people.

When I went up to the single man to give him his tag, I hesitated, noticing his work boots. He had the biggest, widest feet I'd ever seen. Despite his plain clothing, he stood proud and straight. "Umm, we allow normal shoes but I'm afraid yours might damage the floor." It was a part of my receptionist's duties to screen clients for acceptable shoes, although I'd never had to say anything before.

He smiled, his green eyes crinkling. His face was clean-shaven, with a nose slightly flattened at the top, as if it'd been broken before. "They might damage someone's toes too. I'm sorry, we were doing a garden paving job, and I didn't have time to change before coming here. I'll take them off."

Then the woman next to him took his arm and said to me, "This is Ryan. He's a landscaper." She didn't look like the sort of woman

I would have imagined with this guy. She had straight, shoulder-length dark red hair, a light sprinkling of freckles, completely composed in her navy suit and heels. She extended her hand. "I'm Evelyn, his sister."

I shook it, still self-conscious about my hands, although I knew the skin had healed by now.

Untying his boots, Ryan said, "I'm just a gardener, Evelyn."

"No, you're not. Stop it."

I almost laughed. They sounded just like me and Lisa. "Glad you could make it, Ryan, Evelyn."

"And this is my fiancé, Trevor," Evelyn said, turning to the man on her other side, in a pin-striped shirt and a blue tie, which he'd loosened.

"Nice to meet you, Charlie," Trevor said.

I quickly shook his hand, gave them their tags and then moved to the center of the room.

"Welcome, everyone," I said, trying to speak loudly and clearly. I clasped my hands tightly together to stop their trembling. "Today I'll be teaching you just a few basic steps. I need a male volunteer." I'd dreaded this part, but when I scanned the room, I focused on a kind face. "Ryan, since you're in your socks and I know you won't be able to hurt my toes, will you come up?" That got a laugh, which made me feel better.

Ryan rolled his shoulders. Could he be nervous too? Then he came to stand next to me. I positioned him across from me and took his forearms in a double hand hold. "We'll start with a side step. I'll need the rest of you to grab a partner like this and line up with us."

We waited while the room shuffled around.

"Now, we're just going to take little side steps together, toward the door." I thought about how I remembered the movement myself. "It's like you're at the movies and you need to get up to buy some popcorn. You have to squeeze past everyone, so you say, 'Excuse me,' then do a little step to the side."

Evelyn laughed. "It's an excuse-me step."

"Yes. Okay, everyone, come along with me and we'll go 'Excuse me, excuse me, excuse me.'" I felt more comfortable now that the class had started. It wasn't so different from what I'd done before after all.

I held on to Ryan's arms and moved him with me to the side. His strides were so large, he wound up far away from me with every step we took. I ticked him on the wrist. "Stay with me. That's what a gentleman does."

There was a teasing light in his eyes. "Sorry, ma'am."

Ryan stayed up front with me for the rest of the lesson. I'd intended to change partners for every dance, but I was so flustered by being in front of the class that I forgot.

When I had everyone get into dance position and we held hands for the first time, he stared at the floor. "I hope you don't mind."

"What?"

He mumbled so that I just managed to hear him say, "My hands are very rough."

I could feel his calluses, and I saw the knuckles were red and chapped. Warmth flowed through me. I hadn't expected to find someone like me at the studio. "They don't bother me at all."

When I walked around the room to help the other students, Ryan waited until I came back. To my surprise, I was having a good time. The students were all nice and laughing and stumbling over each other's feet. I taught them some of the things Julian had told me, about dance not being about steps but about feeling. When we did rumba, I told them to draw in the sand with their feet. When we waltzed, we pretended to be ladies and gentlemen. I was afraid it'd seem childish but they seemed to enjoy the games.

"Oh, I'm the clumsiest person," one woman said and I automatically answered, "You could never be as uncoordinated as me." The people who could hear us started to laugh. I realized they believed I was graceful and thought I was being modest. They thought I was a real dancer.

At the end, Adrienne came in with her clipboard and started booking lessons for people who wanted to take follow-up private lessons. Most of them stayed around, some thanked me. Evelyn had come up to Adrienne and was asking about planning a dance for her wedding. Ryan grinned at me as he stood by the door, waiting for Evelyn and Trevor.

It was now break time. A few of the dancers started filing through the small ballroom on their way to the teachers' room. I realized Adrienne had the situation under control and that my feet hurt. I stepped into the teachers' room, then took off those high heels, placing them carefully by Katerina's locker.

"How was it?" Nina asked.

"I think all right."

Simone spoke up, "Though you were playing a waltz while you were counting to foxtrot."

I hunched my shoulders. "How would you know?"

"We all swung by to see how the class was going," Mateo said. "You were so busy, you didn't even notice us."

"Well, I'm glad I survived my one and only class. Never again."

Eight

It was early in the morning, and the wintry air was crisp. I stared at the flour sacks piled as high as my shoulder that the delivery truck had dumped in the alleyway behind the noodle shop. A few doorways further, the fishmonger was unloading ice-filled crates from a truck.

Pa grinned. "Just you and me, Charlie, like before."

When I was working at the restaurant, it had always been an understood part of my job to help Pa and his assistant stack the sacks of flour in the basement. Today, the assistant's wife was in labor, keeping him away, so Pa needed me more than ever. The assistant before this one had been my secret steady boyfriend for a few months, and Pa never figured it out. It'd been exciting at first to have a hidden relationship but that quickly became stressful, and when he'd left for another restaurant our relationship had ended as well. I felt a bit hurt that he hadn't wanted to see me afterward, but the truth was, I missed him less as a person than as a distraction. We'd shared an interest in exploring each other's bodies but not much else.

"Come on." Pa hoisted a large bag over his shoulder and headed for the stairs.

I bent my knees, grabbed another one and threw it over my shoulder as well. This was no place for ballroom heels. After a few trips, I was warm enough to shed my coat and sweater. One of the bags had a small leak in it, and now my face and shoulders were white with flour. I rubbed my nose and mouth, trying to clear them. My right shoulder ached from the weight of the bags.

"You want to take a break?" Pa asked. "I can do the rest."

"Of course not." I'd never let Pa do this by himself. I worried about the day that the restaurant work would be too demanding for him.

"You're a good girl." He dropped another sack onto the growing pile in the basement, which was lit by an incandescent bulb. I hated to think which insects were lurking there. "You will make some man very happy someday."

I raised my eyebrows. This I had never heard before. "You don't even want me to date."

Pa didn't meet my eyes, running his hand over his hair. "Uncle and Aunt have been talking to me about this for a while now. Aunt seems to think I should be preparing more for your future."

"What do you mean?"

He stared at a spot on the wall. "I'm not that young anymore, Charlie. Uncle's even older than I am. When I'm gone, I need to make sure someone's here to look after you."

Sudden tears sprang into my eyes. "That's nonsense. You'll live a very long time."

"I'm alone. Your ma's already gone. I've been saving for you girls but I don't know how long that money can last."

Now I understood the money Pa always put aside. It wasn't for our dowries or college, it was for after he had passed on. "I don't want to talk about this. I can't believe you want me to just start going out with men either."

"No! No strangers. Aunt thought maybe a matchmaker . . ."

"Absolutely not!" It was a Chinese tradition for parents to arrange marriages for their children. We were supposed to stay pure until a spouse was chosen for us. "Over my dead body."

"Yes, I thought you would say that. That's why I was thinking, you know that nice boy, that old friend of yours . . ."

My jaw dropped. "Winston. No."

"I always liked him. Maybe you should see him more often."

I rubbed my palms over my eyes. I reminded myself that Pa had no idea Winston and I had already had a romantic relationship and that it had not worked out. Sometimes it was hard to keep track of all the things I hid from Pa but I understood where this was coming from. Winston was a known quantity, or so Pa thought. Pa couldn't stand the thought of his daughter going out with a random man, any more than I could stomach an arranged match. "I'm not about to date Winston or allow a matchmaker to choose a man for me. Look at you. You and Ma fell in love. You didn't let anyone set you up."

Pa's gaze was fixed upon the floor now. "And see how well that turned out. The price of moving to America was too high for her."

My heart broke at the sadness in his voice. This was the first time Pa had ever admitted how unhappy Ma had been here in the U.S. Memories flooded me, of Ma's voice coming from their bedroom, "I wish we'd never left. I want to go back to China." Sometimes she'd sobbed and other times they'd fought. Pa would say that it was hard for him too and she would say he didn't understand, he could never understand. Ma had given everything up for love but regretted it in the end.

"She loved you very much, Pa."

His forced smile was unsteady. "She was a beautiful bird and I clipped her wings. She never flew again after we came here."

"If you had stayed in Communist China, no one knows what would have happened to either of you. There was so much political unrest. And Lisa and I would have been born there with so much less freedom. Instead of washing dishes for a couple of years, I probably would have had to wash dishes my entire life." I smiled at him and took his hand in mine.

Pa laughed even though his eyes were red. "You are right, we never regretted allowing you and Lisa to grow up here. I am very proud of you in your computer job."

I felt the guilt rise in my throat, along with the truth desperate to come out. To change the subject, I said the first thing that came to my mind. "Do you think Lisa is okay?" She was still wetting the bed and having nightmares. I could do so little to help her, I only worked on knitting that scarf for her whenever I could.

His face grew serious. "I am worried about her too. Those bad dreams, they are not good. You say the test is very competitive. Maybe some of the other students have put a curse on her."

"What?" We'd made such progress, I'd thought. Now I was ready to pull my hair out again.

"They are jealous. They do not want her to succeed. Maybe they want her spot for themselves."

"Pa, this is not how things work in America. They might make a mean comment or put garbage in her locker or something, but no one's going to curse her."

"You are young and naive, Charlie. People can have black hearts. It's good you mentioned it. When I get the chance, I am going to talk to the Vision about this."

Pa patted my arm lovingly, then headed up the stairs for more flour. "Maybe Winston can come over for a cup of tea sometime."

When I got home, I showed Lisa the book I'd bought for her. I'd gone to the little bookstore down the street and tried to explain to the clerk what I needed. He swore this book would solve our problems but I wasn't so sure. It was called *English and Math Workout: Test Prep* and was so expensive that it'd wiped out my budget.

Lisa flipped through it. "Charlie, I don't know most of this stuff."

I gulped. "That's why you need the book. We'll work through it together."

"No, I mean, I think this is a college prep book. Not for sixth graders."

"Really? But I told him it was for the Hunter test."

"I don't know, he probably heard Hunter College and thought you needed a general college prep book."

We marched back to the bookstore together. The bell rang as we pushed open the door. The store was cramped and narrow, filled to the ceiling with books, mostly in Chinese, and smelled musty. The same balding clerk came up to us.

I said, "We need a book to prepare for the Hunter high school test. This is for college." I thrust the book and receipt at him.

"This book is very good for test," he said.

"No, we need one for a junior high school test."

He stared at me.

I turned to Lisa. "Can this book help you at all? He obviously doesn't have anything else. Do you want to keep it? If you want it, you can have it."

She said, "It's useless for us. Just get a refund."

The clerk grumbled as he gave me my money back.

Outside, Lisa saw how crestfallen I was. "Don't worry, Charlie."

When we got back to the apartment, I said, "Well, at least let me show you what I learned in the studio this week." I took her hands, then turned her underneath my arm.

Lisa clapped her hands. "Show me more!"

I taught her everything I knew. I did the man's part while she was the lady. By the end, Lisa was shouting, "Quick quick slow!" along with me.

Suddenly, there was a pounding on our floor from below. It was the downstairs neighbor. We must have been making too much noise. Lisa and I collapsed on the couch, laughing.

Later that afternoon, I was leading the warm-ups for the tai chi class at the Yuan Benevolent Association again. I looked down at my baggy shirt and suddenly felt grateful that my tai chi students never cared what I looked like or wore. They'd always accepted me exactly as I was.

Godmother was walking around the room. She put her hand on a woman's stomach and nodded at her as she breathed in and out. "Deeper. Let it go. Don't hold everything in."

I rolled my shoulders, feeling more aware of my body than I ever had before. I reached inward and allowed my feet to sink into the floor.

Godmother met my eyes and smiled. "The core power of tai chi begins with awareness. Our stance is the posture of infinity: not tense but relaxed and upright, expectant. From this nothingness, all things begin."

The next week I was back behind my receptionist's desk again. I was relieved the class was over and I didn't have to be nervous or on display. My feet didn't have to hurt anymore. I wouldn't have to dance with Julian again. At this, a pang went through me.

Dominic came up to me and leaned on my desk. "Almost seventy percent of your class signed up for their free private lesson."

I wasn't sure how to react; I didn't know if this was good or not.

"We'd been getting about thirty percent with Estella. Many of your students said they'd had fun. One group even requested you specially as their teacher."

"Who?"

"The wedding couple and her brother."

I nodded. Evelyn and Trevor. And Ryan. "What did you tell them?"

"No, of course. It is impossible. The couple will still come for lessons. I've booked them with Nina. They said they would call back about the brother. But Julian was right, you do have potential. We would like to ask you to continue teaching the beginners' classes."

A wild combination of dismay and elation rose in my chest.

"We need you. Everyone's booked, we're shorthanded until we can hire a new dancer. Think of it as a little vacation from this desk."

I nodded slowly.

"And the students seem to like you. However, if you are going to be doing any teaching in my studio, even of the very beginners, you are going to start attending dance session. Any problems with that?"

I bit the inside of my cheek. Classes with all of those trained dancers were quite different from bluffing in front of people who had never done a ballroom step in their lives. "Do you think I can?"

"Of course. You will be terrible but we are expecting that. And I see you watching, I see the look on your face. I think you would love to learn something of dance, am I right?"

I flushed that I'd been so obvious. "Yes." It was what I wanted more than anything, only I'd thought I would never be able to do it. If I taught these classes, I would be allowed to train for free, like a real professional dancer, if only for a little while.

It was my first dance session with Dominic and the other professionals. I felt like a fraud walking over to that group, but I kept my shoulders back and my head high.

Adrienne sat at one of the little tables to watch. She sighed as she sat down and took her shoes off. She rubbed her tummy, murmuring a few words to it.

Dominic said, "Okay, take a partner."

Everyone paired up. I saw the others edging away from me. It was Katerina and Viktor, Mateo and Nina, and next to Nina stood Simone alone, looking irritated. I realized I would have to dance with her. Then Nina whispered something to Mateo, gave him a nudge when he made a face, then she came over to me. Thank goodness. Mateo reluctantly held his arms up in dance position to Simone. She slid into them.

We were practicing international foxtrot. There were so many quicks and slows and twinkles and reversals. My head spun. Dominic only had to show a step once and all of the other dancers followed along perfectly, except for me.

I felt like a squid as I hung onto Nina. She just raced after the other dancers and I was happy if I managed to stay attached. My clothing was too hot and inflexible. When I needed to draw a quick circle with my leg and turn at the same time, my heel got tangled in the hem of my skirt and I almost tumbled over.

Dominic stepped over to us and waved his hand, indicating my entire body. "We have to completely rebuild her from the ground up. Allow me to demonstrate what dancing should be. Nina, if you please."

Dominic held out his hand to Nina. Without a word, she flowed into his arms, her head arched back in dance position. He started doing a foxtrot with her, but a foxtrot like I had never seen. It was a far cry from the step, step, side step I'd taught the beginners. They flew and glided, whirling into a pivot turn, then Dominic led them smoothly into a waltz. From there he switched into tango, had her do a number of fans in his arms, dipped her and then twisted her out into a series of spins. As she stopped and faced him after the turns, their bodies changed to the predatory, animalistic pacing I'd seen with Julian. They did a slow and sensual rumba together, then the hottest mambo I'd ever seen. They put every dancer I'd ever seen on television to shame. Dominic spun Nina away from him, then he bowed while she did a deep curtsey. We all clapped.

I was amazed. "How could you dance in perfect harmony to-gether without any music?"

"The music is inside," Dominic said. "We never need music to dance together."

I looked at the others and saw them all nodding. I thought of what Godmother always said about external strength being mean-ingless without inner power.

"What many do not realize," Dominic continued, "is that lead-ing and following are not about one person being in control and one not. It is about yin and yang. It is qi. Necessity. The person moving forward is doing the leading. That person provides the energy and impetus. In advanced routines, that may well be the woman. The person moving backward must flow in harmony with the other, otherwise they will lose balance. Now I need you all to switch part-ners and change roles."

I was surprised and glad that Dominic had spoken about yin,

yang and qi. This time I had to be the man, and I was supposed to lead Viktor. I held him in dance position but he was just so tall, I couldn't see over his shoulder at all.

"Oh my goodness." Dominic came from behind Viktor with a mock shudder. "You look like a driverless car from this side. I hope we all survive this lesson."

Afterward, I was so tired, I wanted to cry. I'd never felt so slow and stupid in my life, not even in school. I should never have left the restaurant; this wasn't like tai chi to music at all.

Nina came up and gave my arm a squeeze. "It'll get easier as you go on."

To my surprise, Viktor bent down and said, "You did good."

I was rubbing my arms. "I made so many mistakes."

"You are judging yourself against us, and we've been dancing for most of our lives," Katerina said. "For a person who had never danced before, you were extremely good indeed. You learned the steps almost as quickly as we did."

"But I couldn't do them together with anyone else," I said.

"Of course not." Adrienne had come up to us. "You don't know anything about leading and following yet. You'll feel like you're wrestling an alligator until you start to understand."

Now Dominic joined us. "You have line."

The rest of the group fell silent. Everyone looked at me.

I gave a broken laugh. "I don't even know what that means."

"Look in the mirror," he said. I turned and saw myself. He took my arm and held it out to the side. He swept his hand from my neck through my shoulder out through my arm. "That is line. It can be developed, but for some it is a gift. You have a great deal to learn, but you want it." He tapped me on my collarbone. "That wanting, that will bring you where you need to go."

Adrienne said, "And now, we need to see you in our office. The rest of you, disperse."

Adrienne, Dominic and I stood in her small office, the same place she'd hired me. I saw her and Dominic exchanging glances. Obviously, they had agreed on something.

Dominic said, "Charlie, we are very sorry but we must let you go."

My head jerked back. How could this have happened? Of course it had. I'd been silly to think I could ever be anything but a dishwasher. It felt especially bitter after I'd just struggled through the dancing, which I'd desired most. My neck seemed to close up, making it hard to breathe.

Adrienne put her hand on my shoulder, her voice gentle. "The thing is, we like you, Charlie, but you are a terrible receptionist. None of us were getting our calls anymore. You kept making mistakes with the roster for the teachers. That booking problem with the beginners' class was the last straw. Dominic and I spoke after that and we agreed we had to take the final step."

I pressed my hand against my throat, blinking. I would never see the studio or the dancers again. I struggled to speak. "I understand."

"However," Dominic said, "you might have a chance as a dancer."

I froze. Could I have heard him properly?

Adrienne cocked her head. "Are you sure you've never had any dance lessons?"

"My mother used to train me, only at home. And I've done tai chi for years, but I'm too awkward, I could never be a dancer."

"Tai chi, huh?" Adrienne said.

Dominic said, "Stop being critical of yourself. That's my job. I'll pick on you and everyone else too. Was your mother a dancer?"

"She was a soloist with Beijing Ballet."

There was a moment while they took it all in. "You're fired and you're hired," Adrienne said. "You'll have to start your training right away."

I couldn't believe it. My heart expanded in my chest and I could feel the smile starting to spread across my face. But I was still worried. "Who's going to do my job?"

They looked at each other. Obviously, they'd discussed this too. "My mother," Dominic said with a small grimace. "She has moved to New York because of the baby. She insisted. And she'll drive Adrienne insane if I leave her at home all day."

"Did you both know before I even taught that class?"

"We hoped," Adrienne said. "When Julian Edwards says someone has potential, we listen. Then you learned so much in that lesson with him, but we weren't sure what you would be like in front of a class of students. You were wonderful. At the beginning, that warmth is so important. You made them feel like if you could do it, so could they."

"That's exactly what I believe," I said.

"See? The dance session today was our final test. And you passed with flying colors."

"I was awful."

"You were, for a professional dancer. But you're only a baby pro. There are others who started ballroom at your age. I've seen you watching the dancing ever since you came here. You have a tremendous hunger in your eyes, and we are looking for a new dancer. I have to tell you that although you'll be paid more, you'll have many extra expenses too, like dance shoes and dresses, coaching sessions. In the long run, I'm not sure if you actually come out ahead financially."

"You'll need to train hard, as fast as you can," Dominic added. "It's much more difficult to learn how to dance than to answer phones, although maybe not for you."

Adrienne snorted.

"How can I start teaching students?" I asked. "I'm hardly any better than they are."

"Never say that. First of all, I would never hire you unless you had much more potential than our average student. Second, you are going to be dancing every day, at least eight hours a day. You will be trained by the best—namely, me and my staff. You're going to learn exponentially faster than any student. In a week, you're going to be far beyond any of the beginner students. In six months, you'll eclipse any student here."

"Will I ever be as good as the other professionals?" I asked.

Adrienne touched a finger to her cheek. "Absolutely. I think you will show us how long that will take."

Nine

I t was the weekend. I checked out my reflection in every window I passed, trying to hold myself long and straight like a dancer. I'd barely been able to contain myself when I told Lisa and Zan. Lisa had squealed and hugged me tight. Zan had cracked up, saying, "I gotta see you doing the cha-cha-cha." When I was at tai chi class, I could barely contain my excitement. Godmother said to me, "You are looking happy today, Charlie" and I'd simply nodded. I didn't dare risk telling her because I wasn't sure how she would react. Like Pa, she might disapprove of my dancing. But most of all, I wished I could tell Pa and that he would be proud of me.

That evening, I headed out to Brooklyn Chinatown in the Sunset Park neighborhood to visit my friend Mo Li, who'd come back early from Boston University for the Thanksgiving holiday. Her parents had an apartment on Eighth Avenue, which was considered extremely lucky since in Cantonese, "Eighth Avenue" sounded roughly like "Road to Wealth." Her father, who'd been an engineer in China, was probably working at a casino in Atlantic City that night and her mother was a cleaning lady doing the night shift at a hospital, so she wouldn't likely be home either.

I was always surprised by how much Brooklyn Chinatown resembled the Chinatown I knew, with Chinese storefronts and signs everywhere. However, the streets were wider and everything was more spread out. You could tell it had developed later because it still had room to grow, while my Chinatown felt dense, like you could barely squeeze another food stand into it.

When Mo Li opened the door to her apartment, I saw her face and recoiled. "Are you all right?"

She wasn't wearing her glasses and one eyeball was huge, while the other one seemed tiny. She looked like a stroke victim. "Yes, I'm just trying on these circle lenses. Come in. Zan will be here soon."

I hugged her, then drew back. "What in the world did you do to yourself?" I still wasn't sure if I'd need to drag her to the emergency room.

"They're contact lenses. I only have one in. I was just starting on the other one when you rang the doorbell."

"No contacts ever made people's eyes look like that."

Mo Li brought me into their little bathroom, where a contact lens case was perched on the yellowing sink. There was a brown lens floating in one compartment, with a dark outer ring and spidery lines painted toward the clear center.

"That is one scary-looking lens," I said. "Is that a colored contact?"

"It's a circle lens. The colored part is larger than your real iris. People use them to make their eyeballs look bigger."

"Why in the world would you do such a thing?"

"They're incredibly popular in Asia. How do you think Grace gets her eyes to look so big?"

I thought for a moment. "Lucky at birth?"

"No, silly. She's wearing these things, plus false eyelashes and a load of makeup. I'll pop the other one in and you'll see."

When Mo Li turned to me again, her eyeballs were enormous. "Now you look like an alien." I peered closer. "There are almost no whites in your eyes anymore."

She studied herself in the mirror, then sighed. "I guess they're not for me."

"Why are you messing with this stuff anyway?"

Mo Li started taking the lenses out. "You know how I'm into the cosplay thing?" Mo Li and her family had moved here from mainland China less than ten years ago, but she had embraced American culture more than any of the rest of us. She loved science fiction and fantasy books. When she got to Boston University, she started hanging out with a bunch of new friends and she began dressing up as some of her favorite characters for conventions. "I got a set of circle lenses to make my eyes blue for my last role. Then this American girl who's also pre-law—she's always really put together—she told me that maybe I needed a different look. You know, to be competitive. I'm graduating this year and they say law school is so cutthroat."

I studied Mo Li, with her soft body, rounded shoulders and horn-rimmed glasses. She'd gained some weight at college but her eyes, now that I could see them, were as lively as ever. "You're the smartest person I know. You don't need googly eyes to be competitive."

"I guess at heart I still feel like a fobby." A fobby was her nickname for what the kids called FOBs, the students who were Fresh Off the Boat, as opposed to ABCs, American-born Chinese.

"That's ridiculous. You haven't been a FOB for years."

"You were the only ABC who would talk to me," she said. "You and Zan were the only people who even noticed me at first." Mo Li and I had met in high school. Mo Li's English was already excellent because she'd studied it as a second language in China, and she soon shot ahead of the rest of us in class. The other smart kids wanted to bring her into their circle then, but she always stayed friends with me and Zan. She'd tried to help us with our schoolwork too, though I had so little time to study. I was already working odd jobs to help Pa out after Ma died.

"Don't you remember that the teachers tried to call you Molly and you refused? You said, 'My name is Mo Li.' You stay who you are and you'll be just fine."

Her smile showed her small, even teeth. "You actually look different." She narrowed her eyes. "I can't put my finger on it. It's like you got taller or something."

"I've got some news too."

After I'd filled Mo Li in and she'd finished jumping up and down, she said, "I can't believe you actually taught a dance class! But then again, I can. You've always had this gangly grace."

I snorted.

She went on. "Really. You'd spill everything in the dining hall, but in gym you could beat even the guys sometimes. Hey, do you want the circle lenses? You could probably use them more than me."

"I'd blind myself trying to get them in."

"True. Well, if you don't need them, I guess I don't either." The buzzer sounded. "Oh, that must be Zan. I'll be right back."

While Mo Li went to open the door, I wandered around her apartment. Unlike ours, her apartment had no religious icons whatsoever. I was used to Chinatown, where almost every store had an altar hidden away in the back. Mo Li had explained that religious rituals had been discouraged by the Communists, so she and her parents were agnostics. There were no red strips of paper with lucky sayings on them. The only thing hanging on her walls was a fine

Chinese landscape, probably brought over from the mainland, and a ragged poster of the periodic table. A bumper sticker that read "Boston University" was stuck on the window, probably because they didn't own a car to put it on.

Since they'd moved to Brooklyn, they had more space than we did. Mo Li didn't have any siblings, due to China's one-child policy, so she had a tiny room all to herself. The living room was cluttered with cardboard boxes and the little kitchen was through an archway. One box was open next to their coffee table, which was covered with decks of playing cards. I sat down on the flowered sofa next to the table.

Zan took off her coat and waved at me as she came into the room. Mo Li called, "Would you guys help me do the decks? The faster I'm done, the sooner I can just hang out. You want some soda?"

Zan and I sighed. We each picked up a deck and started sorting it. Since Mo Li's father worked at a casino, he often brought extra odd jobs like this home. All of the playing cards needed to be re-sorted after use. They got paid ten cents per pack or something like that. I started organizing mine by color, then suits, then number. Mo Li brought a few glasses of cola over to us.

"Why are you home so early?" Zan asked. "It's not Thanksgiving yet."

Mo Li said, "My ma flunked the naturalization exam. She has a chance to retake it next week. I need to help her study."

"Aren't you missing your own classes?" I asked.

"Yeah, but I'll manage. She can't do it without me." Mo Li's ma could barely speak English. "She's been listening to tapes and practicing, but she gets so nervous. She can hardly look at the examiner."

For a moment, we all worked on our cards in silence. Mo Li was faster than we were, probably due to all the practice she'd had. She tied off her deck with a rubber band and grabbed another one from the box. "So, Zan, what's the gossip?"

Since Zan's egg cart was in one of the busiest parts of Chinatown, she saw and heard just about everything that happened. Zan took a new deck too. Everyone was faster than I was. "I saw Winston with a new girl."

My heart sank. Not that I cared. "Who was she?"

"Don't know. Maybe a college student. But I'm sure she'll be gone soon too. And the police were clearing out the park again. I heard the Vision got rounded up."

Mo Li looked up. "Really? For fraud?"

I said, "Come on, she works a lot with my uncle. Many people swear she's for real."

Mo Li sniffed. "There's no scientific evidence that any sort of paranormal activity exists. I think she's just milking people for their money."

Zan said, "They didn't arrest her. It sounded like they just told her to stop burning joss paper in the park."

"Western medicine doesn't know everything," I said. I didn't like them dismissing Pa's and Uncle's beliefs.

"At least it's regulated," Mo Li said. "In the east, you have no idea what you're getting for your money."

Zan sensed the tension and tried to change the subject. "Hey, Charlie, how's Lisa doing?"

"Well, at school she seems to be doing really well. She's going to try out for Hunter high school. By the way, Mo Li, do you think you could help me with something? Did you bring your laptop home with you?"

"Sure," said Mo Li. "I have tons of work to do."

"Can you help me register her for the test?"

"Of course! I don't have an Internet connection here but we can go around the corner to the coffee place. They have free Wi-Fi." I'd been worried about getting through the online registration for the test with my minimal computer skills. Things were so easy when you knew how. "Hunter's a really big deal." Mo Li sounded impressed. "The Hunter kids at BU are fierce. They're so articulate, like they're not afraid of anyone."

I knitted my brow. "I know it's a good school. It's just that she seems so stressed by it. She's wetting the bed at night and having nightmares. I'm worried it's too much for her."

Zan said, "Remember Lisa always used to freak out when she didn't get perfect grades on her report card?"

I smiled. "Yeah. If something didn't go right at school, she'd put her head down and pound her fists on the table. That was a while ago, though."

"People go crazy about those things. Believe me, I know," Mo Li said. "I bet it'll stop as soon as it's all over. Come on, let's go get her registered for the test."

At work on Monday, a heavy older Greek woman sat behind the receptionist's desk. She had hair that was so black, it had obviously been dyed. Her eyebrows were dark against her pale skin and she had a mole on her cheek with a long hair growing out of it. When she smiled wide, her bright lipstick smeared across her uneven front teeth.

Adrienne came over to Nina and me. "Charlie, this is my mother-in-law, Irene. She's going to be taking over your job for a while. We're very grateful she's helping us out like this."

Irene gave me a wink. "She's just getting me out of the house. That's okay, I'll stay here as long as things stay interesting."

I said, "Do you want me to help Irene—"

"No, that won't be necessary," Adrienne interrupted hastily. "Thanks, Charlie, but I'll show her the ropes. We need to get you started on your new job first."

I had dressed carefully that day. I'd worn the dress that Pa had deemed too immodest for the dinner with Uncle. Although it had a square neckline and was therefore open around my neck, it hit me at midcalf and hung loosely around my body.

Adrienne and Nina walked with me into the teachers' room. On the floor were two large shopping bags filled with clothing.

Adrienne started talking. "Now that I know what you can look like, I want an improvement from you. I didn't say anything before because I didn't know we had a choice, and because you were the receptionist. But if you are a dancer, we need you to appear like one of us. So I was cleaning out my closets because I need to make room for the baby's clothing anyway."

"She always brings in stuff for us," Nina said. "At least once or twice a year, she'll bring in a couple of shopping bags full."

"Well, this time, you get first pick." Adrienne considered me. "In fact, just take it all, Charlie."

"I couldn't do that." I could already see from the rich fabrics that the bags were filled with expensive clothing. "What about the other dancers?"

Nina said, "We've been given stuff for years. Now it's your turn."

I pulled out a soft dress in a dark burgundy color and touched it to my cheek. It was a rehearsal dress like the one Nina had lent me. "Why are you getting rid of this? It's in perfect condition." I turned to her in wonder. "You're doing this to help me."

Adrienne rubbed her forehead. "Would I do that? Well, I do go through my things regularly and maybe I got rid of a tiny bit more than usual, but I'm entering a fresh phase of my life. I need new clothing. And Dominic and I have retired from competing, so I don't need most of the rehearsal stuff anymore. A lot of it is Lycra, which will stretch or contract as needed. You can always hem something that's too long."

I walked over to Adrienne without saying a word and hugged her.

She hugged me back. "We are going to make you unveil your beauty, Charlie, even if it kills all of us. Now I have to make sure my mother-in-law doesn't take over the studio while I'm in here, so I'll see you later." Adrienne left.

Nina was grinning at me. "Come over here. This is your locker," she said, showing me one of the gray cabinets.

I touched it, trailing my hand across the metal surface. I really belonged here now, in the teachers' room.

"You can put your things in there. Although you should take those off and burn them." She pointed at my shoes. "You can't dance in those. You'll twist your ankle and get injured. You have to buy a pair of real dance shoes."

I worried about the extra expense. "How much will that cost?"

"You need to get good ones because you'll be in them the whole day long. Shoes are the only tool a ballroom dancer has, so they're very important. There are cheaper ones on the market, but you need to get the ones the professionals wear. So you're looking at about a hundred and seventy dollars for the shoes, with shipping probably close to two hundred."

I gasped. "For one pair of shoes?"

"Yes." Nina opened her locker and took out her Latin shoes, which I now saw were the same as the ones Katerina had. "The strap around the bottom of the foot will give you support. The heel will keep you balanced. You actually need two pairs, Latin and smooth." She took another pair out of her locker. I had seen Katerina wearing this sort when she rehearsed. I had thought they were flesh-colored pumps but now I noticed that the top had elastic around the edges, so that the shoe crumpled up upon itself when no one was wearing it.

"I can't afford that," I said.

"Well, since you're just beginning, you could do everything in your Latin shoes. You'll need to decide at some point what kind of dancer you'll be."

"What?"

"If you'll concentrate on smooth or Latin dances."

"I thought we had to do all of the dances."

Nina sighed. "Of course we do. I don't mean with students. I mean as a pro. When you're a part of a professional couple, you'll specialize either in the smooth dances or in the Latin ones. Sometimes that's determined by your body type. If you're smaller, you have to do Latin. It's always those tall couples with the long legs who win in smooth. They glide across the floor like they're flying."

"Simone is tall and she does Latin with Pierre."

Nina said thoughtfully, "Simone is really talented. I hate to say it because she can be such a you-know-what, but she's good. She trained at Juilliard, could have been a ballerina at the School of American Ballet. And she doesn't let you forget it either. But she's a very versatile dancer." Nina looked me over. "You're right in the middle. You could probably go either way."

"Well, since I have to get a pair of Latin shoes anyway, I'll be a Latin dancer."

Nina burst out laughing. "That's very practical of you."

"I'm a sensible person."

"Your heart's going to pull you one way or another. Take off your stockings."

"Why?"

"Because I need to tape your feet."

I stopped asking questions. It was all too much. I just did as she said.

She took my left foot and started sticking Band-Aids on it, around my heel, the wide part of my foot. By the time she was done, my foot was almost completely covered, and looked like it had been in a car accident.

"Preventative taping," she said. "You are going to get the worst blisters anyway. This will just slow down the process enough that you have time to toughen up your skin before your feet start bleeding too much. Most pros won't tell you to do this. They've been dancing so long that their feet are totally deformed, like mine." She stuck out her foot. It looked fine to me, slender and graceful, until I realized that there were thick calluses across the heel and front of the foot, in exactly the same places she had taped on mine. "But I remembered when I came back after the baby, I'd been out long enough to lose my calluses, and boy, did my feet bleed. I almost couldn't get the blood stains out of my shoes. That was when I decided to be careful and tape my feet again. Actually, it was Simone who gave me the tip. I guess it's a ballerina thing."

"Was it hard to come back?"

Nina raised an eyebrow. "Oh yeah. No studio in the city would hire me, even though I'd been really good before I left." Her voice was bitter. "Only Adrienne took a chance on me, a single mom. You're not supposed to have a baby before you've ever won a title. Come on, let me do the other foot, then we'll go order your shoes."

Adrienne let me borrow from my next paycheck to pay for the shoes, and she used her credit card since I didn't have one. Katerina was nice enough to continue lending me her shoes until my own came.

I rooted through the bags Adrienne had brought for me. There was so much beautiful and luxurious clothing. Velvet skirts, cocktail dresses, silk scarves and, most important of all, Lycra dance dresses and tailored pants that I would be able to move in. I had already felt in that last dance session how hard it was to dance at a professional level in my regular clothing. I would hide these at the back of the closet at home, where Pa wouldn't notice them.

I pulled on a black dance skirt with built-in panties; the skirt flared when I twirled. On top, I added a tight black camisole, and over that, a thin pink silk cardigan. I didn't recognize myself when I looked in the mirror. The pink brought out the flush in my cheeks. I raised a hand to my face. Then I went into the ballroom for my first dance session as a professional.

That dance session, Simone was indisposed. I found out later that she was so furious about my being hired instead of Pierre that she'd walked out. After our class, one of the other dancers would train me. The first day, I had Nina as my teacher. She put a large yellow booklet in my hands. On the front, it read "The Avery Way" and it showed "Bronze, Silver, Gold, and Supreme Gold levels." Inside was a long list of dances and the steps for each one at each level.

My spine was rigid.

"Relax," Nina said, cracking her gum. She wasn't allowed to chew it while teaching but they let her do it when she didn't have a student. "You have time to learn all of this before your exam."

This was like school again. "What exam?"

"We're all certified. You'll be tested to confirm that you know all of these school figures perfectly—both parts, orientation, the count, everything. But don't worry about that yet, just try to get the steps down. Let's start with waltz today. Stand next to me, we're both going to do man's part first."

I stood next to Nina and considered us both in the mirror. Nina was as lovely as ever, but for the first time, I didn't look horrible either. I stood a bit straighter. Nina drew a large circle counterclockwise around the ballroom with her arm. "If you imagine that circle drawn onto the floor, then that is your line of dance, otherwise known as 'LOD.' The left-turning promenade step starts diagonally to the wall . . ."

The rest of the dance session passed in a blur for me. That first lesson, we covered about three steps each in all ten dances, doing both the man's and the lady's parts: foxtrot, waltz, tango, eastern and western swing, rumba, cha-cha, samba, mambo and merengue. I didn't have any energy to wonder which ones I liked best.

At the end, Nina said, "You did really well. Next time, you should bring your cell phone and record the steps. It'll make it a lot easier for you to learn and remember."

I felt ashamed. "My phone doesn't have any video." My mobile only had the most basic functions.

Nina hid her surprise. "We'll use mine and you can watch it when you're free in the studio. They won't book you for private lessons for a while anyway."

I perked up. "Really?"

"Of course not. You've got to learn the entire Bronze syllabus backward and forward, and you've also got to start learning some technique. Believe me, you'll know the whole syllabus by the end of the month but the technique takes years."

Katerina took over for the technique lesson. She slid her foot along the floor, pushing it into the ground with her foot turned out, her leg one long sinuous line.

"Push your foot forward, bring your weight with it, and then transfer your weight. No, too late." She kept her hands on my hips. She was standing right behind me in the small ballroom again. "You are doing American-style Cuban motion here, so you have to transfer your weight, then move your hip, on the bent knee."

This was even harder than learning steps. My entire body ached.

"You are trying too hard to use this," she said, pointing to my head. "Turn off your brain and trust your body. You must learn with your body."

That I could do. When I let go of my attempt at control, I could do what she was asking much more quickly. I took a deep breath and tried to find the silence inside that Godmother always spoke about.

Later that day, I sat in the ballroom at one of the small tables and really watched the lessons. I noticed when Nina had a couple who were beginners, because she was teaching them some of the same things I'd learned. I was surprised at how long it took them to cover one step. I took courage from this, and from the fact that I always saw the pros working by themselves in front of the mirrors. When they had a free moment, they were often walking, rolling their hips or doing turns by themselves in an empty spot.

While everyone else was teaching, I went to an unoccupied corner and started going over material I had learned that day. For the first time, I felt as if I might have a chance to actually be good at something. Like Godmother said, nothingness was the beginning of the universe.

Ten

Lisa and I sat together at our rickety table as the radiator hissed. I pulled the shawl more tightly around my shoulders. It was never very warm in our apartment. She'd printed out some practice questions for the test that she'd found on the Internet. We'd just looked at the reading passage together. I couldn't seem to stop drumming my fingers on the tabletop. Now I read the first question. "The narrator can best be described as (a) curious; (b) antagonistic; (c) ambivalent; (d) miserable."

Lisa said, "I think '(c) ambivalent.' What do you think, Charlie?"

I coughed. "Honestly, I don't know." I'd had trouble reading the passage carefully in the amount of time we had.

"You don't have to do this with me."

"I want to." It was my duty.

"I can tell this makes you so nervous, and I learn better on my own anyway. It sticks in my head that way."

"Those friends of yours, like Hannah, have parents who help

them. You don't, you only have me. What is that other boy doing to prepare?"

"Fabrizio?" Lisa stared at her sheet of paper. I could see she'd lost weight in the past months. "He's enrolled in a course."

"For what?"

"To study for this test."

"They have classes for that?"

She nodded. "He says there are loads of kids in his group and he gets hours of homework for it every week, but it's really expensive. Hundreds of dollars."

"Why would people pay so much?"

"Private school kids try to get in too. Their schools already charge tens of thousands each year for tuition. This is nothing to those students, especially if you consider how much they'd save if they were accepted."

I hadn't realized what we were up against. "That's why I need to be here for you."

"Charlie, you *are* helping me. By being my sister. Just let me study for this on my own. I know how, I promise."

I couldn't keep the relief from my voice. "Are you sure?"

She nodded.

"Maybe Uncle Henry could help you too."

"We're pretty busy at the clinic, Charlie." She looked strained.

"I know, but he's family. I'll get Pa to ask him."

Later, when she was asleep, I worked on the knitted scarf I was making for her present, since it was all I could do for her.

Although I was a dancer now, I approached the training with the steady dedication of the laborer that I was at heart. I practiced day and night. I danced so hard that even with the tape, my feet were often bleeding by the end of the night, but I was used to physical pain from the dishwashing. Even Dominic came up to me to say, "Make sure you rest sometimes."

I would nod but as soon as he left, I'd start practicing again. I lived and breathed dancing. At first, I was embarrassed to watch myself in the mirror, but soon I stopped seeing myself. What I saw was the angle of my foot, the length of my arm, if my weight was pushing correctly into the floor, the rotation of my hip. I practiced my Latin walk with Cuban motion, pushing my feet through each step and rolling my hips. Once, I looked up to see all of the men in the ballroom staring at me before they turned away. But soon I stopped being conscious of other people watching. I grew aware of my entire body for the first time: my hands, my shoulders, my arms, my neck, my thighs. When I danced, I felt alive and free, like I was discovering my true self, that I was more than just a dishwasher from Chinatown.

As I passed Gossip Park, the music of a street band drifted to me. They were bundled up in the cold, yet playing with all their might. I closed my eyes for a moment and counted the music. It was a samba. I gazed up at the bare trees and it seemed to me the entire world was caught up in a dance of some kind. I stepped forward and did two quick turns, spotting the band as I did so. Then I looked around. Luckily, no one had noticed.

Godmother had told me I didn't need to pick her up that Saturday, so I went to the Benevolent Association to meet her there for the tai chi class. To my surprise, the room was already fairly full when I entered and several of the tables had been put together in the center of the room to form one long table, with the chairs placed around it. They must have just had a family meeting of some kind. I spotted Mr. and Mrs. Yuan, Grace's parents, who rarely went there. Two of Grace's aunts were there as well. In fact, most of the people there seemed to be close relatives of her family. I wondered if Grace was in trouble.

Godmother's face seemed tired. Grace's parents nodded to me as they hurried out the door.

As I was hanging up my coat, I said to Godmother, "Is something wrong?"

She shook her head. "Nothing that need concern you. Won't you please help clear the floor for our class?" Then she looked at me more carefully. I'd chosen to wear one of Adrienne's T-shirts instead of my usual baggy one. It was dark green, with a low scoop neck. Godmother pursed her lips. "That doesn't look like you, Charlie."

I forced myself to meet her eyes.

"I'm sorry." She laid her hand on my shoulder. "I'm worried about a family problem. I didn't mean to take it out on you."

I nodded and hurried away but it still hurt that Godmother didn't like the way I was changing.

That Sunday, I woke in the middle of the night to find Pa gone. His bedroom door was ajar and his bed was empty. He wasn't in the bathroom or kitchen. I began to gasp for air, imagining that Pa lay unconscious somewhere.

"Pa?" I called softly, so as not to wake Lisa. "Pa?"

He wasn't anywhere in the apartment.

I hurtled downstairs without my shoes on, the steps stinging my feet with cold. I had vague notions of throwing open the front door and calling for help. As I got close to the ground floor, I felt a draft. I slowed down then, afraid that a burglar had broken in and was lying in wait for me. The door to the backyard of our building was open.

I froze. Pa was on his knees in the moonlight, beating something to death against the ground, with the metal bucket we used for sacred burnings still smoldering in front of him. No, he wasn't beating an animal to death, it was a plastic slipper he had in his hand and he was whipping it against the concrete with all his strength. Parts of the slipper had already broken off.

"Be gone," he wailed, his breath coming in white puffs, "evil spirits of petty people, be gone from our lives!"

I was used to Pa's superstitions: the grapefruit skins he used to ward off evil, making sure that we were always wearing a bit of red for good luck, but this was of another order altogether. I'd never seen him show so much passion. I felt guilty, having caught him in this moment of private emotion, and I quietly snuck back upstairs, hardly daring to inhale. This was his way of trying to help Lisa.

I recognized what he was doing. I'd seen it performed by wailing witches and people in Gossip Park as well. It was a ritual called "Beating the Petty People"; the Vision must have told him to do it. It was supposed to repel attacks from those who would hurt you. When he finally slipped back into the apartment, I pretended I was asleep. I hoped for Lisa's sake that it would help.

On Tuesday, I walked into the studio and saw Simone and her student Keith having an intense talk in the corner. From Simone's exaggerated hand gestures, I could tell she was excited about something, but even with all her enthusiasm, her movements were controlled.

Nina was doing her usual stretches in front of the mirror but skipped over to me as soon as she noticed me. "Charlie, take a look at this!"

She grabbed my arm and dragged me back to the reception area, where the clipboard was. I peered at the poster hanging there. I saw a photo of a smiling older man in a Latin suit and it read, "The Paul Rosenthal Dance Scholarship. A check of $15,000 shall be awarded to the best Pro-Am couple in American Rhythm/International Latin. The talent of both dancers, the professional and the amateur, shall be judged."

At this I stopped and stared into Nina's eyes. Each person would then receive seventy-five hundred dollars.

"Keep reading," she said.

I looked at the poster again. "Two couples, each made up of a professional woman and an amateur man, may compete from each Avery Studio in New York City. The couples shall perform a show number based upon one of the rhythm/Latin dances. The team of five judges, to be chosen and headed by esteemed adjudicator Julian Edwards, will be looking beyond technical ability. Rather, they will be searching for the qualities that Paul embodied in his life: enthusiasm, passion and authenticity."

"I wish I had a shot at this," Nina said, rolling herself up and down on her toes. "I had this wonderful guy but he moved back to Sweden last year. I don't have anyone really good right at the moment. My competition students now are all kind of stiff and scared to be on the floor. But I'm going to do my best to convince someone to do this with me."

"I don't understand."

"This is a private scholarship, which means they can set up the rules however they like. I called my friend at the West Side studio and heard it's being funded by the guy's daughter. He's just passed away. It looks like the daughter's trying to re-create what he used to do: Latin dances, with a professional woman. This prize is a huge deal. It's so much more money than a normal competition and every Avery Studio in New York is going to want to participate for the honor of it."

"So who's going to represent our studio?"

She wrinkled her nose at me. "I'd put my money on Simone. If her Keith wants to do it, and I'm sure he will, the studio will support him."

I knew from my scheduling days that Keith came in three times a week for two lessons each time. "What about Katerina?" She had many competition students.

"She's not a Latin dancer and none of her students compete seriously in those dances. If it were international standard, she'd smoke it but it's not."

"So it'll be between you and Simone. I really hope you win."

"I'd kill to get this."

The only classes I taught in that month of December were the beginner classes. I noticed when Evelyn and Trevor had lessons with Nina. Ryan didn't appear, though. I couldn't believe I was getting paid when I was hardly making any money for the studio.

"They're investing in you," Irene said. "My boy always knew how to do business."

I liked sitting in the receptionist's area with her when my feet hurt too much for me to take another step. Thank goodness Nina had taught me how to tape my feet. Even so, they were so sensitive and sore by the end of the evening that I changed back into my old dishwasher shoes when I left the studio. Now I understood why no one wore even the slightest heel when they changed to go home. Everyone put on the most comfortable shoes they could find.

Irene seemed to fit into the studio as if she'd always been there. She was like a mom to all of us, especially now that Adrienne had left the studio until after the baby was born. As it neared Christmas, the studio was decked out in Christmas trimmings and all of the music started to have holiday overtones.

Irene made mistakes behind the desk as well. Once, I heard Simone complaining to her about another booking mistake on her agenda and Irene said, "Too bad for you, honey. Suck it up."

But I also saw the other dancers pouring their hearts out to her.

"My parents want to meet my girlfriend," Mateo said. "They're pressuring me to bring a date for home for Christmas. I don't know what to do. I just barely got through Thanksgiving alive."

"Don't hide who you are. They are your parents, they will love you no matter what."

"You don't know the culture I grew up in."

"You're a professional ballroom dancer. Believe me, they already suspect."

"Some of the guys aren't gay."

"But they don't know that. They probably think all of the male dancers are gay. How did you get away with this for so long?"

"I convince random women to go home with me."

Nina said, "Oh, thanks a lot. Now I'm a random woman."

"You did a great job, Nina. So good that they kept pressuring me to marry you. That's why I had to tell them our relationship was over."

Irene said, "You've been pulling the wool over your parents' eyes. It's awful to lie to them. Just tell them."

This made me think about my own Pa, and how I was lying to him every day. He had no idea I was working at a dance studio, let alone that I was now a dancer. How long could I keep up the charade?

"We need to do something about your hair," Nina said, craning her neck to read the menu on the wall of the pizzeria. "You have a good face"—by now I was getting used to everyone at the studio commenting on every part of me—"but the hair is a disaster. Whoever cuts it, and I do not want to know who that is, you must never let them do it again. Is that clear?"

I rolled my eyes. Nina, Mateo and I were in line, waiting for her and Mateo to order. I'd started going out to lunch with them, even though I always brought my own food. They must have known that I couldn't afford to eat out but they never commented. That morning, Nina had looked exhausted. I understood she'd had a rough night with Sammy. Even so, I saw the guys behind the counter checking her out. She didn't notice.

Nina continued, "I know someone who might be able to help you. Her name's Willow and she cuts for Jarrett."

Mateo whistled. "Takes months to get an appointment there, and the cuts are like five hundred dollars."

"Are you serious?" It'd never occurred to me that a haircut could possibly cost so much.

Nina said, "Four hundred and fifty dollars for a cut by Jarrett himself. Willow's second-level staff, so her haircuts are a hundred and fifteen dollars, not including tip."

"I can't pay that," I said.

"You don't have to. Willow's a friend of mine. We met at a party in the East Village. We have a trade set up where she cuts my hair and I teach her a Latin class. She's crazy about it. She's been wanting more lessons than my hair can handle. Also, I'm just so wrecked from Sammy, I don't have the time or energy. You'd be perfect."

"So, you mean I'd teach her in exchange for a haircut? But her cuts are so expensive."

"And a lesson with you is worth a hundred and twenty dollars. So it works out, see?"

I hadn't realized I was that expensive too. I wished I could tell Pa. He would have been so tickled. "Is there really any difference between a twenty-dollar haircut and one that's a hundred and twenty?"

Nina raised an eyebrow. "Absolutely. After Willow cuts your hair, it never curls the wrong way. No pieces stick up in the back. The cut will look very simple but it's perfect, and it'll do exactly what you need it to do. I'll tell her about you. She'll be excited."

"And you know," Mateo said, "I'll do your makeup after we get back to the studio."

In the crowded teachers' room, Mateo set me in front of the mirror and started to chuckle. "I've never seen a woman put on makeup like you. You just throw it onto your face with your eyes squeezed shut. Then you go out and everyone's like, 'Oh, what a lovely girl.'"

"They don't say that," I said.

He patted my cheek. "You're different, Charlie. Now, let the expert take care of you, honey."

"What would you know about makeup?"

"Everything."

I shut up. Mateo flipped through my makeup bag. It was a collection of cosmetics other people had discarded and given to me, plus a few pieces of makeup I'd bought after I started at the studio. "This is all wrong for you. You've got makeup for elderly ladies. No, old ladies wouldn't wear this stuff. You're buying senior citizen rejects."

"Thanks."

"I need some tools here," he called out. "Who can help me?"

Nina brought over a makeup case. It was beautiful, with all kinds of colors and pretty brushes. "I got this from my mom for Christmas."

"Some of this will work for her eyes," Mateo said, tapping his full lips with a finger, "but I need cooler lipsticks and powders. Katerina, cough it up."

"Okay." Katerina rummaged in her locker and came over with her bright pink makeup bag. Simone was sniffing her nasal inhaler as she often did and pointedly ignored us.

Everyone watched my transformation while Mateo made me up with a plum liquid eyeliner, which I'd never used before. He put on much more makeup than I was used to. Lipstick, blush. He feathered eye shadow up to my eyebrows. I kept blinking when he tried to put mascara on me, so in the end he gave up and let me do that part myself.

"You don't need any foundation," he said. "Your skin's perfect."

I was surprised by how dramatic the liquid eyeliner made my eyes. He'd emphasized their slanted shape, pulling the line up toward my temples. I paid close attention to everything he did.

"It doesn't have to be expensive," he said, "but you need the right colors. Go ahead and get the cheap stuff but no more of those neutrals for you. You need brighter colors, more blue-based. Your coloring can take a lot of drama."

Pa would explode if he ever saw me like this.

"I don't look cheap?" I asked.

Mateo looked shocked then laughed. "You're gorgeous," he said, ruffling my hair.

I examined my face in the mirror. I still looked like myself, but more so. My eyes leapt out, my cheekbones seemed more pronounced. Instead of looking pale, the way I usually did, I appeared vibrant. I wasn't used to wearing such bright colors, but I had to say it was an improvement.

"You have to blend. It can be bright, but no harsh lines on your face," Katerina said. "On the stage, you'll need even more. But for studio, this is good."

I bought some inexpensive cosmetics in the colors Mateo had shown me as soon as I could. That weekend, I dragged Lisa into our tiny bathroom and made her up. She was giggling so hard I could barely do her eyes.

"Shh! Pa will hear!" I brushed some powder across her cheek. Lisa had lighter skin than I did but she still had the gold undertone that we all shared in our family. She was such a beautiful girl, with her long lashes and almond-shaped eyes.

Lisa peered at herself in the mirror and gasped. I had overdone it a bit but she didn't seem to mind. "I want to look like this every day!"

"Absolutely not."

"Come on, please."

"Pa will kill me if he sees me wearing this stuff. What would he do to you?"

She drooped. "Oh, I wish he weren't so old-fashioned sometimes."

To cheer her up, I said, "Hey, the Broadway show jar is getting fuller. When we go, we'll get all dressed up and I'll do your makeup."

Lisa's eyes shone. "Even Pa couldn't object to cosmetics for a Broadway show."

Willow, the hairstylist, wanted me to come to her apartment in the East Village that Sunday. She was also an artist, and there were large canvases of collages and paintings all over her tiny studio apartment. Many involved tight clusters of newspaper headlines and handwritten phrases. "Buddha Cat!" one said, and stuck all around it were even smaller clippings that said, "Meow!" There were three meows, all in different typefaces, and then the fourth, as a surprise, said, "Vomit in the cafeteria of this nation." I'd never seen anything like this. In Uncle's house, he had traditional Chinese paintings. Most of the art I'd seen before had been soothing and meant to blend in.

Willow was African-American and taller than I was. She was extremely muscular, so much so that I asked if she also danced. She looked very different from the girls I'd grown up with in Chinatown. I wondered if Mo Li or Zan would like her. She was independent too, practicing her art here in her studio, living on her own.

"I hate to exercise," she said. "I'm just naturally wiry, always have been. Hairy, too." She pulled up her loose leggings to show me the thick stubble on her unshaven legs. Wow. The hair on my legs was so fine, I didn't even need to shave. "But I love to dance. The problem is that Nina's so busy, and her hair's long, so she doesn't need to get it cut that much. But now you're here!"

Willow touched my hair, rubbing a few strands between her fingers. "Actually, I like what you've got. It's so free. What do you want to do with it?"

"I don't actually know. I'm hopeless with this kind of thing."

"Hang on." Willow grabbed her cell phone and dialed. When it was ringing, she put it on speaker. I realized she'd called Nina. "Hey, girl."

"What's up?" Nina said. A small child was shrieking so loudly so that I could barely make out Nina's voice.

"I'm here with your friend," Willow said. "Only she's not sure what she needs."

"Oh, so glad you called before she does something dumb to it. She's either got to keep it quite short or long enough that she can tuck it up in a French twist."

"What?" I said.

"That you, Charlie?" Nina said. "Listen, you can't have your hair flying into your eyes or whacking your partner when you dance. It's either got to be short enough to stay out of the way, or long enough to be put up. You guys decide. Actually, Willow, maybe you should choose." The child's voice grew louder, wailing something about a Popsicle. "Listen, I gotta go, but good luck, okay?" Nina hung up.

Willow tilted her head to the side. "I think those Bettie Page–type bangs would look great on your face. Then a layered inverted bob, to accent your cheekbones here, longer in the front than in the back. It'll bring out your eyes."

"Really?"

She nodded. "We'll even out your hair, and take out much of the volume. We'll make sure it retains its movement, but won't get into your eyes." I felt like she'd just figured out my entire life for me.

Wearing a vinyl cape around my shoulders, I sat on a wooden stool in her kitchen and she got to work. When she was done, my hair looked like it had been chiseled out of stone, falling in a clean sweep against the line of my cheeks.

"As it grows longer, we'll keep trimming it until we get the shape we want," Willow said. "You have very dramatic eyes and this will really highlight them."

I'd never known these things about myself. My eyes now did seem much larger. I hadn't realized how much the blob of hair on my head had affected my appearance. After we were done with my haircut, I taught Willow for an hour. She blasted the music and we grooved to some mambo, merengue and cha-cha.

It wasn't until the next morning, after I shampooed my hair, that I fully realized how good she was. It was just like Nina had said. I'd never been able to control my hair, but now it fell into place after I washed it. I hardly needed to style it. If only the rest of my life were as simple to fix.

Eleven

That morning, Lisa waved a letter at me and Pa. "I got my Hunter test ticket!"

"That's great. Make sure you don't lose it," I said.

"I know. There was some problem with Fabrizio's record and now maybe he won't be allowed to take the test."

Pa said, "Ah. Maybe he is being punished for something he did wrong. Bad acts always rebound on the doer."

I rolled my eyes. I knew Pa thought his petty-spirits ritual had reversed some kind of curse the boy had put on Lisa. "He's Italian. I don't think he knows about that kind of thing."

Lisa said, "What are you guys talking about?"

Pa and I both said, "Nothing."

Lisa was examining my hair. "You look different, Charlie."

I couldn't help raising a hand to my new haircut. "Do you like it?"

Lisa nodded emphatically, while Pa said, "It is so flat. You look like a coconut."

"Pa!" It was hard to feel pretty in this family.

He said, "Maybe you could have the hairdresser perm it for you or something. It wouldn't be so plain then."

"I like it simple," I said. "Some people think it brings out my features."

"Oh?" he said. "Like Winston?"

Now I groaned while Lisa giggled.

Everyone gaped at me when I walked into the studio with my new haircut and my makeup done as Mateo had shown me. Julian was back and I saw his head turn as I went by. Viktor gave a long whistle before he was cut off by Katerina playfully tackling him.

"You go, girl," Nina said. "Willow's amazing, isn't she?"

Then Dominic came up to me the way he did every Monday. "However, lovely as you are, you spent the whole weekend walking like this!" he said, hunching his arms over like an ape.

"I did not!" I had tried to remember but I did forget sometimes.

"You did. People lie. The body does not lie," he said, glaring at me. His heavy fingers pinched my shoulders back. "I can see it in the slope of your shoulders. Keep them straight." As he was talking, he pushed in the center of my back and rolled down my collarbones.

I was used to this by now because Dominic was always correcting my body. It obviously offended him whenever it wasn't properly aligned.

Once, Nina had pretended to be Dominic teaching a dance session. "I don't like your feet, your legs, your shoulders and your head. Just cut them all off!"

But the week before, I'd caught sight of myself in the mirror while going to a student and I'd had to double-check that it was really me. This woman, walking proud, shoulders back and neck stretched out long, looked like she belonged here. It was sustaining that appearance that was the challenge.

Julian was leading that morning's dance session. Despite myself, my heart thrilled. I remembered how loose and sure of myself I felt dancing with him. He began by announcing, "We will be doing international tango and the emphasis in today's lesson is standard technique. Simone, if you please."

With a little smile, Simone positioned herself in Julian's arms. He stepped right up to her, so that there was no distance in between their bodies. She arched her back and head back in a dramatic sweep away from him.

Julian adjusted her head. "Don't break the line. It must all come from the spine." He dropped his arms so that he was only touching her with his stomach and stepped forward and back. Simone followed him perfectly. He pivoted, and she did as well, moving as one entity. Then he stepped away from her with a nod and turned to the rest of us. "Gentlemen, when you lead with the true center of your body, you will not need your arms. When we lead with arms, we are only as graceful as an octopus, because that is what we will look like."

Julian pretended he was an octopus. We all laughed. I wondered if he knew how appealing he was. But of course he did. "Take a partner, everyone." Then Julian held his hand out to me and I felt my pulse flutter. "No arms, Silver syllabus international tango across the floor."

The other dancers set off and I was astounded to see how smooth and coordinated their movements were, even though they only touched each other with their middles.

Julian put his arms around me and arched my back, while maintaining contact with our pelvises. Before I could worry about how inappropriate this would seem to Pa, he positioned my spine and head until I was staring at a point on the ceiling. It was so awkward and uncomfortable, I forgot everything else. "How does that feel?"

"Awful," I squeaked. I could hardly breathe in this position.

He chuckled. "That's good. It takes some getting used to. Now, hold that and let me lead. Don't worry about where your feet go, just keep your spine arched and your head up." He took me into dance position and started off. I saw the ceiling spin as we went into a series of lightning-fast pivot turns across the floor. I panicked and started to straighten.

"No, hold the position, breathe into your center. You're doing just fine," he said. We started moving in a straight line again, then he dipped me so that my back was almost parallel to the floor, and we both flowed to the side, then he stopped abruptly and pivoted us around. With a jerk of his arm, our heads snapped to the other side. He swung me into a series of fans around his body. "Welcome to international tango. You're a natural."

I smiled, flattered. I had never been a natural at anything. He let me go and I looked up to see that the others were finishing their round of the ballroom, still without using their arms. Simone swung into a swirl around Dominic without any contact at all.

Then we all assembled again. "Now we switch leads," Julian said. "Still no arms for the rest of you. Charlie, you may lead me with your hands." All of the women got into the leading position and the men, including Dominic, took the lady's part.

"I've been waiting for this day," Simone said, as she positioned Dominic in front of her. Everyone laughed. It was the first time I'd heard Simone say anything funny. I was so used to her being un-pleasant.

The others took off again, with just as much precision as they had the first time around.

"How can they do that?" I asked.

"It's the job of the professional to be able to do both roles equally well," Julian said. "All right, our turn."

He turned around so that he was in the lady's position and I was in the man's. I took him into dance position and he arched back, as perfectly as any woman. I looked at him in the mirror and his position was flawless. It should have looked ridiculous, but on Julian, it didn't.

"I don't know any steps," I said.

"Steps are a crutch," he said, without breaking his line. "Learn to move. That's what takes years of training. Lead me, Charlie."

I took a step closer to him so that our bodies were touching as before. I stepped forward with my left leg and he didn't budge. Julian broke position and looked down at me.

"You were moving with your leg. You need to propel yourself with your center. When our centers connect, then we have dance. Breathe into your middle." He slid his hand in between our bodies and laid it on my stomach. How strange to be touched so intimately by a man I hardly knew. Pa would be shocked—or would he? He'd watched Ma perform too. Maybe he'd understand more of my life than I thought he would, if I only gave him the chance.

I clenched my teeth and stood still. This seemed impossible. Julian settled himself into lady's part again. I forced my body to relax. I thought about how, in tai chi, I told the students we had to move from our centers, keeping our minds and bodies in balance by creating a healthy circulation of qi, the vital life force, within us. I closed my eyes and allowed my body to go forward. I didn't feel any resistance at all.

In surprise, I opened my eyes and Julian was directly in front of me. He'd flowed with me. I did it again, simply propelling us forward but with no awareness of my feet or legs, just thinking about my center connected to his, gliding forward. He moved as if he were a part of me, weightless and effortless. I took a step backward and he stayed with me. I went to the side, he followed. It was like he was an attachment. I laughed with joy.

Julian deliberately turned his head to wink at me. Then he arched backward again. We stepped forward and I decided to try some of the pivot turns he'd just done with me. We spun around and around. I stopped and we broke apart.

He had a broad smile on his face. "You understand. Do you know what I like about you? Not your talent, because although you are gifted, so are we all. Because you have the desire that makes the difference between success and failure. Those who succeed are the ones who are willing to follow their talent into all of the unknown places it will take them."

It was the monthly studio party and I was wearing a dark red dress Adrienne had given me. It fit me closely, with a soft skirt that swung when I moved. Like all of the other dancers, I was wearing a Santa hat. I was grateful the theme this time was simply Christmas, instead of cowgirl or Grecian goddess.

The studio was dimly lit, with platters of cheese, crackers and fruit laid out on the tables. Bottles of wine stood open. We all knew better than to drink. It looked like a party, but it wasn't for us since we were working. The students started to arrive. First came the regulars like Keith, but I also recognized two female students who had been in my beginners' class. They waved at me as soon as they entered. Close behind them came Evelyn, her fiancé Trevor and Ryan, dressed in a crisp white shirt and tan pants.

"Mr. Sexy can come to Mama," Mateo whispered in my ear, keeping his eyes on Ryan.

"Is Mama me or you?" I asked.

He looked at me in some surprise. "I'm Mama, of course." Then he waltzed off.

Like the other teachers, I went to greet the students I knew. While Evelyn and Trevor were chatting with Nina, Ryan approached me, his shoulders backlit by the spotlights.

"So you do exist after all," he said.

"What do you mean?"

"Well, Evelyn's really set on my doing the father-daughter dance with her at her wedding but I wouldn't come back unless you were my teacher. They told us you weren't available then." He looked sheepish. "Guess I'm not that brave."

I couldn't help smiling. "It's intimidating to learn how to dance, but every teacher here is very nice."

"That's what they all say."

I laughed. "So how come you're here tonight?"

"It's a part of that introductory package, along with the beginners' lesson."

The lights flickered, signaling that the dancing demonstration was about to begin, and we all gathered around Simone and Mateo. Much as I disliked Simone, she was beautiful on the floor. They went into a series of bolero moves that ended with her arched backward in a dip, to applause.

When the general dancing started, I found it wasn't as hard to ask the men to dance as I'd thought, since they seemed pleased to be approached. This wasn't personal; it was simply my job. Many of them were beginners and they were excited if we could move around the floor without crashing into someone. I left the more advanced students to the others. Keith and Simone swirled around to a complex Viennese waltz, and I found myself enjoying dancing with the students until one student said to me, mid-foxtrot, "Have you seen the new Gauguin exhibit at the MoMA?"

I stumbled. It was like he was speaking another language. "No."

"It's fantastic. I love all of the postimpressionist painters, don't you?"

"Shall we try a box step with turn?" I knew he wouldn't be able to do it, and instead of all his art talk, he started apologizing for not doing the step properly.

Then Ryan was standing in front of me with his hand extended. When the swing music started, he began to move right in time to the music.

"I see you're not wearing your boots tonight," I said.

"Having enough trouble not getting tied into a pretzel as it is."

I grinned. "Do you remember the underarm turn?"

In response, he led me right into it. I sang a bit under my breath as I did a triple step underneath his arm. He even remembered the variation I'd taught as a challenge, where the man scooted underneath the arm as the lady was turning back. His steps were still too big and he wound up so far away from me that we were only touching by our fingertips.

"I'm impressed," I said as he took me back into dance position. "Are you sure you're only a gardener? No secret ballet lessons as a boy?"

He barked out a laugh. "Definitely not. But I used to box competitively."

I thought about my tai chi background. "That would help explain it."

"And I might have taken some yoga lessons." At my surprised look, he continued, "Lots of boxers do, although we don't tend to advertise it. Not manly, you know. But yoga helps us avoid injuries by building up flexibility and stamina."

I noticed he still considered himself a boxer. "You don't box anymore?"

He started doing a series of basic steps, probably so he could manage to talk to me at the same time. "I left the competition scene years ago. But I still coach kids every weekend. Keeps them off the streets, gives them a place to put all that aggression."

"Why did you stop?"

He was quiet for a moment. "My dad was a cop and got shot in the line of duty. Didn't have time for a lot of things after that."

"Oh, I'm sorry." I thought about Ma. "My mother died when I was fourteen. Things were never the same afterward."

The music faded away. Ryan held on to my hand. "So, are you teaching students now?"

"I'm still being trained." Although I really liked him, I had to be honest. "You might want someone more experienced."

"No, you'll do. You'll be saving my girlfriend's toes too."

Of course he had a girlfriend. I wasn't disappointed, why should I be? I swallowed. "You should bring her with you to the lessons."

"She's studying in California, but she'll be back for the wedding."

"All right, then. I'll get you ready for her."

Zan was sprawled on Mo Li's bare floor, while I had my legs curled up on her bed. Mo Li was back for Christmas vacation. She always wanted Zan and me to e-mail her when she was away, but neither of us had easy access to a computer. Whenever she came home, Zan and I rushed to see her and catch up on all that we had missed. Her parents weren't home again, since they were usually working on Saturday evenings.

Mo Li was digging in her suitcase for something. "Here they are!" She pulled out two large packages and tossed them to us.

I looked at the bright red logo through the wrapping. She'd given us Boston University sweatshirts. "Wow." I took mine out of the plastic. The material was soft and heavy. "This must have been really expensive." We usually got each other things like candles or drugstore cosmetics. Zan tended to make her own things. I still had an embroidered heart with my name on it that she'd given me in high school.

Mo Li said, "I'm on all kinds of scholarships and working jobs on top of it. Besides, I'll be a lawyer soon and then I'll rake in the big bucks. Zan, do you like it?"

I looked at Zan, who was rubbing her sweatshirt against her cheek. The smile she gave me was strange, and then I recognized the emotion on her face as jealousy. There was something new in between us. Things were changing for Mo Li, and now for me too, but not for Zan, with her dreams of driving away out of China-town.

Before Mo Li could notice, I said, "Mo Li, what happened with your ma's naturalization test?"

She broke out in a grin. "She passed! And you know why?"

"Because you helped her prepare so well?"

"Nah, she didn't learn anything. I think it was because I kept jumping up and down outside the examiner's door. The window was set so high, I couldn't see through it otherwise, and I was so worried about my ma. The examiner finally opened the door and told me to either get a step stool or take a seat in the waiting area. I could tell he was trying not to laugh, though. I think he just felt sorry for us and let her pass."

"Thank goodness for kind examiners." I thought of Lisa. "I wish there was something like that for the Hunter test."

"How's that going for your sister?" Zan asked.

I lifted one shoulder in a shrug. "She's practicing on her own, as always. I tried to help her but I just couldn't understand the questions. I think my uncle's doing some exercises with her too, but it's hard for them to find time at his clinic. Her other friends have parents and classes and stuff to help them prepare."

Mo Li shook her head. "No one expects you to be her mother, Charlie."

"I know. It's just there's no one else. Pa, well, you know how he is. He's off in his own world and so busy trying to make ends meet. I wish I could do more for her. She's not happy, something's wrong. I can feel it. If I don't fix it, who will?"

We were all quiet for a moment. Then Mo Li said, "Hey, Zan, what's up with that learner's permit anyway?"

A big smile spread across Zan's face. "I passed the written test! I was waiting to tell you."

Mo Li and I whooped. Then Zan deflated again. "But I don't know what to do now. I guess it's the real reason I put off taking the written test for so long, because I knew I'd hit a dead end after that."

"What do you mean?" Mo Li asked.

"It's no use." Zan echoed my past words. "Who's going to teach me to drive? I could never afford a driver's ed course. No one I know has a car. They wouldn't be willing to risk my driving it even if they had one."

I regretted all of the realistic things I'd ever said to her. "No, you were right. You can do it, you just have to take things one step at a time."

"You think?"

"Look, whoever would have thought that I'd be doing what I am now? I don't know what's going to happen to me but I'm just trying my best day by day. Believe me, if I can become a dancer, anyone could do anything."

Zan sighed. "I'm just the girl at the food cart and that's all I'll ever be."

Mo Li said, "Ridiculous. One day, you'll be waving at us from some big old truck."

Slowly, Zan smiled. "Yeah. *Hasta la vista*, baby!"

Mo Li said, "In honor of this occasion, I'm going to make us some microwave popcorn to celebrate."

As we followed her into the galley kitchen, Zan said, "Oh, have you heard about Grace? She's in deep trouble."

I thought back to the meeting with the Yuans at the Benevolent Association. "What's happened?"

"Her mother caught her in bed."

"No!" Mo Li put a hand to her mouth. We all hid our sex lives from our parents. Until we were married, there could be no exceptions. I wondered if Grace had been found with Winston.

Zan continued, "With a girl."

Mo Li and I both screamed. "I never knew Grace liked girls," I said.

Zan shrugged. "I don't know the details. I only heard her mother stopped by her dorm at Brooklyn College unexpectedly and caught her. Now the family's planning to marry her off, as soon as possible. They say she's too wild."

"She has the right to have a girlfriend if she wants," said Mo Li.

I felt bad for Grace. I didn't want to imagine how Pa would react if he ever found out my secrets. "I agree, but her parents will move heaven and earth to get her tied down to a guy now."

"Speaking of men," Mo Li said, "I have a mission this Christmas vacation."

Zan and I groaned. We knew Mo Li and her projects. She got her heart set on something and we all had to do it. Last time, she'd dragged us all to a karaoke club and made us do vodka shots before singing. Thankfully we were in our own private booth. I didn't really like the taste of alcohol and none of us had any aptitude for singing. Not at all. It was awful.

Mo Li said, "Next week, we are going to Decadence." Decadence was an Asian nightclub on the outskirts of Brooklyn Chinatown. Rumor had it that all kinds of wild things happened there.

I said, "Mo Li, sometimes I think you're shallow."

Zan giggled. Mo Li answered with dignity, "No, I'm exploring what it means to be American."

Zan and I looked at each other.

Then Mo Li said, "My Korean friend says that the most important thing we need to do to get in is to dress really slutty."

Twelve

The following Saturday evening, we all met at Mo Li's house again. Zan and I had told our parents that we were sleeping over at Mo Li's house since her parents wouldn't be home anyway. That way, no one would worry when we were out until late. We would sneak back into Mo Li's apartment before her parents returned in the morning from their night shifts.

The three of us considered each other. We were sorely lacking in sluttiness. Since Mo Li had gone away to college, she'd developed a funky style of her own when she made the effort. She was wearing a fashionable short dress with shiny boots, but Zan had on pants with a high-necked flowered blouse that must have belonged to her mother, and I'd chosen one of Adrienne's simple dresses.

Mo Li said, "Well, at least it's the winter so we'll have our coats buttoned up anyway. They probably won't be able to see much on the street."

"Who's 'they'?" Zan asked.

"The bouncers," Mo Li said. "They decide who gets in and who stays out."

I said, "Is that even legal?"

Mo Li said, "That's New York nightclubs. My friend explained the whole system to me. When you're in line, you need to put the skankiest-looking girl in the front." She surveyed us. "That would be you, Charlie."

"Oh, thanks!" Now I looked like a bimbo. "You're dressed cooler than I am."

"But I'm really short and chunky. You're the sexiest."

Zan studied me. "You do seem different, Charlie."

In this context, I wasn't sure if this was a good thing or not.

Mo Li said, "We should get there just as it opens, when the line's not too bad. We have to try to appear Korean."

"What?" I said.

"We're Chinese so we're borderline acceptable, but if there are lots of Koreans in line, we probably won't get in," Mo Li said.

"Why do we want to go to this place again?" I asked. In high school, the three of us had attended dances at school, and once in a while, we'd gone to parties other kids had given. None of us had ever been into the wild scene. We drank a bit, but said no when drugs, mostly pot, were passed around.

Mo Li said, "It's an experience. I went to a few clubs in Boston, but this type of pure Asian nightlife is really New York. Decadence's infamous. I want to see it before I die."

"That sounds really scientific," Zan said.

"And I want to meet a cute guy," Mo Li added. "We could use some action."

We all burst out laughing.

A few hours later, the three of us were freezing in the line for Decadence. Almost everyone there was Asian and many looked Korean. It wasn't that crowded yet but we could see the two bouncers at the front choosing the people who got in. Most of the pretty Asian girls were admitted. Some of the guys entered too, especially if they were with an attractive woman. Almost all the non-Asians we saw were sent away. Other Asians were stopped too. I wasn't sure why. As we drew closer to the front, I signaled Zan and Mo Li to try to listen in, so that we could maximize our chances of getting into the club.

The bouncer said to two guys in front of us, "Do you have a reservation?"

"Um, no," one of the men answered.

"Good-bye," the bouncer said.

The other man took the bouncer's hand, shook it and said, "We've got the money."

Glancing at his hand, the bouncer said, "Three hundred dollars minimum per table."

The two men consulted each other, nodded and then were admitted.

Mo Li squeaked, "Three hundred! I didn't know you needed a reservation!" I shushed her so I could hear what the other bouncer was saying.

The other bouncer was talking to another group consisting of three guys and two girls. Both girls were beautifully made-up. The bouncer didn't ask them if they had a reservation. He just smiled and said, "You lovely ladies are welcome." He then turned to the guys. One was paler than the others, his hair slicked back above his high cheekbones. The bouncer said to him, "You're in too." Then he addressed the two darker men, who seemed like they might be from Southeast Asia, and said, "No sneakers allowed."

Only one of them was wearing sneakers. That man said, "But he's wearing sneakers too!" He pointed at the guy who'd been admitted.

"They're better sneakers," the bouncer answered.

"What about me, then?" the other man said.

"Wrong type of shoes." The bouncer shrugged. "Sorry."

The girls and guy who had been admitted started to protest, try-ing to get their friends in as well. The bouncer was adamant. Fi-nally, the two rejected men gave up. As they walked away, one of them said, "At least we speak English. We're not like all of the fuck-ing super-FOBs you've got in there." Their friends gazed after them for a moment, then ducked into the club.

It was our turn. I felt Mo Li's hand push me to the front. I looked at the bouncer and forced myself to smile. He smiled back, then turned to my friends. Zan was standing next to me, trying to appear friendly, but it looked more like she was grimacing. He started to frown. Then Mo Li opened her mouth and said something to him in Korean. Zan and I both stared. We had no idea Mo Li could speak Korean. She grinned and the bouncer laughed at a joke she must have made. He waved his hand and let us all in.

As we stood in line inside for the cashier and coat check, Zan said to her, "When did you learn to speak Korean?"

"In China." Mo Li shrugged. "I speak Japanese and French too. I was supposed to become a diplomat if we hadn't emigrated. Asian languages aren't hard when you're Chinese."

"Oh, what about for us then?" I said.

"I mean, when you're a real Chinese. I mean . . ."

By then, we'd entered the main dance area and could hardly hear each other anymore. The DJ was blasting house music. The club was massive. A huge chandelier covered with glittering jewelry hung from the high ceiling. I'd heard it was a Decadence tradition for women to throw their bracelets and necklaces up there. The central dancing pit was ringed with tables, already teeming with men. A balcony above us was filled with tables and guys as well.

I saw passageways leading to what Mo Li had told me were private lounges for larger groups. Some girls were dancing and a few men were flailing around on the dance floor. I almost laughed at what Dominic would say if he could see them. Mo Li bought one of their signature drinks, the Decadent Orgasm, which we shared. It tasted like gin and mango juice. Between the entry fee and the coat check, this night was already very expensive. We'd have to go easy.

People were pouring in. Almost everyone was Asian and the few non-Asians were accompanied by groups of Asians. Everyone around us at the bar seemed to be speaking Korean. Strobe lights played across the shirts and hair of the people on the dance floor. Beautiful go-go girls stepped out onto raised podiums and began to dance a choreographed number while lights spelling out the name of the club flashed across the ceiling. The dancers were pretty good.

I grabbed my friends' hands and pulled them onto the dance floor. I wanted to do some real dancing before it became so crowded that all we'd be able to do was to jump up and down. Huge clouds of steam poured over us. I let the beat pound into me. Zan was leaping from foot to foot like she was jogging. Mo Li threw her fists around as if she were beating someone up. We grinned at each other and I loved all of it.

I raised my arms and spun into a spiral. When I arched my back, my entire spine flowed. Whatever I felt, I could express. It was wonderful, like I could tap into a part of myself I'd never known existed before. I felt in control and free at the same time. The three of us danced song after song. Then I felt someone tap my shoulder, a waiter in a white shirt and bright blue pants. Had I done something wrong?

He grabbed me by the wrist and started to drag me off the dance floor. I pulled back but he was very strong. Mo Li and Zan noticed and followed us. I looked around wildly to see that other girls were being taken away by other waiters as well, mostly under protest. The women all seemed to be scantily dressed. I wasn't wearing anything like that, why was I in trouble?

Then I realized the waiter wasn't ejecting me from the club. He brought me to one of the tables, where a group of young men were sitting. They had a bottle of brandy and a plate filled with appetizers in front of them. The music was too loud for us to be able to talk. The waiter indicated I should sit, then he left. The guys grinned at me and, using hand gestures, offered me a drink. When they noticed Zan and Mo Li, they poured for them too. Now I understood why it cost three hundred a table. The waiters scanned the floor for pretty women, then brought them to the men. I almost wished there was someone there for me, and for moment, an image of Ryan's face flashed across my mind. I shook my head, embarrassed at my thoughts. Well, none of the guys here were likely to want anything more than the obvious. I met Zan's and Mo Li's eyes. They'd caught on too. We smiled, shook our heads and went back onto the dance floor together.

When we finally left Decadence, I was sure I had permanent hearing damage.

Mo Li said dreamily, "Racism, sexism and stupidity all in one evening. What an experience."

It was January and I was back at the studio, sitting in the teachers' room. By now, I was used to the dancers stripping down. I always changed in the ladies' room but the others often stood in front of one another in their underwear. Viktor now wore no shirt and polka-dotted boxer shorts. He was so thin you could see his ribs. Katerina giggled and pinched his bottom.

"What is it with the two of you today?" Simone asked. "Did you have great sex last night?"

Viktor winked. "Even better," he said. "We had great rehearsal this morning."

Everyone laughed.

Katerina said, "That is right. Coaching with Julian. He is a genius." I watched as she danced back to her own locker, singing to herself in Russian. I thought of Julian and felt a sudden pang of longing for a boyfriend and partner of my own. Men had started noticing me and I felt more attractive, more conscious of my body, but it made me lonelier too.

"What happens if you don't fall in love with your partner?" I asked her.

Katerina shrugged. "Why would you not?"

Mateo said, "Honey, even I have slept with my partners. I couldn't stomach it anymore. That's why I stopped competing, until I met Chastity-Belt Nina here."

Nina drew a cross over her body, then pretended to lock herself up and throw away the key. "No one gets into these pants anymore. Your virtue is safe with me."

To my surprise, Simone started talking. Her limpid eyes blinked rapidly as she spoke, and it was like she couldn't keep the words inside. "You do everything with your partner. It's not like you start out the best of friends but you rehearse together, you train every day, you put together your routines. And when you're dancing together, you're constantly trying to create the illusion of romance and passion."

Nina said slowly, "It's a real head trip. It often makes your professional relationship better if you don't have all of the personal junk clouding it up. Sometimes that illusion we're trying to create takes over. We can wind up so . . . ballroom. You know." She struck a series of dramatic poses, with her face going from anguish to elation. "That's what I like about your dancing, Charlie. You're real."

It was almost time for the next class. Most of the dancers trailed out until it was only me and Nina. She was tightening the straps of her Latin shoes.

"Does Julian have a girlfriend?" I asked, attempting to sound casual.

"He might be in between right now, but he's a serial monogamist, you know what I mean? The last girlfriend was some jet-setter from Spanish aristocracy. He's never going to settle down, but at least he's stopped dating dancers."

"Is that a good thing?"

"Well, whichever woman he picked would shoot into the stratosphere with her dancing, so it was great for her, but it exhausted everyone, wondering who would be the lucky one this season." Nina stood up. "He's very attractive."

"I know. I'll be careful."

"It's the nature of the business. When it comes to the professionals, it's a meat market out there. Even good people like Dominic and Adrienne will try to set you up with another pro. It's like date-a-dancer. They have the best intentions but this world will swallow up everything you have if you make the wrong choices. Believe me, I know. And remember that students are forbidden fruit."

Lisa's nightmares had become so bad now that she woke screaming on some nights. I knew the Hunter test was approaching but this was too extreme, especially since she seemed calm about the exam when we spoke. Pa asked Uncle Henry to stop by our place over the weekend, sending Lisa out on an invented errand before he arrived. Uncle shook off his navy wool coat as he came in, appearing out of place in our old apartment with his pressed shirt and expensive shoes. I felt grateful we had someone like him in our family and hoped he could help Lisa.

Pa poured Uncle our finest white tea, in the porcelain set he reserved for company. He also set out a dish with sugared lotus seeds, candied winter melon and dried ginger dipped in red sugar.

"What is your opinion?" Pa asked.

"She's at an age where there are many changes," Uncle Henry said. "With those young girls, it is normal that she has some trouble sleeping at night sometimes."

"She's not just scared when she wakes up, she's stiff with terror," I said.

"I have never seen Lisa like this," Pa said.

Uncle Henry frowned, thinking.

"She needs help," I said.

"There are many possibilities at my clinic," Uncle said. "But probably your best chance is the Vision of the Left Eye."

"You're sending her to the witch?" I asked. "I thought you'd recommend a specialist. Maybe someone she could talk to about her problems."

They both waved their hands at me dismissively. Uncle Henry said, "People like psychiatrists are a bunch of quacks. She needs a professional."

I was silent. Uncle was a successful healer. What did I really know about such things?

"I've seen it before," Uncle Henry said. "Those therapists won't do any good. They'll just ask her about her childhood and all kinds of other nonsense. I think the Vision should start by doing a Release of Life. Then, if necessary, we can consult her further."

"You're absolutely right, older brother," Pa said.

"She has a very bright future ahead of her," Uncle said. "She's not like those other kids who were born here. Sometimes they have less ambition than someone fresh off the boat."

I looked down. I had ambition, I just hadn't been given a chance to draw upon it, but it was still worthless in the context of my family. Even if Uncle and Pa knew I was a ballroom dancer now, they wouldn't think it was an acceptable profession for a girl. Better that I'd be an accountant or pharmacist.

Pa said, "There's nothing wrong with being born here. Charlie's doing wonderfully at her computer firm."

I managed a wan smile.

Uncle said, "Yes, that's very good, but the ambition and drive that we had, it's watered down in the later generations. I just see those young kids hanging out on the street and I think, 'What a waste.' They have it so easy and still do so little with it all. They have the English skills. They know how to fit in. But determination is more important than any of those things. When I first arrived in America, I worked day and night just to make ends meet."

"Pa still does that," I said.

"Well, we need to aid Lisa. I've been having Dennis help her study whenever he's free. I'll start working with her more myself." Uncle paused a moment. "It's imperative that she find some peace, especially with the school test coming up in a few weeks. When you talk to the Vision, Charlie, make sure she knows I sent you."

The police had become much stricter in public places, but I knew that on most Saturday mornings the Vision would be at the edge of Gossip Park, telling fortunes. She sat on a park bench, huddled in a purple down coat, with her assistant, Todd, standing behind her.

Despite the bitter cold, there was a crowd gathered around her. I nodded at Todd, then I held out my gloved hand, showing her the sealed red money envelope.

"Mrs. Purity, Pa asks you to perform a Release of Life for Lisa and me, as soon as possible." Pa had decided that he might as well cover me too, as long as we were consulting the witch anyway. He said it was well worth the extra cost, although the expense worried me.

The Vision of the Left Eye indicated the group of people around me. "I am very busy right now, tell him I speak to him soon."

I'd been prepared for this. "My Uncle Henry asks you to help us as well. It's urgent."

The witch tapped a finger against her cheek. "Come back before twilight."

Things were confusing when she got all mystical. "Do you know what time that is?"

"Try four o'clock," Todd said. "Bring a photo of the person you want to help too."

When I came back with Lisa's photo in my bag, I had to wait another half hour while the Vision finished with her customers. I stomped my feet to keep warm. Todd was still waiting behind her, leaning forward to whisper with her once in a while.

One man, overcome with emotion, gathered the Vision into his arms. "No one could have known he was sick but you. With that knowledge, you saved my boy. Thank you."

I expected us to go to a temple, but instead the Vision led Todd and me to the live poultry store where Zan's father worked. I never liked going in there. A large handwritten sign was plastered across the mirror: "We Slaughter Asian-Style Upon Request," which meant they used a very thin cut across the neck of the bird so that it wouldn't be broken. Chinese needed the head to be attached for religious rituals, otherwise they would go back and request a new bird. The front part of the store was sterile and clean like a regular butcher's, with fowl body parts on beds of crushed ice.

The shop was packed. Many people had been used to eating fresh meat in their home countries and they said it was much more delicious than what you could get in the supermarket. I knew it was hypocritical, since I ate meat, but I hated knowing a chicken had been slaughtered just for me.

When we got to the front of the line, the Vision said to the girl behind the counter, "We want to choose." I took a step back.

The girl gave us a ticket and jerked her thumb toward the rear exit. I exchanged a look with Todd. I really didn't want to go through there. He opened his mouth to say something to the witch but she had already started walking to the door.

We entered a room filled with all types of living fowl stuffed into wooden cages, which were stacked on top of each other. As the Vision went to the chicken section, we passed the doorway that led to the killing room. I caught a glimpse of a man in a blood-stained apron fitting a headless bird into one of the open-ended cones built into the stainless-steel table. His colleague hosed away the crimson blood that poured out onto the floor. There was another large vat of steaming water that must have been used to remove the feathers. I didn't see Zan's father.

I turned to the Vision. "Do you need to buy your dinner now? Can't we do the ritual instead?"

She laughed, exposing her gold canine tooth. Ignoring me, she turned to the man in charge. "That chicken, with the yellow feathers."

"Those are the tastiest," the man said. He opened the cage door and reached in with his gloved hand. He grabbed one squawking chicken by the throat, keeping the rest from escaping with his other hand. "This one?"

"Wait," said Todd. "Mrs. Purity, do you remember what happened the last time you released chickens in the park?"

I blinked, finally understanding what she intended to do with the bird.

The little witch pursed her lips, considering. "I hate those policemen. No respect." She said to the man, "I'm sorry. We won't need the chicken after all."

The man let the chicken go and it fled to the back of the cage as he shut the door. He called, "Next!" and we left.

I was relieved to leave that place but also sorry we hadn't been able to save the chicken. I would have bought it myself to keep it alive, but where would I keep it? The Vision then took us to the fish store, with Todd still trailing us.

"Only the liveliest ones," she said to the fishmonger, indicating a tub filled with live crabs.

"Always the best for you, Mrs. Purity," he said. "You choose."

She selected eighteen live crabs, poking them with a stick to see how well they moved their pincers, which were bound with thick rubber bands. The fishmonger wrapped them up for her in paper, then tossed them in a plastic bag.

"Hold this," she said to Todd. He took the bag by its handles. It looked quite heavy and its contents writhed whenever he set it down.

Then the witch took us through the street of funeral parlors, which most people avoided because they thought it was bad luck, made a sudden turn onto an alley and went up to what seemed like an illegal gambling salon. It was boarded shut. She knocked and a pair of eyes peeked through a slot that had been slid open.

"Release of Life," the witch said. "Wong family." She must have had this arranged by Todd when I was gone.

The eyes blinked and then disappeared. The slot slid closed. I looked down the street to see if any policemen were coming to bust us. It was as if we were trafficking in drugs. Of course, I realized, the Vision couldn't get special religious supplies from the temples because those Buddhists shunned her, and she probably got a discount here. A few minutes later, the door cracked open and a hand covered with age spots thrust a filled shopping bag at us. The smell of incense escaped in a gust from the door. The witch handed it to Todd and we left.

As we started heading west, I said to Todd, "How are you doing? Can I carry one of those for you?"

"Oh no, thanks. I'm used to lugging stuff for her. How's your new job?"

"How did you know about that?"

He shrugged. "You know, Chinatown. Small world."

We went through Tribeca, crossed over the highway, and finally I understood that the Vision was heading for one of the piers on the water. There were only a few pedestrians passing by and seagulls flew overhead, screeching. The Hudson River stretched out before us and the smell of salt was in the icy wind.

Then the witch unpacked the second shopping bag she'd been given. She took out what looked like a plastic model of three sticks of incense in a metal holder, a bottle of rice wine and a paper plate, and set them all on the ground. She flipped a switch and the tips of the incense lit up, as if they were burning. It was battery operated.

I raised my eyebrows. "This isn't real. Are you sure it'll work?"

"The true gods don't mind," she said, shrugging. "It's too cold to light anything. And the police will bother me again if I burn things in public."

She set the electric incense next to the rail, then pulled a red octagon with the Chinese character for our surname, "Wong," written on it out of the shopping bag. She held out her hand to me.

"What?"

She just gestured impatiently with her hand.

Todd said, "Please give her the photo."

I took it out of my bag and placed it in her palm, muttering, "She can't talk because the ritual's too demanding?"

I thought I saw Todd hide a smile.

The Vision tucked the picture in between the sticks of plastic incense, then circled the whole thing with rice wine. I hoped she wouldn't electrocute herself or spray the photo with wine. She closed her eyes and began to invoke the gods. Todd and I also bowed to the photo and my surname. Silently, I asked the gods and spirits please to help Lisa. I wasn't sure if I believed in the Vision or not, but I hoped she could help Lisa.

Then she turned to the other shopping bag. She had me hold the paper plate while she extracted a crab. She slid the rubber bands off each pincer and placed it in the center of the paper plate. I pulled my fingers back in case it started moving as I gingerly balanced the plate from underneath. She took the plate from me, then called, "Gods, accept our release of life. Six for the entire Wong family. May the family be kept whole, may they live in safety."

She flipped the crab into the bay below. There was a small white splash as it hit the water.

"When I have time, I take the train to upstate New York," she said. "The water's cleaner for them and you can let larger animals go there. But that costs a lot extra."

She did this to six of the crabs, one by one. They arched, pincers extended, twirling in the air, and descended into the swirling water below us.

Then she started praying again. "Accept six for Lisa Wong. May the spirits that bother her be laid to rest."

Was that what was happening to Lisa? I wished I knew.

She flipped another six crabs into the water and said in a ringing voice, "Spirits of heaven and earth, accept six for Charlie Wong, older daughter, about to embark on a new life. What one sister gains, shall the other lose. May balance be struck."

I started. How did she know about my new position as a dancer? She was a force to be reckoned with.

The Vision released the final six crabs. She deliberately threw the last crab higher and one of the seagulls swept down and caught it neatly in its beak.

I gasped. "Why did you do that? You didn't have to kill it."

"That too is freedom," she said. "That too is sacrifice. Yin, yang; no life without death."

"What did you mean by what one sister gains, the other shall lose? Are you talking about pounds?"

Todd started to laugh then stopped himself by pretending he was coughing. She tossed the paper plate in the trash, and then she and Todd headed toward the train station. She didn't answer my question. At the mouth of the station, the witch turned and I could see only the white of her left eye before she disappeared inside.

To my relief, Lisa started doing better after that ritual with the witch. She still had nightmares, but they came less frequently and she hadn't wet her bed since it happened. I couldn't get the Vision's words about the two sisters out of my mind, even though I had no idea what they could mean. Lisa and I had less time to see each other nowadays because I came home so late and she left early for school. We were together in the mornings but Pa was there then, and I was afraid to reveal too much about my life if I spoke. I asked her to come to tai chi classes with me on Saturday but she wasn't interested. Sometimes I wondered if she was avoiding me, since she spent lots of time at the library. I supposed she had a great deal of schoolwork. The truth was, I was so entranced by my new life at the studio that I sometimes walked around in a dream world of my own when I was at home.

One evening, though, she woke up when I came in. "How was your day?"

"Hard but wonderful." I crossed over to her and kneeled down. I spoke in a low voice so as to not wake Pa. "I'm learning so much. I feel like the worst dancer in the world, but every day I'm becoming a tiny bit better."

"I wish I could see you dance. I bet you're much better than you think you are."

I kissed her on her cheek. "How was your day?"

I could see the light go out of her eyes again. "Fine."

"Anything special happen?"

"Not really. Good night, Charlie." She turned her back to me and the conversation was over.

Thirteen

I had developed a routine in order to hide my dancer life from Pa. In the mornings, I wore one of my old outfits. Then after he and Lisa had left, I changed into Adrienne's clothes. She'd even given me different bras too. Although we weren't exactly the same size, hers fit me much better than Aunt Monica's had. There were longer skirts that clung to my legs until the knee, then loosened so I could move. I liked the darted dresses, cut on the bias so that they fell softly across my body without being tight, yet showed off the curves I had. I didn't recognize all of the names on the labels but I could tell from the material and cut that they were expensive. Dance clothing was such a specialty market, nothing came cheap. I had hidden Adrienne's clothing in the same sort of bags that held Aunt Monica's cast-offs and knew Pa wouldn't be able to tell the difference anyway unless he saw me wearing them.

I changed and did my makeup as best I could after I had the apartment to myself. Then after work, I'd do the same thing in reverse. At the studio I changed back into my regular Aunt Monica clothing and my dishwasher shoes, and scrubbed off my makeup. The other dancers looked at me oddly sometimes when I did that, but no one said anything. They all put on different clothes as well, only not quite as dramatically as I did. Then I'd go back to my other life with Pa and Lisa.

Although I was used to hiding parts of my life from Pa, I'd never done it for so long, about something that mattered to me so much. I wanted to tell him but then I was afraid he would forbid me to continue. What would I do then? Men on the street turned their heads these days when I walked by, even when I was wearing Aunt Monica's clothing without any makeup. I supposed I carried myself differently now. I wasn't sure how I felt about it. I was glad to be more attractive, of course, but in some ways I missed the old Charlie too, who could wear anything, go anywhere she wanted without being noticed. And although I didn't miss the grimy work at the noodle restaurant, I missed being with Pa every day.

But my love of dance was starting to consume me. Even at home, my head was often filled with everything I was learning at the dance studio. Whenever I was alone in the apartment, I went over dance figures I had learned. I piled up the furniture the way Ma had done for me years ago, yet making sure that I could push it quickly back into place should Pa come home unexpectedly. During the week, I often went to the studio in the mornings before it opened so I could practice by myself while the pros were training with their partners. I was changing, and I couldn't stop it.

At the studio, my old student Evelyn came up to me while I was seated at one of the tables, studying the technical alignments for the steps. I'd seen her and Trevor learning all of the dances, preparing for their fancy wedding in July. They'd obviously decided to make ballroom dancing one of their hobbies as well.

Evelyn was twisting her hands together, nervous. "Charlie, my brother Ryan is coming in tomorrow to take a lesson with you."

"Really?" My heart beat a bit faster. I realized I was excited to see him again.

"Can I ask you for a favor? I've been watching you with your private students. You're a great teacher, no matter what. But would you please just do your best to keep Ryan here in the lessons?"

"Of course I will." There was a question in my eyes.

"I know, I sound like a freak. The thing is . . . may I sit down?"

"Of course." I gestured to a seat next to me.

Evelyn sat down, then continued quietly, "It means a great deal to me to have Ryan do the father-daughter dance with me. Both of our parents are gone now. More than that, I want him to enjoy himself. I owe him a lot, he's taken care of me my entire life. He thinks I'm just trying to impress everyone that I have money but it's not that. The wedding's a fresh start for me."

"Rituals are important."

"That's it. So please be nice to him. He likes you and money is no object. We're giving the lessons to him because he'd never take dance classes otherwise. If he's willing to come every day, just haul his butt in here."

"I'll do my best, Evelyn. You're a good sister."

When Ryan arrived, I was too flustered to notice him. I was in the reception area saying good-bye to a couple who had just finished a series of lessons with me. I'd been teaching private lessons for a couple of weeks now. The man was always neatly dressed in a suit, and as we shook hands to say good-bye, I felt a folded-up piece of paper in his palm. I wasn't sure what it was, so I left it there and turned to go.

"Oh, wait, Charlie," he said, reaching for my hand again. "We really want to thank you for the fantastic lessons."

I felt the piece of paper in his hand again and finally understood he was trying to tip me. Now I remembered the man who had shaken the bouncer's hand at Decadence—that must have been a tip too. I certainly needed the money, but it still made me feel strange. As a dishwasher, I'd never been given a tip, though I knew the waitresses needed to be tipped because they weren't paid much otherwise. Taxi drivers were tipped. I didn't know if dancers were. I wasn't his servant, although I guess they'd paid for my time. In my confusion, I just left it in his palm again.

He stared at the twenty-dollar bill still in his hand, befuddled.

"I told you," his girlfriend hissed. "I said it would be insulting to her."

"But everyone likes the money," he said, as she steered him to the door.

"I appreciate it," I said, calling after them. I didn't want him to feel bad. The door shut behind them. "Really." The skin on the back of my neck was on fire. I was so bad at being tactful.

"Interesting." It was a deep, amused voice, coming from one of the couches. Ryan. He must have been waiting for his lesson there and I hadn't seen him in all of the excitement. He was wearing a plain white T-shirt and jeans.

I said, "Can't you tell I'm smooth? *Not*. Come on, your lesson's about to begin."

He chuckled as he followed me.

"So since you're preparing for your sister's wedding, do you want me to put together a choreographed number for the two of you?" It was easy to assemble little dances for couples. It was just combining a few steps that they knew and having them repeat them.

"Absolutely not."

That was clear. I faced him. "Okay. Are you sure you want to be here?"

His face gentled. "Evelyn's a pain in the neck but she's my sister."

I sighed, warming to him and thinking of Lisa. "I understand that."

The lesson tape began with a steady foxtrot. "Let's see if you can still dance."

Ryan held out his hand to me. "Shall we?"

I let him hold me in dance position. He started off with his right leg and kicked me in the shins.

"Ow!"

"Sorry," he said.

I reached out to slap him on the left thigh, the way I now did to all of the male students so they'd remember which leg was the left one. Before I knew it, he'd encircled my wrist with his hand, stopping me from moving.

I looked up at him and narrowed my eyes.

His lips quirked upward on one side. "I'm not used to allowing people to strike me, ma'am."

"You kicked me first. And it is the dance teacher's right to make sure her students know left from right."

His fingers loosened and he sighed. "I knew I'd regret coming here. Go on. Do your worst."

I slapped him on the left thigh, hard. "The leg that hurts, that is your left leg."

We moved off into the foxtrot basic step and he didn't confuse his left with his right again.

———

Early on the morning of the Hunter test, I bustled around. Pa leaned against the wall, a deep crease on his cheek from where he'd lain on his pillow. He'd already lit incense and we'd all bowed to Ma, to ask her for luck today. I always got home so late from the studio that I hadn't been able to be with Lisa as she studied the night before. I remembered the hopeless cram sessions from my own school days, the desperation that turned into failure at the test. But whatever happened with Lisa today, I hoped everything would go back to normal with her afterward.

"What did you do yesterday to prepare?" I asked.

Lisa was hopping on one leg, then the other. "Not that much."

"Stop that, you'll wake the neighbors." I pursed my lips. I shouldn't have let her study by herself. "Why not?"

"I'd already done the practice test. I went over it again but I didn't have anything else."

"You could have studied vocabulary lists or something. That Fabrizio had hours of homework per week, you said. Maybe you should have borrowed something from him."

Pa said, "Charlie, it's a little too late for this now. I'm sure Lisa will do her best. What happened to that boy anyway?"

Lisa said, "They figured it out with his records and he's taking the test today too. Hannah and her parents have been making it their family project for months now. I'm sorry, Charlie, I should have studied better. I just didn't know what else to do."

"What did you do with Uncle Henry and Dennis?"

She looked away. "They just went over my homework with me, which I knew anyway. Mr. Song said that it was basically an IQ test, which means they don't test so much what you know. They want to see how you think."

"Oh, it's okay. I'm just nervous too. In the worst case, you don't get in and then, well, we'll do something really nice together." I looked at Pa. "Right, Pa?"

He nodded. "Maybe we could go to Central Park or something."

Lisa smiled. "I'd like that." Then she turned serious again. "Yesterday at school, I read on their website that people shouldn't come to line up at four a.m., that it won't help you at all. Really, who's going to do something like that?"

I said, "Hannah and her parents. Come on, let's go. We'd better make sure we're early too."

On the subway uptown to the test site on the Upper East Side, we saw other kids and parents traveling together.

"Do you think they're going to the test too?" Lisa asked.

"Could be."

"It feels weird not to go to school on a Friday." Lisa dug her fingers into my hand. "I'm nervous, Charlie."

"It'll be okay. You know you're smart. What are you scared of?"

"That everyone else prepared a lot more than me. That I'll do something wrong, like I'll fill everything in with the wrong type of pencil and they won't be able to grade my test. Or I'll miss a line and every single one of my answers will be in the wrong place."

I thought a moment, then pulled something out of my bag. "I was going to give it to you afterward but this is for you."

"Oh, Charlie!" Lisa held it up and then started to giggle. "It's beautiful!"

I looked at it and started cracking up too. It was the scarf I'd worked on for her for months. It was riddled with holes where I'd dropped stitches. It grew wider and wider, then suddenly narrowed, then grew wide again. The surface was lumpy because I'd pulled some parts too tightly and some parts were too loose. It looked more like a handkerchief a dog had gnawed on than a scarf.

Lisa tucked it around her neck and closed her eyes with a contented sigh. "No one else could have made something like this, Charlie. Only you."

The test site area was so crowded, we had a hard time finding the entrance. The sidewalk was slippery with ice and slush, and sleet rained down upon us. Finally, we saw policemen and people wearing buttons clustered around a door. So many parents and kids were milling around.

Lisa gasped. Her breath was white. "This isn't just a crowd. This is the line."

What we'd thought were people standing around was actually a long line that already wrapped almost all the way around the huge block, back to the entrance. Lisa and I hurried to join them. We were an hour early, and still all of these people had beaten us here. I studied the others. A woman in a fancy coat and high-heeled boots stood in front of us, holding her son's hand. Behind us was a heavy-set Hispanic man who looked like a construction worker, with his daughter next to him. Everywhere I looked, I saw the same set expression of determination and worry. People were desperate to get into this school. What chance did my little sister have? I wished I'd done more. I should have figured out how to get her into a course, no matter how expensive.

As the line started to move, people wearing buttons reading "Hunter College High School" started walking up and down past us, calling, "Take all water and food out of your bags. Nothing is allowed inside except for your writing utensils. All electronic items will be confiscated. No candy, no snacks."

Lisa clutched the scarf I gave her, her eyes panicked.

Suddenly, I remembered. "Do you have your pass with you?"

Lisa took it out of her coat pocket.

"Whew."

We approached the entrance and I thanked the gods that Lisa had her entry ticket with her. The policemen called, "Parents to the left, children to the right. Make sure you have your pass out." The crowd pushed us forward, the line separating into parents and children. The kids filed inside the building and the adults were left in the cold.

I realized I wouldn't be allowed into the building with Lisa. "How will you know where to go?"

"Don't worry, Charlie. They'll tell me." Her face was white, she was blinking to get the sleet off of her eyelashes. "I wish you could come with me."

"Me too." In a moment, we'd be separated. "Don't forget to go pee before the test."

Lisa said, "Okay" and then she was gone.

I went into a Starbucks and tugged on my hair while I waited for Lisa. She was terrified and all I could do was tell her to pee beforehand. I was so useless. All of the composure I'd gained in the dance studio seemed to disappear when I had to solve real-life problems. People sat around me, working on their laptops and texting on their phones. After a while, I felt embarrassed staying there, so I went out and paced in the cold. It had stopped snowing. The skyscrapers of Manhattan loomed over me. Chinatown was nothing like this. I was fairly close to the studio but hadn't ventured further than the couple of blocks between the subway and the building.

I walked a few blocks downtown to a large department store. Except for a few times when I'd come uptown with Zan and Mo Li to window-shop, I avoided these types of stores, knowing they were filled with things I couldn't afford. I entered the department store, but all of the people lying in wait behind black marble pillars to spray perfume on me made me uncomfortable, so I took the escalator upstairs. I spent some time browsing through women's dresses, wondering which ones I'd be able to dance in, knowing I couldn't pay for any of them. Finally, it was time to get Lisa.

They'd sorted the parents by last name so I waited in the "W" room for Lisa to come back. I leapt up when I spotted her. She was clutching my scarf. We talked as we exited the building among the hordes of students and parents.

"How was it?"

"The beginning was a disaster. I got into the room and it seemed like everyone else knew each other. At least some of the kids."

"They probably took a prep class together."

"Yeah, they said hello to each other and stuff. Then I dropped my pencil case and everything fell out with a big crash so I had to scramble to pick it up. Everyone was staring at me, especially the proctor. She probably thought I was trying to cheat. I even had to ask permission to leave the case on my desk. She checked it first. I forgot to go pee, Charlie, I was too nervous."

"That's okay. So how was the test?"

"The English part was fine and I felt good about it. But then the math was crazy."

"What do you mean?" Lisa had always been great at math.

"It made no sense. There were about forty-five questions, and on some of them, I had a reason for guessing what I did. The rest, I just picked an answer at random."

My heart sank. "Really?"

"Well, I tried of course, but the questions didn't make any sense. There was like a big fraction over another fraction, minus a fraction, times a fraction. I tried to do it and couldn't find my answer any-where. Another question was so messed up, it must have been a mistake. There was no question. It was just smudges of ink."

I tried not to let Lisa see how concerned I was. "Did you freak out?"

"I wanted to. But I figured I wouldn't have time to finish the test if I had an anxiety attack and ran around screaming."

I laughed. "Very logical of you."

"I kept telling myself that if I didn't get in, you and me and Pa would go do something nice together."

We were walking toward the train station by now and I heard someone calling from behind us. It was Hannah and her father, a nice-looking man with a round face.

When they caught up, Hannah said, "What did you think?"

Lisa said, "I thought the math was really hard. Like impossible."

Hannah said, "It was difficult but I didn't think it was impossible. What did you write for the essay?"

I interrupted. "What was the subject?" I remembered Lisa saying the essay was one of the most important parts of the test.

Hannah said, "We had to write about an object or memory that had meaning for us. I talked about our family trip to Washington, D.C., last year and how much I learned at the museums. What about you?"

Lisa twisted a lock of hair around her finger. "Well, we have this jar filled with change, and Charlie and I are saving to see a Broad-way show."

"You wrote about that old thing?" I couldn't cover my surprise.

Hannah said, "What'd you do that for? I mean, that's not so spe-cial. Anyone can go to a show."

Her father jumped in. "Now, Hannah, you shouldn't say that. I'm sure Lisa's essay was lovely. What did you write in it, dear?"

Lisa's cheeks were bright pink. "That the jar isn't just a collection of coins for a couple of tickets but rather a measure of our love for each other and our hopes for the future. That with every cent Charlie drops into that jar, she shows me her belief in our ability to change our lives."

There was a pause, then both Hannah and her pa closed their mouths. Her father said, "Okay! Well, we're going out for some hot chocolate and cake. Do you want to join us?"

Lisa said, "Thanks, but we're meeting our pa to celebrate downtown." This was a lie. I felt sad that Lisa already knew we couldn't afford to go with Hannah and her father.

After they waved and left, I turned to Lisa. "So level with me. Do you think you got in or not?"

She met my eyes. "I have no idea."

I was teaching students regularly now. They were all beginners and I found I really enjoyed it. I was grateful for all of the years I'd helped Godmother with her tai chi classes. My students liked me and many of them signed up for further private lessons after the beginners' group classes, which made Dominic and Adrienne happy.

I was always especially curious about the Asian students, who they were and what their lives were like. In one of my beginners' classes, I had an Asian couple and one composed of a Chinese woman and a tall African-American man. The four of them were clearly friends, chatting together before the lesson began. They were so well dressed and confident. Had any of them grown up in Chinatown? Maybe Mo Li would become someone like this someday. They'd probably had rich families and gone to private schools.

In anticipation of Valentine's Day in a few weeks, the theme at the studio was already "romance." So before we began our class, I had everyone stand in a circle and share a story about love, if they had one. I'd found that if we did a few minutes of talking before we started to dance, the students were much more comfortable with each other.

"Please say your name, what you do, and if you have a memory about how you met someone special, we would love to hear it. If you don't, just skip the story," I said.

We went around the room and the first two people said their names and professions, but didn't want to share anything else. Then it was the Asian man's turn.

He had distinguished features and eyes filled with good humor. "My name is Jason. I'm a neurologist and I asked my wife out on Valentine's Day."

The petite Asian woman next to him giggled. "Yes he did. I'm Naomi. I'm a psychiatrist. I didn't trust him at all because he was so handsome."

The other students laughed.

Jason beamed. "Honestly, I didn't even know what Valentine's Day was. I'd just arrived from Hong Kong."

"And I wasn't sure what to do because he wasn't Japanese like me," Naomi said. "So I asked my mother. And she said, 'He's new in this country. You should be nice to him. Go out with him.'"

"So actually, it was a pity date," said his friend, the African-American man, grinning.

"Hey, you owe me," said Jason. "I set you up with Kimberly here."

I smiled at the next couple, the African-American man and Chinese woman. "So what's your name and story?"

"I'm Tyrone Marshall. I'm a neurologist too. And Jason didn't introduce me to Kimberly, we'd already met in elementary school."

He put an arm around the attractive woman next to him. She was wearing a golden necklace with a jade Kuan Yin pendant.

She smiled and said, "Yes, that's true but we do owe Jason because Tyrone and I had completely lost touch. I'm Kimberly Chang, by the way. I'm a pediatric cardiac surgeon."

Someone in the crowd whistled. "So if anyone feels like having a stroke or heart attack, now is the time."

Kimberly laughed and cleared her throat. "Yes, we shall endeavor to save you. In any case, Jason and I work at the same hospital. One day, while we were chatting, he mentioned this brilliant neurologist he'd met at a conference, a man named Tyrone Marshall. I said, 'That name sounds familiar . . .'"

"And the rest was history," said Tyrone. His eyes hadn't left her face the entire time she'd been talking. Now he bent down and brushed her hair with his lips. I wondered what it would be like to have someone love me like that.

"So you'd actually met when you were children?" I asked.

"Yes," said Tyrone. "She was the smartest kid in the whole school."

"No, you were," said Kimberly.

Naomi shook her head. "They're always like that. It's awful."

Jason added, "We bought them matching T-shirts that read 'Most Disgusting Couple.'"

Everyone laughed. Now that the ice had been broken, they all seemed relaxed as we finished going around the room.

"What about you, Charlie?" one woman asked.

I hadn't expected this. "Oh, well, my name is Charlie Wong. I'm a professional ballroom dancer and I don't want to meet anyone special." This wasn't really true, not anymore, but I wasn't ready to talk about that in front of my students.

The group burst into laughter. "I'd be glad to help you change your mind," a young man said.

"I appreciate the offer," I said, smiling. "I've just got a full plate with my dancing and family right now."

Kimberly said, "Your time will come, Charlie. Just wait and see." There was something honest and generous about her. I hoped she was right.

"Thanks." My throat felt tight. I quickly started the lesson so that no one else would notice.

Kimberly and Tyrone had a wonderful time during the lesson but they were both terrible dancers. Kimberly was laughing so hard, she was almost crying. "You always told me you had rhythm," she gasped.

Tyrone was marching like a soldier, trying to find the beat and failing. "I did, I swear. I don't know what's happened to me. Too much Chinese food, I think."

Kimberly kept moving left when she was supposed to go to the right.

I said to them, "You guys are overthinking it. You need to turn off your brains and let your bodies take over."

Kimberly sobered up. "That is such an intelligent thing to say. You're right." Then they bumped into each other again.

I left them to it and moved on to Jason and Naomi, who were doing much better. He lifted his arm and Naomi did a neat under-arm turn.

After the class, Kimberly and Tyrone came up to thank me. "We had such a wonderful time," she said. "But I'm afraid we're not going to take the risk of injuring you or one of your peers. We're hopeless."

"Oh no, you're not," I said. "You should have seen me when I started."

"You are so kind, Charlie," Tyrone said. "Maybe one day when we're feeling especially brave, we'll be back."

Jason and Naomi did sign up to come back for their private lesson and requested me, as did a number of the other students.

I danced hour after hour. I was either being taught or giving lessons to a student. Nothing can teach you something so well as needing to pass that knowledge on to someone else. I knew I wasn't as good as the other professionals, not even as well trained as the best student dancers in the studio yet, but I'd come a long way in a short time. I could even keep up in most of the professional dance sessions. And although I loved sweeping across the room in a waltz or foxtrot, I had already learned that it was the freedom and exhilaration of Latin that called to me.

One day, while I was practicing by myself, Dominic approached me. "You're getting better. Much better. You should think about competing."

"Professionally?" I gulped.

"Why not? You are starting to look like a professional. Nothing will improve your dancing more than doing a competition. Not that you'll win, not yet, but the training will sharpen your skills like nothing else. I know a few professional men you could try out."

I thought about Lisa and Pa, and the costs of doing a major competition. There would be dresses and new shoes and coachings. I was still wearing my one pair of Latin sandals, which had sprouted holes just like Katerina's. "I appreciate it. But I don't think I'm ready yet. I'll just concentrate on my students for a while."

I woke to find Lisa sucking her thumb in the night. Despite all of my hopes, she had started getting worse again. I told myself it was because we didn't know the results of the test yet but I knew it was a lie. I was so disappointed. The nightmares and bedwetting had started again and she also complained of dizziness and headaches. What if something really was wrong with Lisa? As I gained mastery over my body, Lisa lost control over hers. I realized that it was exactly as the Vision had said. What one sister lost, the other would gain.

I couldn't sleep any longer and slipped out of the apartment into the deserted streets. In the moonlit sky, the clouds rolled thick and close to the ground. The sky was tight with withheld rain. I stood at the foot of the bridge in Gossip Park, which arched over a large artificial pond. I didn't know what was happening to Lisa. My entire life had changed in the past months. I felt like a blind person heading into my future. I was so afraid for her and myself.

I climbed up the broad steps onto the bridge. Pausing, I leaned out over the water and then straightened. I closed my eyes. Slowly, I began to walk, holding on to the stone railing. Keeping my eyes closed, I paused to listen to the wind swirl through the branches of the trees directly over my head. I stepped forward and my fingers trailed over small freezing indentations in the rock.

My feet seemed to drop themselves into the darkness before me. I wanted to make it all the way across the bridge with my eyes closed but the wind across the water was loud and, suddenly, at the halfway point, the bridge seemed to slant more sharply than I'd remembered. Going down, it seemed that any moment, I would fall off the end of the bridge, off the steps, into the unknown.

I opened my eyes. I shook myself and went back to our apartment.

Fourteen

Now that Ryan was officially in private lessons with me, I had to teach him how to dance for real. I'd already shown him all of the different dances and it was time for him to start learning how to lead. We'd managed to wrestle our way through until now, but it was hard to move together with him. Even so, I found myself looking forward to his lessons. Since Ryan worked for an urban landscaping company, the winter was a quieter time for him and he often came in the late afternoons.

"Mmmm hmmm," said Irene as the elevator doors opened and he strode out. We both watched him from the mirror in the reception area. His winter work jacket made him look even broader as he pushed through the first set of double doors, and I noticed the snowflakes on his hair and shoulders. He spotted me, then shook his head in my direction like a dog.

"Hey!" I jumped off of the couch and out of his way.

"Whoops," he said.

"You can shake anything you like my way, honey." Irene gave him a broad wink with her thickly mascaraed lashes, then took his jacket from him to hang it up in the closet. He was dressed casually as usual, in jeans and a dark gray long-sleeved cotton shirt.

His smile lit up his entire face. "Good afternoon, ma'am. May I say that you are looking lovely today."

He never said anything like that to me. "Are you done flirting with the studio owner's mother now?"

Irene came out of the closet, pulled down her bifocals and pretended to look severe. "Widowed mother. And just because you don't know how to have any fun, don't begrudge the rest of us."

"I'd be afraid to have as much fun as you," I muttered as I walked toward the ballroom doors Ryan was holding open for me. I turned to him. "How's your girlfriend doing, by the way?"

"Fiona's just fine. Really busy."

"Must be hard being long distance."

"Yeah, it is. And she's the type of person who's always on the go, so it's not like she's that good with e-mail or on the phone. But we catch up when we see each other again."

I bet they did. I had no right to be jealous, just because she had a feminine name like Fiona and was probably brilliant and beautiful too. And had Ryan for a boyfriend. "Well, today, I'm going to make sure you're a fit partner for her."

I turned Ryan around, put him in the lady's place and then took up dance position with me leading. "Okay, I want you to feel what it's like to dance with you. Don't worry about which leg you're on, just start moving backward when I go." I went forward the way he always did, taking huge strides and only lightly holding him with my hands. He took one step back, and another, then looked over his shoulder.

I said, "You're not allowed to do that."

"But I can't see where I'm heading. I'm not sure where you want me to go."

"Welcome to my world." I kept moving forward, even though he was so heavy to lead; it felt like I was trying to move an elephant. Once in a while, I stopped without warning only to have his momentum jerk us both forward. This was pretty different from the time I'd danced with Julian. I wasn't tall enough to have a clear view over his shoulder so I had to peer around his side to see where we were going. He stopped turning around, although I could tell it took a real effort of will. A few times we almost crashed into each other when he didn't know if he was supposed to walk or not. He sensed it when we were getting close to the wall and squeezed his eyes shut, bracing himself. I stopped him a few inches away from it.

"I don't often have this feeling, but just now I feared for my life," he said.

"That's how it feels for the woman when she is dancing with you. So many men dance as if they were playing a video game. It's like they think that the closer they can get to the wall without crashing, the more points they'll win."

He winced. "Did I do that to you?"

"You hold me too loosely when you're going forward. I have no idea what you want."

"But I'm trying to be gentle. I don't want to hurt you by accident."

"And speaking of being gentle, how does it feel when I turn you like this?" I lifted my arm and stood on tiptoe, then pushed him underneath it with all of my strength. I whipped him around a few more times for good measure. To my surprise, he did the spins flawlessly, even though there must have been three of them.

"I was definitely being manhandled there." He was grinning, as if he'd enjoyed it.

"You use so much force when you turn me. I am not a side of beef. I am a woman. All you need to do is to give me the impetus and I can take it from there." I did the underarm turn again, only giving him a brief push this time. He spun a double, ducking his head to fit underneath my arm.

"That felt great. I could get used to being a lady."

I considered him. "Those were really good spins. You kept your entire body stable. How did you do that?" I'd never seen a new male student be able to whip them off like that. I loved to turn but needed to practice hard just to be able to complete a double without falling over.

"Like I said, years of boxing and yoga."

"It must have been hard for you to give it up."

His face turned serious. "Every change has a hello and a good-bye in it, you know? You always have to leave in order to go on to something new."

I thought of what Godmother always said. "You must empty the cup before it can be filled again."

His smile was slow and warm as he met my eyes. "Exactly."

I liked this guy a bit too much. I remembered Estella and the dance student who had gotten her fired. The way I felt around him was starting to scare me, so it seemed like a good time to change the subject. "Are there any dances that you particularly like so far?"

"I don't know. Whatever works for Evelyn would be fine, I guess."

"I didn't mean for the wedding but for you, personally. Is there anything you've maybe wanted to learn?" When he didn't react, I kept talking. "It's just that I had this student last week who's a curator at the Metropolitan Museum of Art and I asked him how he got into paintings. He said he never really cared about art, but as a kid, he liked to whittle. So he used to go to the museum because they have these intricate wooden frames and he enjoyed getting ideas for his whittling. After a number of years, he began to notice that the frames were holding something interesting too."

Now his gaze was steady. "And your point is?"

"I'm just trying to say that sometimes, if you start with one small thing you like, a whole new world can open up for you."

"Well, someone may once have told me that white guys were too wimpy to do Latin."

"So we'd have to prove them wrong, wouldn't we?"

I was glad to have the apartment to myself that Saturday afternoon so I could go over some of the new steps I was learning. I couldn't do them full out, but at least I could repeat them in my head and mark them on the floor. I was so busy that the time flew by. Suddenly, I realized it was late. I looked at my watch and panicked. I'd completely missed Godmother's tai chi class.

I flew downstairs, not bothering to wait for our creaky elevator, and ran over to Godmother Yuan's apartment. I pounded on the door. She opened it immediately, as if she'd been waiting for me.

"I'm so sorry, I forgot." I was still gasping for breath from my hard dash.

She regarded me. "'No flower can bloom red for a hundred days,' Charlie."

"I don't understand."

"It means that I can't expect a flower to stay beautiful forever. It means you are changing. I can see it." She looked me up and down. "I don't know what's going on but I miss the innocent and lovely girl you were."

"I'm really sorry, Godmother, but you can teach the class without me with no problem. You do all of your other classes alone."

"Maybe the class would be fine without you, but I was not. I missed you and I needed you, Charlie." Then she shut the door again.

I felt terrible and just stood there for a moment, then I knocked on the door again. She didn't answer. I took a deep breath and turned the knob. I called through the crack, "You're right. I am not the same anymore, but didn't you say, 'The sea accepts a hundred streams and rivers'?" I was reminding her of a saying she was fond of, meaning that a good person was flexible and accepting of things great and small. "I'm twenty-two years old, Godmother Yuan. I need to change and become the person I was meant to be. I made a mistake today but please, can't you accept that?"

Godmother sighed, then opened the door wider. "You are right, Charlie. I too am sorry. We did not speak of it but I saw you were becoming different. Growing up. And I guess I was scared of losing you. That you'd become like my own grandchildren, who don't even come to visit me."

I'd never heard Godmother Yuan admit that about her grandchildren before. "They love you. They're just busy."

"Too busy for their own grandmother." She sniffed. "It's more than that. When their parents force them to visit me, I do not even recognize them. They are not the sweet children I knew."

I said carefully, "I heard about Grace."

She stiffened, then to my surprise, began to smile. "I have an idea. You will come to dim sum with our family. In a few weeks."

I'd never been asked to join the Yuans before. "Why?"

"You need a reason for an invitation?"

"Godmother. I know you better than this."

She huffed. "Oh all right. We are having some difficulty convincing Grace to attend. It will help if she has a friend or two there."

"Grace and I aren't friends anymore. We haven't been for many years."

"Of course you are. And you are such a nice unmarried girl too."
My lips parted. "It's a matchmaking session. No way."

Godmother Yuan furrowed her brow. She didn't bother with the Buddhist sayings now. "You owe me."

Ryan, a natural athlete, improved faster than any other beginner I'd seen. When I commented on how quickly he could learn the steps, he said, "It's actually not that different from boxing. It's all patterns of movement. I always had to memorize combinations too." His problem tended to be that he focused on the result rather than the process, so if he knew we needed to end up in the opposite corner, all of his energy was directed toward getting us there instead of how we proceeded. Whenever I saw Evelyn, she beamed at me. Once she blew me a kiss from across the ballroom.

After a few weeks, I asked him, "So do you have a favorite dance now?"

"Maybe the rumba. Or merengue." We were doing the Cuban promenade in rumba. We'd separated and I was swinging in a slow circle around him with a Latin walk, involving much swaying of the hips. At the right moment, he tugged on my hand and I whirled to face him, then went into his arms, back into dance position. "But I don't look quite right."

"What do you mean?"

He stopped dancing. "All that stuff." He waved his hands, gesturing at my hips. "I mean, I don't expect to look like you, but when I see myself in the mirror, I seem kind of stiff."

"Umm, that's because your hips don't sway. At all."

"So I'm still dancing like a white guy?"

"You know a lot of steps." I wasn't sure what to say. I'd always been honest with Ryan. "You're here to learn how to be a social dancer. That means how to partner someone at a party or wedding and have a good time, and you can keep your hips frozen solid if you like. If you really want to learn to move, that's a whole other world."

"That guy doesn't dance like a corpse." He gestured toward Keith, who was doing a routine with Simone. Keith was all long lines and grace on the floor, and he looked wonderful with Simone, who swirled around him with her left leg outstretched in an extended spiral. She wrapped it around his hips, then he turned them both around so they were facing the same way. She unwrapped from him with a swish and they moved toward the mirror in parallel like two great cats. I'd noticed they were doing more set choreography recently, probably preparing for another competition.

"He wins everything. Everyone loves dancing with him."

Ryan studied him, carefully not looking at me. "You too?"

"What?" Then I understood. "Keith's a great, considerate partner. Yes, I enjoy dancing with him at the parties."

He flexed his shoulders. "I could take him in a fight."

I laughed. "You're probably right, but in a dance studio, that's not relevant."

"Yeah. So teach me to dance better than him."

"That's not easy. You've been dancing for a couple of weeks. He's been here for years."

"You don't know how determined I can be once I get my mind set on something."

I saw that he was serious now. "Ryan, the level of technique you're talking about is beyond the number of lessons you were planning on taking. You're enrolled in a program which will be done in a few weeks."

"Well, maybe I'll extend."

Later, in the teachers' room, Nina said, "I was standing right behind you guys, not that you noticed me. Maybe you should try to make a competition student out of Ryan."

"I know him. He's shy about his dancing. He wouldn't want to do it."

"It sounded like he did."

"He wanted to prove some manly thing about how he's better than Keith. That doesn't mean he wants to dance in front of people. He can't even move his hips."

"Give the man a break. He has to be taught. But the thing is, if you can get him into competition, he might blow everyone else away. Some students have had ballroom lessons somewhere else and we need to completely rebuild them. It's better to get someone fresh, like your guy. He's new, he's cute and he's talented. He can go far."

I didn't say what I was thinking: how could I ever afford it? I was giving so much of my salary each week to Pa toward Lisa's treatment and our other bills. "I don't think I can get him to do it, and I don't even have a competition dress."

"So what? Buy one." Nina went over to the clothing rack, which was always filled with formal wear and ballroom dresses, and pulled out one of Simone's Latin costumes. It was two brief pieces, covered in bright gold sequins. "This would look fabulous on you. Try it on."

"No way. That's not a dress, that's a bikini with fringe."

She shrugged and hung it back. "Your choice, your life. But you know what you should do? Ask him to go for that scholarship with you."

I tried not to look as shocked as I felt. "The one for fifteen grand? Aren't you and Simone doing it?"

"Simone is. She's already working on something with Keith. But I don't have anyone who's willing to dance with me, I've tried. So the studio only has one couple in that competition right now and the truth is, none of my students would have a snowball's chance in hell against Keith anyway."

"Come on, if your students are outclassed, what kind of odds would Ryan and I have?"

Nina said cheerfully, "None. Not really. But wouldn't it be fun? And you wouldn't have to worry about school figures and keeping him in the proper alignment. You could just do a little routine together. I can tell you, you'll both improve like crazy if you prepare for a competition."

I'd heard that before. "I'll have to think about it."

We were supposed to hear about the Hunter test near the end of February, but although Lisa ran to check the mailbox every day, there was no letter. The days passed. Then Lisa came home and said that Fabrizio hadn't gotten in. Was this a good sign or a bad one? Were they sending rejections first? We didn't know. Maybe something had gone wrong with her test. Then Hannah's letter arrived. She hadn't been admitted either and was bitterly disappointed. But we still didn't receive anything.

I phoned Mr. Song at school and when I explained the problem, he said, "I'll check with Hunter but I don't think you need to worry yet. Although they give a certain day as the notification date, it's quite common that some letters are delayed." He called me back later to say that we should be expecting the news very soon now.

I didn't even care if Lisa had been accepted or not anymore, I just wanted the whole ordeal to be over. She'd started chewing on the ends of her sleeves, so that I found tiny holes in her shirts near the wrists.

Then, on Saturday, more than a week after we were supposed to have received the notification, Lisa came hurtling upstairs with a thin letter in her hand. It had the purple Hunter logo in the corner. Pa and I came running.

"Well?!" I said.

"I can't open it, I'm too scared. I'm going to throw up. Charlie, quick, you do it." Lisa tossed the sealed letter at me as if it were burning her fingers.

With Pa leaning heavily on my shoulder, I ripped the envelope open and read, "Congratulations, you have been—"

Lisa and I both shrieked. She leapt into my arms and we hugged while Pa wrapped his arms around both of us.

"I can't believe it," she panted. "All those other kids."

"You deserve it," I said. "I'm so happy for you."

"But," said Pa, drawing away, "I haven't decided yet if Lisa will accept or not."

We both froze.

He continued, "There is the long train ride to the school, and maybe it will be too hard for her. I still don't like it that it's out of Chinatown. All of these problems started with this whole Hunter thing."

I read the rest of the letter. "Since we heard so late, we have to decide within a week. They have an event called Hunter Day next Tuesday, that's just a few days away. Students and parents are invited to attend. Then we need to make a final decision by Friday."

Pa said, "You go, Charlie."

"I bet I can go to work later that day. But you should accompany us, Pa. Then you can see what the school really is."

"No. It's not for me. I will ask Uncle Henry if he can go."

"No," Lisa said, "I don't want him."

I said, "Pa, Lisa and I can go alone. We don't need to drag Aunt and Uncle into this. But I think it'd really help if you came too."

Pa was shaking his head. "I have to work that day." And he left the room.

On Monday, I went to Uncle's office while Lisa was at school. It was still early so things were quiet. Aunt Monica had her coat on and was just about to go out, leaving Dennis at the desk. Her gaze dismissed me when she realized I wasn't a patient, then she swiveled back to stare. "What have you done to yourself?"

I'd been careful to wear my old clothing. "Nothing. Why?" Dennis was examining me too, only in a nicer way.

She came around the desk and circled me. "You have changed." It was clear she didn't mean this in a positive way. "Did you use the love spell the Vision gave you?"

"No!" I couldn't wait to get out of there.

Dennis said, "You're looking well, Charlie. Are you sure you have everything you need, Mrs. Wong?"

I shot him a grateful look while Aunt Monica said, "Yes. I'm glad to leave the office in such good hands, Dennis. See you tomorrow."

After she left, I said, "I've never seen her go home early before."

"She's enjoying her freedom. She usually leaves nowadays when it's quiet, or when both Lisa and I are here."

I found it easier to talk to him now that we were alone. "How do you like it so far?"

He had a nice smile. "I love it. I'm learning so much from your uncle. Hey, did you come to see him? He's in the back."

I found Uncle sitting alone in his office, sorting through some papers. When he saw me, he took off his reading glasses. "Charlie."

"Uncle, I wanted to talk to you about Pa. Did he tell you Lisa got into Hunter?"

He smiled. "Yes, he called me. He was very proud, and concerned too."

"I know, that's why I came. Can you please help convince him to come visit the school with me tomorrow? I want him to make the decision based upon knowledge, not fear, that's all."

Uncle hesitated. "You know how your pa is. He hates going to those kinds of events. I can see if I can make time—"

"Oh no." I remembered Lisa's face when this had come up. "You're much too busy and important, Uncle. Anyway, Pa is the one who needs to decide."

"You are exactly right. A parent knows what is right for the child, and maybe he has a point. No one we know has ever gone there. She is a young, innocent girl. She'll need to be on the subways a great deal, she'll be doing things much farther from home: meeting new people, interacting with strangers."

I stared at him, irritated. "It's one of the best schools in the country."

"That's not the point, Charlie. I supported her taking the test, remember? Though I confess I hadn't really thought she would be admitted, I did want to give her the opportunity. I thought studying for that test would help her in school. But your pa wants to keep her safe. Now that she's proven she has the brains, she can go far no matter where she is. If she stays in Chinatown, I give you my word I'll help train her to the best of my ability here."

My jaw was tight with anger. I thought of the way Uncle had only wanted a son. "It'd be different if she were a boy, wouldn't it?"

He sighed. "Yes, but not because I think she can do less than a boy. It's only that, as a girl, she's more vulnerable."

I struggled to find my voice. "Have you been talking to Pa?"

"Some. But in the end, your pa knows best for his daughter."

I stormed into the noodle restaurant. Mr. Hu stared at me as I marched into the kitchen. Pa was using his long bamboo pole set in the wall to press out a large ball of dough.

"Charlie, what—"

"You need to come with me tomorrow. I don't care what anyone else says. You are her father and you need to give this school a fair chance."

Pa dropped the pole and wiped his hands on his apron. "I never attend these things."

"That's exactly right, which is why you owe it to Lisa to go now. You owe it to me." I was breathing hard. Everyone had stopped working and was staring at us. "You never came to a single one of the meetings at my school. No one was ever there for me. All those years, I had such a hard time and you did not come. Then with Lisa, I did my best for her but I'm not her parent. You are. I wish I could make the decisions for her but I can't. It's not fair that I do all the work and then you get to decide. I know you're scared and ashamed. That's too bad. You need to put Lisa first, the way you should have done for me."

Tears threatened to brim over. Through a haze, I saw Mr. Hu and the other workers' faces. Pa had bowed his head. He said weakly, "But I have to work . . ."

Mr. Hu said, "Go."

Pa looked up. "All right. I will come." He came up to me and put an arm around my shoulder, but I was still too upset and shrugged it off. Blinking rapidly, I walked out of the noodle restaurant with my head held high.

The next day, Pa, Lisa and I took the subway uptown to the high school. Pa had put on his best shirt and a wrinkled blazer underneath his worn coat. He looked smaller and frailer outside of Chinatown, with his shoulders hunched and his face down. He shook his head as he saw the beer bottles littering the basketball court we passed on the way to the school. Lisa seemed nervous and awed. But I'd learned to navigate in the outside world now. I walked firmly into the building, which looked like a red brick castle, then gave the guard our information and she directed us upstairs, along with the other parents and kids.

Again, the parents were separated from the students. Lisa gave us a little wave as she headed downstairs to the cafeteria for her tour of the school. Pa craned his neck to follow her until she was out of sight. Then we were sent into the auditorium, which was spacious and imposing, filled with plush red seats. I linked Pa's arm through mine and led him to a seat near the front, where we'd be able to hear everyone well. All of the seats had slips of blank paper and pens on them. Quickly, the entire auditorium filled.

Some people were as posh and well dressed as the students at the dance studio, but some looked just like us. I could tell Pa was surprised that there were many other Asians there. Then a lot of official people stepped onto the stage. They approached the microphone one by one. First, they congratulated us all, then introduced themselves. They were named doctor this and doctor that. One was the principal, one was head of admissions, others were chairs of the different departments. I could tell Pa was too intimidated to follow what they were saying. Thankfully, they kept that part short and then, to my surprise, a bunch of kids walked onto the stage. They were students at the school and those kids ran the rest of the meeting.

One East Indian girl asked the audience to write down our questions on the pieces of paper we'd found on our seats. I wanted to write, "Will Lisa be happy here?" Pa and I couldn't think of anything else so we didn't submit a question, but lots of other parents did. The slips were collected and brought up to the front, then the kids took turns answering the questions.

An African-American boy talked about how he took the train two hours each way for his commute. An older Chinese girl answered a question about how much homework they had—a lot, she said, laughing, but there was still enough time for clubs and fun too. A white girl explained the way security worked at the school. I sneaked a glance at Pa and he was listening intently.

Then the parent associations came up to speak. An older Chinese woman approached the microphone and told us she was the head of the Chinese-American Parents Association and would be glad to talk to any interested parents about any concerns they might have. The head of the Korean-American Parents Association spoke next and mentioned that they held a banquet every year with great food. I saw Pa smile.

When we met up with Lisa again, she was bubbling over. "They have an arts club, and a chess club, and band, and so many different newspapers . . ."

"Slow down," I said, glad to see her so exuberant. "Did you like the school?"

"It's amazing!" Her eyes shone. "You should see their science

rooms, the equipment they have, and they have so many extracur-
riculars. The best thing was, the other kids talked the way I do."

Pa asked, "What do you mean?"

"Well, like, I always make sure I don't use too many big words
because the other kids will think I'm weird. But the girl leading us
around sounded just like me!"

I said, "Did you make any friends?"

"Yeah! One person said to me, 'Hey, what's up?'" She beamed.

I laughed. "Well, that's a start."

Lisa said, "We can sign up right now if we want. The forms are
by the auditorium. We just need Pa's signature."

We both turned to him. He asked Lisa, "Do you want to go
here?"

"Yes. Please say yes."

My heart ached to see the hope in her eyes.

"I should really speak to Uncle about this first," Pa began. "It's
such a big decision."

"Uncle said that it was your decision." I mentally crossed all of
my fingers and toes for luck. "He said a parent feels what is right for
his child."

Pa studied Lisa's glowing face, then smiled. "Let's go find those
forms."

Fifteen

I floated into the studio and arrived just in time to get changed for Ryan's lesson. When he saw me, he asked, "What's happened?"

I couldn't seem to stop smiling. "My little sister just got into Hunter high school. And my father's letting her go."

He lifted an eyebrow. "Wow. Congratulations."

"You know it?"

"Evelyn went there."

Now I was impressed and curious. "What did she do after that?"

"She went to Princeton. That's how she met Adrienne."

At my blank look, he explained, "The owner of your studio. Adrienne was the alumna who conducted Evelyn's college interview. That's why Evelyn chose this studio."

"Really?" I hadn't known Adrienne was so well educated—though I probably should have guessed. She wasn't in the studio these days, having given birth to a healthy baby girl a few months earlier.

"Yep, but I guess dance was what she really loved."

Adrienne had chosen to follow her dreams, just as Lisa was doing. Now it was my turn. I took a deep breath. "Ryan, would you consider dancing in a competition with me?"

He jerked his head back. "Oh no, I don't think I'm ready for that. Even just the wedding's enough of a challenge for me."

I tapped my foot next to him, trying to think. "Look, you wanted to learn to be a better dancer, right?" I parroted Dominic's words. "There is no better way to improve than to train for a competition, and the prize is seventy-five hundred dollars per person."

"Umm, that's really nice but . . ."

I'd known the money wouldn't sway him. "It's all right. I understand." I pressed my lips together and walked back into the ballroom. I didn't know what had gotten into me, anyway. I was just so happy about Lisa and the possibility that she could achieve her dreams, I wanted to give mine a chance too.

Ryan was walking beside me, studying me. "You're upset."

My eyes suddenly felt hot. I looked at the floor so he wouldn't notice. "Do you know why your rough hands never bother me?"

I could feel him shaking his head.

I made myself continue. "Because I worked as a dishwasher for years, before I came here. You should have felt my skin. I was clumsy, and bad at school, and not talented at anything."

He laid his hand upon my shoulder, silencing me. "What would I have to do?"

Startled, I looked up at him. "We'd need to get a dance choreographed. It has to be Latin. We'd have to train hard, really hard, because we'd be up against the best couples from every Avery Studio in New York City and we can't embarrass ourselves."

"So who else is competing from our studio?"

A smile began to cross my face as I said, "Keith and Simone."

Something sparked in his eyes. "You'd teach me to be better than that guy?"

"I would try, yes."

He sighed. "I hate it when people watch me. Especially when I'm dancing."

"I know. Me too."

He chuckled. "Some professional dancer you are."

I forced myself to try to make him understand. "But I'm learning to hone my body. I love using it to express myself, being strong and in control, and yet free at the same time."

He nodded. "Yes, I know that feeling."

He was on the verge of saying yes, but I wanted to be honest. It came out in a rush. "I have to tell you something, which is that since we're both new, we don't really have any chance of winning. It's more that we'd get a lot better and maybe it'd be fun."

When he finally spoke, his voice was quiet. "This means something to you, doesn't it?"

I was just realizing this myself. All my life, I'd been trying to fulfill other people's ideas of who I was supposed to be and failing, and this was my chance to try to become who I was meant to be. I fixed my gaze on the floor again. "I want to do it."

"All right, then."

When I met his eyes, I knew mine were full. I blinked and a tear overflowed down my cheek. He reached out with his broad hand and wiped it away. "Hey."

I took a deep breath. "Come on, we'd better get started."

As I was walking with Ryan to the mirror, he said, "Can I ask you for a favor?"

"Of course."

"I've realized that there is a particular dance I'd really like to learn. It'd be perfect if we chose it for the competition."

"Which one?"

"I don't know what it's called. They do it to that very fast music."

I had no idea what he meant. "Come on." I led him into the small ballroom and went up to the stereo system. I put on a CD with a compilation of Latin music. Then I played the different songs while he listened. He kept shaking his head until a complicated number came on.

"That's it."

I tried not to sigh. "Mambo. You do realize that mambo is absolutely the hardest Latin dance, don't you?"

"Umm, actually, no."

"It is, because the music wants you to step on the first beat. Your entire body will want to step on the one, but you have to hold it in and step on the two. All of the time. And do you know what's going to be the only thing stopping you from stepping on the one?"

"I'll bite. What?"

"Me. I am going to be hanging onto your arm, holding you back until the two beat every single time. That's going to be like trying to stop a rampaging bull. Couldn't we do rumba or merengue?"

"Sure, you're the dance teacher." He was downcast for a moment, then looked determined. "Though if there's one thing I learned from boxing, it's that you need to push yourself sometimes. Reach beyond what you know you can do."

I thought about this for a moment. I didn't want him to be unhappy, especially when he was mainly doing this to help me. "Why do you want mambo?" Then I remembered. "Is it that friend of yours who said white guys can't do Latin?"

There was a long pause before he spoke. "His name is Felipe. He's my best buddy and was my biggest competitor when I was boxing. He lived uptown and I was in Brooklyn, but the best boxing gym's in Brooklyn so we met there. We had the same coach, used to spar together all the time. We're like brothers. He's part Cuban, part Dominican and he's ribbed me my whole life about how I'll never able to dance. And when I stopped boxing, he continued."

"How did he do?"

"Won so many titles." Ryan's smile was sad. "He's pretty famous now in the boxing world. Anyway, I'd like to watch his jaw drop. Just once."

"You want him to come watch the competition?"

"He's not really the type to attend one. Actually, I was hoping that you and I could do it for him somewhere, like at a party. He lives in Spanish Harlem and I've seen lots of couples dancing to this type of music there."

I repeated, "Spanish Harlem."

"I'd be with you."

"Ryan, I'm not really supposed to see you outside of the studio." Though I was tempted.

"What?"

"We're not allowed to fraternize with the students."

"Whoa." He held his hands up. "I have a girlfriend, remember? This is just dancing at a party together. I could even pay you."

It stung a bit, that he hadn't intended his invitation in a romantic sense, although I knew anything between us wasn't possible anyway. I frowned. "They do hire us out sometimes but for more formal events like a showcase or a wedding. I don't think a party uptown would qualify."

"What kind of dumb rule is this?"

I put it as clearly as I could. "If the studio thinks we're having a romantic relationship, I'll be fired."

"I don't want to get you into trouble." He ducked his head. "I guess my friend will just have to keep believing I can't dance."

At the mention of his friend, a thought popped into my head. "Do you own a car?"

"I don't want to drive to Harlem. It'll get stripped."

"So you do have one."

"Yeah?"

I took a breath, then leaned in to say softly, "All right. We'll do mambo for the competition and I'll go to Spanish Harlem with you. No one will ever know about the party, okay?"

He straightened, looking glad. "Are you sure? It's your job."

"We're not in love, so even if they do catch me, I'll probably be all right. They'll believe I'm telling the truth."

His face became impassive. "Yes, good thing you wouldn't be hiding anything."

"But then I'm going to ask you to do a favor for me too. I have a friend who needs a car."

On my way to the studio later that week, I kept tracing an advanced mambo step in my head as I walked through the Chinatown streets. Maybe Ryan and I could use this in our routine. It was swivel swivel hold, then hop freeze, and did I come out on the left or right leg after that? I started to mark the combination on the pavement. Oh yes, it was the right leg. I looked up to see a Chinese lady in boots and a puffy brown coat staring at me. She closed her mouth, gathered up her plastic shopping bags and literally ran away from me as if I were a crazy person. Oops. It wasn't easy to do a mambo in Chinatown.

Just yesterday, our downstairs neighbor had come up to complain again about all of the noise in our apartment. Luckily, I was alone at home then.

"It sounds like a bunch of elephants are stomping around in here," he said. "You two girls were always so quiet. What's happened to you?"

"I'm so sorry. I'll make sure it stops." I resolved to practice at home only in my socks from then on.

I wondered if I could pretend to be sick for the matchmaking dim sum session on Sunday morning with Grace, but I was afraid Godmother Yuan would never forgive me. I chose my clothing carefully. It was a matter of pride that I wanted to look nice, although I still dressed more conservatively than I did at the studio. Pa was already gone and Lisa had left for a friend's apartment.

When I entered the restaurant, I saw Grace and a number of other people seated at a large round table. I knew from watching matchmaking sessions at the noodle restaurant that the girl was usually placed at the opposite end of the table from the intended guy, with all of their family and friends in between. I wondered why it was done this way, since it was so awkward for the potential couple, but I thought it showed whose opinion really mattered regarding the match: the family's.

Indeed, Grace was at one end and I scanned the opposite side for her suitor. My jaw dropped. It was Dennis, Uncle Henry's assistant. Pa was sitting there too. What in the world? Pa stood up to wave at me and I saw he was wearing his best clothes again. To Grace's left were her friends and relatives, including Godmother Yuan, Mrs. Yuan and Winston. Oh no. Now I understood. The official matchmaking session may have been for Grace and Dennis, but Winston and I were a bonus. I glanced back at the door, but by then Godmother had locked onto my arm and was steering me to the table. Too late to run.

Winston stood up so quickly when I arrived at the table that he almost knocked his chair over. Grace was as pretty as ever. However, while I'd always seen her laughing, now she seemed bored and resentful. To Grace's left were people who must have been Dennis's friends and relatives. I greeted everyone at the table and shook hands with the people I didn't know. Pa grinned at me. Winston had been placed far from Grace, to make it clear that he wasn't her boyfriend. There was an empty seat in between Winston and Dennis. I obviously wasn't considered attractive enough to be a threat to Grace or they would never have put me, an unmarried woman, next to the potential suitor. In any case, I tried to head for a spot near Pa instead but Godmother's fingers were like iron. My stomach rolled as I sat in between the two young men.

Dennis's eyes flitted around the room as if he was as mortified as Grace to be there. It must have been doubly embarrassing for him that Pa and I were present as well. When the waiters set several pots of tea on the table, everyone waited for Grace to stand up and pour. She didn't. There was a long awkward silence, which Godmother Yuan tried to break by asking Dennis what he did for a living. She was surprised to learn he was Uncle Henry's assistant. I realized that the two families didn't know each other, but had been set up by a professional matchmaker, probably one of the older women on Dennis's side of the table. Finally, since I was the only other young woman present, I stood up and poured the tea into everyone's china cups one by one, leaving my own for last, as was proper.

I could feel Winston's gaze on me and I didn't want to speak to him so I pretended Dennis was a ballroom student and started talking to him.

He perked up. "I think it's really interesting to apply scientific measurements to age-old techniques."

I thought about the jars in Uncle's office. "I've always wondered exactly which medicines worked and which ones didn't. Although I feel sorry for the animals that get killed for them, especially in cruel ways."

"I was just learning about a technique where they shove an ink stone down the throat of a living poisonous toad and then leave the creature to dry in the sun. The ink is supposed to be very potent in curing certain diseases." His face was more animated than I'd ever seen it.

I grimaced. "I think that sort of thing should be outlawed."

"You're very kindhearted. But don't you think human well-being is more important than some animal's?"

I tried to keep the smile on my face as we continued chatting. The older people picked out the food they wanted from the waiters who pushed the dim sum carts around the restaurant. It was actually pretty easy to be sociable now that I had to do it for my job. Once Pa caught my eye and jerked his head toward Winston. I must have turned beet red and made sure not to glance in his direction again.

When I stood up to refill everyone's cups again, I realized that Mrs. Yuan, the matchmaker and Grace were all watching us with varying degrees of animosity. Of course, the matchmaker wouldn't get her extra fee if Dennis preferred me to Grace. I met Grace's eyes and made a little gesture with my hand to say, "Sorry, go ahead. He's yours." Her lips twitched but she continued to study me instead of Dennis.

For a moment, I remembered our old easy friendship. After we'd grown apart, I'd been jealous of Grace. I'd wondered, if I'd still had a mother and grandma like her, would I have been as attractive? Now I saw her as a girl wearing too much makeup, weighed down by the need to look perfect all the time, by all of those logos on her bags and shoes. I thought about what Zan had told me about Grace being caught in bed with a girl. Maybe Grace was just like me, with desires that couldn't be expressed in our small community. Had she been in love with that girl? Had her parents made them stop seeing each other? Did she feel as lonely as I did sometimes? I realized that in a way, Grace and I were similar, both trying to figure out who we were outside of our parents' world.

I didn't know how Dennis and Grace were supposed to fall in love anyway, when they'd been seated at opposite ends of an enormous table. With all of the disapproval of my conversation with Dennis, I had no choice, so I turned to Winston. "How have you been?"

He was considering me. "You've grown up, Charlie."

"What do you mean?"

"The way you look, the way you carry yourself. You're so confident."

I lowered my eyes to the table. "Well, thank you."

"It's been a long time, hasn't it?"

I didn't answer.

Winston bent in close to my ear and whispered, "I'm sorry. About everything."

I carefully swallowed the dumpling in my mouth, then met his eyes. "It's all right. I'm past that now."

Half of his mouth pulled upward in that smile I'd loved. "I can see that. This new you is very attractive."

"And that's our problem right there."

He looked puzzled. "What?"

"You like the new me but I liked the old you." And with that, I turned away from him.

Pa caught up to me as I walked away from the restaurant. "Pa, you set me up!"

He spread his fingers. "You wouldn't have gone otherwise. Anyway, it was Godmother's idea. She came to the noodle restaurant to ask my permission." Of course. Why hadn't I realized that before? She couldn't have me, an unmarried girl, present at a matchmaking session without Pa's permission, whether or not I was the intended victim.

Pa continued, "So I said it was all right as long as they invited Winston too."

"Pa!" Sometimes I could just strangle him. "Did you know Dennis would be there too?"

"No, she didn't tell me who the suitor would be. I recognized him at the restaurant, but I only got there a few minutes before you did. You seemed to like him better. He must come from a good family if the matchmaker recommended him. You pick."

I breathed deeply to calm myself. "Pa, I want to be free to make my own choices."

He blinked, confused. "But I'm letting you choose."

"Between two guys that you know!" I wondered if a person could get arrested for yelling on the street in Chinatown. "Leave my love life alone. I don't want anybody."

Pa furrowed his eyebrows. "Are you sure?"

I couldn't trust myself to answer and stalked off down the street, fuming.

The next weekend, Lisa and I were making up our beds as usual. She stumbled as she bumped into our old coffee table, which had been in the middle of our room for as long as I could remember.

"Come on, help me set up the mattresses, Lisa." I hated it when she tried to get out of helping me. She staggered over to the sofa and sat down abruptly on the floor. She had missed the couch.

I sped over to her. "What's wrong?" I tried to help her up but it was like she'd lost all connection to her legs. I managed to haul her onto the sofa and laid her on it.

"I can't feel my feet," she whispered.

"Pa!" I yelled. "Something's wrong with Lisa!"

As Pa came running from the kitchen, Lisa said, "No, I'm all right." Her calves started spasming, as if the muscles were out of control.

"She's having a stroke." I placed my fingers against my throat, hardly able to breathe. This was too similar to what had happened with Ma.

Lisa's legs went limp. Gingerly, she lowered first one, then the other foot onto the ground. "No, I'm not. I'm just very tired."

"You lost control of your legs."

Pa was aghast, his skin ashen, the lines on his face deeper than I'd ever seen them.

"We need to call an ambulance." I reached for the phone.

"No, do you remember what happened to Ma? My legs are fine now." Even though Lisa was too young to remember Ma's death herself, she was aware of all the bill collectors who had harassed us for years after Ma died.

I looked at Pa and he pressed his lips together. I understood. We wouldn't be calling.

At the beginning of Ma's illness, when she'd almost fainted from a severe migraine, Pa had called an ambulance and they'd brought her to the hospital. I remember that long night with them both away. Aunt Monica had come over to our apartment and stayed with me the whole night. She'd slept in the living room on the floor by my feet. When I cried, she'd held me until I fell asleep again. Often when I was irritated by her, I remembered that night.

Ma returned the next day, looking frail. They'd run tests on her but they were still inconclusive. However, the bills were clear. We were pursued by creditors and bill collectors for years, until long after Ma was dead. In the end, Uncle Henry paid the rest of them off for us and refused any repayment. That was partly why Lisa had to keep working at his office, to try to pay back a small part of that debt, which both brothers understood, although no one would speak of it.

After that, when Ma's symptoms returned, Pa was afraid to call the medical authorities. He had Uncle help us and when Uncle couldn't, Pa went to the temples and the witches. He returned to our own kind of medicine, which he understood and trusted. In his eyes, the western doctors had failed to discover anything with their tests and had charged us a fortune on top of that, only burdening us with a huge debt. When Uncle Henry fed Ma cool, yin energy foods like pears, lotus seeds and white gourd to help rebalance her energy, Pa believed it helped her headaches. It didn't stop her miscarriages, though, which continued until she finally had Lisa. But then she died a few years after that. None of us really knew what the cause of death was. In the months before her death, she'd started losing feeling in her legs, just like Lisa now. She'd been disoriented and dizzy, until she'd hardly been able to walk any more. Then she died from what seemed to be a massive stroke one night.

Most of Uncle Henry's patients weren't covered by insurance and neither were we, which was normal in Chinatown. I was pretty sure that most of the dancers weren't insured either. It was too expensive. They paid their own bills and desperately tried not to be injured. Most of them were young enough that they didn't have many physical problems. It seemed so wrong to me, now, that we couldn't bring Lisa to the hospital for fear of the costs. But Pa was right that we couldn't control which tests they would do in an emergency room. Who knew how high the bill would be? If I was certain they could help cure Lisa, I would sell my soul in a second, but what if they sent her back to us with no answers and we were then up to our necks in debt with nothing to show for it? We'd be worse off than ever.

Still, we'd spent so much money on the Vision and traditional cures and Lisa was only getting worse. I was starting to doubt. What if she suffered from the same thing as Ma, whatever it was? "Pa, we need to bring her to a specialist who can figure out what's wrong. Maybe a neurologist."

"They won't find anything. They'll just take our money." Pa ran his hands, coarse from all his manual labor, over his face.

That afternoon, Lisa and I sat on the couch in the apartment waiting for the Vision to come, while Pa set tea in the kitchen. This was supposed to be a major emergency ritual.

Lisa had panic in her eyes. "There's nothing wrong with me. Maybe we could make a run for it."

My eyes trailed to the door. I was afraid of that old witch messing around with Lisa, but I was willing to try it if she might help. "Pa's already agreed to hire her, so if she comes and you're not here, he's going to pay her anyway. That's the way he is."

"Do you think she's going to make me eat something?"

"Could be. But I think she's more about spells and incense and that kind of thing."

Lisa shivered and looked like she was going to cry. "I hope they don't move on to Uncle Henry's type of treatments next. I hate taking medicine or being poked with a needle."

I hugged her. "Hey, I thought you wanted to be a doctor."

"I want to be the one doing the poking."

"It's going to be okay, Lisa. Whatever it is, it'll work out."

She started to sniffle for real. "No, Charlie, it'll never be all right again."

I pulled away and looked at her. "What do you mean by that?"

"Nothing." She avoided my eyes. "I'm just tired and scared and I don't want to have all these problems. I wish I could go away and everything would be gone." There was something new in her eyes, a resentment I'd never seen before. "You're fortunate, Charlie. Lucky you don't have to be me."

I felt a spark of anger. "You've always been the pretty one, the smart one, the one who was good at everything, while I was the inept, stupid one. Now it's my turn." I was shocked by my own words but somehow also couldn't stop. "I'm allowed to be decent at something too."

"And because you were so bad at everything, you always got out of things. I was the one who was stuck at Uncle's."

"You're jealous." It had never occurred to me that Lisa might be resentful of the changes in my life. Were her problems a way of calling attention to herself? "All our lives, you've been the one who was praised by Pa, Aunt and Uncle, the teachers, by every single person we knew."

Her eyes blazed. "A whole lot of good that did me. You had an easy way out. If you didn't like something, you just became too clumsy to do it."

"That is unfair!" I wanted to smack her. "I was desperate to stay at the dance studio but I still got fired as a receptionist. I was just lucky they saw potential in me as a dancer instead."

"Well, maybe you should have tried harder. Goodness knows, what you had to do at all your jobs wasn't that difficult."

I gaped. Lisa had never turned on me like this. Perhaps because of the eleven-year age difference between us, we'd hardly ever squabbled like other siblings. "Who are you? Maybe something truly is wrong with you." The moment I said it, I saw the hurt cross her face and regretted it. I shut my mouth before more words came out.

Lisa flung herself onto the sofa so that her back was to me and buried her face against the material. I moved stiffly onto the other chair, looking at anything but her. We stayed that way until the Vision of the Left Eye arrived.

Pa opened the door for her. Then Lisa and I both stood up and said, "Mrs. Purity."

I was surprised she was alone, unaccompanied by Todd. The Vision went with us into the kitchen and lit all of the altars. She'd brought oranges and she set these up by Ma's altar. She took out the sacred papers we would burn while praying, a red envelope and a piece of rock candy.

She said to Pa, "Would you make a pot of plain white rice?"

Then while he was busy, she went back out to the living room and sat next to Lisa. Lisa shrank away from her. Despite our earlier fight, I felt sorry for my sister. The witch took Lisa's hands in hers. The Vision closed one eye and the other one stayed open, wandering far to the left.

I hovered over Lisa protectively, close enough that I could smell the witch's scent of hair wax and sweat. Pa came out of the kitchen and also stood behind Lisa, listening.

The Vision began to speak. "She is infected by an evil spirit."

Lisa gave a little gasp and I felt myself grow pale.

The witch continued, "The spirit has taken hold and must be removed. Today, we will start the process. This is the reason for the nightmares. It is a hungry ghost, one that can never be satisfied no matter how much it consumes. If you leave it, it will take all of her and leave a shell in its place."

I didn't know what to believe. This was terrifying yet also sounded like something out of a story. Pa had wrapped his arms around himself, as if he were cold. Although the witch's earlier Release of Life ritual had seemed to help Lisa, I didn't like her scaring my sister now.

"Are you sure?" I asked.

The witch didn't bother to answer me, though Lisa gave me a grateful look.

I pressed on. "How did you know which items to bring before you even had a chance to examine Lisa?"

"That is standard equipment for those in our trade." The Vision's normal eye glowered at me. "At home, I already made contact with the spirit world and I suspected. Now that I have touched her, I am sure. Not that I need to explain myself to a young girl like you. Put a bowl of plain white rice in front of the altar. Place a pair of chopsticks next to it."

Pa went into the kitchen to do as she said. The Vision turned to Lisa. "Do you have something you wear regularly?"

Lisa went and found the worn blue T-shirt she always slept in. The Vision took it and went into the kitchen while we trailed after her. The witch paused in front of the altars with the shirt in her hands and bowed to Ma and our ancestors. She turned and gestured to the three of us so that we all stood behind her and bowed as well. Then she took the long sacred red-and-green papers that we burned for the ancestors and bowed again.

She brought Lisa forward and held her hand over Lisa's head. The Vision closed her eyes, then took Lisa by the shoulders and forced her to her knees on the bare vinyl floor. Lisa sneaked a look at me, trembling. I tightened my lips. If the witch hurt my sister, I was going to slug her. But all she did was indicate that Lisa should bow deeply, the way we did at temple to the gods. Lisa did it three times. Then the Vision had Lisa rise and she handed her the pair of chopsticks and the bowl that held the rice.

"Eat a piece," the Vision said.

Lisa did.

Then the witch emptied the rest of the rice into the trash. She gave Lisa her shirt, the piece of rock candy, the red envelope, the bowl and chopsticks.

"Keep the bowl and chopsticks safe. Put the red envelope underneath your pillow. Also keep the T-shirt near your bed."

"She sleeps in it," Pa said.

"That is even better. It will protect her."

"Are we allowed to wash it?" I asked.

Pa pinched the bridge of his nose.

"What? I know it's supposed to be a magical item now that you've blessed it, but it'll get dirty if she wears it. Will the magic wash off?"

"It is not magic," the witch said, gritting her little square teeth. "It is power, my power. And it will not wash away." With that, she swept out of the room. We heard the door slam as she left.

I cast my eyes downward, ashamed. "I didn't mean to insult her, Pa."

"I know, it's all right."

I felt bad that I had upset the Vision when I had an idea of how much she cost Pa per session. I hoped she hadn't left early because of me. Years ago, when I was still working at Uncle's office, Aunt Monica had hired the witch to help her get pregnant, and I remembered that to pay for one session with the Vision, my aunt had had me take a hundred dollars out of the cash register. My aunt hadn't gotten pregnant but no one seemed to think that made the Vision any less effective. This visit was surely even more expensive because the Vision had come to our house.

Pa was working longer hours at the restaurant now, going in earlier than he used to and leaving later. When I'd asked, he'd just said times were busy. That meant he was probably helping to set up beforehand and cleaning up afterward for a bit more money. I still gave him almost my entire paycheck, just keeping out the bare minimum I needed. He always hesitated before taking it, asked me if I needed to keep anything more for myself. I would have paid anything if it would help. At the end of every month, I always saw Pa put a twenty-dollar bill into an envelope to send back to family in China. No matter how poor we were, he did this. Lisa and I had been telling him he needed a new coat for the winter but there was no purchase.

"What's in the red envelope?" I asked.

Lisa opened it and took out a yellow piece of paper with red writing on it. It had been folded, like origami, into the shape of an octagon.

"Those are *fu*," Pa said. "Words of power. When written by a master, they can contain demons."

I hoped he was right.

Sixteen

I stood in front of the mirror with Ryan beside me. "Let's start talking to your Irish hips about some Cuban motion. You need to learn how to move your hips. It's like you're waiting for a bus and you're really bored, so you put all your weight on one leg." He did it. "Good. Now you're tired, so you shift your weight to the other leg." He complied. "That's it. So let's do that together."

I straightened my right leg and shifted my right hip back. He did the same. Then I straightened my left leg and shifted my left hip. He copied.

"You're doing a good job but the problem is, your hips are only moving the tiniest bit. If I blinked, I would miss it."

"Years of inhibitions. Hard to get rid of them without alcohol."

"I can see that." I stood behind him and had him do it again, placing my hands above his pelvic bones. As he straightened one leg, I helped him push the hip back. "Great. Now the other way. Shift, and shift. Your body is still resisting me." He was tall and it was hard to see around him.

I stood in front of him and placed his hands on my hipbones and my hands over his. Much better. Now we could both watch what we were doing. "I'll do it with you. Left, and right, and left, and right." His hips started moving together with mine. I released his hands and held mine up high so he could see my stomach. "Cuban motion happens below the waist. The top stays still. It's like there's an ocean in between. Quick quick slow, quick quick slow." I swung my hips back and forth while hardly moving anything above my waist at all. I repeated what I had learned. "The top is celestial: innocent, floating in air, while the hips are grounded to the earth: sensual and heavy. If we don't do this, we'll look like strippers. Without that balance, we don't have art."

"Yin and yang," he said.

I was so surprised, I twisted around to look up at him. "Exactly. Okay. Shift your weight again. Left, right, left." His hands were warm on my hips and his breath was in my hair. The fabric of his pants brushed against that of my skirt.

"I don't think I can do this." His voice was strained.

I stopped. "What's the matter? You're doing fine."

"Excuse me," he said, and practically ran out of the ballroom.

When I stared after him, Mateo, who was leading a well-dressed Indian couple around the floor, leaned into me and whispered, "I think you made that lesson a bit too 'hard' for your friend." He waggled his eyebrows wickedly and strolled off with his students, chuckling to himself.

I gasped, understanding what he meant, but sure he was pulling my leg, as always. Ryan returned a few minutes later, with a few droplets clinging to his eyelashes. It looked like he'd splashed water on his face. "Where were we?"

"Umm, why don't you go ahead and practice that at home?" I said brightly. "Let's go learn some steps now."

Dominic made the official announcement at the Monday meeting. "You all know about the Paul Rosenthal Dance Scholarship. It will be held as a part of the annual National Avery Competition at the Regal Grand Hotel in Connecticut in late July, where every Avery Studio in the country will be represented. This is one of the biggest purses in ballroom today and will show everyone at nationals which New York studio is producing the best dancing. Of course, we know that studio is us. It has been decided that Simone and Charlie will represent our studio to compete for the scholarship with their students Keith and Ryan."

Everyone clapped while Simone gave me a little smirk from her place in the circle.

Dominic continued, "I will personally give the competitors free extra coachings throughout the coming months. I will also do their choreography if they so wish."

I'd seen Dominic's work and he always made the choreography suit the personality and abilities of the performers. It was hard to dance something that didn't suit your body, and especially as Ryan and I were both so new, we needed all the help we could get.

However, even before we got started on the choreography, Dominic needed to evaluate us. Ryan and I stood in the small ballroom as he walked around the two of us, eyeing us both. Then he put on some mambo music and said, "Show me."

Ryan and I started to dance. He only knew the moves from the Bronze Syllabus but I thought he led them pretty well. Invariably, we started stepping on the one beat instead of the two despite my firm grip on his arm, what the female professional dancers called the "Five Fingers of Death."

"Stop." Dominic paused the CD. "You've made a wise decision in choosing mambo."

"What?" I said. Ryan winked at me, which I ignored.

Dominic said, "Because the technique in mambo remains basically the same from Bronze through Supreme Gold. The steps become more difficult but it's not like American foxtrot, where you essentially have to learn a whole new dance when you progress to the higher levels."

I nodded. I'd just started doing Silver foxtrot in dance session with the professionals. I loved its sweeping, gliding form but it seemed to have no connection to Bronze foxtrot whatsoever.

He turned to Ryan. "You have a good body but you still have many traces of the athlete in you. Dance is not about 'what,' it is about 'how.' Not about getting the ball in the goal, any way possible. It's about doing it with grace, precision, balance, emotion and beauty. Still, I foresee that performing the steps well will not be a permanent problem. Your timing is atrocious but I predict also that that will not remain an issue. You will go home, Ryan, and listen to the mambo CDs I give you and you will count out the beat to them, time and time again. Soon, you will learn to step on the two instead of the one. However."

We both waited. "Your hips, they are a problem."

Ryan groaned. "Why does everyone say that?"

Dominic faced me. "Charlie, you have to beat it into him to make sure we have some semblance of Cuban motion before the competition. I'm sure he will improve but you cannot completely rebuild a man in a matter of months. What you need to do is to distract the audience and the judges."

"How?" Ryan asked.

"With this." Dominic tapped Ryan's bicep. "You can lift her."

"You're not serious," I said.

"That sounds all right to me," Ryan said. "Better than that hip stuff."

"You will still need to do Cuban motion," Dominic said. "But if we design choreography that has a number of fairly flashy lifts in it, then you will not need to rely so much on your Latin technique."

I was terrified. "I don't want to leave the ground. I've always been a very stable kind of person. Dancing is one thing, dangling in the air is another."

"What, you don't trust me?" Ryan said, pretending to look wounded.

"Well, I am telling you that if you want to look good on the dance floor, someone has to lift someone," Dominic said. "Would you care to carry him, Charlie?"

I eyed Ryan's frame. "No. But I still don't see why we need them. I've never seen a student doing lifts."

"That is precisely the point," said Dominic. "Students don't tend to do lifts. This will elevate your mambo to a professional level. In regular competition, lifts are not allowed because the floor is too crowded, but for this scholarship, you'll be on the floor one couple at a time. Anything goes. And he can do it, I know."

Ryan looked gratified. "What exactly will we have to do?"

Dominic walked to the door and called, "Nina, come over here, will you?" After a moment, her head appeared in the doorway. "Sweetheart, will you help me demonstrate a few lifts for our friends here?"

Nina was chewing on a big wad of gum again. "Sure. Let me spit this out and I'll be right with you." She trotted into the teachers' room and returned wearing a pair of sweatpants instead of the skirt she'd had.

"Charlie, are you decent underneath that dress?" Dominic asked. Ryan looked at me with sudden interest.

"I'll go put on something else," I said, heading toward the teachers' room. I was already dreading the whole experience.

"Take off your shoes too," Dominic called.

I glanced back at Nina. "She's wearing hers."

"She is not going to wound anyone with her heels," said Dominic. "You, on the other hand . . ."

I sighed, then changed into a tight black tank top and sweatpants. I had to roll up the legs since they'd been Adrienne's and were too long for me. For good measure, I rolled down the waistband too and pinned it with safety pins. I returned to the small ballroom in my stocking feet. I gritted my teeth. "If lifts aren't allowed in regular competition, how come Nina knows how to do them?"

Nina sang, "Because I am a-ma-zing."

Dominic said, "They are permitted in theater arts and show dance competition, and our dancers are trained in everything. Lifts aren't for everyone. People are often too scared, too weak or too heavy. All right, Nina, just come at me, turn around and I'll take you up."

Nina ran at Dominic, turned at the last moment so her back was to him, jumped and he lifted her into the air. She struck an elegant pose as he turned them both, then he suddenly tossed and dropped her, catching her again around her waist and underneath her straight leg, with her other leg bent in a graceful line. They looked incredible together.

"You didn't even tell her you'd do the second lift." I was so impressed. "You know, Nina, I always see you chugging a soda or munching on a hot dog, and I think you're a regular person. And then you do this. I forget what you're capable of."

Nina beamed. "Don't worry, it's easy-peasy."

"Okay, now Nina with Ryan. Ryan, catch her around the lower part of her rib cage and take her straight up. Keep your core and back strong. Don't worry about the fish dive now, just the first part of the lift."

Ryan nodded. Nina ran at him, she turned around, he caught her around the rib cage. His fingers fumbled and then he got a better grip. When he picked her up, he turned them both the wrong way. Then he didn't set her on her feet properly. Still, Ryan was grinning. "I enjoyed that. Better than using weights."

"That was excellent," said Dominic. "Now, Charlie, with me."

I took a deep breath, then ran toward Dominic and turned just as I reached him. He put his hands around my hips. I bent my knees to jump.

Dominic drew back. "What's that?" He traced a few bumps around my waist with his fingers.

"Safety pins. My sweatpants are too big."

"Too big isn't a problem, but anything that can poke your partner is. I don't want to drop you when you're in the air and I don't want to be afraid to touch you because you've got all sorts of needles hidden on your body."

"Sorry." I removed the safety pins and put them on the stereo shelf.

"All right. Run toward me as fast as you can. Jump right here." He indicated a spot on the floor directly in front of him. "I'll grab you and lift you straight up. When you're in the air, keep one arm up and one to the side while I turn us both."

I did like he said and felt myself go high in the air, suddenly dizzy as Dominic spun us. After a few seconds, he put me down. "Wonderful. Now the two of you together."

I looked at Ryan for a moment. Then I repeated the move with him and he took me up. It was exhilarating at first, but then my feelings turned into fear. If he were to drop me, I wouldn't be able to use my arms to break my fall since they were stretched out. As I thought about this, my body realigned itself and I started to flail, off-balance. Ryan caught me in his arms while dropping a few steps back, then we both tumbled onto the floor in a tangle.

"What was that?" Ryan sounded angry.

"Sorry, sorry." I scrambled off of his chest. "I started thinking . . ."

"I could have hurt you!"

Nina was doubled over, laughing. "The problem is that you guys don't trust each other."

"She's absolutely right," said Dominic. "You need to do some trust-building exercises. Come here."

Dominic made me stand in front of Ryan. Ryan extended his arms on both sides of my rib cage. I had to keep my body completely straight and let it fall to the side slowly while Ryan supported me.

I tried not to panic. I didn't want to get involved in any of this. "How come I have to do all of the trusting here?"

"I'm trusting you not to lose your form and squash me," Ryan said.

"This is a man," said Dominic. "He is here to support you. Lean on him, use him."

I heard Nina's voice. "Aw, don't be such a chauvinist."

We got started. It took a great deal of core strength to keep my body in one line as I tilted to the side. It went against all of my instincts to allow Ryan to hold my weight as I headed toward the floor, but he kept me from falling. Then we leaned to the other side. Finally, hardest of all, I had to fall backward while he held me by the neck and rib cage. He didn't seem to be exerting himself too much.

Then we practiced the lift again and I didn't fall on top of him this time. To my surprise, Ryan said, "You went up like a feather. You really helped me get you off the ground. And you're so lightly built. That was great."

"Now a more difficult lift, I think," said Dominic.

Half an hour later, I was lying on my side on the hard ballroom floor, practicing the position I needed to hold. Dominic stretched my entire body backward until I thought it would break. "Arch as far back as you can. Also, you need to keep your left arm by your ear and your other leg bent and pointed at your knee. Hold the arm behind his neck straight. When you feel him starting to put you down, stretch out with your arm toward him so that he can take it to lead you out into the turns you'll be doing the moment you land."

"Anything else? You want a hamburger too?" I muttered. Dance was always like this: millions of details to remember while you were spinning through the air at a hundred miles per hour. I heard Ryan snort back a laugh.

I did the new lifts again and again with Dominic while Ryan worked with Nina. Sometimes, for Dominic's own amusement, he spun us around five or six times instead of the two or three that the choreography required. I had to lose all control, yet at the same time I had to hold my body tight. When he put me down, I often forgot to give him my hand, and I was so dizzy, I could barely find a place on the wall to spot for my last two turns. Finally, I could try one of the lifts with Ryan.

I turned and whirled my outstretched leg toward Ryan as hard as I could. I felt the impact. Ryan stumbled a step backward, then wheezed, "I thought we were dancing, not trying to murder each other."

Dominic said, "Children, children. This is enough for today. You have enough material to work on. Before you leave, Ryan, pick up the mambo CDs at the front desk as your homework. You're both going to need help. Since you must not disgrace our studio, I'll get Nina to work with Charlie and Mateo to help you, Ryan."

"Ooooh, Mateo's going to be happy," said Nina. Ryan covered his eyes with his hand.

"Quiet," said Dominic. "You've made a good choice, Charlie."

"With what?" I asked.

Ryan rolled his eyes.

Dominic stepped in between us while Nina snickered. "I meant in your choice of partner, Charlie. He has a great deal of work to do, as do you, but you fit well together. Dance is about the architecture of the body, and a flexible mind and soul. People who are control freaks don't tend to be very good dancers. You must let go, allow yourself to feel and be honest. I think you both have that." He nodded slowly. "Yes, you are now a disaster together but you are a catastrophe with potential."

I smelled fresh incense in the apartment when I got home. That was unusual. Normally, Pa would light some for the altars in the morning but not so late in the day. Lisa was already asleep but tonight Pa was still up. Even with the Hunter issue behind us, she still wasn't improving. These days, she didn't want me to leave her alone. She said she was tired and didn't want to go to school. Despite all of my probing, she insisted there were no problems there. I thought that maybe she was already anticipating going to Hunter so much that she didn't care about her current school anymore but the truth was, I had no idea. Pa let her stay home a few times, but it didn't seem to make things better.

I went over to Lisa and rearranged her blanket. She had the scarf I'd made for her tucked underneath her chin. I looked up to find Pa watching the both of us, seeming so sad that my heart hurt for him. He had a little ceramic pot in his hand, the one that he boiled his medicines in.

"Was the Vision here?" I asked.

Slowly, he nodded. "She gave Lisa a charm. It's around her wrist."

I looked and there was a bead bracelet around Lisa's wrist, the same type that monks wore. You could buy them at the temple for a few dollars. I doubted the witch had been as inexpensive.

"Here is a bit of the strengthening medicine that Uncle Henry made for Lisa. I saved it for you."

"What is it?"

"Donkey umbilical cord with herbs."

I tried to keep my disgust from my expression. "Thanks so much, Pa, but I don't need it."

Pa stepped forward eagerly. "No, Charlie, you are working so hard and bringing home money for us. I only wish I could afford enough to get you a full dose of everything, instead of just the remains of what Lisa needs."

I realized he was feeling bad, guilty that he hadn't bought two donkey umbilical cords instead of one. "Pa, I really don't need it. And even with my salary, how are you managing to pay for the Vision and all of the medicine?"

"Let me worry about that. The health of my two girls is more important than anything."

I got up and hugged him awkwardly around the shoulder, being careful not to jostle his small pot. "You're a great father. I need to rest now. Good night."

"Are you sure about the medicine?"

"Yes, I'm really fine without it. It's too late for me to be hungry anyway. Don't waste it on me."

With a nod, he was gone.

That wasn't the first or last time I came home to the smell of fresh incense, meaning the witch had been present again. Lisa was sleeping with all sorts of new items. Once I found her with a red veil over her head, which was supposed to protect her from the evil spirits. All I could do was hope that it worked.

One night, as all of my fear welled up in me, I shut myself in the bathroom so I could call Zan on her mobile. Having only prepaid phones, we didn't talk or text too much because of the expense, but sometimes I just needed a friend. She sounded groggy when she answered. I apologized, then told her everything that had been happening to Lisa.

"Oh, Charlie, why didn't you tell me that she was getting worse?" Her voice was fearful. "I assumed it'd stopped after the test."

"I guess it seemed like it would make things too real if I talked about it. When I saw you, I wanted to think about other things. Zan, do you believe in all of that Chinese medicine?"

"I never thought about it. My mother would make me herbal teas and stuff whenever I was sick. I feel guilty when I eat a lot of yang foods—you know, too much fried stuff and so on. It's so much a part of our way of life, it's hard to separate it out."

"I know, I've always accepted it too. But it doesn't seem to be helping Lisa." My voice broke. "I'm at a loss."

"Mo Li."

"What?"

"You need to talk to Mo Li. She'll know what to do."

The next morning, when Mo Li answered her phone and heard it was me, she said, "What's wrong?" since I almost never called her.

I filled her in as quickly as I could.

"I can't believe there's something wrong with Lisa," she said. "I love that girl. She was always tagging along after us. I'm still trying to wrap my head around it. Listen, I don't know a lot about medicine or treatments."

"But you're smart. You study. And read."

"That counts for a lot less than you'd think. But if you're asking for my opinion about eastern versus western medicine, I'd say that both types can be effective. Many eastern remedies have the same drugs in them that western medicine does. It's just not quantified, so you don't know exactly how much or what is in everything. Treatments like acupuncture have been proven to work."

I heard the reservation in her voice. "But?"

"But the thing is that eastern medicine is still very much unknown. You have to trust the practitioner, believe that they know what they're doing."

"It's my own Uncle Henry. And the Vision."

"Well, you know how I feel about all of that mumbo jumbo. I can only tell you that if Lisa were my sister, I'd want to get her to a western specialist as well and hear what they thought."

"I've been thinking the same thing. But we're not insured."

"Of course not. I don't know, Charlie. I can just say that if you have a trustworthy practitioner, that's great. But if you don't, how would you know if they were a fraud or not?"

"Mo Li! You don't mean that."

"I'm simply trying to be scientific here. What you really need is to talk to a medical person."

I pressed my palm to my cheek. "You've given me an idea."

Seventeen

I waited anxiously until Jason and Naomi's next lesson. Jason was a neurologist. I couldn't remember exactly what Naomi did, but in any case, Jason was the one I wanted to consult. I learned a great deal just from chatting with my students as we went across the dance floor. Jason and Naomi were one of my favorite couples and they were so warm, I was sure they would do their best to help me. The moment they really stole my heart was when they were learning to tango.

"By day, I work at a hospital. But by night . . ." Jason waved his arm and suddenly a rose appeared in his hand, which he then tucked in between his teeth. The tango music rolled on. He pulled Naomi into a dip, then stood up, gave her the rose with a flourish. . . . "I am magic itself."

I clapped, delighted. "How did you do that?"

"I'm a magician. This door-to-door fire alarm salesman came by one day and did a few tricks while trying to sell us his alarms. I was hooked, then started hanging out at the magic shop. It's my hobby."

"He does shows in the evenings and weekends," Naomi said, very proud. "He has a partner who covers for him when he has to cancel at the last minute because of his hospital work."

"So you may have two students for life in us," Jason said. "As you can tell, I have a bit of a weakness for performing, and what better way to attract attention than by dancing up a storm with my lovely wife."

Now a waltz was playing, and since they hadn't learned how to travel around the room yet, they stayed in one corner and revolved like a merry-go-round. The other dancers steered around us. I thought about Pa and how grim and lonely his life was much of the time. He spent all of his time working and shunning everything outside of Chinatown. Jason and Naomi had two daughters as well, but if one of them had gotten sick, they wouldn't be dragging witches home, they would know what to do. Of course, it wasn't fair. Pa also worked day and night to earn what Jason probably made in an hour.

"Try an underarm turn," I said.

Jason lifted his arm and Naomi waltzed underneath. "It must have been hard when your kids were little," I said to her. "That Jason's job could involve so much last-minute work."

"Yes, but we're lucky that my work is fairly flexible." Naomi returned to dance position with him and they started revolving again.

"What do you do again?"

"I'm a psychiatrist."

I hesitated. I wanted to get back to Jason, but to be polite, I asked, "How does that actually work?"

"I basically try to treat people's mental problems. And my specialty is something that's even less well known, which is conversion disorder: people who develop physical problems because of a mental issue they have. Maybe you've heard of hysteria? That's what it used to be called."

"I think I remember a bit from school. Isn't that people making things up?"

"Oh no, it's very real. For example, you see people having actual seizures, only if you can manage to scan their brains at the same time, you find that there is a lack of neurological activity. People run the gamut of physical tests before turning to us. It drives the insurance companies crazy because it's expensive to do all of those medical tests, and nothing will help until the underlying psychological problem is treated. But we have to be sure there is no physical cause."

This was getting close to what I truly wanted to know. "Jason, how about trying a balance step now? Good." He stumbled, then recovered. "How does health insurance work anyway?" I tried to sound nonchalant. "If I were to want to get some, for example?"

"Well, luckily, you look young and healthy. It's not such a problem then to get a fairly inexpensive policy."

"What happens if someone already has a problem?" I asked, again still trying to seem as if I didn't really care.

He paused a moment, like he was trying to figure out how to say something difficult. "Insurance companies won't cover pre-existing conditions. They'll charge a hefty premium or put conditions on the payout. It's like someone trying to buy fire insurance while their house is burning down. Although the law is changing and it may soon be possible, the reality is that it's not right now."

I took the plunge. "I know an eleven-year-old girl. She's got headaches, dizziness, nightmares, wetting the bed at night, and the thing that really scared her family was she lost control of her legs for a minute or two."

He stopped dead. "That could be serious. You need to get her diagnosed. Sounds like she needs an MRI scan. There are so many reasons she could be having those symptoms. I'd need to see her first, see how much she can do, before I know which tests she'd need. Take a family history. There are so many different diseases it could be. You'd want to rule out a brain tumor or multiple sclerosis, which is often overlooked in children but can do very serious damage."

My stomach clenched so hard, I felt like doubling over. Lisa could have something very serious. This confirmed it. It was like the nightmare with Ma all over again. I tried to keep them talking and reverted to a standard combination. "All right, let's try two basic boxes, an underarm turn, two more basic boxes and then a balance step."

Jason blew his hair out of his eyes and started.

During his boxes, I said, "If she didn't or couldn't get insurance, about how much would it cost to get her diagnosed?

Jason completely forgot the combination and only did the basic box step while he answered me. I could tell from Naomi's smile that she noticed, but she didn't say anything. "I don't normally treat children so I'm not an expert on health laws concerning them. But if you're just asking about the fees, it's not just the cost of the consultation, which is usually at least around two hundred and fifty dollars, but you'd also need to cover any tests that needed to be done: MRI, EEG, CAT scan. It can all easily run into the thousands. But if you get her to me, I'll help you as much as I can. I give you my word."

Naomi nodded. "You can count on Jason."

Thousands? How could I ever get that much money? It made the Vision look cheap by comparison; no wonder Pa stuck with our own kind. But I could have kissed Jason for his kindness. "I appreciate that so much. Now try the combination and I won't distract you with more questions."

After they'd left, I found myself pacing around the reception area, unable to concentrate enough even to practice. Maybe Lisa had cancer. She could even die. My mind flinched away from the thought of a world without my little sister in it. I remembered a man who was one of Uncle Henry's patients in the brief period I worked there. He'd had a tumor on the skin of his shoulder and didn't have any insurance so he couldn't get it treated. The tumor was already huge by the time he came to Uncle Henry. One day, he'd run into the office with his shirt wet and bleeding, clutching a towel against it, because the tumor had burst. I didn't know what happened to him but I was pretty sure it wasn't anything good, and all because he wasn't insured.

Why was Pa wasting all of our money on Uncle Henry and the Vision? But deep inside, I knew the truth. Even if we'd saved everything he'd spent so far, we wouldn't have enough. At least I had Jason now, who would be able to narrow down the tests so we had a chance of affording the treatment. I wondered how much more I could start saving, how quickly I might have enough. It could take years.

Much as I enjoyed watching Mateo give Cuban motion lessons to Ryan, I was usually being taught by Nina at the same time. Now that all of the choreography had been set, Nina went over every bit of it with me, step by step. After Dominic finished teaching us the number, my head had been spinning. It was only for a few minutes of dance but the amount of information we had to remember was tremendous. For every second we danced, I had to make so many notes to myself: keep the shoulders down, neck long, arms out, turn the hips more to the side, arch the back, get ready for the next step. The mambo was beautiful: romantic, sexy and very difficult. But the lifts—which now included several different approaches as well as lifted turns—were a struggle.

Nina alternated between doing my part and Ryan's, depending on what I needed to work on, although she didn't lift me. At the beginning, she'd given me tips throughout the entire lesson but sometimes, like today, we started chatting while we practiced.

"So, you're never going to date again? Stay alone the rest of your life?" My voice was interrupted by my head whipping from side to side as she led me into a series of double-speed crossovers.

"What's wrong with that?"

We froze into a holding position for a few beats, both hands down while the music pulsed behind us.

"Look at me, I have a list of issues a mile long." Nina spun around and turned me at the same time so that we both did spiral turns, ending up side by side. On the beat, we began a series of forward walks parallel to each other, hips swiveling. "No regular guy's going to come near me. I'm a single mother, I'm constantly gnawing on something. If I ever got my hands on chewing tobacco, I'd probably be spitting it out on the ballroom floor. I'm the most man-like girl there is."

I laughed out loud. "Ridiculous. You're gorgeous. When I first met you, I couldn't stop staring at you because of the way you looked."

She made a face. "Come on. You were amazed by my sagging titties. Take a look." Nina stopped dancing and pulled down the elastic neckline of her peasant shirt, revealing her black lacy bra.

"Nina!" I looked around. Ryan and Mateo were now both staring at us. Even Dominic, Simone and Keith had stopped their coaching session to watch. Dominic made a little tsking motion with his hands at Nina, although he was smiling. "Can't you take a compliment?"

Mateo slapped Ryan on the side of his head and they started working again. It seemed like they were talking about positioning for lifts now, which looked pretty funny since Mateo found plenty of reasons for Ryan to be the girl so Mateo could put his hands all over him. Still, I had the feeling they were becoming friends.

Simone and Keith had already resumed their rumba. Sexy, restrained and elegant: it was the perfect dance for them and they already did it superbly. Dominic was walking around them, correcting Keith's arms. They didn't have any lifts but they had technique and style. The only flaw to me was that Simone always looked a bit too impeccable, as if she were posing for a camera. I preferred Nina, who danced with her heart and soul.

I practiced dancing whenever I was free, and when I couldn't do that, I worked on my body with stretches, sit-ups and push-ups. I was so grateful I no longer had to answer phones or use a computer or fill in agendas for other people. This was work I could do. I'd always been lean but my musculature became more defined. I became stronger and more flexible than I'd ever been, and I could feel the difference when I danced with Ryan. When it worked, it was like we were two halves of the same person. I felt free and strong, beautiful and courageous, capable of anything. I could lose myself in the dancing and know that he'd be there to catch me when I needed him.

Although Ryan and I sometimes argued, I had to respect him. We were both covered in sweat after one of our sessions, but he was the one who had to pick me up repeatedly. I felt guilty when I made a mistake and he'd have to do it again. My body wasn't always in the right place at the right time, I forgot to arch, I whacked him on the head with my arm but he never complained. He just accepted that it was his job to lift me in addition to his own dancing. His Cuban motion had improved, although it wasn't anything to write home about. At least his hips looked like they matched mine. And I appreciated that he always came on time and worked hard without complaining.

Now that it was April, Ryan's work days were becoming longer and sometimes he had to return to the landscaping firm after our lessons. He often came to the studio in his workman's pants and boots again, changing into regular shoes before he danced with me. I didn't tell him that I loved seeing him in his gardener's outfit. He always smelled of earth and greenery then, his body strong underneath the rough clothing.

One afternoon, I saw Ryan walk in behind me, reflected in the mirror. He was early today. He quietly sat down at one of the tables by the edge of the dance floor and I averted my eyes, pretending I hadn't seen him. I focused on myself in the mirror and whipped off a turn to the right, spotting myself. Good, now a single turn to the left. Both clean turns, now the double turns. I stared myself in the eyes and did a double to the right, then a double to the left. Great, now that we're warmed up, how about a triple to the right? One, two, three. Ryan just sat there and watched me with his intent gaze.

Irene interrupted us during our lesson. We were in the middle of a tango oversway where Ryan had just gone from a backward pivot turn to arching me back in his arms.

Irene tapped him on the shoulder. "There's a phone call for Charlie. The girl says it's an emergency."

When I gasped, I broke my position, which threw my entire body out of balance. I floundered.

"Whoa," said Ryan, steadying me. He put me back on my feet. "Take it—"

I'd already raced into the reception area to pick up the phone. The only person who knew I worked at the studio was Lisa.

"Charlie?" Her voice sounded much younger and higher on the phone.

"Are you all right?"

She started to sniff. "School was over and I didn't feel okay enough to go to Uncle's office. I'm sorry, Charlie. I just couldn't do it today."

"Are you sick? What happened?"

"I lost feeling in my legs again." Her voice was thin and scared. "The teacher became alarmed in science class but I told her I'd hurt my ankle. Then it went away and I could walk out, so I did. Please don't make me go to the office today, I feel too bad."

I didn't know what to do. Lisa's school was in Chinatown. It would be the smartest thing to make her go to Uncle's office but to tell them she couldn't work today. At least Uncle could make sure she was all right until Pa and I got home. I couldn't leave the studio with my entire schedule booked full, and Pa would get into trouble if he kept his kid at the restaurant.

"Lisa, you won't have to work today but I think you should go—"

"I'm downstairs."

I stopped. "From Uncle's office?"

"From yours."

I threw the handset back into the receiver and ran to the elevator. I jabbed at the elevator button. Luckily, the doors opened right away and it was empty. When the elevator opened on the ground floor, Lisa was standing there, cheeks wet from the rain and her tears, dragging her book bag on the floor. I hugged her and pulled her back into the elevator with me. Another woman entered with us.

I kept an arm around Lisa as I wiped her face. The woman standing across from us had sparkling high-heeled shoes sticking out of her smooth leather bag. Her silk scarf was tossed casually over her shoulder and I could see she was wearing a leotard underneath her spring coat. "I saw you dancing the other evening."

I remembered I was at work. "You must be a student."

Lisa peeked up but didn't say anything.

"I am. I've been training for years at another studio but just transferred here. I wanted to tell you, you were wonderful."

I was so startled that this elegant woman was complimenting me that I could barely stammer, "Thanks." I smoothed back Lisa's hair. When the elevator doors opened, I took her hand and led her into the studio.

Ryan was waiting for us in the reception area. I'd completely forgotten about him. "I'm sorry, I'll be right with you."

"No, it's all right. Let me guess, you guys are related, right?"

Lisa smiled up at him.

"You're so wet. Are you Charlie's sister?" It was Nina. "Let me take your coat and bag."

Irene said, "I'll make you something warm, dear. Would you like some tea or hot chocolate?"

Lisa said, "Hot chocolate, please." She whispered to me, "Does this mean I can stay?"

I was nodding when Dominic appeared in the doorway to the office behind the reception area. I froze. "I'm sorry, she has nowhere else to go today and—"

He stepped out. "What a lovely girl. Welcome to the studio."

I stared. I'd assumed that he would be angry my sister was interrupting my lesson. She'd always been thrown out of the restaurant when Mr. Hu saw her. "You don't mind?"

"Of course not. Your sister is welcome here as long as she wants to stay. Let her come every day." I remembered that in other countries, it was a tradition to teach ballroom to children from a young age. Dominic was used to having kids study at his studio. Lisa drew in a breath and raised shining eyes to me.

I wished so much I could say yes. Lisa saw my expression and her face fell. "I wish she could. She has a job after school."

She looked so forlorn.

Ryan said, "Do you want to see me throw someone around?" Lisa brightened up. She nodded. He took her delicate hand and went with her into the studio. The moment they passed the doors, he swooped her up and did a series of turns down the ballroom with her in his arms while she shrieked with laughter. When he put her down, he gave her a wink and said, "Now, I didn't say who I was going to do it to, did I?"

Lisa sat at one of the round tables, sipping a cup of hot chocolate and chatting with Nina as if she would never stop. I had phoned Uncle to tell him that Lisa had gone home sick to the apartment and I was accompanying her. If I didn't lie, he would insist on her coming back to his office. Although the studio closed at ten thirty p.m., Pa worked so late these days that I still always got home before him, so I knew we wouldn't be caught.

This was one of the days when I practiced the other dances with Ryan. He still needed to learn to be a good general dancer for Evelyn's wedding. Lisa saw us go from samba to tango to swing. At the end of his lesson, we did a part of our mambo for her. Her face was glowing with pride as she watched me. She didn't look jealous in the slightest.

"She's a great kid," Ryan said as he shrugged on his jacket. "Reminds me of Evelyn, only less annoying."

Lisa was fussed over by everyone, even Simone. I found Lisa in the teachers' room after my last lesson, snuggled up next to Simone while Simone let her try on her collection of rhinestone jewelry. "A bit of sparkle on your upper arm will show off your muscle tone. However, never put something tight around your wrist onstage."

"Why not?" asked Lisa. I wondered myself.

"Because that's the most delicate part of your arm. You don't want to obscure it. A loose bracelet would be all right." Simone made a science out of being beautiful.

"We have to go now," I said to Lisa. "I don't have a nine thirty lesson, so Dominic said I could leave early to take you home."

"I want to stay."

"I know, but you've got school tomorrow."

I gathered our things, changed into my outdoor clothing and shoes, and left with her as she waved good-bye to all of her new friends. On the subway, Lisa snuggled up to my shoulder and fell asleep. She slept like a baby that entire night.

The next day, Nina convinced me to take my food and eat with her in a small park near the studio. It was becoming just warm enough for us to have lunch outside. There was a guy sitting a few benches away from us, fiddling with his nose.

"He's snorting coke," Nina said, unwrapping her meatball sandwich.

I glanced over, trying to be subtle. "How do you know?"

"Because I've got loads of personal experience. I've done way worse than coffee and cigarettes."

"Really?" I'd never tried anything. Although I'd seen other kids doing drugs at dances and parties sometimes, I knew better than to get involved.

"I was young and crazy before I got knocked up. I'd go down Avenue D in a miniskirt at three a.m., trying to score some coke. That's the ugly side to this business, Charlie, you have to watch out for it."

"What do you mean?"

"The drugs, the sex, the romance trap."

"I haven't really seen much of any of that."

"Because our studio's pretty clean, and you haven't been to one of the large competitions yet. Those huge hotels, everyone's there—students, pros, judges. It's insane. Lots of people stay out of it but some of us dancers can get caught up in drugs because we need the energy. The job is so grueling sometimes, especially at the competitions where you're doing event after event with the students, and then you have your own shows with your professional partner too. You're nervous, you're tired, it's important that you dance well. Drugs can seem to be the solution."

"Okay, but what do you mean by the romance trap?" I thought about Julian and Ryan, and how I felt while dancing with them.

"The whole idea that you'll find your perfect ballroom partner and you'll live happily ever after. It's so easy to fall for it. I sure did. The entire system sets you up for it."

I finally dared to ask what I'd always wondered about her. "What happened to you? With your partner and the baby?"

Nina swallowed the food in her mouth and took a slug of her soda. "I started dancing with Brian, Sammy's dad, and we fell in love. We drank, did drugs together, woke up in the morning for rehearsal, danced at the same studio all day, then did it all again. I got pregnant by accident, and Brian proposed."

I understood now. "That's why you kept the baby."

"When I got pregnant, he was really happy at first, and after I got over the shock of it, I was too. Believe me, I cleaned up my act right away, but then we discovered that we got along better stoned than sober." She grimaced. "So there I was, getting huger every day, and of course the studio owners noticed. I was working at the downtown studio then. It wasn't like here. They kicked me out as soon as I started showing. It was all so stressful. Anyway, Brian bailed on me when I was six months pregnant. There was another girl in Florida, a dancer of course. He was afraid. I don't think he's a bad guy." Tears glistened in her eyes. "Hell, I was scared too. But I couldn't run away and he could. If I were him, I don't know, maybe I would have done the same thing. Not saying it's right, just that I get it."

"That must have been so hard."

She nodded. "But Sammy woke me up. Thank goodness my parents helped us out. I knew I had to get myself together. It changed the way I thought about myself. You know, not like I'm all that, but guys always liked me. Then there I was, twenty pounds overweight and a single mom. I wanted to be a lot of things when I grew up, but never a mother. Someday, I thought, or maybe never. I didn't worry too much about that kind of thing. After Sammy was born, I made the rounds at the studios and no one wanted me back. I think rumors about the drugs had gone around, and I was a single mother on top of it. If it weren't for Adrienne and Dominic, I don't want to think where I'd be now."

She gazed me and her eyes were intense. "You're going to come across all of that stuff too, Charlie. I'm telling you, don't screw up. Be careful with the men and the drugs, respect your body. I've been there. I was dancing with Brian, acting like he was the love of my life onstage, and it was so tempting to believe it was all real when it wasn't."

Eighteen

My mambo with Ryan was more intimate than any dancing we'd ever done together before. There was one move where I did a reverse turn in his arms, then he went into a squat so I could lie down across his thighs, arching back until my head was close to the floor. He scooped me up with his arm so I could tuck myself into the right side of his body as he stood up and spun us both. It felt like he was cradling me, as if nothing could hurt me while I was with him. I knew from the texture of his cheek if he'd shaved early or late in the day. When he tried a new brand of cologne, I noticed right away. It was strange to know so intimately the body of a man I'd never kissed. It got to the point where I'd sense he was in the studio the moment he entered, even if I couldn't see him. It was the way the doors shut, the shadow of his reflection in the mirror. I began to understand what Nina had been warning me about.

Then Adrienne returned to the studio. The first time I saw her, I gaped and she started laughing. "I almost forgot. You've never known me when I wasn't pregnant."

"You look incredible. It's only been a couple of months." Adrienne was lean and fit, standing there in a blazer over tailored slacks.

"Do you know why actresses get back into shape so fast after a pregnancy? Because they have to. It's their job to look a certain way. If they don't, people will take photos of them and post them all over the Internet. I'm a dancer and coach. It's my business to get back into shape because my body is my instrument."

"You make it sound easy."

"It's not. The baby's crying all night long. I still get up at five a.m. and get on the exercise bike. I used a treadmill when I was younger but now my knees and ankles are shot after all those years of hard dancing in heels." Then she considered me. I was wearing one of her dresses, fit tight around the bust and hips, flaring out as the royal blue material went past my hips. "You've come far, Charlie. I'm proud of you. So when your competition student comes in, I want you to show me your routine. I've heard a lot about the two of you."

Adrienne watched Ryan and me run through our choreography from beginning to end in the small private ballroom. We were awkward in a few parts, but on the whole, I was glad we'd managed to get through it all.

"Very impressive." She frowned, as if she were trying to put her finger on something. "The two of you have a freshness that more jaded dancers lack. Use it. When you dance, I sense the energy in the movement, which is fantastic. I know you're trying to incorporate all of the technical aspects of the dance at the same time, but what an audience really wants is to be carried away by the emotion between the two of you. In other words, we must feel your desire for each other." Both Ryan and I stared hard at the floor, avoiding each other's eyes. Adrienne ignored us, taking on her lecture voice. "Remember, desire is also a form of friendship, acceptance and connection. If you don't feel it, then you must fake it. Welcome to the world of show business."

A few days later, Adrienne approached us as I was chatting with Nina, waiting beside Ryan, who was putting on his newly purchased Latin dance shoes. "You're ready to be tortured."

"What do you mean?" It seemed to me I'd suffered plenty already. My shoes were as full of holes as Nina's.

"You need to videotape yourselves."

Nina drew in a quick breath. "No."

Ryan shrugged. "Seems like a good idea to me."

Nina said, "That's because you've never watched yourself on video. Every dancer wants to kill herself after seeing herself on film. It's a known thing. Don't do it to them, Adrienne. You'll destroy their sensitive little souls."

Adrienne smiled. "It will hurt, I won't lie, but the pain of seeing yourself will be an impetus for great improvement."

Ryan and I exchanged glances. I took a breath. "Do it."

Nina whispered, "You'll be sorry . . ."

Adrienne used Ryan's phone and taped our entire routine. It seemed to me that it had gone well but that was before I watched it.

Ryan and I sat on the floor, huddled against the wall in the small ballroom, watching the video together. When it was done, we were silent. I glanced over at him. His face was gray. I felt like I wanted to cry.

I whispered, "It's my dinner break now. Are you free?"

He slanted me a look. "Yeah."

"Wait for me at the Chinese restaurant on Lexington Avenue, okay?" Since I never actually ate out, it was the only place I remembered off the top of my head. I always noticed it when I went by. Today, I felt like I needed to do something nice for myself.

"The one on the corner?"

"I'll meet you there in a few minutes. You leave now so it looks like we separated."

When I stepped into the restaurant, he had gotten a table for us. The place was deserted, except for one other couple in the corner.

He squinted up at me. "I've never seen anything more awful than myself on video.'"

I burst into laughter. "Did you see my shoulders, raised all the way up to my ears? And I'm supposed to be the professional."

"I like your shoulders. You looked great."

The waitress came to our table with the menus. She was Chinese, with her hair pulled back neatly from a plain face. I felt like a foreigner, sitting there with a white guy, wearing my ballroom clothing. The menu was long and complicated. I was tired, and as always, it cost me so much effort to read at all. The words blurred into a soup of letters.

I closed my eyes. "Do you mind if I just do it?"

"Go for it. I eat everything."

I quickly ordered in Chinese. My Chinese wasn't great but after all of those years in the noodle restaurant, I could order fluently.

"That was impressive," he said.

I breathed in the faint smell of grease and steam in the air. "I used to work somewhere like this, only less upscale."

The waitress came with our drinks and all of the food I'd ordered. She placed fried rice and noodles on the table as side dishes. Ryan's eyes lit up at the sliced beef with red pepper, green scallions, ginger and watercress. I could smell the jumbo shrimp and a vegetable dish with snow peas, baby corn, Chinese cabbage and bamboo shoots.

I'd automatically chosen chopsticks. Ryan had done the same. He dropped his napkin and stuck his chopsticks into his mound of rice while he retrieved it. Then he saw my face. "What's wrong?"

"I'm sorry." I reached over, plucked his chopsticks out and set them on the table. "You can't do that. It's how we place chopsticks when we do rituals for the dead and it's considered very bad luck."

"And here I thought I was pretty good too. What else do I need to know?"

"Do you really care?"

"Sure. I mean, if I come to dinner at your house sometime, I'd hate to embarrass myself, right?"

I stared at him a moment.

He rubbed his chin, not meeting my eyes. "You wanted me to help your friend learn to drive in my car, right? That was what you wanted from our bargain. She probably uses chopsticks, I could look dumb. Umm, never mind."

I took pity on him. "Okay. Chopsticks are really important to us because they have to do with food and rice, which is essential to our survival. Your chopsticks are like two lovers. They always need to be together, side by side. We never use only one chopstick for anything. Never tap with your chopsticks on the side of your bowl, because that's what beggars do and it's bad luck too. Never gesture toward someone with them or wave them, again, that's impolite. Don't chew on them, that's unhygienic. Never dig for your food with chopsticks because it looks like you're digging a grave and it's bad luck as well."

"Whew. Lots of bad luck here. Okay, let me give it all a try."

He did pretty well and I felt better after I'd eaten.

Ryan was surveying the restaurant. "They thought about feng shui before they designed this place. Those two Imperial guardian lions they placed at the front door—they're needed because of the bank across the street, right? Though I don't fully understand why."

I was amazed. "Yes, because a bank is so powerful, the restaurant is afraid it'll absorb all of the good qi. The lions counteract that stream. I'm surprised you saw that." Many Chinese establishments took feng shui seriously, and they often consulted a feng shui master before making any architectural and design decisions. I'd grown up with that concept of balancing the energies within a space for good fortune, but I hadn't expected anyone non-Chinese to notice.

"We often need to take feng shui into account when we design for some of our clients, whether they're Asian or not."

"Do you do any of the actual planning?"

"Some." He took a sip of his soda. "I'd like to do more. I've been thinking about going back to school to get a degree in landscape architecture. Fiona's always pushing me to do it. But I'm not sure."

"Why not?"

"I love the work, you know? I love being outside, my hands in the soil, creating something beautiful out of the earth. I love know-ing that living things will thrive where I place them. Like Evelyn, Fiona thinks I'm crazy for not calling myself a landscaper, but for me, being a gardener is the best part of the job. I wouldn't want to move too far from that."

I thought about what I'd been through in the past months. "I understand that fear of losing yourself, of changing faster than is comfortable. But in the end, your soul's in your own hands, isn't it? No one can make you into someone you're not, no matter what your title is. It's about becoming your true self."

He gave me a crooked smile. "You're quite something, Charlie. What about you? Do you have a boyfriend who wants you to become a studio owner or something?"

I laughed. "Oh no, being a dancer and a teacher is more than I'd ever dreamed of. That's hard enough."

Ryan tapped his finger against the table. "The thing is, I've been looking at Mateo and Keith and all those guys, and I somehow had the idea that when I was watching them, I was seeing myself. But that wasn't true at all."

"Yes, that's exactly it." I chewed on a snow pea. "Everyone around us is so good and then you watch yourself on video and suddenly you realize how far you still have to go. I guess that's why Nina said not to do it."

He chuckled. "I didn't see anything wrong with the way you looked."

"I didn't notice you doing so badly either."

He reached out with his finger and brushed it across my face. "Eyelash on your cheek."

My skin tingled where he had touched me. I gestured to the waitress for the check. "I'd better be getting back."

I found I couldn't stop thinking about Ryan after that. When he came in for his lesson the next day, I was aware of every step he took. We were attracted to each other, but like Nina said, that could just be the chemistry of dancing together. He had a girlfriend, and I couldn't imagine bringing a white guy home to Pa. Pa could barely accept the idea of me with a Chinese man I'd known my entire life, like Winston. Plus there was the strict studio policy against fraternizing with the students. I could lose my job like Estella had. There were so many reasons Ryan was wrong for me, but when he held me in dance position, he felt just right.

A few days later, Lisa fell from a rope she was climbing in gym class. Although the school nurse could find no sign of an injury, Lisa had a lot of trouble walking after that. Aunt Monica picked her up and brought her to their office. I only heard about it when I got home from work.

Lisa's legs started to fail at irregular intervals, and she sometimes needed a cane to go to school. She told the school she'd hurt herself in a fall. Her symptoms terrified me. She also didn't want to work at Uncle's office anymore. Uncle Henry and Aunt Monica asked her to go there after school anyway, just so they could make sure she was all right.

Lisa said, "I have so much homework now and the office is very busy. I'm sure my legs will get better at home. I'm just over-tired."

Pa said, "I don't like you being in the apartment alone."

"I'm almost twelve years old. And there are so many germs at the office. All of those patients. Maybe I caught something from them."

I said, "You never know. She's been working there the whole time she's been having these problems."

Pa considered. "All right, we'll try letting Lisa come home after school."

"Yippee!" Lisa hugged Pa, then came over and wrapped her arms around me too. "Thank you, Charlie."

I held her tight. "Whatever is going on with you, we are going to figure it out and fix it. I promise."

"However," Pa said, as we both turned to him, "I want Uncle Henry to start working on a treatment plan for her."

At the next tai chi lesson, I hung around Godmother's qigong group, hoping to learn something. Pa was absolutely against letting anyone outside of our immediate family know about Lisa's problems. He was afraid of how Chinatown gossip could destroy people's reputations, but I trusted Godmother, and I knew that after Lisa's incident at school, her symptoms would soon be public knowledge anyway.

Godmother beamed. "Are you finally going to join us for qigong work, Charlie?"

I shook my head. I'd come a long way but I still wasn't ready. "I'd like to ask you about healing after the class if you have time."

She nodded, then returned to her talk of meridians and organs.

After the other students had gone, Godmother approached me. "You seem worried."

"I am." I took a breath, then told her everything that had been happening with Lisa.

Godmother listened, her eyes intent. Then she put her hand on my arm and said simply, "Bring me to her."

Both Pa and Lisa were home when Godmother and I entered our apartment. Pa came up to us with his hands outstretched. "Godmother Yuan, what an honor. I apologize, we were not expecting you. Our home is a mess."

"Nonsense." Godmother went up to Lisa, who had been reading a book. She took Lisa's hands in both of hers.

"Godmother," said Lisa in a small voice.

Godmother said to Pa, "May I?"

When he looked questioningly at me, I said, "I told her." Pa frowned. To him, I had aired our dirty laundry in public, but he also knew Godmother was considered a great *sifu*. Slowly, he nodded.

"Just lie down and stretch out on the couch," Godmother said to Lisa while she sat on the coffee table. "Relax. Do not worry about a thing. I am not even going to touch you. I am just going to try to understand what is happening."

With a glance at me, Lisa lay down warily.

Godmother closed her eyes and suspended her right hand about a foot above Lisa's face. Godmother's fingers began to vibrate. Then she brought her left hand next to her right and allowed both to travel slowly above the length of Lisa's body. Lisa shivered. Godmother's hands reached Lisa's toes, then circled upward again, drawing loop after loop over Lisa's body.

Lisa sat up abruptly, coughing. "That felt so weird."

"That's a good sign," Godmother said. "Negative energy usually leaves via the mouth."

Pa said, "*Sifu*, what did you find?"

"There is a great deal of blockage in her body but I cannot determine the source. I tried to shift some of it. One of the problems is that she is not trained. She has never done tai chi or qigong, correct?"

I nodded. "Very little. But you can heal people who have never trained."

"I can try. It's harder."

I was starting to feel desperate. "I think we should bring her to a western doctor."

Godmother said, "The problem with western medicine is that they look only at the manifestation of the symptoms. For a western doctor, physical pain and emotion are unrelated. They require separate specialists, different treatments. But to the Chinese, physical pain and emotions are two sides of the same coin. You cannot heal the body without healing the soul as well."

Pa said, "Lisa is being treated by eastern medicine."

Godmother raised her eyebrows. "But never forget that in eastern medicine, there can be a tremendous amount of bullshit."

Lisa giggled.

"See, she is better already," Godmother said. "I will return but I am not certain of how much I can do for her."

In the course of the following week, news of Lisa's fall had indeed spread. Neighbors, friends and acquaintances rallied to give us helpful advice on how to strengthen her legs. The hairdresser Mrs. Tam brought us packages of a tea she swore had cured her sister's bad knees. Mrs. Lee told Pa that she'd recently sworn off carbohydrates and it had helped her general health tremendously. Pa was laughing when he told us this story because then he'd reminded her that she was going to put him, a noodle master, out of business with her low-carb talk, and she'd turned beet red. Mrs. Yuan, Grace's mother, was convinced we needed to eliminate all sugar from Lisa's diet. Meanwhile, Winston had started showing up at the apartment as well. He'd come by twice, ostensibly to ask about Lisa's welfare. The first time, Pa was alone at home, and the second, I was just heading to the studio. I hoped he understood from the way I'd hurried off that there was no hope for the two of us.

I watched Julian coaching Simone and Keith in their routine together. It was May, so we still had a few months until the competition, but they were already fantastic. That number was romantic, fast-paced, technically and artistically demanding, and had been choreographed by Julian himself. Of course, it also didn't hurt to have Julian so invested in them since he was the head judge for this scholarship. Ryan and I didn't have the kind of money to hire him, but Keith did.

It didn't seem fair to me to have the head adjudicator coach the people he'd be judging, but Katerina told me, "The ballroom world is so small at the top. Everyone is trained by the same handful of coaches, who are also the people asked to judge competitions. If they were not allowed to judge the people they'd coached, everybody would be out of work."

Ryan and I were now painfully aware of what we'd been doing wrong, and I'd been throwing myself into my dancing, trying to forget everything that was happening at home. Ryan had improved tremendously as well.

As I was correcting Ryan's arm position after a turn, Julian's reflection appeared beside us in the mirror. "Ah, Charlie. My favorite dancer with potential." Julian took my hand and held me at a distance to examine me. "Absolutely beautiful." I flushed with pleasure, then he turned to Ryan. "So this is your competition student. Hmmm. Why don't you show me what you've been doing?"

I knew what an honor it was for Julian to take an interest in us, and for free. Simone stared at us as we left for the small ballroom. When I glanced back at Ryan, he looked a bit annoyed, focused on the hand Julian had laid on the small of my back to escort me into the separate room. I put on our music. Ryan seemed to grit his teeth and we did the routine from beginning to end.

"Lovely, Charlie." Julian turned to Ryan. "You need some work." But instead of giving Ryan any tips, he held out his arms to me.

Julian had only seen us do our choreography once, but he took me through the entire number. His hands were gentle yet firm, and with a minimum of pressure, I felt exactly where I needed to be and where he wanted me to go. When he brought me up into the final overhead lift, the one that still gave Ryan and me problems, it was effortless. Julian was far stronger than he looked. After he put me down and we finished our final series of turns, I felt myself glowing from the exhilaration of dancing with him.

Ryan was leaning a shoulder against the mirrored wall, his arms folded. "Isn't that impressive."

Julian ignored him and gave us both a few general tips, which Ryan responded to with guttural noises. When Julian was about to leave, he kissed my hand and held it clasped in both of his. "I am glad I discovered you."

I couldn't help blushing a bit. "Julian, I'm so grateful to you for everything."

Behind us, Ryan sighed loudly.

Julian turned and said, "Best of luck to you with your charming partner. May you endeavor to deserve her." Then he left the small ballroom.

The moment the door shut behind him, I said, "Are you okay?"

"I don't like the way he looks at you, that's all," Ryan muttered. "He's got the hots for you."

I blew a strand of hair off of my face. "Oh, I wish. There are girls lining up to be Julian's chosen one, why in the world would he pick me?"

"Lining up, huh? He's not all that."

I remembered what Nina had said. "If a dancer's with Julian, she becomes a star, so there are enough women after him. But he wasn't that nice to you, and I'm sorry about that. Still, please try to get along with him the next time you see him because he's judging our event, will you? Julian feels nothing special for me, he's like that with any woman. It's in his job description."

Ryan said, "Yeah, right."

Nineteen

I t was time for Ryan to fulfill his part of our agreement. Zan had been so excited when I told her. She and I took the subway into Brooklyn to meet him at his apartment, a fourth-floor walk-up in a nice residential area.

When Ryan opened the door, I glimpsed a jungle of greenery behind him. "Hey, come on in." His feet were bare beneath his simple cotton pants and T-shirt.

There were masses of plants everywhere in his large studio. His bed was just a mattress on the floor, like mine, although his apartment was much more spacious. The mattress was covered by a red blanket, with a low shelf next to it, filled with worn books. He'd built a tall arched trellis over the bed, the kind you see in gardens, and it was surrounded by several pots of ivy that grew upward, interweaving through the slats. When he was lying down, he'd be able to look up at the leaves and trailing tendrils forming an archway of green above the mattress.

His windowsills held a system of artificial lights shining upon an array of dazzling orchids. The blooms weren't orderly, like the new ones I'd seen in flower shop windows. His orchids were in various stages of flowering, with long and branching spikes: some bore tight purplish buds, some were barren. They'd been cared for and survived, veterans that had bloomed time and time again.

I gestured at the orchids and raised my eyebrows.

He shrugged. "They're my favorite flowers. You guys want a drink?"

"Just some water, please," I said as Zan shook her head.

While Ryan was busy in the kitchen area, I kept pulling my eyes away from that bed, lying in the middle of his room like an open heart. I glanced at Zan, who was fidgeting with her fingers. I was pretty sure she hadn't been in a strange man's bedroom like this before.

A long-haired orange cat with a white ruff wandered out from behind a pot of ferns. I bent down and extended my hand. It waddled over and sniffed.

"That's Sushi." Ryan handed me my glass. "I've been telling him he needs to get into shape but he doesn't listen."

Sushi rubbed himself against my legs as I sipped the water. "So why do you like orchids so much?"

"They're so strong and resilient if you treat them right. They'll bloom repeatedly for you."

"I always thought they were too exotic to be good houseplants. Too difficult."

"In the wrong environment, the most beautiful orchid is like a weed. A weed's nothing more than an unwanted plant."

We piled into Ryan's car, which he'd parked on the street, and he drove us to the middle of a fairly empty parking lot. I noticed a van with the words "Patrick's Landscaping" on it. "Is that yours?"

"Belongs to the boss. I didn't have time to get it back to the company lot last night. He doesn't mind, though."

Zan was staring at the van with longing. "Can we drive that one?"

Ryan chuckled. "Why don't we start with something a bit smaller?"

His dark green car was fairly new. He let Zan sit in the driver's seat while I stayed in the backseat. She glanced at me and I could tell she was about to burst. She bounced up and down a few times.

Ryan slid into the passenger seat next to Zan, then turned to say to me, "You can get out now if you want. You sure you want to risk your life?"

"That's what friends are for." I rolled down the window and felt the sunshine on my face.

He asked Zan, "So what do you know about driving a car?"

"Everything," she said.

"Good. Ever driven one before?"

"No. But I read about it."

"Right. So first you have to—"

Zan reached out and adjusted the mirrors.

Ryan blinked. "Good. Do you know where the controls are?"

She pointed. "Steering wheel, controls for the lights. Brake. Accelerator pedal. Gear selector lever. Has park, drive, neutral and reverse settings."

"You sure you've never driven before? What do you do for a living?"

"I run an egg cakes cart. Can't drive it. No motor."

Ryan and I both laughed. Then Zan revved up the engine and we were off with a jerk.

Zan made a few rounds of the parking lot, then took off for the streets. She was a natural. There were a few close calls because she tended to drive too fast, but Ryan had his hand on the steering wheel and managed to bring us back on track. By the time we got out of the car, she and Ryan were chatting like old friends.

I gave her a big hug. "You were amazing!"

She tipped her head back and turned her face to the sky. "I drove!" Then she remembered Ryan. "Thank you. If you ever want any free egg cakes, just come to Canal Street."

Ryan grinned. "I'll remember that. I taught my sister and a couple of friends to drive but I've never seen anyone learn that fast."

"It's because I want it more," Zan said.

We said good-bye to Ryan and headed toward the subway station.

"I like your guy," she said, slinging her arm around my shoulder.

I shook my head and sighed. "He's not mine."

I needed a dance costume and competition shoes since my Latin shoes were riddled with holes. I didn't mind wearing them at the studio but I couldn't use them while performing so I had to order a new pair, which I would save for competitions. I was sitting in the teachers' room with Nina and Katerina, trying to figure out what I should do.

"How much does a ballroom costume cost?" I asked Nina.

"Roughly between five hundred and five thousand dollars. Some can be even more, cheap ones cost less, but the wrong dress can hurt you on the floor."

I drew in my breath sharply. "Maybe I should just go buy a bikini somewhere. How do you manage it?"

Katerina answered, "It's really hard. You're lucky you're doing Latin."

"Why?"

She looked at me like it was obvious. "No feathers, of course. The smooth dresses cost a fortune because of all the stones, sequins and ostrich feathers lining the hem of the dress. Latin is less material."

I was going through some of the costumes hanging from the rack in the teachers' room. "Much less. There's almost no material at all." I studied one red-and-black number. It was so brief that I couldn't figure out which part of the body it could possibly cover. "I'm not sure I can wear something like this."

Nina said, "Why not? You got it, flaunt it. At least you don't have my saggy boobs."

"Stop it with your boobs. I can't wear this because it'll slip off and I'll be naked in front of a thousand people."

Katerina said, "That happened to a friend of mine. No problem, you just keep on dancing. They've seen it before."

"No, thanks."

Nina said, "She must have put it on wrong. The costumes are made to stay put. Even if they look like they're barely hanging on to your skin, they shouldn't budge."

"What I do," said Katerina, "is I make them myself. The most work is the stones."

"Can you design dresses?" Maybe there was hope for me.

"She made this one," said Nina, pulling out a large sleeveless jade green dress. It was much more modest than the others, looking more like a cocktail dress than swimwear. It shone with rhinestones around the neckline and had a ruffled hem.

I took it and held it up in front of me. It was too big but I enjoyed the way the fabric felt against my legs. "I like that. Whose is it?"

"Designed it for a student. She is probably seventy years old. She's picking it up tomorrow," Katerina said.

"Could you make one like it for me?"

Katerina evaluated me. "Sure, but you could wear something much sexier. It'll also be cheaper if you apply the stones yourself."

"This style is good for me."

"You'd need another color," Nina said. "You can't wear green. You'll look like a frog."

"How about a bright robin's-egg blue?" Katerina said. "It would look great with her skin and hair."

"Yes, that would do," said Nina. "I'll show you where you can buy the fabric and get the best stones on the Lower East Side."

I had trained my body, but it seemed my hands were still as clumsy as ever. I worked on my dress in the teachers' room when I could.

"Isn't glue faster?" I was so tired and my fingers bled from all of the times I pricked myself. I could hardly hold the needle anymore. I had completed so little of the dress after hours of work. Often I placed the stones in the wrong place and had to tear them out and sew them in again.

"Yes," said Katerina, "but I have been watching you. You are not a person who should use glue. Trust me. Needle and thread, when you make a mistake, you can undo it. If you do something wrong with glue, you will smear the fabric and it will look horrible. You'll ruin your dress."

I shut up and went back to sewing. It was painstaking work, finishing the dress stone by stone, but when I was finally done, it glittered and shone. I'd panicked at home one day when I saw one

[283]

of my rhinestones glittering on our vinyl floor and quickly stepped on it before Pa could notice.

Uncle Henry had come up with a treatment plan for Lisa and today was the first session. She begged me to accompany her to the procedure. I canceled all of my evening students and left the studio at the dinner break to meet her at Uncle's office, where she was waiting for me downstairs.

"It'll be all right," I said. "You'll see."

Lisa's face was drawn. "Sometimes I feel like I'm the older sister. No matter how hard you try to be tough enough for this world, you're a romantic at heart, Charlie."

"And what are you?"

"A realist."

I stroked her arm. "It's not going to be that bad. Come on, let's go upstairs."

Her legs seemed worse and I let her lean on me until we got to Uncle's office. In addition to Uncle Henry and Dennis, both the Vision of the Left Eye and Todd were in the waiting room; so they were pulling out the big guns. The Vision saw us and sniffed. I guessed she still wasn't happy with me. Todd gave me his easy smile and I noticed a number of paper shopping bags at his feet.

As we greeted each other, I heard the Vision say to Lisa, "It was your birthday recently. Did you wash your hair on that day?"

I knew what was coming. Pa didn't want us to wash our hair on birthdays or holidays because it was supposed to bring bad luck.

"No, I didn't." Lisa was telling the truth. She tried to please Pa when she could.

"That is correct." The witch turned to me. "But you did."

How had she known? "I can't remember," I lied. With my job, I had to shower every day. Dancing was physical and I was constantly close to the students, but in my defense, I washed my hair on my own birthday too.

"You must be more careful of your sister." Then the Vision addressed Uncle Henry. "We may proceed."

"What are you going to do?" I asked. Lisa's hand was trembling and I clasped mine around it.

"A moxibustion procedure," said Uncle. I knew what that was. Acupuncture needles were inserted into the skin. Then the herb mugwort was burned near the needles to enhance their effect. "The Vision will pray for her at the same time, also exorcising any spirits."

I shuddered at the thought of a malignant soul preying upon Lisa.

"Which type of moxibustion shall we perform?" Dennis asked. There were several levels of intensity, which ranged from uncomfortable to severely painful.

Uncle smiled at Dennis. "What would you do?"

Dennis didn't hesitate. "Given the severity of the situation, the best would be direct scarring moxibustion."

I heard Lisa's gasp of fear as I pulled her behind me. "Absolutely not." With this type of moxibustion, a small cone of mugwort was placed on the skin at an acupuncture point and burned until the skin blistered. The skin scarred after it healed.

Uncle Henry was shaking his head as well, looking a bit surprised.

Dennis said, "Of course, that may not be necessary. A less invasive procedure might be adequate as well. We wouldn't want Lisa to be uncomfortable."

The Vision said, "Her father has given permission to do whatever we need. We mustn't hold back just because of a young girl's squeamishness."

I said, "But no one knows if this will work or not. You say I'm hurting my sister because I wash my hair on her birthday and then you want to scar her?"

Uncle Henry said, "Don't worry, Dennis was just making a suggestion. I don't think there's any need to go so far. We can do repeated treatments of the milder sort instead. But she will need to return more often."

I took a deep breath and turned to Lisa. "What do you say?"

"I want you to come in with me." She darted a glance at Uncle and the Vision, avoiding Dennis's eyes.

"Not possible," said the Vision. "The room is too small. Dennis is needed to assist the doctor with the burning of the mugwort, I'll be there to drive the evil spirits away, and there is no space for anyone else."

"It would be a danger to Lisa," Uncle Henry said. "You know that, Charlie. We are only trying to help her. We will do acupuncture with nonscarring moxibustion. I am also her family. I would never hurt her."

Lisa was looking at me pleadingly.

"The door stays open," I said. "I'll be in the hallway."

Uncle Henry sighed. "We'll do it your way this time, Charlie, but you cannot be so difficult or we will never get your sister healed."

Todd followed me out to the hallway and we leaned against the wall. Through the open door, I could see the Vision undressing Lisa down to her underwear, then having her lie face down on the examination table. While Dennis held her steady, Uncle Henry took a thin acupuncture needle and attached a ball of spongy mugwort to the top of it. Slowly, he inserted the needle into Lisa's calf. I saw her tense. I clenched my fists as well.

The Vision closed her eyes, starting to invoke the gods and spirits. "Come cleanse this girl. Purify her and remove all that is tainted."

To my surprise, I felt Todd wrap his hand around my left fist. "Gentle. You're going to need that hand."

I looked at him with some irritation. He was jittering his leg up and down, and it was distracting. "What?"

"Forgive yourself, forgive the hand."

"All right, Todd." Sometimes I thought Todd wasn't completely right in the head. No one normal would work for the witch anyway. I turned my attention back to Lisa and winced to see Uncle inserting needles all along her legs and spine. I didn't have a view of Lisa's face from where I was but her body was rigid. Then I smelled the sweet smoke as Uncle and Dennis started to light the mugwort. If any of it fell onto Lisa's skin, it would burn her and be almost impossible to remove because of the density of the needles. After allowing the mugwort to burn for some time, Uncle and Dennis blew out the fire. They removed the needles and Lisa was allowed to get dressed again.

"That wasn't too bad, was it?" said Uncle Henry to Lisa.

She didn't meet his eyes. "I want to go now."

"She's going to have to come back," Uncle Henry said. "I'll make the appointments with your pa."

The next week, I thought up an exercise program for Lisa. I would start by getting her to stand for a few minutes to strengthen her legs, and before we knew it, she would be back to her old self again. At the beginning, she had only lost control over her legs for short, discrete periods, but now it seemed they were just weakening in general. The school nurse checked her again but didn't find anything unusual. Lisa needed the cane most of the time these days, but still Pa asked me not to accompany her to her second session with Uncle Henry on Saturday. He'd heard I'd been difficult the first time.

When Lisa returned from the session, the skin on her face lay pale and worn, like the surface of an empty plastic bag. She looked thin and hunched over. The weather was finally warm—spring had arrived—and she was wearing a long skirt.

"Let me see." I flipped her skirt up over her bare legs.

Lisa leapt back in her chair. "Don't touch me!"

I held up my hands. I'd never seen Lisa react like this. "I only want to make sure they didn't scar you."

"They didn't," she said bitterly.

"Are you sure?"

"Yes. Get away from me."

Lisa was just upset after her session. I would have been too. I wished we didn't have to do this now but the weekends were the only time we had together. I placed an aluminum walker that I'd borrowed from Godmother Yuan in front of Lisa's chair. Godmother still had it from when she needed one after her fall last year.

"Are you sure about this?" Pa looked worried.

"It's good for kids to exercise, right?"

He didn't seem convinced but he didn't say anything else.

I placed Lisa's small hands on the bars of the walker. We hauled her upright so that she was standing. I timed it with a stopwatch in my left hand.

Almost immediately, Pa said to Lisa, "Are you tired? Do you want to sit?"

Lisa looked straight ahead, swaying slightly on her skinny legs.

I pressed my lips into a thin line. "Pa!"

He ignored me, only focusing on Lisa. "I think she wants to sit."

"She'll be all right a little longer," I said.

Lisa said, "Just because you think you're the expert in everything these days doesn't mean you're always right, Charlie."

I bit back an angry retort. Finally, when Lisa got tired, she whimpered. Her legs began to buckle and we let her sit. I wrote down the date and time in a little pad.

I started exercising Lisa every weekend.

"You're being too hard on her," Pa would say to me. I felt as though I were holding both him and Lisa upright. There were days when she would resist us angrily, dragging her weight back into the chair and dropping her hands from the walker. Sometimes, it was as though she wasn't present at all. I was always exhausted afterward.

After two weeks, Lisa could stand for a longer amount of time. But her eyes were still hopeless.

"I want to take Lisa to a neurologist," I said.

Pa was outraged. He slammed his hand down on the rounded edge of the kitchen sink. "No, no," he yelled, slapping with each "no." "No! She's just a child, leave her alone."

I tried to speak in a reasonable voice. "We have to find out what's wrong, Pa."

"Uncle is helping her," he said, turning his back to me. "He said she's coming along well. She just needs a few more sessions."

"Pa, Uncle doesn't see every—"

He put his hands over his ears. "You're trying to kill me." He turned on both taps full blast and bent over the sink. The conversation was over.

———

"Just a little longer," I said quietly.

Lisa kept trying to sit down. Her face crumpled up like a little child's and she began to cry, not even trying to hide it. She made small whimpering sobs and her cheeks glistened with tears.

We let her sit down.

"Oh dear heart." Pa wiped her eyes with his white handkerchief. I couldn't watch.

That night, as I lay on my mattress, I felt Lisa's anguish rip through me. It was as though each sob tore into the soft flesh on the inside of my chest. I longed for Ryan's arms around me, to hold and comfort me. And then I turned away and I was crying, stifling my sobs so she wouldn't hear.

A few days later, Ryan and I were in the small ballroom, practicing the overhead lift again. We were now able to get through it without someone spotting us. I'd done this lift easily with Julian, but Julian was in a class by himself. I had to run to Ryan and jump, then he held me by the hips and lifted me straight into the air while I arched backward. It was terrifying because I was so high, probably eight or nine feet up, in a position where I couldn't do anything to save myself if he dropped me or I lost my balance.

Today, for some reason, I glanced down in the middle of the lift. I could see the top of his tousled hair, the highlights gleaming in them, and then all was lost. I pitched forward and Ryan threw himself underneath me so that I wouldn't get hurt when I landed. We wound up in an undignified heap on the floor.

He lay there beneath me, unmoving. I was terrified he'd hit his head on his way down. "Ryan! Are you all right?" I felt his neck, trying to figure out where his pulse was. That was when I realized his eyes were open, and he was laughing silently. "What?"

"That's your idea of first aid? Strangling me?"

I leapt off of him. "Very funny."

"You almost killed us both, and you're mad at me."

"You're right." I reached out a hand to help him up. "I'm sorry. I just lost my concentration."

"I was watching you in the mirror. Why were you looking at my hair in the middle of our most dangerous lift? Do I have dandruff?"

The truth popped out before I could stop myself. "You have these pretty bronze highlights."

His expression became this complicated blend of embarrassment, irritation and satisfaction. Then he said, "Let's move onto the next part."

That was the body ripple. With his body covering mine, one arm wrapped around my stomach, my right hand in his left, my other arm behind his head, we undulated together before I twirled out into the whip turn. At the beginning, we had been out of sync, so that his chest was moving upward while mine was going down, and his hips were done before mine got started. But now we had it perfectly synchronized. We were supposed to look sexy during the move, which meant he bent down so I had my head against his jaw, my face partially turned to his, as if we were about to kiss.

I tried to take the step into my turn but found I couldn't move. Instead, Ryan tugged on my hand until I'd turned around and was wrapped in his arms. His eyes were closed and he was rubbing his cheek against mine as he bent me backward over his arm.

"Would you still rather dance with Keith than with me?" he whispered against my ear.

I felt hot, as if my veins were filled with wine. "Maybe not."

As he turned his head, I felt his breath fall upon my lips, and I forced myself to say, "We can't."

"It's all right, I'm faking my desire," he murmured.

I smiled despite myself. Then he kissed me. His taste, his smell, I'd waited so long for this. I lost myself in that kiss, my hands entwining in his hair before I remembered where we were, and what would happen if someone walked in on us. And Fiona, and Pa. Ryan was just reacting to touching my body, while I was in danger of losing my heart and soul. I drew back, my lips throbbing.

He cupped his hand to the nape of my neck. "I'm not sorry I kissed you." He bent in to kiss me one more time and I let him before I pushed gently against his chest. Slowly, he pulled back and let me up. He held my face with his hand and let his finger brush against my jaw. I felt his hand tremble. Then he dropped it and turned away.

I busied myself collecting our CD from the stereo. "Lesson over." My voice was hoarse. The door quietly opened and shut, and then he was gone.

Ryan canceled all the rest of our lessons that week. I didn't know what it meant or what to do. Was he ever going to come back? What would I do if he didn't? Walking in the park in the June sunshine with Nina a few days later, I spotted a gardener tending the flowers and my heartache must have shown on my face.

Nina said, "Are you all right?"

I ran my hand through my hair, then told her about Ryan and the kiss.

"I knew it." She was speaking quickly, frightened for me. "If you get involved with him, not only will they fire you but no other studio in New York will touch you. You'll be blacklisted. No one wants a pro who sleeps with the students. It's bad for business."

I pressed my lips together and shivered despite the sunlight on my face. "I don't want to go back to my old life. If Ryan leaves, I don't have a partner, and if I get involved with him, I won't have a job. I have nothing." I felt the dread deep in my stomach.

"No, you'll always own something that no one can take away. Even if you were faced with losing your job, you'd keep the knowledge in your body, your passion for movement, your understanding of its power. That's yours."

I kicked at the dirt on the ground. "I'm so confused." She was talking about career and love of dance, and I shared that, but mostly all I could think about now was Ryan. "Sometimes I think he cares about me a little. But it'd be such a shock to my father, I'd feel so guilty about dating a non-Chinese guy. And the worst thing is, he's got a girlfriend . . ." My voice trailed off.

Nina turned her face away.

"I know it's bad."

"Yes, it is. Charlie, you shouldn't even be thinking about him in that way. He's a student. I'm so sorry, honey, but it doesn't matter about him and the girlfriend. He's bad for you. You remember what happened to Estella. I heard they've broken up by now. You have such a bright future ahead of you as a dancer and a teacher. Go find yourself a nice professional man to play with. Listen to Doctor Nina here. Get this student out of your system."

I rubbed my eyes. "I'm finished with him as soon as the competition is done. I'll turn him over to another teacher."

After my talk with Nina, I was resolved to break things off with Ryan. I didn't want to call Ryan from the studio, just in case we got into personal territory. I copied down his mobile number from his file and then waited until the next day, Saturday, to phone him. I wanted some privacy.

It rang a few times and then his deep voice answered. "Ryan Collins."

"Ryan, it's me."

He immediately knew who I was. His voice gentled. "Hi."

I made my tone very businesslike. "You didn't come in last week. I wanted to make sure you were all right."

He coughed. "Umm. Yeah. I'm fine. Just a bit of the flu." Like I was born yesterday.

"Feeling better now?"

"Yeah."

I cut to the chase. "Are you going to bail on me and the competition?"

There was a silence. "No. I'm in until then."

"Me too." I forced myself to say it. "After that, it might be better for you to go to another teacher."

There was another pause, then his voice sounded strained. "I'll be done with dancing by then. I'll be ready for the wedding. That was the goal, wasn't it?"

My entire chest ached. "Okay, well . . . thank you for staying with me through the competition."

"Listen, should we just get the rest of our bargain over with? There's a party uptown tonight."

I wasn't sure I'd heard him correctly. "After what happened?"

"I want to take you, all right? I missed seeing you this week."

Despite all of my resolutions, I felt myself soften. I kept my tone cool. "I promised, didn't I? What do you require from me?"

"Bring shoes you can dance in. And wear something sexy, will you?"

Twenty

I lied to Pa again and told him I would be going to a birthday party at a colleague's house in Far Rockaway, which was hours away from Chinatown by subway. I said it'd last until late. I wondered if this dynamic of our relationship would ever change or if I would be deceiving him until I was old and he was gone.

As I knew he would, Pa said, "But it'll take you so long to get home."

"Don't worry, Pa, I'll be all right."

"No, I don't want you coming back that late alone. Is your friend a woman?"

"Yes."

"Can you stay at her house?" As he fell into my trap, I felt the guilt rush over me.

"Probably, I'll call her and see."

He was relieved when I told him that I would be allowed to stay over at my fictional female friend's house. I could then sneak in after he was asleep and say that I'd returned much earlier. Otherwise he'd wait up for me. Lisa knew me well enough to understand I was lying but she didn't say anything.

I tried to decide what to wear. Although Adrienne's cast-offs had greatly helped my dance wardrobe, I hadn't bought much new clothing for wearing outside of the studio. And as Pa and Lisa were home, watching our little television, I had to look like my old self when I left. In the end, there was nothing for me to do but wear Adrienne's clothes underneath and my old clothing on top, even though it was already mid-June and quite hot.

I snuck into the bathroom and put on a miniskirt and a tight gold cropped top, daring for me since it bared my stomach. Over that, I threw on a long flowered dress of Aunt Monica's. The only shoes I could really walk in were my clunky dishwasher shoes. I peeked out and Pa and Lisa both still seemed to be staring at the television, although I didn't think they were really watching it. I didn't want to risk wearing too much makeup in front of Pa, so I put on just a minimal amount before slipping out.

Outside, I hurried past the Canal Street jewelry stores, their displays glittering with pure gold, which Chinese believed warded off evil. Though it was evening, the streets were still packed. Our plan was to meet at the subway station, but my heart skipped a beat when I saw Ryan leaning against the pole, silhouetted against the setting sun. He was in my neighborhood. It was as if he could be a part of my real life.

I approached him and his face lit up. "Charlie, you look beautiful." He'd never said anything like this to me before.

I had to laugh. "Are you serious? You asked me to wear something sexy and I have this on." I gestured at my long dress and dishwasher shoes.

He shrugged. "I guess it feels like a long time since I last saw you."

I fiddled with the handle of my bag. Should I mention our kiss? It probably wasn't even a big deal to him. "Are we okay?"

"No, I'm not, anyway. What about you?"

I raised my eyes to his. "How's Fiona?"

"Charlie, I've known her forever . . ."

"It's fine, I understand." I bit my lip.

"And what about Julian?"

"That's hardly comparable."

He ran his hand over his face. "He's an open door. All you need to do is walk through it. And you feel something for him too. I can see it when you dance together. I hate to say it but he'd be right for you in all the ways I'm not."

Now he was trying to set me up with Julian. How much could my heart hurt? I looked away. "Can we talk about something else?"

"You can get fired just for seeing me tonight. I don't know, I'm so confused." He hugged me from behind and then, so lightly that I wasn't sure if I'd imagined it or not, he kissed my hair.

I closed my eyes and gathered myself, then turned around. "No more of that."

He backed away, holding his hands up. "All right. Friends?"

Slowly I nodded.

It was a long ride all the way uptown. Ryan was leaning back next to me with his eyes closed, the curve of his neck and jaw revealed above his T-shirt. How strange to be sitting there with him, not rehearsing. It was hard to be heard above the noise of the subway. "Where are we going, anyway?"

"Some friend of Felipe's is giving a party. A whole bunch of people will be there."

"Are they your friends too?"

"Nah. You might meet some of the kids I coach, see some street dancing too."

I was excited for this, even apart from being with Ryan. I'd never been to this part of the city, but even more, I'd never been to a party where the social capital was dance. I wondered what Mo Li would think—to her, it'd be an investigation, an exercise in self-broadening. I just couldn't wait for the music, and the space and freedom to move. I knew I wasn't supposed to, but I tucked my arm underneath his and leaned my head against his shoulder. The subway rocked us back and forth. He felt so comfortable, his body familiar. His arm was covered in downy hair, his shirt soft against my cheek. "Ryan?"

"Mmmm?"

"I wish you were a girl."

I shut my eyes and didn't hear his answer. The next thing I knew, he was telling me that it was time to get off the train.

But then, as soon as we emerged from the subway station, my happy excitement drained away. The sidewalk was dark, lit only by street lamps, and in front of me, a pyramid of black garbage bags was stacked high next to a bus stop. We headed up a street that was deserted except for a few homeless people who were talking to themselves, huddled against the buildings.

"Do me a favor and take my arm, will you?" Ryan said.

We rounded a corner and saw a group of young Latin men, hanging on the street. One was sitting on a fire hydrant, a few were leaning against the buildings, but most of them were huddled around one guy in a dark T-shirt. I grabbed Ryan's arm and tried to redirect him. I didn't want to make any sound that would alert them to our presence, but he kept moving forward as if he hadn't seen anything.

"Ryan!" I hissed.

"It's all right." By now, they had seen us and everyone was giving us the once-over. I felt panicked. I kept walking with Ryan, hoping they'd let us through. The man with the dark T-shirt held up both his arms. Ryan released me and strode up to him. I couldn't breathe.

"Hey, man." They hugged while I exhaled heavily. Ryan said something to the man in Spanish, to my surprise, and then everyone turned to me. The man Ryan had embraced was looking at me with curiosity, then he extended his hand. "I'm Felipe."

I shook with him. "Charlie."

The entire group gathered around us as we started walking.

When Ryan threaded my arm through his again, I whispered, "I'm a little nervous here."

"You're fine. You're with me."

"When did you learn Spanish?"

Ryan shrugged. "You know, boxing, my job. Lots of the guys speak Spanish. They tell me my accent's awful."

Felipe joined us and said, "My mom misses you. She says you have to come over for dinner soon."

"Yeah, I will. She still worried about you?"

"Every day I hear, 'Felipe, when you going to stop that boxing? A few more fights, you'll be in a wheelchair. You're gonna get Parkinson's.'"

"She's right. Wise woman. You should stop getting your butt kicked."

"I'll kick your butt. How's Evelyn?"

"Great. You coming to the wedding? It's next month."

"Got my tux ready. Just need to find a date." Felipe glanced at me and winked. I noticed he didn't mention Fiona: code of honor among men. I already knew she'd be back for the wedding.

Meanwhile, even though I was holding on to Ryan tightly, all of the men around us were eyeing me. This was something new. For the first time, I was grateful for my sixty-year-old-lady outfit. We halted so someone could get a light for a cigarette, and to my surprise, the young guy walking next to me dropped onto the concrete sidewalk and started doing a rapid series of push-ups. Then he popped up and strode along with the rest of us again.

Ryan bent down and murmured, "I think he likes you."

I ignored him and said to Felipe, "So, tell me about how you and Ryan met."

"We met at the mecca of all boxing gyms in Brooklyn and spent our teenage years trying to knock each other out. Just about every serious fighter winds up there. Then we started hanging out in each other's houses and neighborhoods too."

Ryan said, "I'll never forget how that place smelled. No AC, if you slipped on all the sweat, you just went down on those concrete floors. Weights held together by duct tape. But it wasn't for show. People were polite and respectful and no one cared how much you could bench. It was about doing the work. But boy, could those trainers break your back."

I looked at him a minute, picturing him in that world. He could feel my eyes on him and turned to me. "What?"

I shook my head. "It's just—you've got this whole macho boxing past. But then you have an apartment filled with orchids and a fluffy fat cat."

Felipe whooped with laughter. "She's seen your green thumb, eh?"

Ryan smiled. "I'm a very peaceful guy. I just had a bit of anger to work out in my adolescence, that's all."

Felipe snorted. "A bit of anger. Don't let him fool you, this guy's got some serious talent. I have the dents in my head to show for it."

We finally arrived at a large apartment building. Even from the outside, we could hear the music blasting from the top floor. Mambo. We all trailed in. Ryan, Felipe, me and a couple of the other guys fit into the rickety elevator. The rest disappeared into the stairwell. When we stepped out, the hallway was dank and smelled like cabbage. My heart was still pounding hard. Then Felipe banged on the door and we went into the apartment.

Inside, the music was so loud, my eardrums began to ache. I could smell marijuana and a more bitter stench, like kerosene, although I knew it had to be something else. The apartment was filled with young Latin men. Most of them were sitting on the floor against the wall. There were only a few old armchairs and little tables scattered across the room. Small groups huddled by the tables. I followed the guys into the kitchen, which was crowded with bottles of liquor. Felipe turned to me. He was a bit shorter than Ryan, and moved with compact efficiency. Since it was too loud to speak, he made a drinking gesture to ask me what I wanted.

I shrugged. He held up a bottle of Coke and pointed to some rum. I nodded. While he was making my drink, a girl with long dark hair and a prominent Greek nose stepped into the kitchen. I was relieved not to be the only woman there. She smiled at me, then made a smoking gesture with her hand, pretending to bring it up to her lips. She was offering me something other than cigarettes. I smiled as I shook my head, then noticed Ryan in front of me, holding both of our drinks.

Together, we squeezed our way out to the living area, where we settled into a spot on the floor. Ryan leaned back in his cutoff

T-shirt and jeans. I wrapped my long dress around my legs, feeling safer in it, even though it was very hot in the room. I saw to my relief that there were a few other women scattered throughout the crowd. Still, we were vastly outnumbered. I started to feel disoriented. What was I doing here? The other girls were so secure, smiling and flirting with the men, and I was just out of my depth. Ryan put his arm around me as he handed me my drink. I felt a bit better. It'd been made with a lot of ice and tasted delicious.

Most of the other guys had stripped down to their undershirts. The windows were wide open and a light breeze blew through. A lot of people were smoking, cigarette butts littered the floor. I scanned the room and noticed a table ringed with people. Ryan got up, strode over to a muscled young teenager who was hanging around there, and whacked him on the back of his neck. The boy grinned as he shuffled away.

Then Ryan returned and yelled something into my ear. ". . . outa here?"

I nodded. We squeezed our way through the crowd until we were out of the apartment. Were we leaving? But instead of taking me back to the elevator, Ryan guided me to a ladder leading up to the roof.

Since it was a bit quieter in the hallway, I asked, "What was at that table and who was the guy?"

"Cocaine. He's one of the kids I coach, that idiot."

I emerged into a fresh night filled with stars and moonlight. The roof was huge and flat, with occasional pipes and cables cutting across the chimneys. The building was much taller than the ones I was used to in Chinatown and we were so high up that we had a great view of the streets. A lot of people were sitting on the tar, leaning against the high ridge at the edge of the roof. Someone had brought up a boom box and the music was blasting here as well. In the middle, a space had been left for dancing. I was delighted. I'd never been on our roof at home and I was sure no one danced Latin there in the night. When we found a clear spot, Ryan brushed some cigarette butts away with his foot and we sat down.

One couple was doing salsa, the street version of mambo. Although it was night, there was enough reflected light from the buildings all around us that I could see fairly well. She had on a bright yellow flouncy skirt that flew as she turned. They were pretty good, fast and on the beat, only with a limited repertoire of steps. They did some moves I'd never seen before. Soon another couple had joined them, and another, until all of the girls on the roof were dancing with someone, and the other guys watched with longing eyes.

A wide hand appeared in front of my face. It was Felipe, asking me to dance. I glanced at Ryan, who was watching me with a neutral expression. I felt nervous dancing here, in front of all these people I didn't know, but at the same time, my limbs were buzzing with the desire to join in.

I took Felipe's hand, then stood up. I had to get rid of the old lady dress or I'd trip in it. First I kicked off the dishwasher shoes. I retrieved my old Magic-Markered pumps from my bag and slipped them on. I was good enough to dance in them now and I didn't want to destroy my dance shoes. Felipe nodded approvingly. I felt awkward as I pulled the huge flowered dress over my head, showing the more revealing outfit underneath. A breeze brushed my bare midriff below the tight gold top. Everyone seemed to be watching me. I stole a glance at Ryan. His jaw was slack as I dumped my excess clothing and stepped onto the floor with Felipe, who was now grinning broadly.

As soon as we started to move, I relaxed. Felipe was a phenomenal street dancer and kept us right in time to the music, his hands firm yet gentle. He led me into combinations I'd never seen before, although I recognized some of the elements. He threw my hand up, caught it, then twisted us so that both of us were dancing in parallel with our arms interlinked. He untangled us, spun me out and caught me again. It was exhilarating. I never had any idea what was coming next, yet we always stayed in sync. Then there was a tap on my shoulder and it was Ryan.

I saw the surprise on Felipe's face. He stepped a few feet away from us to watch as Ryan took me into dance position and we started to move. Ryan wound me in, then gave me a push on my shoulder blade to spin me out. I did one and a half turns to return to facing him. Then he picked me up and tossed me onto his shoulder, where I perched for a moment before dropping onto his side, where he spun us both around and around. It was thrilling to just let go and dance, without anyone telling me about my arms, my legs or my head. I hadn't had so much fun since that night at Decadence with Zan and Mo Li. I was free and joyful, powerful and sexy. I loved moving together with Ryan, we were a unit yet we each had our own roles. I felt as if I had left my body behind and Ryan and I simply were the dance.

Everyone had cleared the dance area and was watching us, drumming on the roof in time to the music. Ryan nodded at me and we started running through our choreographed routine from the beginning, going from lift to lift as if we'd been dancing together our entire lives. When Ryan brought me up into the overhead lift, people started to cheer. It was dizzying, being up in his arms, high against the stars. We did the final turns that ended the number, and finally Ryan bowed as I curtseyed. There was a moment of silence before the crowd applauded, then Felipe came over with a huge smile and gave Ryan a high five.

Then I felt someone nudge my arm and realized this time it was the girl from the kitchen who wanted to dance with me. Ryan smiled as he stepped aside. She started moving in front of me, expecting just to dance facing each other, but then I took her into dance position and began to lead her. She beamed. Her body was strong, and when she turned, droplets of sweat flew off her hair. We did a few basics, then side breaks and underarm turns. She didn't know any steps but was a natural turner. I spun her for a triple, then dropped underneath my own arm for a double myself. When our dance was over, she leaned over and kissed me on the cheek before walking away.

I returned to the spot on the roof where Ryan and I had been sitting and was immediately surrounded by other men who wanted to dance with me. How things had changed. I kept shaking my head with a smile until Ryan found me and wrapped his arms around me. They stayed away after that.

We sat on the rooftop together watching the dancing, with me resting my head against his chest. What a different world I had lived in. It wasn't only that I used to have a different job, I'd been another person, and now, dancing had freed me. It felt like a hallucination—the music, the night air, Ryan by my side. I sighed and closed my eyes with the city twirling its skirt of lights around me.

Hours later, Ryan and I stood outside looking for a taxi. Felipe had accompanied us to help. Even though it was now quiet, my hearing was still dulled from the hours of music. Felipe and I stood on the sidewalk while Ryan stepped into the middle of the avenue, trying to flag down a cab. None rode by.

"You were incredible," Felipe said with his light accent. "When I first saw you with Ryan, I didn't understand, but now I do."

He thought I was the new girlfriend. "Oh no, he's still with Fiona."

Felipe's bushy eyebrows shot up. "You know her name."

"Of course I do. Ryan wouldn't hide her from me." I couldn't stop myself from asking, "So, what's she like?"

"Great woman. A bit bossy, but you know, that's life. Very pretty."

I blinked and stared at the pavement.

"I've hurt you. I'm sorry."

Was I that transparent? Apparently. "No," I lied, then added, "We're not involved. We only dance together."

"How interesting." Felipe bent over and slowly kissed me once on my left cheek, then on my right. He smelled like rum and smoke. For the third kiss, I felt his lips a hair away from mine when he suddenly wasn't there anymore.

"What the fuck are you doing?" Ryan was still holding on to Felipe's T-shirt. He'd just yanked him off of me.

"She's not your girlfriend," Felipe said. "She just told me."

"She's my partner so stay the hell away from her." Both men had squared off, facing each other. I stepped in between them and pushed them away with one hand on their rib cages.

"It's late and we're all tired," I said. When they didn't seem to be listening, I pounded on both of their chests with my fists. "Stop it!"

Ryan looked down at me and started to chuckle. "Only you would get in between two boxers. You have no sense."

Felipe began to grin as well. "I didn't know you felt that way about her, brother." He walloped Ryan on his shoulder, leaned down and mock-whispered to me, "Never got that reaction from him before."

I said, "If you guys aren't going to tear each other's throats out, how about I try to get a taxi?"

"Go ahead," said Ryan, "But nothing's around for miles."

I stepped out onto the street. Behind me I could see Felipe had his arm wrapped around Ryan and was whispering something to him, gesturing toward me while he did it. I raised my arm and a cab pulled out of the shadows, coasting to a stop in front of us.

Ryan stared. "How did you do that?"

"I think they were afraid of you. I'm a woman. Get in."

I waved good-bye to Felipe as we drove off and he blew me a kiss.

"What did he say to you?" I asked, leaning back against the vinyl of the seat.

"Some crap about how great you are. I think he was still hoping to get your number. I hate that guy."

I smiled in the darkness. "I liked him."

"I've never seen Felipe so surprised. It was all worth it."

"I'm glad," I said softly. "So did you spend your whole youth sitting through those parties, unable to dance with anyone?"

"That about sums it up."

We were quiet. However wonderful this night had been, it was the end of something. We'd completed our deal. He was committed to Fiona, I was committed to not losing my job, and Pa wanted me to find a nice Chinese man, a Dennis or Winston. I sighed.

"You sound sad." The lights from the street slid across his face.

"I guess I am."

I felt his hand on the side of my neck, pulling me toward him. "Don't be," he said.

I gazed up at him. "Ryan, we can't do this."

He closed his eyes and swallowed. "I know. Come on, just pretend I'm a girl."

I sighed as I rested my head against his shoulder.

When we stopped near my apartment, I pulled out my wallet but he waved it away. As I opened the car door, he caught my hand. There was something open and pleading in his eyes. I touched his cheek for a moment, then I pulled away and stepped out of the taxi.

Twenty-One

There were only about ten days left before Lisa's school went on vacation for the summer and I had an appointment to see Mr. Song again. I wasn't sure there was anything he could do to help Lisa, but I had to try. Through his window, I could see the hot blustery weather outside. It was drizzling.

Mr. Song was wearing a pale blue shirt with no tie. He shook my hand vigorously. "I was just thrilled to hear that Lisa will be going to Hunter, although we will miss her here, of course."

"We're very grateful to you."

"Oh, that's nothing. What can I do for you today?"

I chewed on the inside of my cheek. "The thing is, we're worried about Lisa." I made myself explain to him about Lisa's symptoms, that she hadn't actually fallen as she'd told the school, but we didn't know why she was becoming so weak.

He looked concerned. "Some of her teachers have noticed a change in her but we assumed it was the combination of the physical injury and her leaving our school soon. Many kids start to mentally check out when they know they'll be going someplace else next year, but it's much more worrisome if there was no physical injury to begin with." Mr. Song got up and started rifling through his file cabinet. He pulled out a number of forms. "If you can get your physician and father to sign these, the school nurse will be able to begin constructing a health plan for Lisa. It'll allow the nurse to communicate directly with your medical practitioner and then she can pass the information on to the right person at Hunter. The only problem is that we're approaching the end of the school year so we'll need the forms quickly."

"We don't have a family doctor." Uncle Henry had always taken care of us, despite his lack of a medical degree, and we'd gone to a public clinic for standard vaccinations. "My father is pretty resistant to western medicine."

Mr. Song frowned and said, "That's unfortunate," which made me defensive.

"It's because when my mother died, the medical bills were astronomical. We don't have any health insurance."

"But times are different now. Recent changes in the law don't allow insurance companies to deny children under nineteen coverage on the basis of a pre-existing condition." He'd lost me. He must have seen the confusion on my face because he explained, "It used to be that if Lisa did have a condition, the insurance company could refuse to cover her, but now they can't do that anymore. She could get free or low-cost health insurance."

I'd had no idea. I felt torn between fear at the thought of Lisa with a disease and elation at the possibility of providing health insurance for her. "What would we have to do?"

"I'll give you the right forms. The main thing is for your father to sign them. If the parent refuses to diagnose or treat the child, then we enter into a gray area of ethics. Usually, unless actual threat to the child's life can be proven, the school's hands are tied."

"I don't know if I can convince Pa."

"I'd be glad to come by and talk to him."

Pa was so intimidated by school officials, I didn't think he would hear anything Mr. Song had to say. "I'm afraid that might do more harm than good."

Mr. Song scribbled something down on a business card and passed it to me. "That's my personal cell phone. If you think there's any chance I could do anything, day or night, just give me a ring."

"Thank you. It helps just to know you're out there."

I couldn't wait to talk to Pa about Lisa and her insurance, but I didn't want to barge into the noodle restaurant again. This was too important. I needed to keep my head level. I'd talk to him tonight or maybe even tomorrow morning, when we were both calm and rested.

When I got to work, Simone wasn't there. As Adrienne started the Monday meeting, she said, "I'm sorry to have to tell you that Simone is in the hospital. She won't be coming back to the studio due to some personal problems."

"What?!" Mateo exclaimed. "Is she all right?"

Nina looked sad. She knows something, I thought.

"She is fine now." Dominic continued, "She has had some health issues and we must respect her privacy. She sends all of you her love. We will miss her greatly and wish her the best. We'll also need to redistribute her students and will be speaking to you individually as soon as we've made our decisions. For starters, Nina, since you're our remaining competitive Latin dancer, we are hoping that you'll take Simone's place with Keith in the competition."

Nina glanced at me. I gulped. The last thing I wanted was to have to compete against her. I closed my eyes for a moment. I knew that whatever happened, we'd be friends first and competitors second. When I met her eyes, I managed to smile. She relaxed, then said, "Sure."

It had never occurred to me that Simone would leave. In the locker room, the teachers were abuzz, but I noticed again that Nina kept silent.

Katerina said, "Why would she go?"

Mateo said, "Sweetheart, those wet eyes of hers, the acne, the way she was so jittery. The nasal spray?"

When Katerina still looked blank, he said, "Cocaine. And probably a whole load of other stuff too."

I talked to Nina alone as soon as we were both free. "You knew about Simone and the drugs." It wasn't a question.

Nina nodded. "Simone and I worked together at my old studio in the East Village. We used to be pretty tight, then I had to stay away from her for my own health because she was still using."

"But why did she do it? She seemed to have everything."

"Simone had a hard upbringing. I think she was sexually abused. She even worked in a strip club for a while."

I gasped.

Nina wasn't meeting my eyes. "I was embarrassed to tell you this before, but when the dance studios wouldn't hire me back, I auditioned at a club to be a cocktail waitress too. I had a baby at home. It was so gross. I was still me and, God help me, I thought about taking the easy way out. Simone told me about it because she knew I was hard up. They're not allowed to touch the waitresses at that place and it'd be a couple of hundred a night. I'd be able to clear out my bills, take care of Sammy, help out my folks. So it sounded okay to me, you know?"

"Did you go through with it?"

"Well no, because I bombed the audition. The guy just looked at me for a long time at first. I guess I passed that part, because then he asked me three questions. First: 'Do you do drugs?' I'd stopped so I could say no. Second, 'Do you have a boyfriend?' I didn't like that because it sounded like he was hitting on me but I thought, 'Hey, I can handle guys,' so I said no. Last one wasn't really a question. He said, 'Take off your shirt.' I asked him why and he said the management wanted to know. I got it."

I stared at her blankly. "I don't."

"The management was planning to have sex with me. They probably did all of the new girls and he needed to check me out first. I told that guy to screw himself and walked out. I have to live up to my little dude. I need to be a mommy that will make him proud when he grows up."

"I can't believe Simone went through that."

"Like I said, the childhood stuff will mess you up. Her dad died when she was young and I think her stepdad . . . Well, all of her relationships with men were crazy. It was like she had no boundaries left."

I thought of Ryan, who'd also lost his father. Nina had just shared so much with me and I trusted her too. I blurted, "I went to a party with Ryan this weekend. I really like him, Nina."

But her reaction was less forgiving than I'd hoped. "Charlie." Her face was stern. "Listen to me. I've been through it. You're dancing with him. He's your partner. You rely on him, he counts on you. It's so easy to fall under the spell, but is it real? And what about being a dancer and a teacher?"

I pressed my lips together. "I know all those things and yet I still want to be with him."

"Everyone wants to be with their partners. Take the energy and use it on the dance floor. Don't make that leap and then regret it the rest of your life, like me."

I braced myself to see Ryan again after our date in Spanish Harlem. Now that it was summer, he came to the studio fairly late in the evenings because he basically worked until the sunlight was gone. This was one of the busiest times of the year for him, yet he was still making time for our lessons.

Following everything that had happened and my latest conversation with Nina, I had once again resolved to be absolutely professional with him from now on, but the moment he stepped into the studio in his big boots and gardener's outfit, I melted.

I stood by him as he bent to change into the dance shoes he'd bought. "Do you think anyone on earth has wider feet than you do?"

"I often think they're like two loaves of bread." Then he peeked at me through his hair, which had fallen into his eyes. "Sometimes I worry I might embarrass you when I come in straight from work. Not the kind of clothing Keith would wear."

"No." I cleared my throat. "I'm proud you're my student. Come on, let's get started."

It felt better than right to dance with Ryan again, but I blocked any other thoughts from my mind and heart. He must have decided to do the same, because he didn't bring up anything personal again. I told myself it was better this way.

Pa wasn't home yet when I got back from the studio that night. I decided to wait until the next morning, when we both wouldn't be exhausted.

At the breakfast table, Lisa poked at her steamed bun. Pa was praying long and hard at Ma's altar. I knew he hoped her spirit would be able to help us. He'd been going to temple more often as well. When he finally joined us, I brought out the stack of forms that Mr. Song had given me. "Pa, I went to see Lisa's guidance counselor yesterday about her health problems."

They both looked up. Pa said, "Why did you do that? Now the school will think she's a bad student."

"That's crazy. Why would they do that? She's having a medical problem and they should be aware of it."

"It'll bias the teachers against her. They'll think she's a sickly child." Pa had grown up in Communist China, where the less you said to any official, the better.

Lisa said, "I like Mr. Song. What did he say?"

"He told me that we could probably get low-cost or even free medical coverage for you. That means we'd be able to send you to doctors and get your tests. We could find out what's going on." I could barely contain my excitement. "The money wouldn't be a problem anymore."

Both Lisa and Pa looked taken aback. Lisa shrank into her chair. "I don't know, Charlie. I don't want to be tested by loads of doctors."

"Who knows what they will do to her?" Pa added. "They told Mr. Lee he had asthma. He had needles, inhalers and then it turned out he had lung cancer. Within five months, he was dead. Almost bankrupted his family as well."

"We'd be insured. We wouldn't have to pay."

Pa's face was bitter. "They lie. When your ma was in the hospital, the doctors told me not to worry too. They didn't tell me what the bills would be like. Those big companies tell you one thing, but when you owe the money, it's a whole other story."

I struggled to stay calm. "Pa, this is different from China. There are laws. They can't say you're insured for something and then suddenly, you're not."

"You don't know the way the world works, Charlie. Uncle Henry doesn't believe in it either and he's an educated man. And I don't want Lisa to disappear into a hospital where they're doing all kinds of things to her. They can use her like a test rabbit."

I finally understood. For Pa, it wasn't even about the bills. It was about losing control to a foreign system and watching someone you loved die slowly. I felt my face soften, but I knew this was important. "All I want is to help find out what's going on with Lisa and heal her."

"That's what I'm trying to do!"

"Pa, don't you realize how much Lisa's symptoms are like Ma's? Aren't you scared?"

Lisa drew in a quick breath. I immediately laid my hand over hers, regretting I'd frightened her.

The veins on Pa's forehead bulged. "I'm thinking about it day and night. It would help me if you would work with us instead of deserting us for that foreign world of yours. Ever since you've started working at the computer company, you've changed. I don't even know who my daughter is anymore." He stood up, grabbed his keys and walked out of the apartment.

I clenched my fists. Lisa had her head down on the table. I tried to keep the anger out of my voice. "Lisa, why didn't you help me there?"

"I don't want to go to the hospital."

I was on my own.

The first time I saw Nina and Keith dance together, a pang ran through me. She was simply stunning. Simone had been a brilliant dancer but when she danced, it was her technique that stood out. It had sometimes seemed as if she was going through the motions. Despite any strip clubs she might have worked in, Simone had been uptight. I'd heard her laughing when Keith made a joke, saying, "That is so humorous," which took the fun out of anything. I saw now that she had been constantly trying to fill a role that only she could see in her mind.

Nina existed in a relaxed glow that just made you want to be near her. She made it all look easy. I saw Keith smiling with her and knew that her popularity in high school hadn't been because of her looks. It was just Nina. Despite their age difference, Keith and Nina looked fantastic together. He blossomed as well, dancing with a passion and freedom I hadn't seen in him before. Watching their rumba, my heart rose with the thrill of the dance, then sank as I thought of the competition. Of course Nina had learned their routine in a heartbeat. They would undoubtedly win. For a moment, I was consumed by jealousy.

Then I remembered something Ma once said to me. "The hardest part of making a sacrifice isn't the moment when you do it. That's the easiest. You're too busy being proud of yourself for being so noble. What's hard is the day after that and the following one and all of those days to come. It's needing to make that sacrifice over and over again, the rest of your life, while in your mind, you can still taste that which you lost. Or what you think you lost."

Now that Lisa was out of school for the summer and didn't need to keep up appearances, I felt like she wasn't even really trying anymore. I gripped Lisa's upper arm with one hand and the stopwatch with the other. Pa was on the left side of Lisa, propping her under her armpit, straining a bit from the effort. Lisa let us hold most of her weight. I hated being at home more and more. But I continued to make Lisa do her exercises, not because I still believed I could save her that way, but because I couldn't think of anything else to do for her. I'd told Mr. Song that my father refused to sign the documents. He'd offered again to talk to Pa but I knew that would do more harm than good.

"I'm tired," she said. "I hate this. Let go of me."

"Just another minute and then we can stop, Lisa," I said. There was no response. She swayed, then tried to drag herself back into her chair.

"Lisa? Hey." I had to struggle with her body to keep it upright. "Stop it! Stop!" I yelled. Her left arm flailed out and struck Pa in the stomach. He hung on.

Suddenly, all of the frustration and fury burst inside me. I grabbed Lisa's arms and held them to her sides. "Stop it! Lisa, what are you doing? Do you care about anything anymore? What is going on? Just talk to me!"

"Charlie, it's all right," Pa said. I barely heard him.

"Let her go," he said, pulling at my arm. I didn't look at him.

Lisa was staring into the distance, beyond my face, still leaning her body backward. I shook her, twice, hard.

"Let her go!" Pa cried.

"Lisa!" My entire body was boiling hot. "What is happening to you? Why are you like this? Tell me!" I was shouting into her face.

Lisa stirred weakly. "What?"

"No! Stop being like that. Stop it!" I grabbed her under both armpits and shook her. Lisa slumped, off balance. Her head rolled back and forth. I swung my left arm and slapped her hard.

"Enough." Pa's face was wet with tears. "Enough!" He grabbed me and pulled me off of my sister. She sank into a chair, while I batted weakly at Pa's arm. Her cheek was crimson. She was gasping, as if she was too stunned to cry.

I ran from the apartment.

There was nowhere I could go to escape myself. I fled to the temple and knelt on one of the burgundy cushions in front of the goddess Kuan Yin. I bent my head so no one could see my expression. I felt like I was running a fever, nauseated by what I had done. A woman was kneeling next to me, shaking a tube filled with bamboo *kau cim*, which were fortune-telling sticks called the Oracle of Kuan Yin. One stick with a number inked on it fell out. She retrieved it and went to find the corresponding written oracle slip, which would give her the answer she'd sought. I was glad to be alone when she left. I laced my hands together and set them against the bridge of my nose. I closed my eyes. I couldn't even speak to the gods.

After a while, a figure approached. I looked up to find one of the monks, clad in his saffron robes. "I apologize for the intrusion but walking meditation is beginning." I realized another monk had been beating on the ornately carved wooden drum that signaled the start of the ceremony.

"I'm sorry." I stood up with haste and wobbled for a moment on my feet.

He steadied me with a hand. "I wish you peace." His face seemed ageless and kind.

I could feel the weight in how he held my forearm. He was present in every gesture. "I just hurt someone I love."

"The great gods have great compassion. They have already forgiven you. You did not act from evil."

I took a half breath, unable to fill my tight chest completely.

"She's young and defenseless. We promised never to hurt her." Corporal punishment was common in many traditional Chinese families but Pa and Ma had never believed in it. Even though Uncle had told Pa he was spoiling us, Pa had never raised a hand. But now I'd struck her and, more important, I'd betrayed her trust in me.

"To be human is to be under assault. So much around us leads us to close ourselves off, to harden. And sometimes we act thus. But in spite of all this, we must choose to open, and to open again. Breathe. Open. You will be all right." With that, he left.

I did as he said and felt the scent of oranges and incense seep into me. I moved to the back of the room to join the line that was already forming for walking the winds of fate, which was what we called this form of meditation. We believed that this was a way to turn aside the evil winds of fate that entered every life. Slowly, I gave myself over to the chanting of the monks as I followed the line of practitioners circling the temple. I did not find salvation, but something of the turmoil inside quieted. When the walking meditation was over, I realized Todd had been a few feet behind me in the line. I'd always thought witches avoided temples since they were willing to engage in darker rituals the monks would never condone. Monks had contact with the true gods, while witches trafficked with the petty ones. I avoided his eyes and hurried away before he could greet me.

I returned to the apartment, where Lisa was sleeping on the couch. I bent over and kissed her on her hair. She stirred, realized it was me, then turned away, huddling into the cushions. I deserved it. I held her anyway. "I'm so sorry, Lisa."

A heavy hand clasped me on the shoulder. It was Pa. He looked at my face, then without a word, he took me in his arms.

Twenty-Two

A week later, I was surprised to find a text from Grace on my phone saying she wanted to see me. She must have gotten my number from Godmother Yuan. I met her on a park bench in Gossip Park the following Sunday in the early afternoon. She was waiting for me, as perfectly made-up as a doll, with huge and darkly fringed eyes. I wondered if she was wearing those circle lenses Mo Li had.

I felt strange as I stood there. "Hi, Grace."

Grace held her hand out to me. "Charlie, it's good to see you. I know we haven't been friends in a long time." Her honesty made me more comfortable, and I gave her hand a quick squeeze as I sat down next to her. She gave me a rueful smile. "I just don't know who to talk to anymore. I need your help. My family is going nuts and I don't know what to do." She stared into the distance. "They want to marry me off. You remember that matchmaking session back in March was a disaster. So now they're taking things a step further."

"You could have given Dennis a chance."

She exploded. "That's not the point! I've been ordered around my entire life. I'm not going to be told whom to marry on top of it all."

I remembered she'd been caught with a girl. Maybe she didn't even like guys. "Are they still so upset about that other incident?"

"Oh, you heard about that. Whole Chinatown thinks I'm a flaming lesbian."

This was the Grace I'd known all those years ago and I couldn't help chuckling. "Are you?"

A tiny smile played around the corners of her lips. "Maybe."

I thought about that for a moment. "Did they make you break up with her?"

Now she looked tired. "They're trying."

I deliberately leaned against her so that our shoulders touched, and nudged her elbow the way I used to when we were kids. "No one's better at getting around parents than you."

She burst out laughing. "Thanks. All I want is to have control over my own body. Can't I choose for myself? Is that so much to ask?"

"No. I guess they're just a bit freaked out."

"It's not the first time. I dated a Triad guy last year."

I stared. The Triad was the most dangerous gang in Chinatown. Most of us tried to stay away from them. I knew many of the stores had to pay "protection money" to different gangs, depending on where they were located, otherwise the owner would find his store ransacked. I'd heard rumors of them putting out hits on people they didn't like.

"He dumped me. He thought I wasn't paying enough attention to him. I guess I wasn't really interested in him anyway, I was just trying to prove to myself that I still liked guys."

"You're lucky he was the one to leave you."

"I know. My folks found out later and panicked. I swore I'd be better and then they caught me with this. They're now planning to send me back to China to find a husband. They've already got five men picked out. I just have to choose one of them, marry him there, and bring him back to the U.S."

I gaped. Traditionally, men who couldn't find a wife here had been sent back to China to choose a bride. Nowadays, it'd become much harder for anyone to find a bride in China because of the one-child policy. If a family could only have one child, they usually wanted it to be a boy, so many had illegally chosen to abort female fetuses or given girl babies up for adoption. The result was that there were now many more men than women there. I guessed it made sense that women could return to find grooms these days, but I'd never expected someone as westernized as Grace to be sent back. "What do you want me to do?"

"Please speak to my grandmother. She loves you. You should hear her talk about you, it's like you're the best thing since the invention of chopsticks. And you always know what to do. At the dim sum restaurant, you did it all correctly, with the tea and the serving of the dishes and everything."

"No one looked that happy with me."

She giggled. "Believe me, I was grateful you were there. Why don't you go out with Dennis?"

"Oh no, thanks. My life's complicated enough." I thought of Ryan and ached.

"So will you talk to her? For old times' sake."

I gazed at Grace's troubled expression and missed her usual bright mischievous eyes. We'd always gotten into trouble together as kids, and had so much fun doing it too.

"All right."

I knocked on Godmother Yuan's door. She had dropped by our apartment several times to try to heal Lisa further, but it hadn't seemed to make much of a difference yet. When she called for me to come in, I let myself inside. The fan whirred. Her flowered couch was still covered in plastic, her few furnishings tidy. Although her place was very simple, she was lucky to have it. Most elderly women in Chinatown were still working at factories or shops. Godmother could survive on teaching her classes and the gifts she received from students. She bustled into the kitchen area to make me some jasmine tea.

Once we were settled, I said, "I wanted to talk to you about Grace."

"'The tiger takes the leap, the eagle spreads its wings.'"

"Excuse me?"

"You two are so different and each creature must follow its own nature."

"Godmother, tell me the truth. Do you study those wise quotes so that you're ready when you see me?"

She wrinkled her nose. "Maybe a little. An old woman has to have something to keep her mind busy as well as her body."

"Okay. I just heard that she's being sent to China to find a husband."

"It will be good for her. She is running wild."

"Don't you think she has the right to choose her partner? Or to decide if she wants to marry at all?"

She sat up very straight. "She can pick! Who says she can't?"

"Out of a handful of men that the family has selected for her."

"The family is very wise, often much wiser than a young heart."

"Godmother, I know it isn't my place. I am younger and more

foolish than you. I am not a Yuan. It's just that Grace asked me to say a few words to you. She made mistakes and she deeply regrets them. She's building a fine life here. She has just graduated from college. Do you think it's wise to uproot her? Pair her with a man who may be more traditional, expect her to play a role she can't fulfill?" Godmother took a dainty sip of tea. I knew she was listening and pressed on. "We both know how Grace is. She's not going to submit docilely. Even if you manage to force her to marry someone, she'll find a way out. She always does. How will this end?"

She sighed. "You may not be a Yuan but you are family. Perhaps you are right. Knowing Grace, the marriage will be a disaster. I will speak to her mother. It was only that your uncle was going to China anyway and it seemed to be the ideal opportunity. He'd be the perfect chaperone until Grace met up with our own family."

"Uncle Henry's going to China?"

"You didn't know? He's going to take your sister there, so she can be treated properly."

I raced back home to our apartment. Pa was in the kitchen, stirring something over the stove, while Lisa was lying on the couch with her eyes closed. "Why didn't you tell me?"

Pa could see from my face what this had to be about. He turned off the flame and came into the living area. "It would have upset you."

"I have the right to know. Have you told Lisa yet?"

She said, "Tell me what?"

"So you and Uncle were planning to ship her off to China without informing either of us?"

Lisa's eyes grew enormous.

Pa said, "The temples and witches there are much more powerful. It will be better for her. The Vision says she must escape the evil that resides here."

"Lisa hardly speaks any Chinese," I said, enunciating carefully. I had to stay calm.

"That's why Uncle Henry will be going with her."

I gripped the sides of my head as if to cover my ears. "What about his practice?"

"Aunt Monica and Dennis will stay here and keep the office open for the regular prescriptions. Dennis can handle the simpler cases, he's been doing so for months. Uncle's always wanted to go back to China and this is his chance. And he'll be able to help Lisa at the same time."

I still had a terrible feeling about this. "How can we afford it?"

Pa let out a deep breath. "Uncle Henry will pay for it. We are very lucky to have such a generous man in our family."

"I think it's an awful idea. We don't even know if any of this stuff works. They could do anything to her there, scar her, both physically and emotionally."

"Uncle Henry will accompany her to every treatment and the Vision is a very powerful witch. We must trust their advice."

"I don't know about the Vision."

"She has helped many people in Chinatown. Charlie, I know you're worried about your sister but she won't be alone. Uncle Henry wants to help her as much as you do. He'll make sure that nothing bad happens to her. You must have more of an open mind."

"I still can't believe you're going to send her to a country she's never been to."

"I'm just letting her go home."

"No, this is our home. America. Lisa and I were born here and this is where we belong. You too, only you don't realize it yet. If you went back to China, you'd see how much you've changed as well."

"Ridiculous. We are Chinese, and in the end, we belong to China. Uncle and I know and love all of the people she'll be staying with. You don't, but they are our friends and family."

"How long?"

"Uncle must return after a few weeks. He cannot afford to keep his practice shut for longer than that. Lisa . . ." His voice trailed off and he looked away.

"Will stay as long as necessary to heal her," I finished for him, folding my arms. "What about Hunter?"

"This is more important. A Chinese family has the right to send a child back to China. We have to do what is best for her. We cannot be selfish and keep her here."

Lisa had been quiet this entire time. Now she spoke in a voice that trembled. "Please don't make me go to China. Please." She started to tear up.

I went over to her and took her hand in mine. "I won't let them." I took my left hand to brush her forehead three times, as I always did, to brush away her fear and bad luck. I thought about how I'd slapped her. How could I ever forgive myself? Then something occurred to me. What was it that Todd had said, back in the hallway at Uncle's office? "Forgive yourself, forgive that hand." He'd known I would hit her. Suddenly, I understood the Vision's secret and realized maybe I had someone who could help us.

Todd lived in an old apartment building on East Broadway with his older brother. When he answered the door, I didn't give him a chance to speak. "It's you, isn't it? You're the power behind the Vision."

He stiffened, then said, "Do you want to come in?"

We sat on his folding chairs in the tiny studio. "Why do you work for her? Why don't you start for yourself?"

He gave a half-hearted shrug. "What would they call me? Prophecy of the Strange Haircut? She's got it going: she's old, she's got the freaky eye. You want a glass of water? That's all I have."

"No, thanks. So what exactly do you do for the Vision?"

"She handles most things on her own. The incense burning, releasing of life, the spells, that's her. I do the real psychic stuff."

"Like when she has to predict the future."

"Yeah. Or talk to spirits, that kind of thing. That's why she's so successful, partly because my predictions usually come true and partly because people like to believe in mumbo jumbo."

He stared out the window for a moment, then said, "I buy egg cakes every day. On Canal Street."

"What?" He was so different.

"She never sees me."

Ah, this was about Zan. "A lot of people buy egg cakes. If you want her to notice you, maybe you should speak to her. So will you help me?"

"With your sister? The Vision does most of the exorcisms and stuff."

"But I don't think there's anything to be exorcised."

"There usually isn't. Spirits enjoy their space. She didn't bring me with her when she did your place so that means you're right."

"So she's cheating people? When she did the Release of Life, Lisa seemed to get better."

"Well, who knows what really happened? Any act of compassion is powerful. She's got the same power we all do, that of our souls and desires. Sometimes her spells work just because people believe in her. When you pay that much money, you want to think it was effective or maybe it was coincidence."

"But she doesn't have any psychic abilities whatsoever? She told me my new job would amount to nothing, and I've never stopped thinking about it."

"No, you don't need to worry about that. Completely untrue."

"This is crazy, Todd. How can you work for her? Knowing you're the real thing and she's the fake?"

"I gotta make a living too. At least I get to use my skills sometimes to help people. No one except for the witch would hire me. I'm not much use otherwise. I'm constantly having to tune things out and I get distracted. Don't you remember me in high school? I was so strange, no one would talk to me."

I clasped my hands together so tightly that the knuckles were white, then slowly asked, "Can you tell me what's wrong with Lisa?"

"I haven't had that much access to her. The Vision's kept me mostly off of her case. Even with your uncle's treatments, she had me stay outside, probably because she didn't want me to reveal that there was no spirit possessing your sister."

"But I'm here now and I can give you something that belongs to her. But are you going to do something . . ." I paused a moment. ". . . weird with it?"

"No, what do you think I am, a witch? I'll just try to make contact with her energy and see what I feel. The best would be to get me something that is around her a lot."

I took Lisa's T-shirt and an envelope out of the bag. "Actually, I brought you the T-shirt she sleeps in and a photo. The Vision wanted them when she was doing her rituals, so I figured you might want them too."

"She's just copying me." Todd held out his hand for the T-shirt and envelope.

"That prophecy about what one sister gains, the other shall lose—was that you?"

"Of course."

The only photo I could find so quickly of Lisa was an old one of her and Pa together. I didn't want to go through the boxes in the closet to find her old school pictures and I figured it wouldn't matter that much. I'd slipped the picture out of its frame and then stuffed it in the envelope.

Todd simply draped the T-shirt across his lap, then held the sealed envelope and closed his eyes, frowning. "This is strange, I feel a young female energy and an older male one."

That was impressive. "That's because I couldn't find a photo of her alone. That is of her and Pa. Don't you want to take it out and look at the picture?"

He ignored my question, keeping his eyes closed. "That explains it. You removed it from its frame this morning. They are standing by water, with some kind of wooden structure near them."

My breath caught. I'd been alone in the apartment when I took the photo and he'd never been to our place so he couldn't have seen it before. The photo was from when we all went to Coney Island together. "How did you know that?"

He opened his eyes and, for the first time, I saw Todd look hurt. "Despite what you truly think of me, I am not a fraud."

"I'm sorry. I don't quite know what to make of you."

"It's okay. I should be used to it by now. To be honest, some of this stuff is fake and some is real. I don't really know how I feel about it myself. It's hard to tell which is which."

He closed his eyes again. He started jittering his left leg, like he was having an epileptic attack. "They love each other very much.

The girl's very unhappy. It's like there's a darkness touching her. There's another man. He has too much influence over her. He's a cold, dominant person." Uncle Henry.

"What about her illness? What is wrong with her?"

He furrowed his eyebrows. "I don't really feel an illness. There is darkness but I'm not sure if it's located in her body. It may be a more psychological condition."

I thought of what Godmother had said, about the physical and the emotional being linked. "But she can hardly walk anymore, her legs are so weak. She's not faking it."

"It's like there's a mountain weighing her down. She has a secret. I can't tell what it is, but I think it has to do with the man. They are wrapped up together in some kind of dance but it's not a healthy one."

"Uncle Henry. He's planning to bring her back to China for more treatment. My father won't listen to anyone else."

He reached out and took my hand. I could still feel the movement of his leg. It was disconcerting, made it hard to think. "Your own future is in constant flux. I see two paths in front of you. Be wary of what looks like right but is actually wrong."

I was irritated. Couldn't anyone speak clearly? "Now you sound like the Vision."

"Follow your heart. Choose to become the woman you should be, the one your ma would wish for you." His leg stilled. He was done.

The studio was wound up in excitement about the upcoming competition. Ryan and I performed our mambo from beginning to end at one of the studio parties. Everyone clapped and whistled, especially Evelyn and Trevor.

"What did you think?" I asked Nina afterward.

"You were amazing! I can't believe how fast you both have improved."

"Do you think Adrienne is right, that we need more emotion between us?"

"That's hard to say, Charlie. It does seem a bit . . . well, you know, flat at moments, but that's a lot better than not knowing what you're doing."

Ryan and I had been careful to be restrained with each other, so it was probably that deadening of feeling that she sensed. Although I still felt the same way about him, I made sure not to let it show. Evelyn and Ryan took a few lessons together, so they could practice their father-daughter dance for the wedding, which was to be the weekend before the competition. After all of their lessons, he and Evelyn had no trouble dancing together at all. I was grateful I didn't need to teach Ryan and Fiona. She'd be coming back soon and they'd catch up. It shouldn't hurt this much.

When I told Evelyn how wonderful she and Ryan looked, she said, "You've done such an incredible job with him. Thank you."

Ryan rolled his eyes. "Just keep talking about me like I'm not here."

When I laughed, he'd looked at me, just a moment too long, a shade too intensely. Although I immediately changed the subject, I saw Evelyn watching us both throughout the rest of the lesson.

During a private lesson with my Asian doctors, Jason and Naomi, I said, "Tango basics across the room, left turns around the corners and, if you feel like you can handle it, throw in a couple of fans." Sometimes teaching dance reminded me of ordering food at the noodle restaurant.

In the middle of one of Naomi's fans, Jason whipped a handkerchief out from behind her ear. "This is for you, Charlie. For good luck at the competition."

"Thanks so much," I said, touched. It read "Mambo #1."

Jason said, "And don't forget my offer about your friend. Just let me know if you need my help."

"Actually, I've been wondering about something." Todd's words that there might not be an illness involved had given me some hope. I turned to Naomi. "What was it you said about your work? That sometimes a physical problem can come from mental stress or something? In Chinese medicine, it's the same. They believe emotion and physical pain are always related. Could that possibly be what's happening?"

Naomi nodded. "It's always a possibility. A traumatic event could cause symptoms that are physical. I had a girl who went blind. After therapy, just talking about the problems in her family, she regained her sight."

Jason said, "I'd have to caution you there, Charlie. It's tempting to believe that, so we don't have to face that something could be seriously wrong with someone we care about. We always have to rule out the physical causes first. Most of the time, a disease is going to be the reason."

In the week before the competition, I came home from the studio to find Pa waiting for me. Lisa was already asleep. Without a word, he beckoned to me to come into his room so we wouldn't wake her. He held out something in his hand. It was my salary slip, which I was always careful to hide. He must have found my stack stashed in the back of the closet where we kept our mattresses. Underneath was a copy of my entry form for the scholarship. I was sunk.

"What is the meaning of this?" he asked. "You've been acting so difficult, I decided to look through some of your things to see if something else was happening that I didn't know about."

The slip read "Avery Dance Studios."

It was on the tip of my tongue to say, "That's the name of the computer place I'm working for." I even constructed the entire lie in my mind. I'd tell him that even dance studios needed a data team and they just happened to be my employer. But I'd had enough of falsehoods. The studio, the dancing, my entire new life flashed before my eyes and I found myself saying to Pa, "That's where I work."

His voice was tightly controlled. "As what?"

"A dancer."

He pulled his hand across his face. "How can you disgrace us like this?"

I stared at him until I understood what he meant. "I am not a stripper!"

"What are you then?"

"A dancer! Like Ma was."

Everything about him stilled. "Don't you talk about your ma like that."

"I'm a professional ballroom dancer. Why can't I compare myself to Ma? I'm her daughter."

"Your ma was the most beautiful—"

I cut him off with a fierce whisper. "No one loved Ma more than I did, but you have to stop that."

"What?"

"Stop making me feel like I'll never be as good as she was. I'm not her, I'm me. And I have a right to be myself."

He gentled. "I never meant to make you feel that way, Charlie.

Just, your ma was a trained classical dancer. Who would hire you as one?"

My voice was weak. "They didn't. They took me on first as a receptionist but I was terrible."

Pa stared, confused.

"So they gave me a job as a dancer."

He scratched his forehead. "They're crazy people."

"Yes, they are. They taught me. I'm not bad. I teach lessons— waltz, tango, mambo."

"Are you dancing with men? And what is this, then? Is this for lessons?" He waved the competition form in his hand.

I decided to pretend I hadn't heard the men question. "No, I'm doing a show."

"You are a showgirl! How can this be, my own daughter?"

"Pa! I have never given you any reason to—"

"I was too easy on you, I know it."

It all flowed out of me. "You've always been living in your own world. You think that if you stick your head in the sand, everything will go away. Well, it won't. I'll tell you something. Winston and I already dated. He left me because he didn't think I was cool enough. And I love to dance. It means everything to me. I've had to hide what I really did, what I actually cared about, for so long. But it's my fault too. Maybe I should have given you a chance."

Pa's throat turned bright red. "You are not going to this competition show. This wild society, this America is no good for us. We need to go back home. Lisa has to return to China, and you too."

"You see! This is why I could never trust you." I felt the blood pulsing in my ears. Behind the anger, I was scared of losing every-thing: my dancing, Ryan. "I am doing the routine and I'm not going to China."

"I am your father!"

"Hush! You're going to wake Lisa. There is no way you can stop me from doing the competition or make me go to China. I'm an adult, Pa. You can't dictate my life."

He looked as if I'd slapped him. I hated how much this had hurt him, that he couldn't understand.

"Then Lisa will. I will have Uncle book the tickets as soon as possible. I can save one of my daughters at least!" He opened the door and waited until I left his bedroom, then shut the door hard behind me.

Twenty-Three

R yan went to Evelyn's wedding. I couldn't stop picturing them in my mind that entire weekend: Ryan dancing with Fiona, Ryan and his number with Evelyn, Evelyn and Trevor doing their wedding dance. I wondered how Ryan felt when he saw his girlfriend again. I would have been out of place there anyway. I'd only seen western weddings in films, with the bride in white, the Chinese color for mourning. If I ever married, I'd wear red and gold.

On Monday, all Ryan said was that it'd gone well and then he changed the subject. Evelyn and Trevor were on their honeymoon. A part of me had been afraid Fiona would come to the studio, but she didn't appear. Ryan and I practiced nonstop. And then, the competition was upon us. The studio closed on Wednesday and the other dancers headed to the competition. I didn't need to be there until the next day. Pa still wasn't speaking to me after our fight. He was so angry while I packed to leave. I'd never seen him like this. Even so, I couldn't still the hum of anticipation underneath my skin because Ryan would be picking me up soon.

On Thursday morning, Ryan would drive the both of us up to

Connecticut. I could have taken the train since the hotel was very close to the station, but he'd insisted. I was ashamed of how it thrilled me to think of being in a car alone with him.

As I left the apartment with my suitcase, Lisa said in a small voice, "I hope you win, Charlie."

I hadn't even known that she'd been paying attention. I looked back at her, sitting in her usual spot on the couch, with her cane and walker by her side. I swallowed a lump in my throat. "I'm going to do my best." I walked over and gave her a hug.

Instead of Ryan's car, I saw the "Patrick's Landscaping" van pull up in front of my building. Ryan waved at me and I ran out. After I'd thrown my bags in the back and settled in next to him, he said, "I hope you don't mind. My car's in the garage. The boss let me borrow this."

I laughed. "Everything's an adventure with you." And we were off.

I enjoyed sitting up so high in the van, looking out over all the other cars. I understood now why Zan wanted to drive a truck. He had the air-conditioning on and it was wonderfully cool inside.

I said, "So tell me more about the wedding last weekend." What I meant was, how are you and Fiona doing?

"Everyone was really impressed with our dancing. Evelyn was thrilled."

I didn't want to ask directly but I had to. "What did Fiona think?"

He gave an awkward laugh. "She was blown away. I think it made her feel a bit inadequate."

I tried to pretend I was a professional with no feelings whatso-ever. "She should probably take lessons sometime." I chewed on the inside of my cheek, then I said it. "Maybe not with me."

There was a pause. "Maybe not." He was staring straight ahead through the windshield, then took a breath. "So . . . what type of men do you like?"

"What?! That's quite a change of subject."

"I mean, in some ways, I don't know a lot about you. Do you get hit on by students a lot? Do you ever like any of them?"

"All the time. And no, not in that way." It'd surprised me at the beginning but then I realized it was a type of automatic reaction. Some single men seemed to think they had to ask the dancer out, just as no one wanted to date the dishwasher. Ryan was the only one I found attractive, and in many ways, I considered him my partner, not a student. "But most students are tactful. They'll beat around the bush a bit and if you don't bite, they'll stop. In the worst case, you can always tell them it's just studio policy."

"So what are dancers supposed to do if you're not allowed to date the students?"

I looked at him in some surprise. Of course he wouldn't know. "Dance with other professionals. Dominic's been trying to match me up with another pro for a long time now."

His smile seemed forced. "Any good candidates?"

"I haven't looked yet. I've been so busy with our routine. There are a few I'm supposed to meet here." Dominic had told me about a guy from the West Side studio, and another from Long Island.

"I guess two pros are a perfect match."

"They can be." I looked out at the moving traffic for a few minutes. We were crossing some bridge. I blurted out what I'd really been wondering. "Is Fiona still in town?" I needed to brace myself if she was going to show up in the audience.

"No." Then Ryan was silent and we didn't talk much more until we arrived at the hotel.

———

When we arrived in front of the enormous hotel, one of the doormen saw the van and tried to wave us through to the back, probably where the landscapers usually parked. I glanced nervously at Ryan and he shook his head for me not to worry, pulling the van up to the curb. I stepped out, then removed my dance costume from the back. The man took one look at the glittering dress in its transparent bag and said, "Oh, you're one of the dancers for the competition. I'm so sorry."

Ryan grinned as he pulled out his garment bag too. "Not a problem."

Already, other doormen were holding the massive doors open for us. I stared in awe when we entered the grand hotel. A pianist played quietly next to a waterfall over pale marble shot through with gold threads. Everyone there seemed so elegant and assured. I tried not to stutter when I gave the hotel clerk my name. I'd never done this before. The clerk told me Nina had already checked in for the room I was sharing with her. All of the dancers doubled up with each other, and I was grateful Nina would be there with me. The clerk handed me my key, then Ryan checked in for his single room.

I said, "Do you want to meet back here soon?"

He smiled. "I thought I'd be on my own."

"I'm supposed to take care of you." Dominic had told us we were to stick to our competition students like glue.

"I'm glad there are some perks to being a student."

We walked deeper into the hotel toward the elevators, and I saw a flock of women in brightly colored ball gowns coming toward us, checking Ryan out and giggling. I looked up to find him studying me. He hadn't even noticed.

He said, "So I guess this is our last dance together, isn't it?"

"Yeah." I busied myself with my bags, trying to hide my emotions. When I finally glanced at him, he was wearing his neutral expression again. He took our bags and we went to the elevators.

When the doors opened, a woman wearing a white bathrobe and slippers was standing inside the elevator. By the way she held the robe closed, I could tell she wasn't wearing anything underneath. Although her makeup and heavy mascara were smudged, I recognized her as one of our students. She said, "You have to try the sauna before you leave. It's fantastic."

I only had a vague idea of what a sauna was. "Where is it?"

"Downstairs, by the pool. Nothing will relax you better than all that steam after a hard day of dancing and stress."

I was completely out of my depth. I'd never been in either a hotel or a sauna. It was like the first day I stepped into the studio for my job interview, where everything was new and everyone else seemed so comfortable. Now the studio was like home to me, but this hotel and the people in it made me feel inexperienced and insignificant. How could I possibly think of competing here? We would place last, we'd be the laughingstocks of the entire session.

Someone squeezed my arm. It was Ryan and his eyes were kind. "Don't look like that. I believe in you. Together, we're going to be just fine."

I nodded, relaxing a bit. Sometimes it was like Ryan could read my mind. I only had time to give him a grateful look before the elevator doors opened again. It turned out our rooms were on the same floor, only at opposite ends.

"Are you all right with your bags?" He was always such a gentleman. How I hated lucky Fiona.

"I'm fine, don't worry about me. I'll meet you back here at the elevators in ten minutes, okay?" The thought of Ryan accompanying me to my room was too tempting.

He gave me a nod, then strode off to his own room.

I had to fumble with the room key for a while before I figured out how to open the door. Nina wasn't there. She was dancing so many heats with Keith, she was probably already on the dance floor. I opened the closet door and an explosion of sequins and feathers greeted me. She'd hung up her gowns—she needed several different ones for the events. The bathroom was littered with false eyelashes, makeup, glitter, bottles of hair spray and bobby pins. Good old Nina. It reminded me of our teachers' room, and I felt better seeing this evidence of the ballroom world I knew. I hung up my competition dress, quickly stashed away the rest of my things, then went out to meet Ryan.

The main ballroom was enormous and packed with men in black tie and women in ball gowns. Every size, color and shape were there. I sucked in a breath. I hadn't understood the scope of the ballroom world. So many incredible dancers and students, and I had no idea how it all worked. The men who were competing had numbers pinned to the back of their tuxedos or black shirts, while stunning women swirled around them. A voluptuous woman in a bright orange Latin dress was doing a sensual samba with her teacher. Video and professional photo cameras were set up all around the edges of the ballroom, their lights dazzling my eyes. Stands selling dresses, shoes, bags, every dance accessory imaginable, lined the walls.

"Come on," said Ryan, shouldering his way to an empty table on the edge of the dance floor.

From there, we could see the competition. To the right, the couples for the next heat were already being lined up. We were in the middle of a series of Latin events. "Oh, there's Nina and Keith." I was so glad to see their familiar faces as they were waiting to go on.

The heats began. There were so many couples on the floor because this was nationals, and every Avery Studio in the country was represented. We watched as heat after heat was danced. I felt more comfortable as I analyzed the dancing and was grateful I'd been trained in such a good studio. Some were excellent and some were poor. I was glad to see no one was as good as Nina and Keith. It was grueling, even to watch.

I felt a hand on my shoulder and looked up to find Julian, very handsome in black tie. "Charlie and Ryan. So pleased you're here."

"Oh, I'm happy to see you, Julian," I said warmly. In my peripheral vision, I noticed conversations around us pausing as people concentrated on Julian and us. Even Julian's reflected glory was heady.

Ryan nodded, trying to stay polite.

"Don't miss the party tonight. Penthouse at ten p.m." Julian turned to Ryan. "Sorry, pros only." Then with a little pat on my shoulder, he left. I watched him go, saw other heads turning as he passed by.

Ryan's jaw was clenched. "He just has to rub it in."

"What?"

"That you're invited and I'm not. That I'm not a professional, and therefore not supposed to be with you."

"I don't think he worries about us that much."

I went to the party together with Nina. I kept thinking about the fact that Ryan was somewhere in the hotel but I knew it was better to focus on other things.

"You should find yourself a pro tonight," Nina said as she put on her makeup for the party. "If you need the room, just let me know."

"For what?"

"Sex, what else?"

"Where would you go?"

She shrugged. "I'd bunk with another dancer. We always help each other out."

"I'm not going to be needing the room."

"We'll see. You haven't been to a professional party yet."

The penthouse was filled with dancers. Women were leading other women, men leading men, and of course, men and women together. A rap song was blasting at full volume. We passed Mateo dancing up a storm with a man I didn't know. Mateo saw us, gave us a wink and a kiss, then said to his big handsome partner, "Okay, baby, I'm leading now," and they switched leads. The other guy kicked his heels back in a flip as Mateo dipped him. An old friend of Nina's grabbed her when the music changed. She winked at me as she was whisked away. I didn't know what to do. Everyone else had years of history together. I wasn't sure I should have come.

Now Adrienne was at the stereo, changing the music and calling, "Hustle time!" Dominic took her in his arms and they started spinning and breaking at high speed. I'd never seen them dance together before. They were incredible.

Then someone took me into dance position and I found myself face to face with Julian. He was wearing a T-shirt and jeans, looking much younger than I'd seen him, and he was more attractive than ever. I felt as if I'd been picked by the prince himself. It took me a second to figure out the hustle steps, but once I understood it was similar to western swing, I caught on pretty fast. Julian could move. It was so effortless, I could let myself go, trusting my body to his magical hands. I must have been glowing with pleasure.

I tilted my head and asked, "How am I doing, coach?"

"Beautifully." He had such a sexy smile.

The music changed to cha-cha and I said, "My turn to lead."

Julian grinned as he took the lady's part. Of course, he was as light and fast as the best woman I'd ever danced with. I felt as if I'd been driving around in a rusty old heap my entire life and now sat behind the wheel of a Lamborghini. I had only to give him the slightest tap and he spun like a dervish. Then the music changed and he took me in dance hold again. We were dancing number after number together, and I knew people had noticed, but I was enjoying myself so much, I didn't care. When I was with Julian, I was someone, I belonged.

As the night went on, the dances became more intimate until I found myself backed against a darkened corner, doing the lambada with Julian. He had one hand braced against the wall, holding a glass of champagne. Our hips were rocking together in tiny circles, while his other arm was wrapped around my waist. He leaned forward, then brought the champagne glass to my lips and fed me another sip. My eyes fluttered closed. The party, the dancing, Julian. It was so intoxicating. I didn't want to think or worry anymore: Pa, Lisa, Ryan all seemed like heartaches I could ignore, if only for one night.

Then Julian had gotten rid of the glass somehow and had my hand in his again. He rubbed the back of my hand against the faint stubble on his cheek. "We feel good together, don't we?"

He had lowered his forehead to mine now. His breath was scented with strawberries and champagne. He turned my hand so that it lay against the side of his neck. I felt the silk of his skin, the sweep of muscle revealed by his thin T-shirt. Then his lips were on mine and the tip of his tongue was tracing the curve of my lips, parting them. He started to trail a line of kisses along the side of my neck. I drew breath and tried to clear my mind. "Julian."

"Mmmm?"

My voice was barely a whisper. "I don't want to be the next woman on your girlfriend list."

Julian drew back and looked at me reproachfully. "How can you do the lambada with a man, then tell him no?" I smiled, as he'd meant me to, and he continued speaking. "You think I say this all of the time, Charlie, but I don't. You're special to me. I'd like to discover how special. I know I have a reputation, please don't hold it against me. Give me a chance." His eyes were sincere, and just a shade vulnerable.

What would it mean to love the glorious Julian? To have him for myself, to be a dancer with him by my side, if only for a while? I could go to bed with him tonight. We'd have a wonderful time. How everyone would be amazed and impressed that he'd chosen me. Would it be so wrong to give him the chance he'd asked for? Julian bent forward and lifted my chin with his thumb. He kissed me on the lips while his fingers caressed the vulnerable skin of my throat.

An image of Ryan, how he'd looked at me when I left the taxi that night, flashed across my mind. I opened my eyes. I reached up with both hands and gently pulled Julian's away.

He studied my eyes. "He's forbidden, you know that."

I nodded and couldn't keep the sadness from my face. Ryan wasn't mine.

"Am I such a poor substitute?"

"You're too good to be a stand-in for anyone, Julian." I reached up and threaded my fingers through his hair. "I'm flattered. I admire you. You're so sexy. But I'm just realizing that maybe I love him."

Hurt and anger crossed his face. He drew back as I let my hands drop away from him. "Do you know why I won so many competitions?"

I said nothing.

"Because I can't abide losing." And with that, he released me and walked away.

I didn't want to stay in our room and have to answer all of Nina's questions when she returned. I couldn't sleep now anyway. I thought about what that student in the elevator had said about the sauna. I undressed, grabbed a robe and followed the signs to the sauna downstairs. I hadn't brought a bathing suit but it was deserted anyway. I took off the bathrobe and hung it up, wrapped a towel around myself and lay down on my stomach on the heated wooden bench. I cradled my head in my arms. What had I done? I'd hurt Julian and now he was angry at me too. What a mess I'd made of everything. I closed my eyes in the steamy room.

I'm not sure how long I lay there but I must have fallen asleep because I woke as the sauna door clicked closed. It was Ryan. He was naked to the waist, wrapped in a towel, with droplets of water dripping from his chest. He must have gone swimming. All of my longing was in my eyes. He crossed the room and knelt in front of my face.

As he reached for me, I stopped his hand. "What about Fiona?"

"We broke up last weekend."

I blinked, trying to take it in. Ryan was available. "Why didn't you tell me?"

"I tried. I'm not the smoothest guy, in case you haven't noticed. I'm not like Julian."

I had to say it. "I just came from him."

His face stilled. His open hand clenched into a fist. "Did you—?"

"No. Being with him made me understand how I feel about you."

I felt him exhale. I peeked from under my lashes. His face was exultant. Then his palms were on the nape of my neck. I let my eyes close again and felt his hand push my towel aside and run down the length of my spine. His lips were at my neck, making their way around to my collarbone. I reveled in his touch; I couldn't believe that, finally, Ryan could be mine. None of the rest mattered: what Pa might say, what the studio might do. With Julian, I'd been infatuated, carried away by his glamour and charm, but Ryan recognized me as I truly was and filled my soul.

I turned over and wrapped my arms around his neck, pulling him down for my kiss. I arched up and when my naked breasts touched his skin, I felt his sharp intake of breath. Still kissing me, he wrapped his arms around me and stood up slowly, until I was cradled in his arms. Now he let my legs go and I was standing nude on the sauna bench, pressed against him. I was taller than him this way. I bent over and started licking the droplets of water from his neck and shoulders. He tasted of chlorine and salt.

"Come back to my room with me." His voice was hoarse.

I kept licking. I was kneeling, at his chest now. His hands ran across my body.

One palm cradled my head and tilted my face up. He traced my eyebrow with his finger. "Will you come?"

I nodded. He picked me up and set me by my bathrobe. I put it on, then he tied the sash neatly around my waist. He shrugged his on, took my hand, and we headed upstairs.

The next morning, I woke up with Ryan's arms wrapped around me and turned to him with a smile.

"Good morning."

With his eyes still closed, he started to stroke my body underneath the sheets. I kissed him and his beautiful eyes opened. He murmured, "I was afraid I'd dreamed it."

"Me too." I studied his face, so close to mine.

"Do you regret it?"

"Never."

His face filled with joy. "I've been crazy about you ever since you gave that guy his tip back."

He kissed me again and again. When he gave me the chance to breathe, I said, "So I think I missed the part where you tried to tell me you and Fiona had broken up."

"In the van. I was going to say it but I was scared you'd say it didn't matter, that you didn't feel that way about me, so I tried to figure out first if you cared about me. You know, pave the way a bit. That's when you told me you weren't attracted to any of your students."

"Oh. I meant my other students."

"Great, that was very clear. Not." His smile was crooked. "I wasn't sure if I should tell you at all. I'm a risk to the job you love, while Julian fits into your life perfectly. He could make you a star. I guess I didn't know if you'd pick me over him, I wondered if you even should."

"I realized when Julian kissed me how I felt admiration and affection for him, but no more than that. It's like you see who I am beneath it all, underneath the dancer and the dishwasher and all of the other labels."

He pressed his thumb to my lips and started stroking them, then kissed me tenderly. "What about your job?"

"You're leaving the studio anyway. I think if we keep our relationship quiet for a while, we'll be all right. What happened with Fiona?"

"I'd known for a while that it wasn't working, I just didn't want to hurt her. Then I met you and started to have feelings for you. You contributed to the timing with Fiona, but it would have happened anyway. When I saw her at the wedding last weekend and people started asking us when it'd be our turn, I knew it was all wrong."

"It must have been hard to tell her."

He simply nodded. "And how did Julian receive your rejection?" His voice was casual but his eyes were intent.

"He was hurt. He might take it out on us in the competition today."

"Let him do his worst. What other people think of us, whether we place last or first, isn't what really matters. If we feel that we've danced well, that's all that counts."

Now I laid the tips of my fingers against his temple. "I wish I'd met you years ago."

"I feel the same way."

"Thank you for sticking with this competition. It meant so much to me that you agreed to do it."

He grinned. "I couldn't resist getting to spend more time with you. Now I want to know everything else there is to know."

My worries about Lisa and Pa came rushing back to me. I rolled over onto my back. "Well, first, I've been lying to my family about everything. My father didn't even discover I'm a dancer until a few days ago, and he was very angry. I think he believes I'm some kind of stripper."

"Charlie, you're one of the most honest people I've ever met. You must have had good reason and he'll probably see that someday. Can't your little sister help him understand?"

I blinked and gazed at the ceiling, trying not to cry. "Lisa's sick.

There's something wrong with her legs and she's having trouble walking. She's been acting strangely. I'm so scared."

"That sweet girl I met?" I heard the emotion in his voice. He pulled me to him and hugged me tightly. "What burdens you've been shouldering alone."

Later, Ryan and I separated so we could go down to the ballroom discreetly.

Nina raised an eyebrow when I slipped into our room. "Well? Was it the smart choice or the dumb one?"

"Brainless is my middle name."

Nina came over and put her arm around me. "That's my girl."

"How did you know?"

She snorted. "So obvious."

Early that afternoon, Nina and I got dressed for the scholarship competition together. When we were done, she was in a slinky red dress covered with fringe, her hair in a French twist. My bright blue dress glittered with the stones I had spent so many hours sewing on. If only the world could know how many thumb pricks it had cost me. Catching sight of myself in the mirror—the way the dress clung and swung when I moved, the way the light hit my face—I realized for the first time: I looked like Ma.

Then we joined hands and went downstairs to meet our partners.

There had to be at least a thousand people sitting at tables watching the dance floor. Cameras were set up everywhere for video, and the professional photographers circulated through the crowd, taking photos during the competition. Ostrich feathers and stones hung everywhere, with the many fragrances perfuming the air. It was now social dancing before our event. The couples on the floor could all actually dance, so it looked like a scene from a Broadway show. The entire crowd in motion rotated counterclockwise as it was supposed to, with the women swirling in their brightly colored evening gowns.

A man came up to me and said, "You're from the New York studio, aren't you? I've heard of you. You must be the Princeton graduate."

"No, actually, that's her." I pointed to Adrienne, in a dark green dress that clung to her body as she danced with one of our students.

"Oh, I'm sorry. Since you're Asian, I just thought . . ." His voice trailed off.

Then I caught sight of Ryan and my breath hitched. Instead of the traditional black shirt and pants that most male Latin dancers used, he was wearing a white tuxedo shirt and black pants, without a jacket. He was staring at me as if he couldn't stop. I went over to him and he swung me into a waltz with the rest of the social dancers. I danced with the crispness of his shirt underneath my fingers, the scent of his cologne embracing me.

As Nina and Keith were finishing their rumba, just before we were to go on and perform our routine, I spotted a Chinese man at a center table. He had gray hair, angular features, and was watching the dancers with great intensity. Pa. I gulped for air. What was my father doing here? And, oh gods, Lisa was sitting next to him, looking very young here.

Ryan noticed my panic. "What's wrong?"

"My father and sister are here."

He squeezed my hand, and we were on. I could hardly breathe. The crowd was immense. I was going to forget my steps. I was only a dishwasher. My mind was a complete blank. But then I met Ryan's eyes. He held out his hand to me and our music began.

My body must have remembered the hours of training we'd done, but I was only conscious of the music and of Ryan. I moved with him, and even when he wasn't touching me, I could almost touch our connection as if it were an invisible bond between us. I felt the ache of all the months we hadn't been able to be together, the satisfaction of our love now, and the exhilaration of finally accomplishing what we set out to do. We were two people who a year ago hadn't met or set foot in a dance studio, and now we were doing our dance together in front of some of the best dancers in the country. I had done it.

When the music stopped, I saw that Dominic and Adrienne had risen to their feet applauding. Ryan's eyes were only focused on me. He turned me out under his arm and I sank into a low curtsey. It was hard to tell under the stage lights, but I allowed myself to believe the judges were beaming at us. Julian was writing notes, his head down, and I couldn't make out his expression.

We stepped off the floor, then walked back on while the other contestants joined us. The judges tallied their scores as I scanned the crowd for Pa and Lisa. They seemed to be gone now. Perhaps I had conjured them for inspiration. Nina rushed up and gave me a quick hug.

"You nailed it," she said.

I held her by the shoulders. "You were fantastic too." I turned to Keith, who was standing beside her. "You were both stunning."

"I couldn't take my eyes off the two of you," said Keith.

And the announcer was naming winners. We weren't the sixth

place couple, nor the fifth. I couldn't believe it. Then the announcer said, "In fourth place, Georgina Petrov and Hendrik Stevens!" We all clapped politely. My dress felt too tight, I was gasping to breathe.

Now it was only Nina, Keith, Ryan and me, and one other couple left on the floor. It was the first time Ryan and I had ever competed and we were still in the running. I closed my eyes. I had danced better than I ever had before, we both had. Then the master of ceremonies called out another set of names for third place, and they weren't ours. Could this really be happening?

The announcer said, "And in second place, Charlie Wong and Ryan Collins!" My jaw dropped, then Ryan and I were walking onto the center of the floor to accept our bouquets. I was thrilled. I sought the judges' table and saw Julian there, his eyes now upon me. He blew me a tiny kiss, then turned away.

Nina and Keith had been announced as the winners by now and she was laughing and crying at the same time as she grabbed me. I hugged her back. Then we were whirled away by everyone waiting to congratulate us.

It was hard to push my way through the throng of people. Everyone wanted to tell us how captivating we'd been, but Ryan must have understood what I was trying to do because he made sure we kept moving forward. I reached the spot where I'd seen the Chinese man. Had I been mistaken? Then he was in front of me and it was Pa, with Lisa by his side. He dashed a hand across his eyes, took me by the shoulders and embraced me. "It was like I caught a glimpse of your mother again, when she was young, but it was all you, Charlie. I am proud of you, dishwasher daughter no more."

I could hardly keep my balance, this was all so much to take in. "I'm so glad you came, Pa."

I turned to my little sister, who was staring at me as if she were in shock. "I almost didn't even recognize you out there, Charlie."

I slung an arm over her thin shoulders to hug her. "You remember Ryan."

Ryan bent down to give her a kiss on the cheek and I saw his intelligent eyes taking in the walker she leaned upon, how pale she was.

When he straightened, I laid my hand on his arm and addressed Pa. "My partner . . ." I took a breath. ". . . and boyfriend, Ryan."

Pa had already been eyeing him. Now he swallowed hard. Slowly, he extended his hand and they shook. "Are you a dancer man too?"

"No, I'm a gardener, sir."

Pa nodded. I could tell he liked the gardener and the sir part. "Maybe you can come to have a cup of tea sometime."

Twenty-Four

Ryan drove all of us back to New York City that evening. Most of the other dancers stayed since the competition would continue through the weekend. In the van, I asked Pa, "How did you get here, anyway?"

"We took the train. The lady at the train station helped us figure it out." He looked proud of himself, then ashamed. "I was going to barge in and save you from yourself. I didn't understand."

"It's all right, Pa. I'm so glad you and Lisa saw me dance." I glanced over at my sister, who'd been quiet and withdrawn. The trip must have exhausted her, plus the bewildering array of new people.

As Pa and Lisa got out of the van, Ryan caught my hand and kissed my knuckles before I could leave. I leaned toward him and whispered, "See you very soon." Both Pa and Lisa were watching us. Pa made a brave effort to stop wincing when I exited, but I couldn't read Lisa's expression at all.

The next morning, I was humming to myself as I made breakfast for all three of us. It was just toast, and for once, I didn't burn it. I set it in front of Ma's altar and bowed. "I know you've been guiding my steps, Ma. Thank you."

At breakfast, I said to Lisa, "To celebrate, I'd like to buy something pretty for you today."

"Really?" She perked up, and for a moment, she looked like the old Lisa. "But it's hard for me to walk too far."

"We could just go to one of the bigger stores in Chinatown, and maybe you could come with us, Pa. You don't have to work today."

He said, "I am not so good at shopping."

"But if Lisa becomes too tired, you could help me walk her home. We'd be able to stay out longer that way, and I'd really like to do something fun with the three of us." I could barely contain my happiness: the competition, my dancing, and I had a date with Ryan that evening. I pushed my worries about Lisa away, just for today.

Pa muttered, "This will be fun?" But he was smiling.

A few hours later, Lisa and I stood in one of the dressing rooms at a large boutique in Chinatown. We'd chosen the handicapped dressing room so we'd have enough space for Lisa's walker. I hung up the cute dresses I thought she might like. She hadn't wanted to try anything on but I'd insisted. Pa was hovering around outside the curtain, waiting for us.

"This is such a lovely color for you," I said, taking a dark rose sundress off its hanger. "Let me help you."

Lisa just stood there in her walker, staring at our reflections in the mirror.

"Come on, give me your hand and we'll get your top off."

She batted me away. "No, don't touch me. Just stop it, Charlie."

I stopped. "What's wrong?"

"I didn't want to come here, I don't want a new dress, but you wouldn't listen to me."

"I was just trying to get you out of the apartment for a while."

The expression on her face was bitter. "It's all about you and what you want, isn't it? You, the dancer; you, with your great boyfriend; you, Pa's wonderful daughter. You don't care about me at all."

The blood rushed to my head. "So you're jealous, is that it? It's finally my turn and you can't take it." Then I caught sight of us in the mirror: me standing fit and straight, and Lisa's hunched body in the walker. I was immediately overcome with remorse. "Sweetheart, I'm sorry."

Her eyes reddened. "You used to read with me every night. You were there for me. This past year, you've only been thinking about yourself and your dancing, you even fobbed me off on Uncle Henry to study for the Hunter test. You haven't been paying attention."

"Oh, Lisa. I didn't mean to make you feel that way." I gathered her in my arms, the way I had from the time she was a toddler.

She started to sniff. "You left me. And I needed you."

Now Pa poked his head through the curtain. "Are you girls all right?" When he saw us, he quietly slipped into the dressing room and stood in the corner.

I was trying now to blink the tears back too. "I always love you, Lisa, and even if it seemed like I was distracted, you were never far from my thoughts. I've been so worried about you."

Her voice was muffled against my shirt. "You were right too, I am jealous of you. I watched you at that competition, you were so strong and beautiful, and everyone was applauding for you, even Pa, and I just hated you for it. I couldn't stand it anymore. Ever since then, it's been like there's a balloon inside me, and it's getting fuller and fuller until it has to pop. But I don't really hate you, Charlie."

"I know."

I could barely hear her now. "I'm not a good person. I've done things, I'm so ashamed."

Above her head, I met Pa's worried eyes. "What kind of things? Nothing can be so bad that you can't tell us."

She shuddered like a small animal.

I stroked her hair. "Whatever it is, we'll help you. I promise. We won't be mad at you."

"Dennis . . ."

My forehead furrowed. "What about him?"

She took a deep breath. "He was like a big brother to me, he was so smart and cute, and I'd follow him around the clinic, and then I started to like him even more, you know?"

I nodded, relieved. Lisa had a crush, that was all.

She continued, "I tried to make myself as pretty as possible whenever I went there. I wanted him to like me back. Then one day, he kissed me."

My entire body stiffened. "What?"

Pa went white.

"I was so happy and it felt nice. But then he went on and on, and it didn't stop." She started to sob. "It didn't stop, Charlie."

Pa stepped forward on rigid legs. He laid a careful hand on her shoulder as his voice trembled with anger. "Dennis touched you?"

There was complete stillness, then her dark head, smelling of sweat, gave an almost imperceptible nod. A cold creeping feeling stole into my lungs and my pulse started to trip over itself. It was all I needed to know. It all fit now. Lisa's symptoms, the way she'd been acting. And even when she'd stopped working there, she'd undergone the treatments at Uncle's office—it must have been awful for her to see Dennis all that time, to have him brush against her as he helped Uncle. I squeezed her so tightly I was afraid I'd hurt her.

She whispered, "He made me do things to him too."

The veins stood out in Pa's neck.

I couldn't seem to stop shaking. "Why didn't you tell us before?"

"It was my fault. I started it."

Now both Pa and I held her. He said in a broken voice, "No, it was not your fault. You are an innocent child. Did he rape—" Pa's voice broke off and he covered his face with his fingers.

Lisa shook her head. "No, but it was getting worse. Thank goodness my legs started failing and I didn't have to work at the clinic anymore. Uncle and Aunt had no idea. Dennis would get me alone when they were gone or busy. I was so scared and ashamed."

I said, "He's a grown man and you're a child. Whatever happened was completely his fault. You had a crush on him, that's normal. He took advantage of you. What he did was criminal." I thought back to what Lisa had accused me of and my stomach started to heave. "I should have seen it. I was too selfish. I blame myself."

Pa said, "No, Charlie. No one could have known. Not even your uncle and aunt saw, and they were there every day."

Lisa whispered, "Is everything going to be all right?"

Pa and I looked at each other. "Yes. We're going over to the clinic right now."

Since it was Saturday afternoon, the clinic was packed. There were so many people crowded behind the door, we could barely get it open. Aunt Monica rose from her seat as the three of us entered. "Is something wrong?"

Pa said, "Yes. Where are they?"

Aunt Monica pointed toward one of the treatment rooms, then trailed after us. "What is happening? You can't just interrupt them, they're with a patient."

I stood close to Lisa as we went down the hallway. Her body looked so fragile and she was shaking. "I'm here, Lisa. The only person who should be worried is Dennis."

"Dennis?" Aunt Monica echoed.

By now, Pa had pushed open the door of the treatment room. Uncle Henry, Dennis and the patient, a heavy middle-aged man without a shirt on, looked up. I saw fear cross Dennis's face when he saw us.

Pa said to the patient, "Get out." The man grabbed his clothing and fled.

Uncle Henry said, astonished, "Brother, what is wrong?"

Pa's mouth opened but no sound came out.

I had my eyes fixed on Dennis. I felt my breath in my throat, choking me. "You asshole."

Aunt Monica shoved us all fully into the room and shut the door behind us. "You're going to cause a panic with our patients. What is going on?"

Pa stepped over to Dennis, grabbed him by the shirt and shook him. "This son of a dog has been doing things to my daughter."

Uncle tried to step between them. "I know you're protective of Charlie but—"

Pa pushed Dennis away from him with a violent gesture. "Not Charlie, Lisa!"

They all froze. Uncle's face paled until only a few red blotches were visible on his cheeks. He whispered, "You cannot make those kinds of accusations. How can you even think that?"

"He's been molesting her." I almost gagged to get the words out. "That's why she's been so ill. All the times she was alone there, he took advantage of her."

Dennis met my eyes, his face blank. He seemed relaxed, only I'd learned to read bodies by now and I could see that his shoulders were rigid. "That's ridiculous. Lisa was all over me, following me around, everyone saw it. Now she's trying to blame me for her own fantasies."

Pa reached for Dennis again but Uncle kept himself in between them. I'd never seen Uncle look so upset. He said, "We need to get to the bottom of this in a rational way. Lisa, what happened?"

Lisa had been standing in her walker, frozen and breathing shallowly. She didn't speak. I went over and helped her into a chair, then stood in front of her with her hands clasped in mine. I looked into her wide frightened eyes. "Now is the moment, Lisa. You just have to tell them what you said to us."

She pressed her lips together.

"The child is upset," Dennis said. "You can't listen to anything she claims anyway. She just wants attention and will do whatever's necessary to get it. I can't believe you're taking her silly talk seriously."

Uncle turned to him and gave him a cool look. "My family would not be upset for no reason."

Aunt Monica crossed her arms. "This is ridiculous. Dennis would never do such a thing."

Lisa pulled away from me and buried her face in her hands. We could still hear her muffled words. "I wanted to stop but he wouldn't. He just kept going."

I heard Uncle's sharp intake of breath.

Dennis's eyes were shifting wildly from side to side. "None of this is true, I never touched her. All I'm guilty of is that I didn't want to break her heart so I was nice to her. Honest."

Aunt Monica said, "I believe him. He's the most trustworthy person around. That child just wants to cause trouble."

I glared at Aunt Monica. "Don't you dare say that."

Dennis said, "Where's the proof? There isn't a mark on her."

I hadn't thought of that. Lisa didn't look up or respond, only seemed to shrink further into herself. That clever bastard. He'd been careful. "She's had all these symptoms this past year. It started soon after Dennis arrived. The bedwetting, the nightmares, the weakening of her legs."

"Wait," Dennis said. "How can you blame all of that on me?"

I thought of what Naomi had told me about conversion disorder. "We'd need to get her examined to be sure, but mental trauma can lead to physical symptoms exactly like those." I appealed to Uncle Henry. "Every Chinese medical practitioner knows the psyche and the body are one."

Uncle's quick eyes scanned Lisa. He turned to Dennis and slowly clenched his fists.

Dennis started to back toward the door and began to babble, "I didn't do anything, I couldn't help it. It wasn't my fault—she asked for it!"

Uncle roared, "I trusted you!" He and Pa both stepped toward Dennis.

Dennis grabbed the doorknob, yanked the door open and fled down the corridor.

Uncle yelled through the doorway, "I will prosecute you to the fullest extent of the law!"

By then, Dennis had run out of the clinic. Uncle strode down the hallway to the crowd of shocked patients and said, "The clinic is closed today. Leave now."

When Uncle Henry returned to us, Aunt Monica said, gasping, "There is no proof. How can you be sure? What will everyone say?"

Uncle ran a visibly trembling hand through his hair. "I am certain. This will already damage his reputation in Chinatown beyond repair. We won't bring Lisa's name into it, just allow people to believe what they want of him." He bent down and spoke gently to her. "Why didn't you tell me?"

"I didn't think you would believe me. I'm only a girl."

He looked stricken. "What a fool I've been. This happened under my nose." He stood and turned to Pa. "I failed you, brother."

Pa took him into his arms and the two men held each other for a moment. "That man has caused enough damage. Do not let him hurt us any further by feeling guilty. He alone is to blame."

Summer was ending. I started getting both Lisa and me up at the crack of dawn on Sunday mornings so we could join Godmother Yuan to do tai chi at six thirty in Gossip Park. The first time we got up so early, Lisa protested. "Why do you always have these crazy self-improvement programs? Now that we're reading *Pilgrim's Progress* again, isn't that enough?"

"Come on, I've always wanted to do tai chi together with you."

"Why can't we go to the Saturday afternoon classes you help teach?"

"Because I want to be a part of the group with you, not leading it. And since I've started qigong training with Godmother, I need my full concentration for that." I'd finally consented, and while it was hard for me to lose control of my emotions, I could feel it healing me. "Anyway, Godmother says the most powerful tai chi sessions are at dawn, in the open air."

I hoped it would help bring Lisa back into her body. Although it would mean getting painfully little sleep, I thought it was exactly what she needed right now to heal her body and soul. She'd been so damaged. She still wet the bed sometimes and often she woke up screaming, but the problems with her legs had disappeared. Mr. Song had guided us through everything. Pa had signed the insurance papers and Lisa was fully covered now. The western doctors could find no physical problems, which was a great relief. She was talking to a very good psychiatrist every week—Naomi, my dance student. Now I wanted to start the eastern medicine part of her healing as well.

We stood at the edge of the group in Gossip Park. This early in the morning, even the late August heat wasn't too bad yet. I caught sight of Godmother Yuan, who waved at us. Lisa shifted from leg to leg, nervous. Then the group started to move as one, and I could feel the energy flow outward to surround us. I nodded at Lisa to encourage her to follow along, as I was.

We rose from the basic position of having our weight balanced into the Pouncing Tiger, where our arms guarded our faces as cats do. We swirled and flowed from position to position. We went from High Horse stance, where we bowed our legs as if we were balanced upon a horse, to the Crane, where we stretched our arms out like an ascending bird, with the left knee raised. I stopped worrying and just felt my life force flow through me. In many ways, it was similar to doing ballroom when I felt most grounded. And it was hard. Lisa made mistakes several times but managed to keep going. By the end, I was sweating and Lisa's cheeks were pinker than I'd seen them in a long time. The old Chinese people seemed as calm as ever. They bowed to each other and us, then left.

"Come on." I jerked my thumb in the direction of the street. "I'll get you a bowl of congee and some fried dough." Lisa clasped her hands together. That was one of her favorite dishes.

We went to a tiny restaurant that had some of the best breakfast food and seated ourselves against the wall. Lisa dipped a segment of fried dough into her congee and took a big bite. "I love this place."

"I know, I think I'd starve if we didn't live in Chinatown." I blew on my steaming congee. "What did you think of the tai chi?"

She nodded, chewing. "It felt good. Difficult, but peaceful too. It's nice to do something with you again."

I felt a dullness grow in my chest. "I'm so sorry."

She stared at her food.

I pushed on. "I let you down. You were right, I was so busy with myself—"

"No." Lisa's eyebrows drew together in concentration. "It wasn't your fault, Charlie." Despite the heat of the congee, she was shivering.

"Do you forgive me? Of all people, I should have seen it."

Her voice was husky. "There's nothing to forgive. I was just trying to block it all out. No one could have done more than you. You always said I did better than you in everything, but do you know the reason why? You know what the only difference between you and me is? That I grew up with you to help me, and you didn't have anyone."

I got up and went over to her side of the table. I hugged her and we held each other.

When Lisa and I got back into the apartment that day, the Broadway jar was sitting on the table. Lisa ran to it, picking it up. "It's so much fuller."

Pa came out of his bedroom. He'd aged a decade in just a few weeks but he was making a real effort to spend more time with us. "Now that I don't have to pay for so much medicine, I had something left over for the jar. I think we'll have enough very soon."

Lisa laughed and ran into his arms. "Thank you, Pa!"

"Anyway, I promised you we would do something nice if you did not get into Hunter, right? Well, I think we should do something extra special since you will be starting there in a few weeks."

Lisa said, "Which show? And when? I want to pick!"

To tease her, I said, "No, I want to choose!"

We grinned as we stuck our tongues out at each other.

It was mid-September and the weekend of the Autumn Moon Festival celebration. I strolled through the blocked-off streets arm in arm with Mo Li and Zan. Something had caught Ryan's eye and he'd told us to go on ahead, he'd catch up with us soon. The Moon Festival was one of the most important holidays to us, a time when people reunited in a circle like that of the full moon. To many Asians, it was similar to Thanksgiving, and Mo Li had come back from Boston University for it. I loved the streets packed with tables and tents, the colorful lanterns that hung over our heads. No regular food stands were allowed, which was why Zan had the day off too.

We stopped by a stand that sold paper lanterns and traditional cookies in the shape of pigs and fish. Mo Li bought a lantern in the form of a butterfly, I got one that looked like a colorful glass rabbit and Zan, of course, bought a modern one in the shape of a bulldozer. As a child, I'd been so excited to walk through the streets at night with my lit paper lantern swinging from a stick in my hands.

Zan said, "Do you want to buy one for Lisa?"

I shook my head and pointed to the large roped-off area we were approaching. A sign read "Lantern-Painting Contest." Among the many families sitting at the long tables were Pa and Lisa, both frowning in concentration over the round white lanterns they were working on. Lisa looked up, saw us, waved and bent over her lantern again.

Mo Li laughed. "Better not disturb them further. They look serious."

I said, "First prize is a couple of boxes of mooncakes and you know how much Lisa loves those." Mooncakes were dense, sweet delicacies filled with white or yellow lotus-seed paste, with a salty egg yolk in the middle, looking like the full moon.

Zan asked, "How is she?"

When I'd told them what had happened, they'd both been horrified. "It's something she'll need to carry with her for the rest of her life but she's working on it. She's happier than I've seen her in a while. She's started at Hunter and loves it."

Behind us, Ryan's voice called, "Wait up." He was holding a beautifully wrapped orchid, which he must have bought at one of the stands. "This is for you."

While Zan and Mo Li cooed, I swallowed. "It's in a pot. I don't think I can keep it alive."

Everyone laughed. Ryan said, "I'll help you."

As he trailed behind us, I asked Zan, "Did you ever see Todd at your egg cakes cart again?"

She blushed. "Every day. Actually, we've taken a few walks together after I finish work."

Mo Li and I raised our eyebrows.

Zan said, "He's stopped working for the Vision. He's setting up as a psychic for himself and he's already doing pretty well."

I asked, "How's the Vision taking it?"

"She's so mad, but there's nothing she can do about it. I think she's going to lose most of her customers to him."

Mo Li tapped me on the shoulder. "There's your old noodle restaurant."

I turned to Ryan. "That's where I worked as a dishwasher."

He said, "And look at you now."

Later that evening, Ryan was waiting for me downstairs from our apartment. His white shirt beneath his jacket glowed faintly in the gathering shadows. I took his arm and led him down the street. When we got to the park, the sky was half lit by the sunset, balanced between day and night. The sky grew darker and it began to rain. We went slowly because the ground was uneven. The rain made the wisps of his hair stick to his face. We were at the foot of the bridge. The water roared underneath.

"Ryan, will you help me with something?" I told him about trying to cross the bridge with my eyes closed, how steep and dark it had seemed. I took his hand and we stepped onto the bridge. I closed my eyes, then reached my right hand out to the wet stone. Ryan held my hand on the other side. His hand was warm in the chill evening air. We began to walk. The rain in the leaves overhead swirled with the wind, roaring like an ocean above us. I stumbled, but now we were guiding each other. We fell into step together as I kept my eyes closed. The water droplets felt cool against my eyelids.

We went a bit faster, and a little more, and then we were at the place where the bridge peaked. The rain seemed to fall harder. The slope began and we went faster and faster, the rain drenching our wet clothes, and we began to run. I let go of the rail, I heard Ryan laughing as we took flight. I was half afraid that any moment we would tumble off the steps, but we were still going and then we were at the stairs, racing down them, and somehow the steps were behind us and we were running into the unknown on the other side.

ACKNOWLEDGMENTS

First of all, I'd like to thank all of my readers for their support and great kindness. And to those who have connected with me on social media, via my website, e-mail or in person—your friendship and your stories mean a great deal to me, thank you for sharing. I hope very much that my writing touches your life in a positive way. I'm also extremely grateful to all of the organizations, libraries, booksellers, high schools, colleges and universities who have stood behind me and my work—you've made my deepest dreams come true.

There are so many people who have contributed to this book. The two foremost in my mind are my incredible agent, Suzanne Gluck of William Morris Endeavor Entertainment, and my phenomenal editor, Sarah McGrath of Riverhead Books. I could not have done this without you. I owe a great deal to the rest of my team at WME, especially Tracy Fisher and her foreign rights team, Anna DeRoy for film rights, and to all of my foreign publishers.

I'm indebted to all of the wonderful people at Riverhead Books and Penguin Random House. You've worked so hard for me and my books,

Acknowledgments

and I consider you both friends and colleagues. Thank you for believing in me, most especially Geoff Kloske and Susan Petersen Kennedy. I'm also in awe of the rest of you, including Kate Stark and the Riverhead marketing department, Jynne Dilling Martin and the Riverhead publicity department, Craig Burke and the paperback publicity and marketing department, Leigh Butler and the subrights department, Helen Yentus and the art department, Alan Walker and the academic marketing department, Tiffany Tomlin and the Penguin Speakers Bureau, Linda Rosenberg, Tony Davis and the copyediting department, and finally the entire hardcover, paperback, and digital sales forces, in particular Kevin Che for being the first to lead the way.

I'm so thankful to everyone at Fred Astaire East Side Studio in New York City, especially legendary dancers and coaches Marina and Taliat Tarsinov, who trained and supported me as a ballroom dancer from the very beginning. It was a dream to dance with Jungie Zamora, plus Sheena Daminar, Tina Gerova, and Sonya Fil are inspirations to me. Armando and Laura Martin have been there for me from the start. I'm also very grateful for the talents of Emeka of Montage Production, the band Son Asi, singer Alja Weerts, photographer Chris Macke, Web designer Ilsa Brink and makeup artists Michelle Coursey and Roberto Gonzalez.

My dear writer friends and readers Katrina Middelburg-Creswell and Sari Wilson—thank you so much for your wisdom, support and insight all along the way. So many others have contributed to this book and I'm thankful to you all, especially psychic Etty van der Graaf, William Guo, Stan Lou, Hoi Wing Louie, Meridith Messinger, neurologist Scott Mintzer, Gary Lao Hu Mono, Patrick van Rij (Van Rij Hoevenier), Jet Robnett, David Roodman, Jason and Naomi Tong, Elliot Wolf, and authors Benedict Jacka and Pete Jordan. Close friends who have always stood by my side include Julie Voshell, Alex Kahn, Stuart Shapiro, Jon Sherman and Lisa Donner. My gratitude also goes out to Esther van den Berg, Liesbeth Broers, Saskia de Bruijn, Gerhard Koning, Karel and Marianne ter

Acknowledgments

Kuile, Shih Hui Liong, Joost Lucassen, Jan Paul Middelburg, Jet and Hans Omloo, Merijn Scheffer-Teunissen, Dania Schoonenboom, Natasja Slob, Leonie Teunissen, Gracia Tham, Hilda de Vries, Meta van der Wal and authors Patty Chang Anker, Margaret O'Brien Dilloway, Holly Kennedy, Sinead Moriarty, Leo and Tineke Vroman, and Patricia Wood. Hugs to the Beck/Nolan family, especially Buddy, Charlotte and Emily.

All my love to my family, especially Chow (Joe) and Justine, who helped me so much with research and their great insight. Also thanks to Alex, Amanda, Choi, David, Diana, Elaine, Elton, Eton, Jennifer, Jonathan, Kam, Kitty, Lai Fong, Min, Ping, Walter, Wendy and York. I'll always keep my late brother Kwan in my heart, alongside my parents, Shuet-King and Shun. I also can't forget the Kluwer family: Gerard, Betty, Michael, Sander, Matz, Meijs, Otis and Renée van Duren, Yvonne Kruis, plus Anita, Tommy and Eva Racz. Finally, my deepest love and gratitude to Erwin, Stefan and Milan, who put up with me through all those months of writing, traveling and burned food. And I must mention our three cats, Anibaba, Sushi and Timoto, who did a great job of lying across my keyboard to keep it warm.